Paul Magrs (pronounced Mars) was born in the North East of England. After seven years at the University of East Anglia teaching English Literature and Creative Writing, he now lives in Manchester and lectures part time at the Manchester Metropolitan University. The rest of his time he devotes to writing. He has published fiction for both adults and children. His novels include *All the Rage* and *To the Devil: A Diva!* and *Never the Bride*, the first novel to feature Brenda and Effie.

Something Borrowed

PAUL MAGRS

headline
review

First published in 2007 by HEADLINE REVIEW
An imprint of HEADLINE PUBLISHING GROUP

First published in paperback in 2008 by HEADLINE REVIEW
An imprint of HEADLINE PUBLISHING GROUP

1

Cataloguing in Publication Data is available from the British Library

ISBN 978 0 7553 3291 5

Typeset in Garamond by Avon DataSet Ltd,
Bidford-on-Avon, Warwickshire

Printed and bound in Great Britain by
Mackays of Chatham plc, Chatham, Kent

Headline's policy is to use papers that are natural, renewable and recyclable
products and made from wood grown in sustainable forests.
The logging and manufacturing processes are expected to conform
to the environmental regulations of the country of origin.

HEADLINE PUBLISHING GROUP
An Hachette Livre UK Company
338 Euston Road
London NW1 3BH

www.headline.co.uk

For Tiffany Murray

Chapter One
The Shame of Sheila Manchu

Good morning!

I love waking up in my gorgeous, multicoloured attic at home. I love the north-eastern light and the angry calls of gulls across the sheer blue sky; the ghostly aromas of a hundred thousand cooked breakfasts and the steam rising from the spouts of a hundred thousand teapots over the slate blue rooftops.

Friday morning. There's a spring chill in my room and I'm pushing back the night with the thick bedclothes and I'm doing my stretching exercises briskly when there comes the clattering of the letter box at the bottom of the stairs.

I need to be up and about! Doing things! Getting on

with business! I start jogging on the spot. Star jumps. Thump thump thump on the bedroom floor. Not bad for my age, eh? How old would you say I was, hm?

You'd be wrong.

Thump thump thump down the stairs.

Ah. This morning, a note shoved through by hand. I recognise the prim italics of my neighbour and best friend, Effie. She hasn't written much:

Brenda, dear. We're needed. Are you free today? I will meet you at 9.30 a.m. in our usual spot at the Walrus and the Carpenter. Coffee and walnut cake are on me.

It isn't at all like Effie to offer to pay. And what does she mean, we're 'needed'? I hope she's not determined to get us involved in any more funny business. We had enough of that at the end of last year.

This is supposed to be my retirement. This is my quiet bed and breakfast, and my quiet landlady life. But I'll meet Effie at the Walrus and the Carpenter nevertheless, and see what it is she wants. Just in case it's something important.

I feel as if I am in the swim of things here, at the heart of Whitby. My establishment is quite close to the harbour and the seafront and the bridge across to the old town. I am surrounded by hundreds of these intricate Victorian streets. Living here, looking after guests here, I am in the middle of all the places and things I think I'll ever need. This morning, togged up in my heaviest coat and fleece-lined boots, I'm taking deep lungfuls of sea air and I nod and exchange a few good mornings with people I know.

I skirt round the harbour mouth and I'm watching the fishing boats bobbing at their moorings. The rooftops over the bay are shining in the morning sun and, when I look up, there's the ancient abbey, hulking and dark and jagged against the horizon. I try not to look too hard at it. I hurry over the bridge and into the old part of town.

Whitby still feels like the perfect place for my well-earned semi-retirement. Last year, setting myself up in my B&B, I decided I would take in a few, select, paying guests. I would fuss over them, and make my rooms luxurious for them. I would keep my head down and live out a quiet life in my seaside retreat.

That was my plan, anyway.

When I arrived here, descending upon these higgledy-piggledy streets, I established a gentle routine of none-too-strenuous work, cookery and contemplation. I made friends here, with a few quite ordinary-seeming souls. I enjoyed mornings of coffee, cake and conversation with my new friend Effie from the junk shop next door. We ventured out to the occasional not-very-extravagant restaurant along the seafront. We went to a bingo night or two, even a tea dance in one of the stately hotels on the Royal Crescent.

Above all I felt that I was fitting in at last. I was happily inconspicuous. A little tall, perhaps. I am a heavy-set woman, with undistinguished features. My hands are rather large. I tend to keep them out of the way, and try not to gesticulate when I speak. My accent is difficult to pin down, for I have lived in many different towns and counties. I slather my face in thick make-up, so that it always has a slightly unnatural hue to it. Not out of vanity, you understand. I look more like someone covering something up than I do someone deliberately flaunting herself. I hear people wonder: burns? Scars? My clothes are rather demure and modest; old-fashioned.

I don't look in the windows of the shops as I pass them this morning. I glide past the sweet shops, the jewellery and novelty shops, and I'm not tempted to glance sideways at my reflection. I'm less self-conscious than I was before. I'm out in bright sunshine, in full make-up, and my head's held high. Things are better for me these days.

People find it difficult to tell exactly how old I am. And that's just as well. That's how I like it. I appear old enough to be harmless. Old enough for folk to believe I live a blameless life. A life above suspicion.

Oh, dear.

My life has been rather fraught with terrors and disasters. And it still is.

I seem to have the knack for drawing into my orbit people and things, events and occurrences, that can only be described as *macabre*.

The Walrus and the Carpenter is a very small café, tucked away in the old part of town, halfway up the long sloping street that leads to the one hundred and ninety-nine steps that take you up to the church and the abbey. If you sit inside that café by the chintz curtains of the bow windows, you can watch everyone traipsing up and down the cobbled lane. After a while you'll see everyone in Whitby passing by. Maybe that's why Effie and I have made it our regular morning coffee haunt.

The bell chimes as I let myself into the small parlour. I'm inhaling the welcoming scent of hot coffee and freshly baked cake. And there she is. There's Effie, already at our usual place. She's looking stern and watchful in a new beige mac. She's also – when I approach I can see them under the table – wearing what can only be described as running shoes. Ambitious, in one knocking on seventy.

The waitress is very polite. She takes our order and leaves us to our conversation.

'Are you free this evening, Brenda?' Effie asks airily as she takes a first, scalding sip of coffee.

'I am,' I say. 'What do you have in mind?'

'Oh, nothing in particular ...' she says, and I know she has something very definite in mind. But I play along, and concentrate on a forkful of moist walnut cake.

'I simply thought,' Effie continues, 'that our previous experiences might come in handy, that's all.'

'Previous experiences?' I shoot her a suspicious look. 'Which experiences are we talking about here, Effie?'

'Oh, don't be coy, Brenda. You know very well . . . the kinds of things that the two of us encountered last year.' I get a dark look from her. She dabs her thin lips with a cotton napkin. 'And there's a certain person who might be needing our particular brand of expertise.'

'What have you been telling people?' I ask her, more sharply than I mean to. 'Who have you been talking to?'

'Now, Brenda,' she says, dropping her voice. 'I'm not going to tell you anything at all until you calm down. Eat your cake.' Her eyes are actually twinkling. She's loving this. 'I merely happened to mention to someone who I know is in trouble that you and I have a little experience in . . . well, sorting out situations of a rather delicate nature.'

'Delicate!' I have to laugh at this. 'Effie, the situations that you and I got ourselves into last autumn were downright bizarre. They were weird. They were shocking and they were absolutely hair-raising. They were exactly the sort of thing that I used to get involved in during my previous life. My old life, before I came here for some peace and quiet.'

'Exactly!' Effie cries. 'And so we've both got a bit of expertise in dealing with the . . . supernatural.'

I sigh. She won't be put off. Effie has developed a taste for strange goings-on. Things have been a bit quiet during the winter and the early part of this year, but now I can see that she's all worked up at the idea of something a bit spooky coming our way. I could do without it, myself.

'We were brilliant!' Effie says, all gung-ho. 'Remember how we dealt with that nasty, slimy Mr Danby and his Deadly Boutique? When he was offering makeovers to all the women of Whitby and everyone was flocking there to get rejuvenated? And he was sucking their life essences out of them! Well, we soon put a stop to that, didn't we?'

I frown. 'More by luck than design, though.' I'm still a bit embarrassed to recall that particular escapade. I was the one who clambered naked into his Deadly Makeover machine and made it explode. I was the one who brought an end to his evil boutique, and I'd rather forget the fact.

'And what about that business of the pies at the Christmas Hotel?' Effie hisses. 'When we heard that they were made out of the flesh of the waiting staff? Who was it went investigating then? Who was it found the dead body in the meat lockers, eh?'

'It was us,' I admit. 'But . . . just because we got caught up in all of that, it doesn't make us experts . . .'

'Yes it does!' Effie chuckles. 'Last autumn we faced all sorts of terrible, supernatural dangers together. Ghosts in my attic! Those awful monkey women from the Deadly Boutique! And we even had to hoist poor rejuvenated Jessie out of her grave, when she came back as a zombie, poor thing. As if she hadn't already been through enough.'

'Hm,' I sniff. 'I'd have thought you'd seen enough funny business. After your fancy man and all.'

Effie stiffens and I wonder if I've gone too far. 'Well,' she says. 'You're right. I fell a little in love. Rather foolishly in love. With a supernatural being I should have kept right away from. And I lost him, didn't I? And if that doesn't qualify me for dealing with . . . spooky investigations, then I don't know what would.'

We sit in silence for a while, and I pour us some more coffee. Effie first clapped eyes on the dashingly handsome and urbane Kristoff Alucard in this very café. From that first moment she was transfixed by him. She was lost. She who had never had her head turned by any man in all her long life. And I think he probably had true feelings for her, too, but he was more interested in the books of arcane lore she has stashed in her attic rooms. It was those that led the suave Alucard to his doom. Using those books, he found his way to the hidden gateway to hell – or Bitch's Maw – in a forgotten corner of the abbey ruins. Then Effie and I were both there with him in the dead of one freezing night when the tiny, ancient abbess suddenly appeared and sent Alucard spinning off into hell. And that's where he still is. And here Effie is, with a supposedly broken heart.

'And besides.' Effie perks up at last. 'What did the old abbess tell us, that night, eh?'

I shrug. 'Something about the Bitch's Maw. Something about us.'

'Aha!' cries Effie. 'So you do remember. She told us that hell is bursting at the seams. And there are tortured souls escaping all the time. Coming through that portal, Brenda. Escaping here, into Whitby. Here we are, standing on the very doorway into hell. And we have a duty of care. To deal with the monsters, for good or ill.'

'All right, all right,' I tell her. 'I know. I remember.' I wish I didn't, though. I can still see that tiny abbess's wizened face in the moonlight, up at the abbey. The way she told us that we were stuck with this job. It felt like a life sentence. And I realised then, all at once, that this must be the reason I was drawn here to this town by the sea. It wasn't in order to live a quiet life at all. I had been dragged here unwittingly, to team up with Effie, the descendant of generations of Whitby witches. And together we had to fend off the forces of darkness.

What a palaver.

'So what is it?' I ask her. 'What's this latest spooky thing?'

Effie taps her beaky nose. 'You'll just have to wait till this evening. Glam yourself up. We're going somewhere surprising.' And with that, she slurps up the last of the molten sugar in her cup.

When I walk back home, leaving her in the town to do her shopping, I'm thinking that, really, she's a lonely old soul. She's been in the dumps since her fancy man Alucard was banished into hell. Maybe being asked to investigate something will keep her mind occupied. It might do her good to feel wanted, I suppose.

The afternoon whooshes by in a blur of scouring powder and self-raising flour. I'm in my most welcoming landlady mode as my guests arrive in enthusiastic dribs and drabs, fresh from the railway station, throughout that afternoon. They are a polite, undemanding bunch. I see them settled in with minimal fuss and they seem genuinely delighted by the airy, immaculate rooms I have provided for them. I explain rules and routines and, as I'm in such a good mood, I even consider cooking Sunday lunch for them.

I like it when I have a full house.

I roll up my sleeves and get on with my work. All around me, the other landladies of Whitby are doing likewise as we advance into the sun-warmed weekend.

Teatime rolls round and I pause with spicy tea and ginger biscuits. I'm thinking about Effie again. Effie and her mysteries. She'd be gutted if I didn't go out with her tonight. I suppose I should show willing. My work here is finished for the day.

What did she say about glad rags?

I wonder where it is she's taking us. And who it is who needs our help so badly.

It's quite a walk up the hill. We're heading out of town in our best outfits, on foot. We're passing other B&Bs, other guest houses. This area is a good fifteen minutes away from my place, and the sea. I'm sure the advertising for these establishments doesn't say that.

At last we're standing in front of a particular hotel. It's a sprawling stucco monstrosity, freshly painted in ice cream shades of yellow and pink. Banners advertise 'Big Screen Sport' in the lounge bar and others proclaim 'Seventies Nite Tonight!' in the basement nightclub.

'Here?' I can hardly believe it. Effie leads me across the road determinedly. I might have known, though. Effie's in her dancing shoes. She's in a glitzy black frock, too, topped off with a fur wrap. A vintage outfit, fetched from some deep wardrobe in that museum-like house of hers. And here I am, ready for a proper night out, clumping along in my nicest shoes, with a smart print dress I chose in the sales. I've set my wig nicely, in a modish way, and I'm ready to face the world on Friday night. 'But here? The Hotel Miramar? You always say it's a terrible den of vice, Effie . . .'

She shrugs. She purses her lips. 'It's not so bad,' she tells me, linking one of her skinny old arms into my much heftier one as we dodge the traffic. It's a balmy spring evening, with the sun just sliding down over the headland. The breeze is warm and, given a choice, I wouldn't be spending the evening sitting in some sweaty bar. And certainly not one with the reputation that the Hotel Miramar has.

'You came here last year, didn't you? When you were courting?' I shoot her a quick look.

'Indeed,' she murmurs, hunting through her beaded clutch bag as we stand outside the main door. 'Look. Membership card. You can come in as my guest.' We're standing under one of the ubiquitous flashing signs. This one is advertising the nightclub (or 'niterie') in the basement of the hotel: the Yellow Peril. When Effie opens the heavy double doors to the foyer, there's a sickening smell of spirits and chicken Kiev.

'I wish you'd warned me that we were coming here,' I said. 'I don't feel dressed right.' I'm buttoning up the cardy I've slipped over my dress.

'You look fine,' Effie tells me. She's gone into concentrated, alert mode, her eyes glinting about suspiciously.

'Who are we here to help, anyway?' I ask. 'You haven't told me anything yet.'

Effie is just about to explain something to me when we're descended on by a woman in a lime green blouse. 'Terrible with the complexion she's got,' Effie hisses. She's never liked Rosie Twist, who is a journalist on the local rag, *The Willing Spirit*. (And features editor on its hedonistic weekend supplement, *The Flesh is Weak*.)

Rosie has frizzy magenta hair and a salon tan like meat paste. I think the poor woman is colour blind.

'Well!' she says. 'I never thought I'd see you two here.' You can feel her mind whirring over the possibilities. Her fingers twitch, itching to fetch her notebook out of her bag. She'll have us in her tawdry gossip column, I just know. Respectable ladies on binge-drinking jolly at local hellhole.

Effie is frowning at her. 'Hello, Rosie.' She's never forgiven Rosie or *The Willing Spirit* for a feature article on her shop which described the place as a danger to local health and safety. 'A bit of dust!' she had bellowed at the time, tearing the page to shreds. 'A bit of dust never hurt anyone! Why does everything these days have to be gleaming, antiseptic and safe? What kind of world is it turning into?' Ever since then – last Christmas – Effie has despised Rosie Twist.

'Come on, then,' Rosie jeers. 'Tell me. What are you two doing in a place like this?'

'None of your business,' Effie huffs. 'Come along, Brenda.'

'This isn't your usual old lady kind of place. You must be here for a reason . . .' Rosie follows us with a glint in her eye.

Effie draws herself up proudly and glares at Rosie. She glances to make sure none of the other hotel guests – propping up the bar – can hear. 'We simply fancied having a nice dance.'

'Oh, come on.' Rosie laughs. 'I've got my eye on you two. Nothing good happens when you two are around. So tell me. Is something going on here at the Miramar? Something weird?'

I cough politely, in order to gain their attention. Rosie has been fixated on Effie – like a mongoose. I can see Effie's about to lose her temper. They both look up at me. 'I'd keep it quiet, if I were you, Rosie, love. You see, you're right. We are, in fact, involved in all sorts of dark and nasty business . . .'

'I knew it!' she snaps triumphantly.

'And wherever we go, danger is bound to follow. Terrible things have happened.'

'So?' she says. 'That's good! That's the kind of thing I want to know. I knew there was a story about you two . . .'

I lower my voice again, and stare unblinkingly into her eyes. 'Terrible things might happen to *you.*'

She gulps. She backs off. I can see I've jarred her composure. 'Oh, rubbish,' she stammers. 'I'll find out what you're doing here, don't you worry. It'll all come out in the end.' With that, she totters off to the ladies' lav, and slams the door.

'Blue eyeshadow with that tan,' Effie tuts.

'We'll have to watch out for her.'

'Yes, but let's not threaten too many people, eh?' Effie tells me.

There's a throbbing and a pounding from the basement. The monogrammed carpet underfoot is pulsing like a gold and scarlet migraine. The disco has started up downstairs in the Yellow Peril, and it's time for us to show Effie's membership card and to descend into the underworld.

There's a surprise waiting for us at the little desk at the bottom of the stairs.

'Robert!' He's sitting in a bubble of light, crouching over the membership book. Next thing I know he's giving me a swift hug.

It's weeks since I've seen Robert. He's my young friend who used to work at the Christmas Hotel, and who helped us during some of our investigations last year. 'I *am* glad you've got yourself another job,' I tell him. Though, secretly, I wish it was somewhere nicer than this.

Mind, he looks very dapper in his black tie and tails. He steps back for us to admire him. 'Better than my work clothes in the last place, eh?' he grins. Handsome boy. I turn to see Effie gazing at him with her usual wry disapproval.

'Good evening, young man,' she says, passing over her card and bending to sign us both in. 'How is your aunt keeping these days?'

Oh, dear. Robert's face falls at that. Poor Jessie. He tries to rally. 'As well as we can expect. Some of the things she's been through . . .'

Effie straightens up and nods briskly. 'Quite. We can't expect miracles, can we?'

Robert's eyes widen. 'But I think it's a miracle that she's still here, in the land of the living. That's a miracle to me.'

'Hm,' says Effie. 'Are we ready to go in, Brenda? I believe it's Seventies Night, isn't it, Robert?'

I ask him, quietly, 'Is she still living in the same place?'

He nods quickly. 'It's not ideal, of course. But it's where she wants to be. I wouldn't want to argue with her. She can flare up very quickly.'

I pat his hand.

'She'd love a visit from you,' he says impulsively. 'Both of you.'

'I'm not so sure about that,' Effie says, not at all keen. Robert is looking at us imploringly.

'We'll see.' I smile. Of course, we will have to go and check on his Aunt Jessie. I feel responsible, in a strange way, for how she's ended up. Of course we'll go.

'So how come you're here?' Robert asks. 'Are you going to dance the night away?'

The disco noise is already overpowering. I can see Effie is keen to get through the swing doors into the inner sanctum.

'I quite enjoy a nice bop,' I tell him playfully. 'But actually, it's Effie who's dragged us here. Something's up.'

Robert's eyes go wide. 'You're investigating!' He grins at me.

Effie swings round on us. 'Do you two have to go blethering on about our business? Keep a tin lid on it. That idiot journalist Rosie Twist will be coming down the stairs after us. We don't want just anyone finding out what we're up to.'

I roll my eyes. '*I* don't even know what we're up to.'

Robert clicks his fingers. 'It's Sheila, isn't it?'

Effie twitches. 'Sssh,' she hisses.

Robert lowers his voice and leans in. 'You're here to see

17

Sheila. I just know it. Oh, thank goodness. I'm glad she took my advice. It was me who told her that you two are . . . good at looking into . . . mysteries and that.'

I bite my lip, because I don't want to yell at Robert. But I'd rather the whole town didn't know about my and Effie's adventures. Instead I ask him, 'What's wrong with Sheila?' I don't really know the woman. I've met her a couple of times. Busty, glamorous type. Owns this place. All this silver hair, right down her back. Feathers and satin and fussy make-up.

'She's been in a proper old state,' Robert says. 'Since yesterday morning. I've never seen anything like it. She's inconsolable.'

'Come on, Brenda,' Effie says firmly, grasping my arm.

Rosie Twist has appeared behind us, brandishing her membership card. 'Who's inconsolable?' she pipes up.

'The DJ,' Robert puts in smoothly. 'Snapped her twelve-inch Donna Summer right across. No more "I Feel Love"! On a Seventies Night! What a disaster!'

Rosie scowls and bends to sign the book. I wink at Robert and Effie drags me into the noisiest disco I've ever been to.

It's like the Belle Epoque inside, mixed with Lucrezia Borgia and *Saturday Night Fever*. The place is heaving with half-familiar faces, surging between Hawaiian bar and the lit-up dance floor, which is pulsing its amber checkerboard like crazy. Effie seems quite at home, slipping through the mostly older crowd. She's intent on getting to the bar; cutting a swathe through the electric boogaloo and all the hullaballoo. She orders drinks and soon we're perched on chrome stools. Effie has a slim flute of something sophisticated-looking and I feel foolish holding a half-coconut of a funny-tasting concoction that I'm sucking through a curly straw. I wasn't made for high stools.

'What's wrong with Sheila?' I ask her.

'I don't know yet. I only got the message this morning.'

'Inconsolable, Robert said.' I suck up a whole mouthful of my cocktail. I'm just about getting used to its weird, foamy texture. 'I never knew you were such great pals with her.'

'I'm not,' Effie says. 'I'm intrigued. She didn't sound like herself on the phone. She said Robert had told her what a great help we had been with his poor Aunty Jessie.'

'I'm not sure that's true,' I say. Poor Jessie. She turned into a Neanderthal – or, what was it? An Australopithecus-type woman in that makeover machine. Then she died of a heart attack, and then she came back to life. It was a horrible do all round. Still, it was nice of Robert to say we had been a help to him.

'So Sheila said she'd like to talk to us. She offered us a free night out here at the Yellow Peril and that's why we're here.

That way she can have a word with us without drawing attention. We look like we're here for a night out, rather than actually investigating. Do you see?'

'I do.'

'I must say, poor Sheila sounded rather spooked on the phone.'

Spooked. I nod understandingly. That sounds like one for us.

And then there's a change of record and a shift in atmosphere for the crowd standing immediately around us. The red-faced drinkers draw back a little to allow the owner and manageress to pass like a whisper to the bar.

She's like their queen in here, is Sheila. Some of them go so far as to applaud her appearance as she steps across the sticky floor to greet us. She looks composed and beautiful in a long silky dressing gown affair, trimmed with blue feathers. She's come down in her nightie, it seems, though somehow that doesn't look out of place. When she smiles her whole face crinkles up and, oddly, all her extra flesh only adds to her sexiness and her allure. She greets Effie as if she is a long-lost best buddy. As Sheila kisses my cheek I realise that what she seems most of all is grateful. She is brimming with gratitude that we have turned up on a Friday night in response to her plea. She looks as if we have agreed to save her life.

'Come into my office for a moment, would you?' she asks. 'Not for long. It won't take long to explain.'

Of course, of course. There's no turning down a request from her. Without a word, Effie and I are off our stools, shouldering our handbags and holding our exotic drinks aloft. We swim through the crowd in Sheila's wake. We're both agog to learn what's behind all this. We don't even question the wisdom of getting involved.

Something is telling me this must be very murky business indeed. It must be nasty, to have spooked a woman like Sheila Manchu.

She sits down at her desk very gracefully. Effie and I pull up chairs and prepare to listen carefully to what she has to say.

'I imagine that the two of you have heard all sorts of gossip about me.' She raises an eyebrow. 'I know how people here in this town talk. I know the kinds of thing they say about me. Perhaps they don't mean to be unkind, but I do have feelings, you know. I'm not impervious to the harsh opinion of the world.'

Effie says kindly, 'Tell us, Sheila. What's happened?'

Sheila's chin trembles. The whole of her large body is trembling. 'I'm sorry. You might well think I'm over-reacting. I'm taking it too much to heart. But it's the kind of thing that can really get to you, this. It can knock your confidence.'

Effie takes a handkerchief out of her clutch bag and passes it to her. 'Start at the beginning,' she tells Sheila.

And Sheila does.

'I suppose I've never really felt accepted here. I know how long it takes to be accepted by Yorkshire people. Well, we moved up here in 1974 and that's over thirty years ago. Still I feel like some southern interloper. Someone who'll never fit in.' Sheila spares me a glance here. She knows that I'm a much more recent interloper. 'I realise this hotel of mine is vulgar and silly. And that people here think I'm trashy. And I can't help that. But I didn't think anyone actually meant me any harm.'

'Harm?' I ask. 'Has someone threatened you?'

She smiles sadly. 'In the old days, death threats and so on were ten a penny. We'd get them arriving in the post almost daily. Every time I picked up the phone there'd be some anonymous sinister voice promising my husband or myself a grisly end.'

'Why?'

'My husband was rather notorious in his line of work.' She sighs. 'When he lived in London he was a proper terror, I suppose. Some people would say he deserved everything he got, all that aggro, when all he wanted to do really was retire from the shady scene he was involved with.'

I cast a glance at Effie and she's nodding patiently.

She already knows all this, it seems, about Sheila's old man.

'I met him late in his life, you see,' Sheila explains. 'When he was wanting to turn his back on all his schemes and nefarious plots. He'd had enough. He was worn out. A jaded skeleton of a man. But he had such panache and charm about him, even then. What was I? Just a girl. A dolly bird in Soho. I was a waitress in a go-go bar when he met me. I was seventeen and he was a hundred and nine.'

'That's some age gap,' I say.

Sheila nods. 'My husband was a unique man.'

'You married when you were so young?'

'You have to understand what he was like. He had been a criminal mastermind of truly global reach. He was a mandarin. A genius. He could flatter and charm like no one I had ever met. He was so sophisticated, so witty. And there was still some glamour about him, some remnants of the handsome man he had been so long before . . .

'And also, he couldn't do enough for me. He was so powerful, he had only to snap his fingers and his will was done. My will was done. Now, that's very seductive to a girl from nowhere. A girl who had nothing. But still . . . at first . . . I had my qualms about him. He had, he admitted, been rather wicked in his past. He sat me down and told me exactly how heinous his crimes had been. He had a flat deep

23

under the ground in Limehouse and I remember sitting there, in this opulent pleasure palace, and thinking: I don't care. He could be the very devil and I wouldn't care. Because I wanted him, do you understand?'

'I think so,' I say.

Effie looks less sure. 'I think you were making a whole lot of bother for yourself.'

Sheila smiles, as if she should have known Effie wouldn't understand. 'I told him I didn't care what had gone on in the past. So long as he treated me proper. I know all his other girlfriends and wives, even his grown-up daughter, hadn't met very pleasant fates. He was a dangerous man to be around. But I was seventeen and gorgeous and I thought I was invulnerable.' She pauses and says, 'Let me show you something.'

Sheila leads us to a concealed door and opens it with great ceremony. The space inside glows like a shrine and she lights a stick of incense and mumbles a prayer of greeting to the assemblage of objects within. Effie and I draw in our breath sharply at what we see.

A gold and green silken robe stands suspended, as if still occupied by his withered body. On a shelf above, a skullcap, and, beneath that, several jars and pots elaborately lacquered in gold and black. There is a photo in a blood red frame, of a refined-looking Chinese gentleman of advanced years. His hooded eyes are blank and dark and yet they still seem to project amazing malevolence across the gap of years.

'Sweetheart,' Sheila sighs. 'This is Brenda and Effie, and they are here to help us. I know you would approve of them. They will get to the bottom of all this. They'll find out who it is who's wanting to hurt your Sheila.' She looks to us and smiles proudly. 'Isn't he handsome? Look how wide his brow was. Just imagine how magnificently huge his brain used to be, plotting away inside there! He was a criminal mastermind! A complete genius!'

What do you say in these situations? I stammer politely and say, 'I like his robe.'

'Ah.' Sheila chuckles. 'That's how he got his name. Mu-Mu Manchu. It was my pet name for him and it stuck.' Gently she closes the door and bolts it carefully. 'Good night, my darling.'

Effie is shooting me sideways glances.

Sheila picks up her story, sitting back heavily on her swivel chair. 'So. 1974. We leave the big smoke. The dirty city. We leave the bright lights of my Soho and the dingy lights of his East End behind for ever. My husband gives up his various schemes to conquer the western world. It hadn't worked out in the end, but he wasn't completely disheartened. He didn't think his life wasted. He'd had a smashing time, he said, and I don't think it's vain of me to think of myself as some small consolation.'

'Indeed,' Effie says.

'So he was happy when we came here. He set me up with this place. The Hotel Miramar. He knew I would need some security after he passed on. Obviously, being ninety-two years older than me, he knew that I'd need something to see me through. And I flung myself and all my energies into this place. Into making it work. But, like I say, people weren't always welcoming. They looked down at me, and I was just doing my best. "Never mind them, girl," Mu-Mu would tell me. "You just do your thing." So I did, vulgar as they might have found it. All-night gambling and the discotheque. Strippers and Grab-a-Granny Nites. Swingers' weekends. Whatever I could think of to bring the punters in.'

Effie looks uncomfortable and I realise that hers must have been one of the voices commenting disfavourably on the Hotel Miramar back then.

' "Just be yourself, girl," Mu-Mu would tell me. "There's nothing wrong in doing exactly what you want and stuff the rest of them." And he was right, bless him. He passed away three years after we got here. He didn't get a chance to see this place at its best. He didn't get to see what a success, a gold mine, I've managed to turn it into.

He'd be so proud to see the naysayers so jealous of me. He died in 1977. During a street party for the Silver Jubilee. A fit of anti-British apoplexy.' Sheila sighed. 'I always told him he'd do himself a mischief, one of these days.'

We fall quiet, respectfully, at this turn in the tale. Effie is still trying to catch my attention subtly. I can't look at her to find out what she wants.

'So . . . what can we help you with?' I prompt. 'Won't you tell us what's happened?'

Great big tears are welling up in her green, glittering eyes. 'I . . . had a letter, yesterday morning. What you might call a poison pen letter. It was saying the vilest things. Horrible, vindictive things. All about me and Mu-Mu and the long-buried past.' She lets out a shuddering sigh and dabs her eyes with Effie's lilac hanky. 'Whoever wrote it knew all about everything. Everything that ever went on in our lives. They knew things that shouldn't be known. Impossible things. Damaging things . . .'

I gulp. 'Where is it? This letter? May we see it?'

Sheila looks at us sharply. 'You'll help me then? You'll look into this?'

'We'll see what we can do,' Effie says. Her voice is calm and determined, with only a hint of warmth to it. 'But we'll need to see the evidence, of course.'

'Oh, thank you both,' Sheila gasps. 'It has really upset me, this. You wouldn't believe how hideous it's been. Someone dredging up the past like this . . .'

'So where is it?' asked Effie. 'The letter?'

'It's in my room. Upstairs in the hotel. Locked away. I didn't want to take any chances of it slipping out of my grasp. And I wanted to be sure you would help me before I passed it over to you.'

'Sensible.' Effie nods.

'Is the writer of the letter threatening you?' I ask her. 'Or trying to extort money from you?'

'No, nothing like that. Just saying awful things. Gloating. Jeering. Letting me know that they . . . know absolutely everything about . . . Mu-Mu and me . . .'

I reach across the desk and pat her dimpled hand. 'We will do our best. You asked the right people for help.'

Sheila tells us to enjoy ourselves. We have come all this way to see her and listen to her woes – the least she can do is offer us a few free drinks and a decent night out at the Yellow Peril. 'Don't even think about my dreadful story for the rest of this evening,' she says, showing us out of her office. 'Put it out of your minds. Enjoy. Make merry. And, if you will, return tomorrow and I will hand the horrible document over into your care.'

'Very well,' says Effie. I can see her eyes light up. She can't wait to find out what the letter says.

At first I'm not so sure about us sticking around at the Yellow Peril for the evening. Effie's not the kind to make merry at the drop of a hat, and it really isn't my scene at all. But when Sheila opens the soundproof door and lets us back into the subterranean discotheque, something about the wild drumming and pounding of the music gets into me. It gets into Effie too, like a demon, like a spirit of devilment.

Next thing we know, having bidden Sheila good night, we're having a twirl around together on the fringes of the dance floor. It must be a very popular tune this one, as it seems everyone is up on their feet, bopping about and grinning. Sheila has melted away into the crowd and it's as if she has taken all her sadness and gloom with her.

Effie is puffing and panting and strutting about with her hands in the air. What's got into her? Shimmying about. Dancing rings round me. Shaking her skinny old bottom! But I'm the same! I'm hopping about on one leg and then the other, the slightly slimmer one, the one that's better at dancing. I'm clapping my hands in the air, in time to the beat. It's a long time since I've gone on like this. We're up on the checkerboard dance floor. We're moving towards the centre. Somehow the crowd of busy, jostling show-offs has opened up a space and we're bang in the middle! We're in with the in-crowd! It's Friday night and we've gone dance crazy!

'What are we doing?' I lean in, laughing, and ask Effie at the top of my voice.

'I don't know!' she gasps. 'But isn't it great?'

'What do you think about Sheila?' I ask.

'Were those tears put on, do you think?' she bellows over the blasting music. 'There's certainly something going on here. Something a bit nasty.'

I pull a face. Sheila seemed genuine enough to me. But what do I care? I'm dancing! I'm spinning around! I can hardly catch my breath!

And then I notice something that slows me down a bit.

There's someone watching us from a table at the edge of the floor. He's drinking a green cocktail and nodding in time to the music. An older gent with a crimson bald head, which he mops now and then with his handkerchief. He's wearing a tweedy three-piece, rather antiquated. He must be lathered in here. The mirrored walls are misted up with steam. What's he looking at? What's so amazing about Effie and me? How come he's not eyeing up all the young ones in their hotpants and what-have-yous? But he isn't. The old gent with the silver 'tache – I nudge Effie and point him out to her – he's watching us. He catches my eye and raises his glass to us.

'Cheeky old thing,' Effie mouths at me. We pretend to ignore him, shuffling our feet and jogging our elbows to a slower track.

And so the night goes on at the Yellow Peril.

I'm awake at three twenty. I'm sitting up straight in my bed and my heart's thudding like an old boiler with its blue pilot light flaring like mad. Outside, in the hall, there're these awful noises. Scritch. Scratch. And I'm frozen solid. I can't budge an inch.

What is it with me? Come on, Brenda. You're old enough and ugly enough. But I want to scream. There's a scream wedged solid in my throat, as if I've swallowed a whole frozen chicken. Tap tap tap. Is it one of the guests? Have they come up the top flight of stairs to taunt me? To scare me in my bed?

There's the hollow, clopping sound of tiny feet on the wooden stairs. I'm being haunted by midgets. Heavy, determined, club-wielding midgets.

Now I'm shaking. This is ridiculous. I've faced worse things than this.

But not in my home. Not up here in my attic.

There's a pause. There's quiet again. Then a distant tapping. Trip-trap-trap. Whatever it was is moving away. Trap-trap.

It's gone.

I don't want to go out there. I sit on my bed. I wrap my duvet about me and I sit there for more than an hour, staring at my door. Once, twenty-odd minutes later, I hear scuttling noises. Giant mice in wainscoting. But that's an end to it for tonight. The worst night yet.

There have been several of these weird visitations in recent weeks. Each one has rattled me more than the last.

But I have to pull myself together. I have guests and responsibilities. I need to stow these terrible thoughts away and sleep a little more. Just a couple of hours. I need to rest in order to face the day.

I manage almost two hours of sleep. And then I'm up, doing star jumps, bathing, dressing, and seeing to my duties.

Soon I'm bustling between kitchen and breakfast room, seeing to cooked breakfasts and pots of coffee and tea. My guests are in pairs at the floating islands of their tables, bleary-eyed and crunching away on their triangles of toast, their cereals. As I pass back and forth with steaming plates I can see them casting each other sidelong glances. One of them – a young woman in a tracksuit – takes me aside when breakfast is just about finished. She's used the pretext of asking me about local walks, and she expresses her concern about the noises in the night. I wring my tea towel in my hands as she leans in and looks so earnest and polite. 'We just wondered . . .' she said, 'what it was, and whether everything is all right . . .'

What can I say to her? I try to allay her fears. But what can I tell her? I mumble something about my blundering into a small coffee table in the dark. Cheerfully telling her that's what they must have heard. Even laughing about it, I am! But it must ring hollow, because she still looks concerned as she moves away. What will they be thinking? That their landlady's a secret drinker, staggering about and falling on things at three in the morning.

I plunge into the kitchen and set about the washing-up. I listen to them all leaving for their Saturday out in the town; exploring the abbey and the winding streets. I've not given any of them my usual, upbeat spiel about what to do and what to see. My nerves are too shattered to do my job properly, and they all know it. This is no good. I'll be losing business. I try to assuage my fears in the hot frothing water and the dinful clatter of claggy plates.

And I try to clear my head with a brisk Saturday morning walk of my own, togged up against the April breeze. I head down to the harbour and take huge lungfuls of salty air, watching the fishing boats sliding and jostling and the tourists getting pecked by undaunted gulls. I'm hurrying across the bridge then, on to the path through the old town, to meet Effie for morning coffee.

I dash through the narrow arcades of shops – yellowing books; glutinous home-made toffee and parkin; Celtic jewellery and dense, carved jet. Peering in one of those jet shop windows I notice a man in serge green tweeds, gaiters and walking shoes. As I scoot by, he obviously feels my eyes burning into the back of his head, because he turns and his ruddy face lights up. He grins under that silver 'tache of his, and gives a strange kind of salute.

It's the old bloke who was sitting in the Yellow Peril last night. The old geezer who was watching me and Effie bopping about on the glass floor. I nod at him brusquely – not at all encouragingly – and hurry on by. He could be anyone. A pervert. Anything. But his smile snags a memory for me. I don't know. I'm sure I've seen his face before. His manner is very familiar.

Never mind him, though. Effie will be getting cross as two sticks, waiting all this time.

I'm watching Effie divide up her sticky fruit cake with her fork. 'Sheila Manchu lived the life of Riley,' she hisses. 'What was she saying? Swingers' parties? Gambling and all sorts. And I'm guessing that's not all. I bet that's just the tip of the iceberg. Oh, yes. Whatever is written in that poison pen letter must be pretty strong stuff.'

'I bet she's got some hair-raising secrets for someone

to expose,' I say, blowing on my black coffee.

'Yet she said that it wasn't trying to extort money,' says Effie. 'Not that sort of letter at all. She really did sound spooked to me, by whatever it said.'

There's that word again, I think. *Spooked*. Well, I'm spooked as well, as it happens. I'm always spooked, and just lately I'm more spooked than ever. And who can I tell? Who's going to care? Who's going to come to my rescue? No one will. Of course no one will. I'm on my own with whatever has started to trip-trap around on my bare attic boards in the middle of the night.

Effie goes on. 'We have a job here, don't we? To look into these queer affairs? Isn't that what we were told late last autumn?'

I nod. 'The abbess told us that we are both here for a reason. We are meant to team up and guard the gateway into hell. To keep an eye on who comes popping out. If you believe in that kind of thing, I mean. Destiny. Karma, all that stuff. I'm not sure whether I do or not. I believe in free will.'

'You *would* do,' Effie says pointedly.

I raise an eyebrow. 'What's that supposed to mean?'

'I just mean that you've had to look after yourself, haven't you? And take care of your own destiny.'

I pull a face. She's quite right. I've had to make up my

own rules for a very long time, and I hate the thought of being a pawn for someone else.

But we're getting off the subject. I bring us back: 'I still don't think we should go running to help just anyone . . . and drawing attention to ourselves. If people think we go looking for trouble and danger, then we're bound to find a whole lot more of it at our door.'

'I thought you liked Sheila more than you expected to,' says Effie through a mouthful of cake. 'I must say, I was very happily surprised. I'd always thought she was a boring, blowsy floozy. But I found her rather simpatico, actually. And I was quite touched by the tale she told.'

'I never thought I'd hear you talk like that about the owner of the Hotel Miramar.' I shake my head. Then I remember, and tell Effie about the silver-haired bloke in the green tweed, saluting me in the street.

'Perhaps you've got an admirer,' says Effie dryly, casting her eyes up and down my outfit.

I snort. 'I doubt that, lovey.' Then I think – what if? Wouldn't that be something! But surely not. Surely never again. I'm past all that. I've had my day. I don't draw the stares the way I used to. I don't catch the passing fancy of ageing men any more. But . . . maybe I do! Maybe I have! The thought is a novelty: a suddenly delicious one. I slurp my tea, just thinking about it, and have to dab my chin quickly. I'm light-headed with sleep deprivation and the idea of someone paying attention. I need to pull myself together.

'Where would we start?' I ask her. 'Poison pen letters. That's like real mystery-solving. Proper detective work, isn't it? We don't have those skills, do we?'

She shrugs, as if skills are the last thing you need.

I persist. 'I mean, we say we can help. We claim to be investigating things. But really, we don't know anything, do we? We can't really *do* anything. We just blunder in . . . and often make situations worse than they were before . . .' I've lowered my voice because there's a new party arriving and shuffling in at the table beside us. This place is so tiny, it's easy to give away all your business.

'I can see you're going to be no help today.' Effie sighs. 'Does a night on the razzamatazz always put you in such a negative mood the next morning?'

I bite my lip. I want to tell her about my noises, about the haunting. Somehow I can't. Effie's the one who really believes in ghosts. I'd be mortified to have spirits of my own, polluting my place. Effie would smirk, I'm sure.

'I think,' I say, 'since we've as good as promised Sheila Manchu our help, we had better just get on with it. We need to see the letter itself and then we'll get to the bottom of it. Somehow.'

'I knew you'd do it!' Effie smiles. 'I knew you were looking forward to getting your teeth into a new mystery.'

'Well . . .' I say modestly. 'I didn't really mean it, when I said we had *no* skills. I think we're quite talented, actually. Intuitive, rather than logical and intellectual.'

'We follow our noses,' Effie says. 'So . . . let's follow them back to the Hotel Miramar.'

Sheila greets us effusively in the foyer of her hotel. This time she's wearing a silken oriental shift, which strains over all of her curves. She shows us to the lounge bar and has a tray of drinks brought, so we can wet our whistles as we think over her case.

Effie sips her bitter lemon and realises Sheila is staring at her with a curious kind of respect. 'I understand that there is a tradition here, in this town,' Sheila says quietly, so that guests at the other bar tables won't hear.

'Pardon?'

'For women in trouble like me, going to the women of your family, Effie. And begging them for help. I understand this tradition goes back for generations. Hundreds of years, even.'

Effie is frowning. 'I'm not so sure about that.'

'Oh, I am.' Sheila smiles. 'Like it or not, you're the local wise woman, you are. And everyone knows it, somehow.'

'I assure you—'

'And you're lucky, because you've got Brenda to help you.' Sheila glances round at me, clinking her half of shandy to mine. 'You're a formidable team, I understand.'

'Who have you been talking to?' says Effie darkly.

Sheila shrugs, suddenly inscrutable. She sips her drink in a very ladylike fashion, and a great wash of sadness seems to come over her again. 'You will help me, won't you?'

I pitch in. 'Maybe you should think about whether you have any enemies here in Whitby. Start making a list of those who might resent you so much they'd be prepared to write you a poisonous letter . . .'

'I don't know!' Sheila bursts out, going red. 'There could be dozens! People here have resented me for years. They think I'm sleazy and rich. They come here to enjoy themselves, and then they go whispering about this being a house of ill repute . . . a decadent pleasure palace . . . It could be just about anyone . . .'

I nod, thinking: those are just the terms Effie always used to use when talking about the Hotel Miramar. Most people, when mentioning the place and Sheila herself, would allow a pleasurably thrilling note of scandal to creep into their tone. But would someone like Effie, say, actually write to Sheila with the express intention of upsetting her?

'I think we need to see it, Sheila,' says Effie gently.

We both watch as Sheila glances round to make sure she is unobserved. Then, almost reverentially, she reaches into the gold-embroidered clutch bag on the table in front of her. The envelope and paper are a very plain white. She unfolds the letter and lays it in front of us. It's typewritten, so not many clues there. Effie and I crane forward to read.

Sheila Manchu, you fat old hag, you are a vile strumpet and a festering harlot. You and your husband came here, you slag, and you shamed us all with your nasty and devilish ways. You used your hotel as a front for crime and drugs and sexual perversion, all sorts of wickedness. Everyone in this town despises you! And all of us are glad your old husband is dead and gone into the fiery pit like he has. The gateway into hell is right on your doorstep, Sheila Manchu, and it's waiting for you next. You'll be shoved in there quicker than you can blink one of these days, oh yes. You and your horrible hubby, you'll be writhing on a spit as Satan turns it through all eternity . . . You've never fitted in here, and everyone here has hated your stinking guts for thirty-odd years. The people of Whitby would burn you if they could get away with it. Everyone makes snide comments about you. When you walk through town people turn aside to comment, and to tell each other how horrible you are. There's whispering behind your back all the time. Behind every smile there's venom and bile.

I must say, it would have given me quite a turn too, had it arrived on my doormat with the day's usual freight of junk and business correspondence. I read it through a couple of times and what snags my eye most is the mention of the gateway to hell. Funny thing to drop in, I think. Very specific. Almost as if someone knows it is a proper geographical location rather than a metaphor. Who else in Whitby would know about the Bitch's Maw? Who else besides Effie and myself? Not many, surely, would be aware that the gateway is concealed in the ruins of the abbey. I shudder at the very thought. But for now, I keep it to myself.

'I can see why that would be distressing,' says Effie, stiffly sympathetic.

Sheila is close to tears again. She's shredded her beer mat into fluffy pulp. 'It's that bit about everyone whispering and making snide comments behind my back. That's the worst bit.'

She stops and lets this sink in. I realise that what she's just described is a familiar paranoia of mine. On my worst days, that's exactly how I imagine the world works, with everyone sniggering, pointing and commenting behind my back. Poor Sheila!

'Yes, well,' says Effie. 'That's very helpful, seeing that. May we take it away with us?'

'Of course,' Sheila tells us, and watches as Effie carefully stows the letter in her own plain brown handbag.

No sooner has she done this than we are suddenly joined by a fourth person. She pops up as if out of nowhere, all garish colours and insinuating manner. Rosie Twist is in our midst and we all clam up. How long has she been listening? What has she gleaned? She'll know something juicy is in the offing: we all seem so guilty and quiet.

'Hello, Rosie,' Sheila says, with a sniffle.

'I'd heard something has happened to upset you, Sheila. What's up?' Rosie's manner is, as it is with everyone, pushy and peremptory. There's never any standing on ceremony with Rosie.

'It's nothing,' Sheila says, mopping her eye make-up.

'Come on, I've never seen you like this. You're indestructible! You never get upset! You could have the seven plagues of Egypt unleashed on the Miramar and you'd take it in your stride . . .'

'Just leave it, Rosie,' Effie snaps. 'Whatever it is, Sheila's hardly going to tell you about it, is she? Unless she wants it splashed on the front page of *The Willing Spirit*.'

Rosie shrugs. 'Please yourselves. As it happens, I was

asking out of the spirit of friendliness. Not anything else.' She moves to turn away, sulkily.

'Oh, Rosie,' Sheila bursts out. 'I didn't mean to offend you—'

'I'm quite used to it,' Rosie says. 'Everyone thinks the worst of me. Just because of *The Willing Spirit.*'

'That's because it's the most awful, gossipy rag,' Effie tells her.

Rosie glares at her and storms out of the bar.

'Silly woman.' Effie sighs.

'You shouldn't upset her,' Sheila says. 'She wields a lot of power with that paper. She could destroy anyone in this town. And she knows it.'

'She's *nowt,*' Effie says, using a very precise Yorkshire term. 'And she doesn't scare me. Hardly anything does.'

Now I know Effie is saying this for effect. There are plenty of things that scare her. And somehow, as the shandy goes right through me like a fizzy wave of foreboding, I feel we're straying close to something that's going to scare us both daft.

I have an early night, Saturday, because of all the sleep I've been missing. But round about one in the morning I'm awake again and I'm afraid I make something of a fool of myself.

Who can blame me, though? After the ghastly, wakeful nights I've had, when I hear the noises at one a.m. of course I assume they come from the same source as the sounds that have taunted me for a fortnight or more. I leap out of my bed, furious with fatigue, and I lumber heavily to my bedroom door.

Now, if I had stopped to really listen to those noises, I'd have realised they were different from what usually comes to haunt me. These weren't pitter-patter, scritchy-scratch. These were heavier treads on the stair carpet; these were doors slamming downstairs. These were tipsy giggles from my paying guests. But I hurtled out on to my landing, bellowing at the top of my voice. I'm squirming, even as I remember this, and the spectacle I must have made of myself in my voluminous nightie with my wig not on. I must have been terrifying as I came crashing down the top flight and then the bottom flight of stairs, screeching and howling like a great bald golem.

I came face to face with Mr and Mrs Marsden from Room Three. They were struggling with their keys and they looked appalled to see me. In fact, they looked horrified at the sight of me. They both shrieked and I was brought to my senses with a jolt.

Almost immediately, others were coming out of their rooms to see what was going on. The couple from Room

Two, across the landing, looked bleary and perplexed.

I started stammering apologies. They must have thought I was a wild woman. A maniac. They would all want to leave early in the morning, I was sure of it.

'I thought we had burglars . . . It's so very late in the evening, you see . . .'

Mr Marsden had a protective arm round his wife. He waggled his Yale key at me. 'We have been out dancing. Enjoying ourselves. We didn't expect to be greeted like this.'

He looks me up and down. And then I see that all of them, all four of them – and the other two, now coming up from downstairs to see what's going on – they're all looking me up and down, somewhat disturbed by my physical presence. Mrs Marsden is still whimpering in her husband's arms, she got such a fright when I jumped round the corner. And I think: I've got no make-up on, nor my wig. All my scars are on show. I might as well be standing here in the nuddy. I'm here before my paying guests in all my glory. My horrifying glory. No wonder they're looking at me like that.

I apologise again and beat a hasty retreat.

'Get an alarm fitted!' Mr Marsden yells after me, and I colour with shame.

He's right. But an alarm would be no good against the noises I usually hear in the night.

I lie awake in my bed for some time, imagining what

these couples under my roof will be whispering to each other in their rooms: what will they be saying about me? Will they leave straight away in the morning? Have I disturbed them that much? I'm dreading getting up to do the breakfasts. Imagining their snide looks. Their smirks.

I toss and turn, dreading the coming of the real noises.

I try to distract myself by thinking about Sheila Manchu's case.

On our walk back into town at teatime, Effie talked a bit about her experience of Sheila over the years, which didn't amount to much. She wanted to fill me in on the things I didn't know, since I only arrived here last year. There wasn't much to tell me, beyond the tittle-tattle I had already heard. For over thirty years stories had circulated about the town, of the petty crimes and misdemeanours and the scandalous things that went on at the Miramar. Effie tried to make me appreciate quite how wicked it all seemed, back in the seventies. People would discuss Sheila's doings in whispers. And, while Mu-Mu was still alive, there was always that threat: the glamorous danger that came with his name. People were scared of Sheila and her husband. They were connected to all sorts of badness.

This is how my thoughts go swirling round in my head, over and over, as I lie there in the night, spent and exhausted. Waiting for my haunting to start up again. But nothing comes. Not tonight. Or if it does, I am insensible to it. For the first night in ages, I sleep like a dream.

And I wake feeling marvellous. And if my guests give me funny looks over their breakfasts I hardly notice. Luckily, no one leaves early, and no one asks for a refund.

The next day or so passes in a haze of hard work. I feel obliged to smarm up to my house guests by cooking them a proper Sunday lunch. I know it's not the kind of thing most B&B ladies do, but it's my firm belief that extras like this are what draw the punters back. My guests this weekend are rather surly and ungrateful, I think. In the end I regret spending my time basting the joint, straining the greens, fluffing up the Yorkshire puddings. I am pleased to see the back of my visitors, come Monday morning. Funny, some of these people passing through your life, you just don't seem to take to them. By lunchtime on Monday I can hardly recall their faces.

My memory's not the best though, as you know. Especially when it comes to faces.

Still, Monday afternoon gives me one of those rare moments when the synapses (is that the right word?) fire off in the right order, and the old skeins of cobweb come floating down from the rafters of my mind and suddenly something comes back to me. Light dawns! Sparks shoot across my vision. My face cracks out in a huge grin.

I have remembered something so gobsmackingly obvious I can hardly credit the fact I would let something so important slip out of my head.

I'm in the beer garden of the Hotel Miramar when it happens.

I've had a wander up there alone, just mulling things over. Sometimes I think better when I'm not accompanied by Effie's constant chatter. I can't tell her this, of course. She'd be mortified. Anyway, it's a stuffy, standstill kind of afternoon, and I know Effie is home, stewing over the puzzle of Sheila Manchu's letter. As ever, I prefer to be up and doing. Before I know it I'm up at the Miramar and I'm delighted to bump into Robert, who is on duty for the afternoon.

We're out in the beer garden – or the scrubby bit of grass at the back that Sheila wants to turn into a beer garden – when I have my blinding revelation. We're standing on the terrace and Robert is describing to me what the garden will look like.

'A barbecue?' I'm saying. 'Marvellous. I'm surprised she's never had one before.'

'She's going for the whole Polynesian, Tikki look,' Robert's enthusing. 'Waitresses in grass skirts and what-have-you. She's ordered all this very expensive bamboo garden furniture . . .'

'It'll take her mind off her upset,' I muse.

'That's what I think it's for,' he says. 'She's throwing herself into this beer garden project so she doesn't have to think about whoever it is who means her harm.'

I turn back to him. 'Do you have any ideas who it might be?'

Robert looks uneasy. 'Loads of people in Whitby have secrets. There's lots of shady characters, too. People who enjoy making others suffer. What I'm thinking is, what if there's a whole rash of these letters? Who knows what might come tumbling out into the open?'

He loves a bit of melodrama, does Robert. Still, the thought makes me shiver, as we stand in the afternoon sunshine. And that's when I have my revelation, or my flash of remembrance, or whatever it is.

'Oh, look, it's him!' I hiss, clutching Robert's arm.

There's the old feller, coming out through the French windows, into the garden. He's stretching and yawning, presumably after a post-lunch nap. He's in his green tweeds again and his walking boots.

'It's really him! I know who he is! I remember now!'

Robert looks alarmed. 'Who? Brenda, what are you on about?'

Very dapper and self-possessed he looks, too, as the sunshine gleams off his bald pate and his immaculate moustache. He hasn't heard me squawking out – luckily. I'm drawing Robert back behind the box hedge, so we can watch him unobserved.

'I know who he is!' I whisper harshly into Robert's ear.

'Brenda,' he says impatiently. 'You are acting very oddly.' Bless Robert: he feels it's his duty to alert me to these moments. As if I could rectify them somehow and start to behave properly!

'Henry . . .' I gasp, as memories come floating back to me through the past's vortex. 'His name is Henry.'

From afar we watch the old gent take a few deep breaths. Then he strides out, wielding his walking cane. He toddles off happily down the garden path.

Robert frowns. 'What's the big deal, Brenda?'

I watch the old feller disappear round the corner, off on his walk.

'I've seen him about the place. In the nightclub, and then in town. He recognises me too, but he hasn't come over to talk to me. He's just nodded and winked . . .'

Robert laughs at this. 'You've got an admirer, Brenda!' He's chuckling, but I'm disturbed by all of this.

'Henry Cleavis . . .' I say. 'But . . . but it can't be. It really can't be him.' Now I'm pacing heavily around the yellowed grass of what will become Sheila's beer garden. I'm just about pounding my fists into my brow, forcing the memories to return. 'Think! Think! When did you last see him? When did it end?'

Robert's after me, concerned. 'Brenda . . .?'

'It really can't be him, Robert,' I gabble. 'There's something wrong here . . .'

And then I'm off, before Robert can say anything more. I'm pulling my anorak back on and hurrying round to the front of the hotel, even trampling on the flowerbeds in my haste. Back to the main road. But Henry Cleavis has gone. I've missed him again.

But it can't be him, can it? Surely he'd be dead by now.

Me, with my long-lived life: I'm used to knowing people and leaving them and losing them and having to forget them. Just for my own sanity's sake. Otherwise there is just too much to remember. Too many memories to fit inside one body.

And so, in order to ensure that I go on surviving, I have to quite deliberately make sure that I forget them. And so these people – these lovers, friends, allies and enemies – they vanish somewhere, back in the past. That's the cruel way it's always been. No one – hardly anyone – endures as long as I do.

But now this . . . Henry Cleavis. Here in Whitby. He has come back. He has reminded me that he was once in my past. Here he is, sprightly and cheery as ever before.

If I knew which way he'd set off walking, I'd go chasing after him. I would. Now I know it's him, I'd hound his footsteps.

But I've missed him. All I can do is hurry home, back down the hill into town. I knock up Effie and she's been having a siesta. She looks rumpled and cross when she comes to the door. I don't know how she makes any money in that shop of hers.

'What? What is it?' she demands.

I drag her on a walk over to the old part of town, to our favourite confectioners, where we can buy home-made dark chocolate and black treacle toffee. So we have something to chew on as we go over our quandaries.

We often wander like this, pausing to peer in the tourist shop windows as we go by. We are wending, that's what we're doing. Wending our way up the cobbled lane that leads to the one hundred and ninety-nine steps going up to the abbey that overlooks Whitby. I'm not sure we'll clamber all that way today. In recent months Effie and I have kept away from that Gothic monstrosity, and not without reason.

We're happy simply peering through the thick pebble glass and sucking on our shards of treacle toffee. Except Effie is crunching hers. I can hear it, as I bend in close to look at a brooch she points out to me. How can she crunch things with her false gnashers in?

'All this jet,' she says, gesturing to the shelves and shelves of matte black jewellery. 'In years gone by it was supposed to have a function quite other than being purely decorative, you know. The townspeople would take a cross, say, carved out of jet, and nail it above their front doors.'

'To ward off the devil?'

'Amongst other things.' She squinches up her mouth. 'Jet is supposed to emit a foul vapour of some kind, quite lethal to evil spirits or evil-doers . . .' She harrumphs, as if dismissing the idea. 'I believe that several of my ancestresses were seen off that way. According to local legend, anyway.' She shrugs lightly.

'Oh really?' I go quiet, wanting her to go on. It's rare that Effie talks about her witchy forebears. She certainly doesn't expound upon the topic of their ultimate demises. But then she sighs and straightens up and rustles in her paper bag for the last sticky hunk of toffee. We amble up the sloping path and she changes the subject.

'Two names stand out for me,' she says. 'Two possible suspects. I don't know yet why they would be doing such a thing. I don't know what they have got against Sheila Manchu. But the two women I am thinking of are two who know plenty of secrets. They know more than anyone else here . . .'

I have dressed up too warm for this spring afternoon. Woolly tights . . . what was I thinking of? My old heart's yammering and banging away with all the exertion. My palms and the backs of my knees are itching and trickling with perspiration. 'Which two women?' I ask Effie. What I really want to say is: Oh, do let's have a sit in the Walrus and the Carpenter, Effie. But Effie's in full flow.

'For one,' she says, 'Rosie Twist.'

The crowds are denser here, near the antiques market and the shop where they smoke kippers. Effie should keep her voice down. 'Oh,' I say. 'You just don't like Rosie. Why would she send letters like that? When she can write whatever she wants – very publicly – in *The Willing Spirit* every week? Why would she need to sneak around?'

'Hmmm,' says Effie.

'Who else?'

'Mrs Claus,' Effie says, in a much more tight-lipped and ominous fashion. By now we are at an ironwork bench at the foot of the famous steps. Gratefully I plonk myself down on it and Effie perches beside me, rather more elegantly. From here we can look out and survey all the blue and purple rooftops across the steely sheen of the harbour. We can see right over the other side and the Georgian splendour of the hotels on the Royal Crescent.

'You've a point there,' I mutter, and find that I'm staring

at the tall windows of the Christmas Hotel. I am glaring at that gaudy tribute to bad festive taste: that tawdry establishment where the grotesque Mrs Claus rules her own fantasy empire.

'She knows many things she oughtn't,' Effie says.

'Don't I know it.'

'She is malign and powerful. She will stop at nothing.'

'I know that too,' I say. In fact, thinking about it now, I am astonished that no one has tried to put a stop to her. Why haven't the authorities intervened? Are the police all terrified of her? She seems to run the whole town. Her fingers are in every single pudding. How come no one has got rid of that monstrous yuletide hag?

I am embarrassed that Effie and I – after tangling briefly with her evil schemes last year – haven't been back in order to sort her out. We have just let her continue, getting up to whatever nefarious doings she fancies.

Surely it's about time that someone put an end to the evil reign of Mrs Claus?

'But why would she be threatening Sheila Manchu in particular?' Effie sighs.

'They're business rivals. Vying for the holiday trade.'

'They have very different clienteles. Mrs Claus has the elderly and the Christmas-obsessed. Sheila caters for an altogether racier crowd.'

'That's true.' I think again. I click my fingers. 'What about Robert? He left the Christmas Hotel in order to go and work for Sheila. Perhaps Mrs Claus is very sore about that?'

Effie gives me a withering look. 'You may think a lot of Robert, Brenda, but I hardly think Mrs Claus would declare war over the loss of a single elf.'

I shrug. 'We don't know how her mind works. There could be any number of twisted reasons behind this.' I sit back on the groaning bench and pretend to be mulling it over. My mind is elsewhere, of course, and Effie realises it. She turns on me with a shrewd look in her eye.

'What is it?'

I've been caught out. 'I've remembered who he is. The old bloke I've seen round and about the town; staying at the Miramar. He's someone I used to know, a great deal of time ago.'

'Oh, really?'

I nod firmly. 'And I've got a funny feeling in my water' – Effie makes a squeamish face at this – 'that Henry Cleavis is here in order to see *me*.'

'You?' Effie cries. 'How can you be so sure?'

'You don't understand. A lot went on in the past. Between me and Henry. I don't recall all of it – yet. But it's coming back to me in dribs and drabs. Like his name did. I'm sure the whole thing will click into place, and then I'll know. I'll know why dear old Henry has come looking for me . . .'

Effie's face softens. Now she looks concerned. She shields her eyes against the sun's glare and stares at me. I know I must sound a bit crackers to her. So sure. So convinced. 'Oh, Brenda. Don't go setting yourself up for a disappointment.'

I assure her that won't happen.

'I mean, if he was here to see you, then surely he would have popped over by now and said something? He's noticed you, hasn't he? He's looked straight at you. So how come he hasn't come over and said anything. Hmm?'

Cheeky mare. *And* she's finished the last of the toffee.

These midweek days with no guests booked in, I'm at the mercy of my nightly brouhahas. The skittering and pattering on the staircase. The terrible footfalls. The profound pauses – which are even worse. At least there is no one to hear me crying out in the night. I have no need to stifle my shrieks of alarm. I don't have to be embarrassed by these terrors of mine. Terrors that are growing wilder and more uncontrollable with each passing night.

But why should I be scared?

Who on earth could hurt me, really?

I am the indestructible woman. I have survived so much.

So many years. So many adventures. I've always come through the other end. I've hardly ever been injured or ill. Nothing much has disturbed the remorseless plod of my life. So why should these noises get under my skin like this? What is the matter with me? Am I turning soft in my advanced old age?

Wednesday morning and the phone goes early.

It's Robert, on an early desk shift at the Miramar. It's his first chance to check the bookings. 'You're right,' he tells me, without preamble. 'Henry Cleavis *is* his name. He booked in a week ago. Gives an address in Cambridge.'

My heart's banging and I'm starting to see whirling spots. I grip the receiver more tightly and thank Robert profusely. 'I knew it was him.' But it's something else again to hear proper confirmation.

Robert says, 'You sound disturbed by all of this. Is he an old friend of yours? Aren't you glad to see him again?'

I swallow hard and tell Robert: 'I last saw Henry Cleavis in . . . it must have been 1946.'

'That's a long while,' Robert says, clearly unsure of my point.

'Sixty years or more.'

'So? Were you brought up in the same place?'

I smile. 'You flatter me, Robert. But you know I'm considerably older than that.'

'Oh,' he says. 'So you are.'

'And so is Henry Cleavis,' I add. 'If I recall correctly, he was in his mid-fifties in 1946. He was a don and erudite as anything. He was bald as a coot even then. He must be well over a hundred now and he hasn't aged a day. So what's that all about, eh?'

Of course, Robert can't possibly know what it's all about. Once again the poor boy is out of his depth. Just as he was last year, when he and his poor Aunty Jessie ran into trouble at the Christmas Hotel, and Effie and I had to do our best to rescue them (with mixed results). Anyway, I thank Robert for his efforts and the info, and I struggle into my housecoat and the day ahead. I've a family of six called the Pinkneys invading this afternoon.

Downstairs, picking up provisions in the grocery store beneath my B&B, I discover that my pre-dawn hullaballoos haven't gone unnoticed by shop-owners Leena and Rafiq. They live right next door, of course. I hadn't even thought they might hear my shrieks and wails. Now Leena is staring at me, full of concern, as she rings up my comestibles on her antiquated till. 'I really wouldn't be complaining,' she's telling me, 'and it's not like we really mind about the noise and everything. It's just that we are worrying about you, Brenda. This cannot be right. Shouting out like that in the dark.'

I am mortified, packing my stuff into my shopping bag as quickly as I can. I want to be out of here, and right away from Leena's unctuous care. 'It won't happen again. I've got some sleeping pills now.'

'Nightmares, is it?' Leena simpers. 'Only Rafiq could have sworn he heard you running up and down your stairs. Throwing things about. Heavy things, too. I told him, don't be silly, Raf. Anyone can have nightmares.'

'Quite,' I say stiffly, thrusting cash into her eager mitts.

At last I escape from the shop. And I try to put all of that nonsense out of my head. The hauntings are something best kept for the night. If I think about them at all in the daytime I could really start to believe that I'm cracking up. And I don't want to think about that possibility.

I hurry home. It's time to get to work.

But: on my doorstep there's a hand-delivered letter.

I frown as I stoop to snatch it up. Someone's dashed up the side passage with this in the small span of time that I've been fetching my groceries. It isn't one of Effie's urgent spurs to action. And then I think – jarringly – what if it's a poison pen letter? What if I have received my very own envelope crammed full of bilious hatred and spite? What if persons unknown – armed with a rattly typewriter, somewhere out there, at large in Whitby – what if they know me and all my (admittedly terrible) secrets?

I quell my ragged breathing. I slam the front door shut. I struggle with my bag up the stairs to the cool seclusion of my kitchen. And I make sure I am quite settled and calm when I rip open the mysterious communication.

The handwriting is awful. Erratic, all over the place. The stationery is serviceable and plain. There's an air of distraction about the whole thing: as if it's been written by a man (I see at once that it must have been written by a man) with much on his mind. A very brilliant mind.

Halfway down there is a spot of what might be jam.

My dear Brenda —

Oh, my dear, is it really you? Why haven't you said anything? Why don't you say hello? At first I couldn't be sure. You were squinting at me, and I was squinting at you. The two of us were squinting like mad across the crowded dance floor, weren't we? And then I was sure. And I saw you again in the town! And I knew, I knew it had to be you.

I would love to take you to dinner this — no — tomorrow night — evening — Thurs. We have so much to say to each other, I am sure. I hope you are free and available.

All this time! So long! So much to say! Hello, my dear!

I thought you must – felt sure you must be – dead – deceased – by now. Luckily you are not.

I thought you were long gone. Remember the last time? You ran out on me, didn't you? I never saw you again after that terrible scene down in London. What happened then, Brenda? How did you survive?

I'm sorry. I am being impolite. Firing questions at you like this. But I can hardly believe it! Who would have thought we'd just bump into each other like this, all these years afterwards.

Here we are! Two great survivors of the twentieth century! In the land of the living!

How do you feel about fish and chips? I've noticed somewhere down on the harbour front – looks promising – Cod Almighty. Do you know it?

Well – enough of me for now. There will be time enough to discuss everything on Thursday night. Don't go dressing up.

I will call for you at seven, shall I?

Oh, you are a treasure! You always were!

With very best wishes and my admiration,

Henry (Cleavis).

I should have guessed it, but Effie is sceptical about the whole thing. Thursday morning, we're having coffee together, and I wish I hadn't told her anything about my impending date.

'I thought you'd gone a bit coy,' she says, sucking liquid sugar off her spoon.

'Coy!' I laugh.

'No wonder, if you're running about the town with old men. No wonder you've lost interest in the job we've been asked to do.'

I sigh, mashing up the layers of my custard slice. 'I haven't lost interest . . .'

'Have you asked me about the latest development then?'

I frown. 'Is there one?'

'I received a phone call early this morning. Sheila had thought of someone who she has confided in in the past. Someone she told all her secrets to.'

'Who's that?'

'The Reverend Mr Small,' Effie says. 'I've never liked him much. Fancy telling that old gossip all your secrets!'

'But surely he would never write a letter like that . . .'

Effie shrugs. 'Who knows? But I'm going over to the church to have a word with him, this afternoon. I'm going to check him out. Will you come?'

Now I'm torn. I've work to do. I've got to get a lot done this afternoon, if I'm going out this evening. I tell Effie this as we leave the Walrus. She doesn't look impressed. 'You need to prioritise,' she tells me, clipping off down the cobbles.

'That's what I am doing!'

'So I have to go and see the Reverend myself? While you go gallivanting? I thought we were a team, Brenda!'

She's laying it on a bit thick. 'It's hardly gallivanting, Effie. It's only Cod Almighty. And can't you see? There's a mystery here, too. I mean, how can Henry Cleavis be as old as he is? And why's he here? In my experience of him, wherever he was, there was always something fishy going on.'

We're striding out over the low bridge, across to our part of town.

'He'll be after something from you,' Effie warns me. 'You mark my words. This isn't some cosy, harmless little reunion. This old chap will have ulterior motives in getting in contact with you. It won't make you happy.' She's shaking her finger at me. Suddenly I want to be away from her. I make my excuses and dart away to Woollies. I'm embarrassed when she starts yelling at me across the busy road: 'Hanging about with strange men only leads to disaster, Brenda! You should nip this one in the bud straight away!'

People are looking. They'll think we're both crazy. I give her a hurried wave and slip into the shop. I'm using it as an escape route, for the door at the back – but while I'm here there's no harm in picking up my usual bag of pick 'n' mix.

As I'm scooping up my favourites and having them weighed, and then hurrying off again, Effie's words are ringing inside my head. I try to clear it. She's gone bitter because of Kristoff Alucard. He gave her the proper runaround. I was the one warning her about him. Does she think this is payback time? Has she been put off men for ever? Can't she even conceive of a gent's wanting to take me out on his arm?

Poor Effie. Beneath that respectable frontage of hers, it's all confusion and just a little bitterness. She's not a very happy soul.

Now. Put it all out of my thoughts. I have the Pinkneys' rooms to attend to. They've left such a mess. They've come through my house like a boisterous whirlwind. I've my work cut out for me today. But that's okay. Tending to them will take my mind off my nervousness. I need to press my new outfit, and tease my best wig into some sort of style. I've got to exfoliate. Consider my make-up. Consider what to say to him. And try to remember as much as I can.

I feel as though Cleavis is coming towards me across a vast gulf of years. He's bringing me gifts. That's how he was in my troubling and nebulous dreams last night. He was bringing me the gift of myself. Bits of forgotten me. Whatever it was we got up to together, in the 1940s, he's bringing those memories back with him. On a funeral barge, moving through the mists. Like something from the Egyptian Book of the Dead. He'll have organs of mine, and slices of my raddled mind in ornate jars with dinky lids and handles. His job will be to reunite me with these forgotten parts. In my strange dream of last night he was passing me these beautiful vases and jars and restoring me to myself.

Everything I have deliberately put away and forgotten. He'll be bringing pieces of it back to me.

I slept so deeply, so contentedly, I never woke once. I don't even know if those wicked noises came again.

I was standing on a sandy beach, clutching these jars with my organs inside, and my memories were flooding back. Then I was watching Cleavis set sail again in his ancient barge, on the black and oily water. He cut an impressive figure in his tweedy suit, drifting away from me across Lethe or Styx or whatever it was.

I'm having a little sit as I wait for Henry to arrive. I don't want to spoil the perfection of my ensemble: to muss my hairdo or wrinkle my dress.

There's his gentle rapping at the door downstairs. After all this time he has come for me. It's all I can do not to leap up and fly down the stairs. But I don't want to seem too keen. I don't want to frighten him off.

He's examining the peonies in the tubs in the side passage. He turns to beam at me. 'Brenda, my dear.' And he embraces me. His mustard worsted jacket is rather tickly and mothbally and it's this that sets my eyes watering. That's what I tell him.

'Sixty years!' he gasps, holding me at arms' length and sighing with pleasure. 'You're still the same! How?'

I'm rather blunter with my own, almost simultaneous question: 'Why aren't you dead?'

He laughs at this. 'Still the same! Still the same!' Then he takes my arm. I check I've got my bag, my keys, everything I need. Then I walk out with him, into the high street, and allow him to guide me to Cod Almighty, which just happens to be my favourite restaurant in town.

I'm aware of Effie's upstairs window and the raggy curtain billowing. She's desperate for us not to see her but I catch just a glimpse of her eager expression.

Cod Almighty isn't particularly smart. It's homely and quick and does the best fish and chips in town. My own favourite is whitebait, which arrive steaming and golden in a neat little heap. It's like eating a whole miniature shoal of fish.

Cleavis nibbles at a triangle of white bread and he explains why he isn't a day older than the last time I saw him. 'Ah, yes. Um. Well – that's hard to – explain. It's – not the easiest. Well. Um. Well, you know how I was wont to go on my little jaunts and adventures. And. Um. I went all over the world. Underground societies. Spy rings. Satanic cults. That sort of thing.'

I smile and nod encouragingly. He doesn't mean, of course, that he was actually *involved* in satanic cults or spy rings, or whatever. What he really means is that it was often his job to infiltrate them, and to destabilise them from within. Under the guise of a bumbling, middle-aged, harmless academic – an Icelandic specialist at that – it was relatively and surprisingly easy for Henry to inveigle himself into the most alarming of places.

'I remember your adventures, yes,' I say. In fact ... I remember that we were embroiled in hair-raising adventures together, once or twice. It's starting to come back now. I think.

'Anyway, in the fifties. Some time. I was sent to Africa. Deep into the heart of Africa. I don't know. Some hidden-away place. Lost city kind of thing. High priestess. Gods and goddesses. Funny business with old treasure. Elixirs of life, that type of. You know, malarkey. Blah-blah. And terrible danger, I don't mind telling you.'

'I can imagine,' I say, spearing up a whole load of whitebait and crunching them up. Delicious.

'Anyway ... well. The upshot was. Yes, I did. I walked

into the blue flame. Absolute sacrilege. They were horrified. As they might be. And their old queen is lying there, dead as a doornail. And the city is shaking and rattling and falling down about their ears. And I say, "Whoops," or something and everyone's a bit stunned. And there I am, with eternal youth! Well, eternal middle age. I live for ever! Hurrah!' He turns his attention to the chips he's left cooling on his side plate.

'Are you sure?' I frown.

'Seems to be the way. I'm over a hundred now. Not doing too bad. Lived a bit of a quieter life, since the seventies, anyway. Fewer adventures and all. I've taken up writing. Marvellous fun! Lovely!'

'I don't believe you, Henry,' I tell him.

He slurps his tea. His moustache is soggy with it. 'What's that?'

'I don't believe you've given up the adventure business. Secret cults and elixirs. Monsters and demons. I can't see you ever giving that up.'

'Ah, well. Maybe. Maybe not. It's different these days. The other Smudgelings are all dead. It's hard. Watching everyone die before you. You know. You know that, of course, better than. Better than anyone, Brenda.'

'You're right. I do know. But I know that I've got to go on. I can't just get sad and stop living, much as I might want to.'

'Oh, I'd never feel like that,' Henry says happily, chomping on his chips. 'There's still so much to do! So much! Busy! Busy all the time!'

Now I want to get down to business. 'Why are you here?' I lower my voice and my head, until I'm staring him dead in the eye. Milky blue, bright, alert. He blinks at my question. 'Did you come looking for me, Henry?'

'Why . . .' he says, slowly smiling. 'Do you want me to be here, looking for you?' And now he has dropped that somewhat affected stammering manner. He's staring back at me and holding my gaze.

I look away first. 'I'm not sure. My memory is patchy, you know. Far too patchy. I can't even remember how and why we parted. I don't know where it was, or when. Some time in 1946. But under what circumstances, I have no idea. Not any more.'

'Really?' He's produced a huge paisley handkerchief and he's dabbing at his 'tache. 'That's a shame. Memory. Funny thing. My own . . . well, it's quite good. Surprisingly.'

'Lucky you.' We go a bit quiet for a while. I'm not going to beg him or blurt out all the questions. I know I could ask him what it was we were up to, on that adventure together in London back then. But I'm not going to ask him. I must have had good reason for putting those memories away. And so I am content to trust my younger self and her reasons for forgetting, and for protecting me now.

This is my new life. I'm happy here. He can't make it any better than it is. Whatever he might tell me. Whatever missing pieces he might bring back to me.

At last he says, 'I had no idea you were here, Brenda. Came as quite a shock. Really. Seeing you there. Amazing! What a coincidence! I mean, really!'

I'm such a foolish old woman. Of course he's not here for my sake. Of course not. Why would he be?

'So . . . why *are* you here, Henry?' I ask him, and my voice is thick with disappointment.

'What else?' he chuckles. 'Same old. Funny business. Demons. Satanic stuff. All that terrible stuff!' He grins at me, as if he expects me to share his delight. Old fool.

But I'm a worse fool, of course. I grab up the dessert menu and waft it savagely in my face to dispel my embarrassment. 'Knickerbocker glory? There's a glorious one with crème de menthe . . .'

So we finish off our night spooning up green ice cream and acid-coloured minty sauce.

'You know, Henry,' I say airily, as we finish. 'Your business and mine, they're not so very different these days. Demons and whatnot.'

He looks at me quizzically, but I just tap my nose. Let him stew over that for a bit.

71

*

After all the excitement, Friday night sees me quite content to slop around at home in my dressing gown. I'm brewing up a pot of spicy tea when Effie comes knocking. Of course she wants to hear all about my date, and you can tell she's miffed I haven't already been round hers to report.

'There's nothing to tell . . .' I try to protest. We carry out tea things to the living-room area of my attic and curl up on the two squashy armchairs. I turn my attention to the record player, flick through some old albums.

'Come off it, Brenda.' Effie chuckles. 'I want to hear every detail. You must be bursting to tell me.'

So I tell her everything I think she might be interested in. Everything about my reunion with Cleavis that she might find amusing. What we ate. How he looked and how he treated me (like a lady, though I insisted on paying half. 'What?' Effie gasps, incredulous). I put on a nice old soothing Billie Holiday album.

What I don't tell Effie is how Cleavis has jogged my memories of the 1940s. I don't know why I withhold this. My longevity isn't exactly a secret from Effie. Poor old Effie has been made privy to most of my secrets. Somehow, still, I don't like alluding to them when I'm talking to her. It doesn't seem very tactful, reminding an old lady like her that I'm nearly immortal. So when it comes to my erstwhile adventures in 1946 and all that, I keep schtum. I focus on the events of last night which were, of course, rather pleasant. He walked me back to my door and came in for a mug of this gingery, peppery tea. He was sitting where Effie's sitting now and we shared a companionable silence in which nothing particularly earth-shattering was said or done.

'Will you see him again?'

'Oh, I'm sure I will.'

Effie frowns and slurps her tea. 'It's not sounding like the romance of the century, so far.'

'It's not,' I said. 'Just a meeting of old friends.'

'But he came here looking for you . . .?'

Sadly I shake my head. I have to own up. 'I'm afraid not.'

'What?'

'I asked him. He said no. He's here for other reasons altogether. Seeing me again was just a shocking bonus.'

'Ah, Brenda. I'm sorry. Are you disappointed?'

I think about this. 'Not really,' I tell her.

'I did warn you,' she says, 'about setting yourself up for a disappointment.'

I'm thinking: how could he have come looking for me anyway? After all, I've left no trail that I know about. I'm missing off official records, aren't I? It's a tangled old route that leads to my door. Not even Cleavis – not even if he had been really looking – could have found me. Not through any normal channels.

I let the topic slide. I don't want to be discussing my Henry with Effie like this. I try to get her talking about poison pen letters.

'Sheila Manchu's gone a bit quiet and ashamed and won't be pushed. She says she wants to forget about it all. And, meanwhile, the Reverend Mr Small didn't give anything away whatsoever.' She sighs, and holds out her mug for more tea. I wrestle with the knitted cosy.

'I really don't think he could have written that letter. Not the Reverend.'

'I suppose you're right.' Effie sighs wistfully. I can tell she'd enjoy pinning the blame for the letters on him.

'I think it's got to be Mrs Claus who sent it,' I say at last. 'Only she would be rotten enough. Anything bad in this town, and it always seems to be her behind it.'

'Perhaps.' Effie pulls a face. 'But I still fancy it's that idiot Rosie Twist. Just think of the way she looked the two of us up and down. Last weekend at the Yellow Peril. She has this insinuating manner about her, like she knows far more than she's telling.'

'You're just being paranoid, Effie.'

'Am I?' Effie tuts. 'I still think it's her. With her nasty tan and her awful clothes. I think she's gone crackers. I expect to get one of those wicked notes myself, any day now.'

'What can she accuse you of ? What have you done that's so bad?'

Effie gives me a peculiar, dark look at this.

The record finishes and I get up to turn it over. I hobble across the sheepskin rug because one of my legs has gone to sleep.

And then – I don't know why – I launch into the tale of my almost-nightly hauntings. I haven't told Effie anything about them yet. I've kept all of that quite private because it makes me feel a bit foolish. But now, for some reason, it seems time to share.

So I tell her. Every detail. The scratching and tapping. The tiny footsteps in the hall. The creaking doors. The whumps and thumps. And me: sitting up rigid in bed, holding my breath and passing out with fear in the wee small hours of nearly every night.

'Brenda!' she cries. 'Why didn't you say something before? That sounds awful!'

'It's been really horrible,' I tell her. 'I don't know what to do about it.'

'Do?' She frowns. 'I'm not sure there's anything you can do about it. Not if your ghosts are like my ghosts. I've got them, too, as you know. My hauntings are a bit gentler than yours, though no less persistent. My female forebears are there all the time: hanging around, disapproving of me. Trying to get me to do precisely what they want. They mutter and agitate and peer down at me from the walls. But I have learned to live with them. I ignore them. It drives them crazy! But I simply won't give in to them. And you must learn to do the same, Brenda. You've just got to rise above all this fuss and nonsense.'

'I'm not sure I can . . .'

She's looking at me oddly. She's surprised I'm so disturbed. I've shown my weakness to Effie and now she doesn't know what to say. We finish our tea in quiet, and then it's time for Effie to go home, and nothing more is said.

And I am left alone in my attic, once again, to face my night terrors.

They come again, of course.

It sounds as if there's an octopus dancing on the wooden landing outside my bedroom door. Or a giant spider, maybe, trip-trapping so softly out there. I can see its shadow creeping under the gap of light.

But the biggest shock and the worst thing comes with first light. Effie's back at mine, banging on the front door with bad news. She's heard something dreadful. Gossip in the downstairs shop while she was fetching her newspaper and milk. She thinks I need to be up and witnessing this.

She thinks it's germane to our investigations. And she's right. But I still resent having to fling on my clothes and follow her out into the chilly town before eight o'clock on a Saturday morning. I follow her, though. I'm tingling with weariness and pins and needles as the sun warms up the whole of Whitby. I follow her through the centre of town and up on to the cliff edge in front of the Royal Crescent.

Just yards away from the corner of the Christmas Hotel there are police vans and a cordon that's only just been set up. Ghoulish spectators are gathering and that's what we are, too, as we approach and bustle our way to the front: craning our necks to see.

At first I think the cordon and police activity are to do with the Christmas Hotel. Perhaps there's something dreadful going on there again. Or perhaps Mrs Claus has been busted at last. But, no. The police are scared of her. They'll never take her in. And now I can see that the cordon is over on the grass: around the very edge of the cliff. The vans and cars have pulled up to the edge. There are police down on the beach, far below on the narrow strip of dirty sand.

'It's a jumper,' Effie says.

I look at her curiously, thinking it's an article of clothing she's seen, but then I realise what she must have meant by that. The small crowd around us is whispering, muttering, pointing. The surf below is lashing at the rocks and it's hard to hear anything. We peer down at the coppers and the medics by the body of the jumper, which is spreadeagled there in their midst and obviously stone dead.

Just before they cover it up and roll it away we see enough of the body and what it's wearing. That lime green dress. That red overcoat. That dayglo tan.

We don't have to say anything to each other. Effie and I both know who it is who's gone plummeting off the tallest and cruellest of these cliffs.

It's Rosie Twist lying down there. She'll be missing her weekend deadlines, I think. For both *The Willing Spirit* and its supplement, *The Flesh is Weak*.

Effie's a bit heartless. 'This makes things more complicated,' she says, with a sniff. 'I could murder some breakfast. What do you say, Brenda?'

Chapter Two
Womanzee Must Die!

It's guilt that drives us, I suppose.

That's why we go out there, so early Monday morning. Me more than Effie. She doesn't see how we are responsible for Jessie. She doesn't feel guilty at all. But still she accompanies me, at the crack of dawn.

We're taking kippers to Jessie, who is living rough.

She used to be so smart. So particular. Now here she is, hiding out in what amounts to a cave. She lives in a hole in the cliff underneath the abbey. Her nephew Robert found it for her. It's the safest place for her to be.

Effie doesn't agree. 'She should be handed over to the authorities,' she grumbles, yet again, as we make our way through the deserted streets. The light is a gentle gold across the bay, and the air is very cool and soothing. Effie's constant mithering is the only irritant this morning.

'Robert can't simply turn her in to the police.' I sigh. 'He feels responsible for his poor aunt. And how she's ended up.'

'The zoo might take her. Does Flamingoland still have Baboon Mountain?' There's not a flicker of a smile on Effie's face.

'Don't be cruel,' I say.

We have to walk past all the tourist shops, and past the bottom of the one hundred and ninety-nine steps. Then there's a row of tiny holiday cottages, and finally a quieter, scrubby path, which skirts round the headland towards Jessie's hiding place.

'The silly woman brought her downfall on herself,' says Effie. 'If she hadn't been so keen on regaining her lost youth and messing about at that boutique last year, she would never be in the mess she is.'

Effie knows it isn't as simple as that. True, Jessie did go mad on the weird rejuvenation treatments on offer at the place known as the Deadly Boutique. Lots of women in this town trooped into that dodgy place: lured by the promise of having decades knocked off their natural ages. They should have known, however, that miracles of the sort they were experiencing come at a ghastly price. Effie and I watched in appalled wonderment as these duped women swanned about Whitby, looking young and beautiful again. Jessie – who was a waitress at the Christmas Hotel – was the most amazingly transformed of all. She had knocked off about forty years.

These things always come at a cost, of course. When Effie and I investigated we uncovered the vile schemes of Mr Danby, who owned that decadent parlour up Frances' Passage. It turned out that he was placing these women in his mysterious Deadly Machine and robbing them of their life essences, which in turn he was feeding to his tiny, vampiric mother who lived in the flat upstairs. Anyway, no need to go into the details of it now. Suffice to say that Effie and I were both nearly killed during our adventures in the Deadly Boutique. And Jessie was somehow turned into something from the dawn of time. She reverted far too much and now resembles what Effie calls an Australopithecene woman, the poor thing. Worse was to come for Jessie, though.

'I don't like seeing her.' Effie shudders. 'Especially now she's dead.'

And it's true. We were all there for Jessie's funeral, at St Mary's church, at the top of the hill by the abbey. Her heart had packed in as a result of the makeover traumas. We were there when they laid her to rest. And Effie and I – embroiled in another adventure completely – were there in the dark graveyard the night that Jessie had clawed her way out of the grave.

Jessie the primitive woman – the womanzee, as Effie mockingly calls her – is now a zombie womanzee. And she is a very disconcerting person to visit.

She is sitting there Monday morning, by a smouldering camp fire outside her small cave. She's crouched over, glowering at the horizon. Filthy dirty and hairy as anything. She's caked in all sorts of muck. We can hear her growl at us warningly as we approach. Effie's cracked voice gives out a jaunty 'Good morning!' as she struggles to give the impression that we have tramped out here because we really want to. I am swinging the shopping bag of kippers and the flask of tea, and I find myself waving airily at Jessie and Robert. Her nephew is crouching beside the fitful fire with her, gallantly toasting muffins on a sharp stick. He waves at us, glad that someone has turned out to visit.

'I'm amazed no one's noticed her living here,' Effie hisses at me, before we get too close. 'Anyone would have the screaming abdabs, bumping into her.'

'Sssh.' I pat her arm, and call out loudly, telling them what I've brought.

And then we are squatting uncomfortably on the damp sand, having a picnic with Jessie and Robert. For all of Robert's effusiveness and delight at seeing us there, Jessie seems – as usual – monumentally unimpressed. Though it's true she doesn't express much these days outside a vague crossness and ravening hunger. This morning she looks both me and Effie up and down and goes, 'Glooop,' in a very melancholy tone. It's the only human word she still has in her vocabulary and, as Effie points out, it isn't even a word.

Robert is very brave, carrying on as if we've chosen to have a picnic out on the beach as a silly whim; a pure piece of pleasurable indulgence. He unwraps the kipper we have brought and holds it out to his aunt and, for a second, he looks like some supplicant, kneeling with his offering before his primitive goddess. 'Gloop,' says Jessie, and snatches the flat fish out of his hands. She crams one end hungrily into her mouth and I sense, rather than see, a shudder pass through Effie's body.

'It's good of you to come, Brenda,' says Robert. 'It's so easy to feel that Aunt Jessie has been forgotten by the whole world.'

I smile at him. 'It's the least we can do, lovey. It's no trouble, really.'

'I'm glad it's warmer now,' he says. 'The winter was terrible for the poor thing. I never thought she'd survive.'

Effie coughs politely, looking away from Jessie as she devours her breakfast. 'How long can this go on, though? You can't keep her here indefinitely, Robert.'

Robert blinks sadly. I feel my heart go out to him. 'I really don't know, Effie. This is a pretty unique situation. I'm not sure what I should do . . .'

Effie purses her lips. Then she says, 'It's not just about her safety and well-being though, is it?'

I narrow my eyes at Effie. I just know she is about to put her foot in it. 'What do you mean?'

'Well . . .' Effie casts another glance at Jessie, who is happily crunching up fish bones and flesh, in a world of her own. 'She is out here, free as can be . . . and we know what a temper she can have now, in her altered form, and . . . frankly, who can blame her? It must be absolutely terrible to find herself . . . in these straits. She used to be a quite attractive woman. So who's to wonder at her going off the deep end, now and then?'

Robert is opening the flask of hot tea we've brought. I'm holding out the plastic cups. Robert pauses before he pours, frowning. 'I don't know what you're saying.'

Effie takes a deep breath. 'I mean, what kind of danger is she to the public?'

'The public? Why, none . . .'

'How do you know that?' Effie says. 'You can't watch her all the time. She goes roaming around here at night on these beaches. She could be up to all sorts that you don't even know about, Robert. She could be . . . I don't know . . . doing anything. She's a wild woman! A monster!' These last few, terrible words have emerged from Effie in a breathless rush.

We stare at her. So does Jessie, with a mouthful of kipper. It's as if even she realises the awful thing Effie has said. 'Gloooop,' says Jessie, with just a hint of animosity.

'You shouldn't have said that,' Robert tells Effie. 'My Aunty Jessie would never hurt anyone.'

Effie scowls. 'You don't know that. The way she is now, no one knows what she is capable of.'

I put in, 'I don't think she'd attack anyone, Effie. It's not in Jessie's nature . . .'

'*But she isn't Jessie any more!*' Effie bursts out. Then she stands up, and dusts crumbs of damp sand off her new mac. 'Oh, look. I'm sorry if I've offended you. I feel I just have to say my piece. I think you're going to come a cropper hiding your aunt out here in the caves.'

Robert simply stares at her, his trusting face full of hurt. I don't know what to say. I feel ashamed of my best friend. Jessie has turned back to her rough meal.

'And think of this, too,' Effie goes on. 'Jessie might get blamed for things. Like Rosie Twist, going off the top cliff the other day. They still don't know who was responsible for that. Now, if anyone gets wind of Jessie the wild womanzee camping out on the rocks . . . Can't you see how easily they could fix the blame on her?'

Effie has a point. I hadn't thought of it like that. It would be a simple matter, should Jessie come to light, for the whole town to demonise her. That could end very nastily indeed.

Robert's hand shakes as he pours out milky tea. He doesn't say anything to Effie.

'It's all very well going into denial,' Effie snaps. 'It's all very well ignoring the sense I'm talking . . .'

'I'd prefer it if you didn't come to see my aunt again,' he tells Effie in a very level voice. 'She only wants her real friends to visit her.'

'Glooop,' says Jessie, as if to underline his point.

Robert adds, 'You're still welcome, Brenda. I know you'd never turn against my aunt.'

I wince. 'Robert, I think . . . maybe Effie has a point, perhaps . . . It's not entirely safe here for Jessie . . .'

He looks at me with tears in his eyes. 'Then where can she go, Brenda? Where does a woman like her hide herself away, eh?'

And I can't tell him. I have to tell him that I don't know.

It's a very gloomy little party that Effie and I leave behind us on the beach that morning. We shuffle back home after our visit, feeling that we have made things somehow worse.

*

The Christmas Hotel is the last place I want to go for dinner. But when Henry calls me I don't feel I can refuse. Is that weak of me? I think it is.

I doll myself up, feeling cross with myself. But I could hardly go into all the reasons why the Christmas Hotel is my least favourite place in Whitby. Not over the phone, at any rate. You don't know who might be listening in.

What could I say? The place gives me the creeps. Mrs Claus is always up to no good. Effie and I were held captive there during our investigations last autumn – bound and gagged in the attic – and we only just escaped with our lives. That was to do with the business of the human flesh in the pies. I don't want to go into all of those details with Henry just now.

On go my glad rags. I even slip on my mismatched dancing shoes, in case he asks. I smarm on my lipstick and I examine myself from every angle for flaws. I'm not perfect, but I'll do.

When he calls he's extremely smart, in a smoking jacket and a cravat. I'm proud to be seen walking out with my professor in the early evening.

We stroll along the prom and I could almost feel that we are strolling in a different age. The rowdy kids at the amusement arcades simply melt into the background. Their noise, along with that of the tiny fairground and the honking traffic, dulls down into a persistent buzz, harmless as the noise of the sea. Henry and I simply bustle along happily, towards our supper date, and it's as if none of the hurly-burly of modern life can even touch us.

'I could tell, my dear. That you weren't keen.'

'But I am! I am keen!' And I make a note to myself not to seem *too* keen.

'On coming to the Christmas Hotel. I could tell by your tone. On the phone.' Now we're puffing slightly, clambering up the winding steps to the front of the Royal Crescent. We pause at the top, surveying the brilliant blaze of lights along the hotel fronts: how welcoming and classy they look. And we look out at the bronze smoothness of the sea; the cankered, jagged blackness of the cliffs and the abbey. And I find I'm searching out the caves along the front. But of course I can't see Jessie skulking about on the beach: the shadows have grown long and it's too distant anyway. But I know she's down there, ekeing out her miserable afterlife – as my new beau accompanies me to the hotel where she was once such an accomplished waitress.

'The thing is,' Henry says thoughtfully, 'it's a place I want to see. For myself. You see? Things there. Of interest, hm?'

He's so elliptical. But I think I get his gist. We scurry across the road and the porter opens the main doors for us and suddenly it's Christmas time all over again. The foyer is swagged and festooned with more tinsel and glitz than ever before. The muzak carols are booming out at an even more ear-splitting level. Henry turns to glance at me quizzically, and bursts out laughing. He looks completely delighted by the staff who are helping the elderly guests to their places. As always, the staff here are dressed in green and scarlet elf outfits.

'I think it's quite marvellous.' Henry grins, once we are settled at a table in the restaurant. We're in one of the best: a bay window right out on the front, so we can watch the sun slide down behind the sea. 'Scampi!' Henry exclaims, flapping the menu. 'Steak and kidney pie! Yum!'

I shake my head quickly. 'Don't eat the pies here,' I tell him.

He raises an eyebrow and then I have to explain about the whole cannibalism business from last year. I mean, we didn't actually prove anything. It was just Robert's strong suspicion. And he was the one working here: he saw what went on. And we did, after all, find his Aunt Jessie's then-dead corpse in the walk-in freezers . . .

'What a life!' Henry chuckles, shaking his head. 'What a life you lead, Brenda!'

'Hm,' I say, wishing he'd lower his voice slightly. 'I'd stick to the vegetarian option, if I were you.'

But Henry wants turkey and all the trimmings. He wants the full yuletide experience at the Christmas Hotel. While we eat and drink I notice that his shrewd eyes are flitting about the place. He's taking in every detail as the guests chunter, chatter and chew on their mince pies and puddings. He's alert to everything and suddenly I am compelled to ask him: 'What *are* you investigating, Henry?'

'Hm? Me? What do you mean, my dear?' He holds out his cracker and, momentarily forgetting my own strength, I pull it and almost have his poor old arm out of its socket. He laughs ruefully, rubs his shoulder, and insists that I put on the party hat.

'When I used to know you, back in the past,' I persist, 'you and your fellow dons were always up to something. You were always looking into your secret cults and wicked goings-on. You're still doing it, aren't you? The Smudgelings are still active.'

'Oh,' he sighs, and a greyness settles over his face. 'They're all dead, Brenda. Tyler died in 1972. Most of the others went before he did. My brother John, bless him, went to his Maker in the late seventies. He was in New York. Nasty things lurking on the disco scene. So there's just me. Only me left. I'm the only Smudgeling still going.'

He's smiling at me sadly, and I feel silly and cruel in my

paper hat, asking brusque questions like that. But Henry Cleavis is gentle and he doesn't mind, I can tell. Then he wants to ask me a question in return.

'Why did you go?' he asks simply. 'You ran out on me. Poof. And at such a moment! I never understood. We were friends. How could you? How could you leave, Brenda?'

I flush. I look down at my half-eaten lentil bake. I don't know what to say to him. I really don't. With a shock, I realise my eyes are misting up. I can't look up at him again. I can't meet his gaze. He'll think I'm ridiculous, crying as easily as this. He won't understand. How can he understand?

I end up mumbling into the crockery: 'I don't remember, Henry. I can't remember how . . . it finished. I don't remember things in detail. Running out on you . . . is that what I did? I don't know.'

'You did,' he said. 'You left me. Alone in that terrible place. Right at the worst possible moment.'

Now I do look up. 'What terrible place?'

Henry's eyes widen. 'You really don't remember, do you?'

'It was over sixty years ago, Henry . . .'

'But I don't forget. I couldn't forget an escapade like that one in Limehouse.'

I frown at him. Limehouse? I can't remember ever having been there, I don't think. Something stirs and ripples in my mind. Then it's gone. I shake my head to clear my thoughts. 'I'm an old woman, Henry. A lot of my memories simply aren't there any more. I've had to let them go. There's only a certain amount of room in one addled old head. Can we drop this now?'

'Of course,' he says gallantly. But he looks very troubled. And, truth be told, what he's said tonight has put the willies up me, as well.

As the evening wears on there is one of the hotel's frequent festive singalongs and Henry and I try to make good our escape. We hurry through the tables as the old people start to clap and bawl. When we pause to pay our bill the elf at the counter introduces himself. He's somewhat plump and young and shifty-looking.

'I'm a friend of Robert's. Martin. I know he's pals with you, Brenda. How's he doing?'

'Oh, fine,' I say airily. I don't want to give too much away. I don't trust anyone here at the Christmas Hotel. 'He's very happy at the Miramar.'

The elf nods gloomily. 'He was never happy here, really. Not since . . . well, what happened to *Jessie*.' He doesn't fully vocalise the name of Robert's aunt. He just mouths it at us.

'Who's Jessie?' says Henry.

'Long story,' I tell him.

'I'm surprised you're here, Brenda,' Martin says, in a queer tone. 'I don't think there's much love lost between you and Mrs Claus, is there? I've heard her talking about you.'

I shrug at this, though I hate to hear about people talking behind my back. This Martin sounds like a stirrer to me, a trouble-maker, and I don't trust him. I smile tightly and turn away.

'Not very comfortable. Were you? Eating here tonight?' Henry asks me, as we scoot across the gaudy carpet of the foyer and out of the place.

'I'm just glad we didn't come face to face with Mrs Claus herself. She's a terrible, hectoring, bullying sort of person. All bright red and shouting heartily. Wanting everyone to join in the fun. She seems all jolly on top, and then you realise there's this terrible emptiness and hollowness and savagery inside her. She's an utterly self-centred and depraved creature inside . . .' I shiver at my own words as we step out on to the prom.

'I'd have been fascinated,' says Henry. 'To meet such a person.'

As we walk back along the seafront it takes us a few moments to realise that there is more noise than usual coming from the amusement arcades. It hardly seems possible that they could get any louder, with all their screeching music and jangling and whining of electronic gewgaws. But tonight there are screams of horror lifting eerily into the darkening air. Screams?

'Something's up.' Henry's nose is twitching with alarm. He seizes my arm and we both hasten, instinctively, *towards* the source of the noise.

What we see down there sends a shudder of dismay through me.

'What is it?' Henry shouts, over all the clamour. We are stuck in the path of teenagers pelting out of the Silver Slipper arcade. Boys and girls alike are white-faced and panicked. 'My God!' barks Henry. 'What have they seen in there?'

Even before I catch a glimpse of her, I know who it is. And I know that Effie was quite right, this morning, to express those few badly received words of caution.

I can see that Henry is about to plunge bravely into the coruscating lights of the Silver Slipper. His dander is up, I can tell, and he must know what is happening inside there. I warn him. I tell him to be careful.

'My dear.' He smiles, puzzledly, as if he didn't know what circumspection was.

But it turns out that we needn't go in there at all. The source of the noise and the panic is coming out to greet us.

More cries of abject horror. The last few stragglers are hounded out into the open air. And then we see the rough beast they've been so scared by, as she comes slouching out on to the prom.

'Oh, Jessie,' I moan, falling back.

Jessie has been on a rampage.

Somehow she has been drawn to the golden lights of the arcades. Tonight she has loped across the sands at low tide, drawn by the shallow entertainments on offer on the western pier. She has arrived here, naked and smeared in filth, shrieking and gibbering like the womanzee she is. Behind her I can see cracked and smashed-open machines. She has destroyed these things with her bare hands. I push Henry back, out of her way, as she hurries by us, into the open air. She gives a huge roar, throwing back her great shaggy head. She doesn't recognise me.

More screams as she crosses the road. A taxi swerves. Jessie roars again and the sound is an ancient, primeval one, echoing across the bleak bay.

Then she's gone. She's nipped down the steps, back on to the beach. We cross the road after her and peer down over the edge and she's been swallowed up by the shadows. Just in time. There are sirens. Police, an ambulance, arriving in the minutes following her departure. I hope she hasn't hurt anyone. They'll get her if she has. Even as it is, I think Jessie's days must be numbered. People know she's here now. They know she's a pest.

'That was amazing!' Cleavis can't quite catch his breath. 'I've seen nothing of the sort before! Not in this country, at any rate. You say she's called *Jessie*?'

I nod grimly, looking out over the bay. 'She used to be my friend.' And I hope she makes it back, across the wet sand, to the sanctuary of her cave.

It takes me some time to get over the shock of seeing Jessie there, and everyone's reactions to her. And even *I* was looking from the outside, frozen on the pavement, clutching my handbag, all dressed up, thinking she was monstrous. Me! This time, it was me, Brenda, thinking that somebody else was the monstrous one. Novel for me. Though I had neither the time nor the inclination to gloat about it.

How could I gloat? I was watching the normal human beings – the holiday folk – running away and shrinking from Jessie's touch. They fell back in horror at her approach. She has mutated so far into something from their prehistory: they seem to have an atavistic dread of the woman, with her matted fur, distended swaying breasts and long, yellow fangs. She is unforgivably far removed from what they regard as human. And so they will want her taken away. They will want her destroyed.

Henry and I talk about this in anguished whispers as we walk back through the town. We can hear the news passing from mouth to mouth amongst the night-time crowd: the truth becoming elastic, exaggerated, as it spreads into the consciousness of the place. There's a monster on the loose. A female monster.

Even as Henry and I discuss the matter, I am thinking private thoughts I would never say aloud. I am thinking that I can suddenly appreciate how I might be seen by the normal folk. Looking at Jessie from the outside, I am suddenly aware of what it is like to gaze upon a monster.

And what if my disguise ever fell away? What if people saw through all the fragile bits of my human alias? Some night when I thought I was blending in, and mixing with the everyday mass of people . . . what if all the wigs and the outfits and the skilfully applied make-ups simply dropped off? What if they could see through my feeble attempts to remain inconspicuous? And they saw me as a freak. A beast. A creature to be hounded out of town.

Well. It's happened before, hasn't it?

It's very easy to turn back into the monster. I just have to stop making the effort. I could revert, easy as anything.

And then I'd have to move on again. I'd have to leave this latest home behind. I've done it so many times before. But not here. This time I'm staying. I can't let those shrieks of horror get under my skin and discombobulate me. I have to hang on to myself. My heart goes out to Jessie, though, and I hope there's something we can do to help her.

Does Henry Cleavis expect to be asked up for coffee? It doesn't even cross my mind. I plant a swift peck on one of his shiny red cheeks and push him firmly off in the direction of the Miramar.

My head's splitting now, from thinking about monsters.

Funny thing happens, Tuesday morning. I'm actually feeling quite cheery and ready to face whatever the world can throw at me. I've had a decent night's rest again. I'm managing to catch up with the sleep my ghosts have robbed me of. But I wake to the sound of somebody else moaning and wailing and full of upset. It's next door. I can hear a woman crying and a man's voice, trying to calm her down. With a shock I realise it's Leena. I realise that, in all the time they've lived next door, I've never heard their voices coming through the rough plaster walls. They are the quietest neighbours in the world.

Of course, I have to find out what the palaver's about. I have a quick breakfast and make my way to the shop at the front. They haven't opened up. The place looks so strange without the boxes and boxes of dew-covered fruit and vegetables ranked outside. Their lack makes me think something absolutely awful has happened. I knock on the front door. No answer. I bang hard on the front door. I start to get impatient and keep on banging till I get a result. These are my neighbours! I need to know what's going on!

When he opens the door just a crack to speak to me, Raf looks drawn and pale with worry. He explains that they are taking a day off, and I'll have to walk to the new supermarket for my supplies this morning.

'That doesn't matter.' I shrug. 'I'm more worried about all the crying I could hear through my walls . . .'

Raf gulps. 'I'm sorry about this. If we disturbed you . . .'

'What's the matter with Leena? What's happened?'

He darts a backward glance. She's calling for him from upstairs, sounding like an invalid. 'Look, I shall have to go, Brenda. Leena's needing me.'

'But what is it? Maybe I can help. What's happened? Do tell me, Rafiq.'

He frowns heavily. Such a good-looking boy, even when he's distraught like this and peering through a tiny gap in the door. 'She got a letter this morning. She doesn't know where it comes from. She started crying as soon as she read it, at breakfast. I've never seen her like this before.'

I nod grimly. 'She isn't the only one.'

'What do you mean?'

'Where is this letter?'

'She put it straight down the sink. The whatsit, the waste disposal. I never got a look in. I don't even know what it said. She's been hysterical ever since. Look, Brenda . . .' Leena's pathetic voice is more persistent now, wafting through the shop.

'Will you let me in to speak to her?'

'Not yet,' he says, looking panicked. 'She's in no fit state. I've never seen her like this before. Come later, maybe, huh?'

He just about slams the shop door in my face as he darts off to see to his wife.

Well. I wonder what was said in Leena's letter. Something awful, to make her react like that. I turn away, musing. Why didn't she keep the evidence? Was what the letter said really that bad? Was she really that ashamed of its contents?

Seems to me that whatever the letters are saying, it must be true.

Of course, I have to tell Effie about this latest development.

I have to suffer her awful tea in her messy living room.

It's rare that Effie actually lets anyone into her home and, when you're there, you can see why. Fastidious as she is, the old thing isn't very house-proud. There's dust an inch thick everywhere. The pictures and mirrors are opaque with it. When I ease myself down on the old horsehair sofa, I imagine I can feel the dust mites jangling about inside the old fibres.

Effie's brewing up some of her tarry black tea and listening with pursed lips as I tell her about Leena and her reaction to her letter.

'Hmm,' she goes. 'I've always thought that girl's got something to hide.' This morning, Effie doesn't look at all sympathetic. She tutted and rolled her eyes when I told her about the waste disposal. 'Whoever is sending these things knows just the right thing to say. In order to make the maximum impact. Quite a skill, really.' She hands me my tea.

'Something else,' I say. 'I thought we'd seen the last of these letters.'

Effie knows what I mean straight away. 'You mean, because of Rosie's death? Murder, suicide, whichever it was.' She passes me a plate of rather grey-looking biscuits. 'You thought that was the end of it?'

'She was one of our best suspects . . .'

'Perhaps.' Effie crunches into a custard cream. 'Unless . . . the letters went second class . . .?'

'Hand-delivered, remember? At least, Sheila's was. No stamp. We'll have to check with Leena later about hers.'

'Hand-delivered, hmm.' Effie frowns. 'Someone very local. Very handy. Making mischief. Deadly mischief.'

I realise, watching her, that she's quite enjoying this whole business.

My phone's ringing when I get back home. Sharp, insistent, clamouring for my attention: I get the feeling it's been ringing for some time. I pound my way up the stairs and burst into my attic. It's Robert.

'We've missed you, up at the Miramar. Haven't seen you in a few days.' He's on early shift at the front desk again, running up Sheila's phone bill.

'Sheila clammed up on us, Robert.' I sigh. 'Said there was nothing else she could tell us to help our investigation.' And then, lowering my voice slightly, I let him know what happened next door this morning.

'So it couldn't have been poor Rosie writing these things . . .'

I sigh. 'That's what Effie and I have just worked out. I feel bad for suspecting her now.'

'There's something else,' Robert bursts out. 'Someone else got one of those letters this morning.'

'Who? Not you, Robert?' My heart leaps up at this in dismay. I realise that I'd go ballistic should anyone see fit to threaten him.

'No, no. Guess who, though? Mrs Claus! She woke up this morning to one of these insinuating missives. And she just about exploded with wrath! She'd been dreading getting one of these things and went into meltdown as soon as she saw it on her breakfast tray this morning. Apparently she's had a right bad turn!'

I frown. 'But how do you know this?'

'Martin the elf. Remember him? Friend of mine from the Christmas Hotel.'

'Oh yes.' Indeed, I remember him better for having seen him last night, when I was there myself. I didn't like the look of him. I never have. Sneaky-looking sort.

I'm distracted for a second then, realising that I've had tea and mouldy biscuits with Effie and she never once asked me about my date last night. Jealous old thing. And, as a consequence, I never thought to tell her about seeing Jessie on her rampage through the Silver Slipper. Well, perhaps it's just as well not to confirm Effie's prejudices. Now I'm thinking: do I tell Robert? Will he want to know that his aunt is running about the town, monstrous and in the nuddy?

Best keep it for a while, that news.

Right now he's telling me something else, in that endearing, urgent way he has.

Midnight tonight, is what he's saying. Out on the west pier. Can you make it, you two? He's saying it's the only time he can get safely out of the hotel. When he can get away without anyone noticing. Well, I know that's true, the way things are at the Christmas Hotel . . .

'Sorry, lovey,' I interrupt. 'I've lost your gist there. What are you on about midnight for? What's that about the pier?'

Robert is very patient with me. He repeats: 'Martin says there's *more* news. Something else. And he wants to tell you and Effie. Tonight. On the pier. He's got some info for you two in particular.'

'Us two . . .?'

'And midnight is the only time he can get out from under the control of Mrs Claus.'

I nod slowly. 'We'll be there,' I tell him.

'Gotta go. Here comes Sheila!' And his phone slams down.

It's a remarkably clear night tonight. There's no cloud cover at midnight and the day's heat has departed. Luckily, Effie and I had an inkling of this and we've wrapped up warm for our jaunt on to the west pier. The moonlight is stark: drenching us in blue. Our footsteps sound very loud on the old, worn stone.

'Are you happy then, Brenda?' Effie asks.

I glance at her. 'With what?'

'You know.' She smirks. She sounds a bit schoolgirlish and coy. 'With your feller.'

'He's not my feller.' I look around then, knowing that he's up there, on the prom somewhere. He's watching us from one of the memorial benches, through an ancient pair of binoculars. When I told him about his meeting he wasn't at all pleased. He insisted on spying on us from the shore. The shore's a long way back, though, from the end of the pier. I'm not sure what kind of help he could be, if anything kicked off. But I like the fact that he still wants to be there. On the alert.

'You *look* happy,' Effie observes.

Well. I haven't even really thought about it. I suppose that means I *must* be happy.

Henry Cleavis is behind it all, of course, and shrewd Effie realises this. At least she is being a bit more gracious and she has stopped openly criticising him. Meeting him on the prom tonight – Henry gallantly clutching his binoculars – she allowed herself to be formally introduced to him. She has started to act as if she is glad for me. I know she's impressed by his smartness, his classiness. And, as we stroll nervously down the curving pier, she is showing a genuine, open interest in him.

'An academic, eh? An expert on the Icelandic sagas, you said? And he's retired, is he? And where was he a don, hm? Oh, very nice, Brenda. Very nice indeed. He sounds like a fascinating person.'

She's making a proper effort, is Effie. And I'm glad about that, as well.

It's a long time since I felt anything like this.

It's funny, to wake up in the mornings and to know that most of the things I'll do today will be just ordinary, mundane things. The humdrum things I always do. Buying sausages and tea leaves. Making up beds. Scouring out bath tubs and polishing brasses. But I also know – in the instant that I spring awake – that I'll see *him* today as well. I know that chances are we'll spend some portion of the day together. We're in those early days of (say it!) a romance, when time concertinas up. The gaps between sightings are short but, subjectively, very far apart. We'll make time to meet, or we will just happen into each other, easy as you like. This town is small enough for some benign, gentle force to guide us into each other's orbit. I will see him today, and tomorrow, and the next day. I feel that he is part of my life now. I have never felt so pleased and . . . buoyed up.

Effie is peering off into the dark realms of the sea, leaning over the railings. She scans the flats of the sands, all the way across to the eastern pier, which bends to almost touch the end of this one, like a gigantic pair of calipers. The harbour is the safe space between the piers: the town's huge maw. Effie can't see anything yet. Neither can I, even with my heightened senses.

I haven't opened my heart to Henry Cleavis. I haven't told him anything yet. I tell him I'm pleased to see him when I do, but that's as far as confession goes. I don't want to go making a fool of myself. It could be fatal, to start slobbering over him and getting over-emotional. But tread easily, Brenda. Don't come on too strong. (But, really! What a thought! I feel ridiculous for even writing it down.) I shouldn't go on daft, getting my hopes up. I can't go acting like a girl.

I never was a girl, was I? I was always as I am.

I don't think Henry will ever really feel anything for me. He's a timid, bookish bachelor. He's over a century old! There's no place in his life for a woman like me.

There's no way he would ever feel like this – this wonderful! – about me.

I'd best keep it all under my woolly hat.

'Ah,' says Effie, jolting me out of my reverie. I blink.

'What is it?'

She's facing back down the long stretch of pier we've covered. She's looking back down that avenue of wrought iron lamps. There's a man coming towards us. He's hurrying along: a tubby, unathletic figure, making for the end of the pier. Furtive, keeping his head down.

'That's him,' Effie says. 'This Martin person.'

And as he nears us at last, we see he's in the Christmas Hotel's regulation red and green figure-hugging elf suit.

'That doesn't do *anything* for him,' Effie says.

I shush her as the young man approaches. His face is twisted with exertion and near-panic. There's something about the look of him that disturbs me. And suddenly I know that Effie and I will have to tread very cautiously with this one.

'I know you are big pals with Robert,' he says. He stares right into my face. There's something in his eyes that I don't like at all, but I return his stare bravely. What can he do to me? There's two of us here. There's Cleavis ready to come running. But still something about this young man unnerves me. 'If Robert trusts you, I can trust you,' he says. His breath is shuddering out of him. He keeps darting looks back at the bright facades of the hotels.

'Look here,' Effie says. 'What is all this about? What makes it so imperative that you drag the two of us out here . . .' I can hear St Mary's bonging out midnight over the harbour and a chill sweeps through me.

'I needed to get away from her influence . . . right away . . .'

Effie raises an eyebrow. ' "Her"?'

'I don't know how much Robert has told you,' Martin goes on. 'About the way Mrs Claus . . . has everyone under her thumb . . .'

'Drugs in the cocoa,' I blurt. 'That's how Robert reckons it's done. Mind-altering whatsits.'

He looks surprised. 'You know, then. You know how she gets everyone doing her bidding.' He looks on the point of tears. 'Terrible things, sometimes.'

'Calm yourself down,' Effie says. I'm amazed to see her patting and rubbing the elf's back. Not like her at all. But this boy seems as if he's about to have a nervous breakdown on us.

'She was so scared, you see. She was convinced that . . . Well, she's got a lot to hide, see? And she thought it was the only thing to do . . . Of course, she never does her dirty work herself, does she?'

'Hang on,' I say. 'You're rambling. Slow down. Deep breaths.'

'I take it by "she", you mean Mrs Claus?' Effie asks, darting me a quick glance. I swallow hard. It looks as if we are about to be drawn once more into the malign world of Mrs Claus's eternal Christmas.

'Of course I mean her,' Martin says resignedly. 'She controls us body and soul, you know. We have no will, no volition, outside her. We are her puppets, in that ghastly hotel. The staff and elderly guests . . . all dancing to her insane whims . . .'

'What has she done now?' asks Effie steadily.

'Robert escaped,' Martin goes on. 'He got away from her. So it isn't impossible. But I am weaker than him. I must be. I can't get away. Only . . . sometimes . . . like tonight.' He looks as if he is wrestling with himself: as if part of him wants to go tearing back to the hotel. The words are leaping out of him in fitful bursts. He's like man possessed, and I dread whatever it is he wants to tell us. 'Robert said that I must confess to you two. That you will help. That you will know what to do. He says that you are good women . . .'

'Cut the flannel,' Effie breaks in. 'What has Mrs Claus made you do?'

I look at her sharply, alarmed by her tone, but it seems to have done the trick. Martin gets to the point: 'Mrs Claus was terrified of getting one of those letters. Word's gone round town about Sheila Manchu. Terrible secrets coming to light. Mrs Claus has got a lot to hide.'

'I bet she has,' Effie breathes. 'And what conceit the woman has! Imagining that she would be next on the list!'

'She had a good idea who's been sending these things, these letters, out. She's had her eye on this person a good long while. Never trusted her an inch.'

Effie and I draw even closer as Martin lowers his voice. He's talking more quietly than the gentle sussuration of the sea, but we don't miss a word of what he's saying.

'Mrs Claus was certain. She's always so certain. She's

always right. And so she sent me out . . . on a little errand.'

'No!' Effie gasps. 'Murder?'

Martin's face squinches up and he sobs desperately. 'There was nothing I could do! We can't resist her! She has hooks into us, into our flesh and our minds. We can't resist her . . .'

'What did you do?'

'I lured the victim here. On to the western cliff. Back there. I phoned her. I told her I had information. I had the dirt on Mrs Claus. Well, I knew that would draw her out. She'd go anywhere for a story like that. She couldn't believe her luck. So she came. Late at night. She came up to the cliffs to meet me.'

I can hardly credit it. He's confessing in such a deathly and calm monotone.

'Rosie Twist,' Effie says. There's an edge to her voice – bitter and harsh as old coffee grounds. 'I thought nowt of her, but she never deserved to die like that.'

There's a pause. Martin looks down at the mossy stone underfoot. His face is hawk-like in shadow. I instinctively draw away from him.

'I lured her there. Right to the edge. Making promises. Sure she was the one sending the letters. It was obviously her. She knew everything about everyone. She was in a position to threaten people. That's why she always seemed so . . . superior and sardonic. Rosie Twist.' Now he looks savage. He looks murderous once more. But hold on. Don't panic, I tell myself. Stay with this.

'You shoved her over the edge,' Effie tells him. 'You murdered her.'

Martin nods. 'Because I had no choice. I had Mrs Claus inside my brain. Instructing me. All this pressure building up. And . . . once I'd charged at her . . . and shoved her in the stomach with both hands, and then . . . it was so easy. The pressure was off. It was a huge relief! I just had to watch her. She reeled backwards with a squawk. An awful noise. But it was cut off, abruptly. As she vanished.'

'She fell over two hundred feet,' Effie said. 'Like a rag doll. Shoved out of the way because she knew too much. We saw her. Lying there, broken up. The next morning.'

Martin cries out then, and thrusts his face into his hands.

'She didn't do it.' I speak up hesitantly. 'You know that, don't you, Martin? Rosie Twist never wrote any letters.'

He's still howling, blubbering, feeling sorry for himself. I can't even tell if he can hear me.

Effie slaps at his hands. 'Listen to her, son! You just listen. Rosie Twist never wrote any poison pen letters. Because *more* have arrived since . . . since she died. Since you murdered her.'

Martin looks up at us. He looks just about dead himself.

'You killed her for nothing,' says Effie.

'I know that,' Martin whispers. 'I realised that. When I heard about these latest letters. When Mrs Claus got hers this morning. I realised what I'd done. And I needed to . . . tell someone . . .'

'Well,' says Effie. 'What do you expect us to do about it?'

I shuffle nervously. I don't know what Effie's planning. What can we do? Grab him? Drag him to the cop shop? I try to read Effie's expression, but in the shadows this is impossible.

'I should give myself up,' Martin says. 'I should tell them. What Mrs Claus is like. Stitch her up.' Suddenly he cries out in pain. 'But she's in my mind! I can feel her!'

I glance ashore and see that Cleavis is up on his feet, silhouetted on the headland. He's heard the cries from Martin. He gives a quick wave. Do we need his help?

Oh yes, I wave back, as surreptitiously as I can. We could do with a hand all right.

Martin's not watching me, though. He's squealing and shrieking as if his guts are bursting open inside him. Effie and I take uncertain steps backwards.

'It's an illusion,' Effie cries in a commanding tone. 'She isn't really inside your mind. And she can't really control you. It's all an illusion brought on by the drugs . . .'

'No!' he howls. 'She made me do it! She made me commit murder!'

And now I can hear Henry's sensible brogues slapping on the wet stone of the pier. He's running here to help us and the noise puts the fear of God into Martin.

The elf whirls and dashes to the railing. I yell out instinctively to stop him, and Effie stays my arm. 'But the sea . . .!' I screech and watch, appalled, as Martin springs and flings himself over into the darkness. With surprising agility, he has taken himself off into the night.

Effie and I bolt to the edge of the pier. 'The tide doesn't come in this far,' she's gabbling. 'Look. Sand. He's on the beach.'

There was no splash. No sudden suicide. Only an escape attempt: the whump of a podgy hotel elf landing heavily on wet sand. 'There!' Effie shouts, and we catch a glimpse of Martin scrambling desperately across the flattened dunes. He's running with the leaden persistence of someone plagued by nightmares.

Effie's heading for the stone stairs that lead down to the beach. 'Come on!' she barks. 'We have to get after him!'

I hesitate for a second.

'Brenda, *come on*!' bawls Effie.

Then Henry is dashing up to us, breathing heavily, and brimming with concern for our welfare. 'What has he done? Has he hurt you?'

'We've got to get him back,' Effie tells us grimly, and hurriedly plunges ahead of us down the green sea steps.

I can't imagine what we must look like. The three of us, three daft old so-and-sos pelting hell for leather over the soft, cloddy sand. It's like running through demerara sugar: flying up in flurries as we press on. The three of us are so old and out of condition, how can we hope to catch up with the elf?

He's plump but he can put on a turn of speed when need be, it turns out. The three of us are wasting our breath yelling after him:

'Martin! Martin, you've got to stop!'

'Come back, you young fool!'

'Give yourself up, it's the only way! Look, we can tell the police that you were brainwashed! Anything! Just stop!' This last voice is mine – rambling on, as usual. By now I've got the most horrible stitch, all down one side.

Still Martin won't stop. We can hear his ragged breathing; it sounds like surf heaving up the shingle. At first he runs for the sea, then seems to change his mind and loops back across the bay. He's striking out towards the darkness and we seem powerless to stop him. We plunge on heedlessly, in pursuit.

It's midnight and surely people can hear us? Not

everyone in Whitby is abed yet. Aren't people staring from the prom? Can't they see the three of us chasing this murderer? We're making enough noise to wake the innocent from their beds, surely . . .?

'Martin! Martin, come back!'

He puts his head down and flees. Who knows what's going on in that scrambled young mind of his. He came to us in order to confess; to give himself up. But now he has changed his mind.

I have to stop. I can't keep this up. I'm seeing luminous spots in front of my eyes. I feel as if I'm going to have a stroke, here and now, in the mouth of the harbour. Henry stops, too, and he's as whacked as I am. He rubs my back as I bend and Effie starts shrieking at us. 'We can't let him go!'

'We can't catch him up, Effie,' I pant. 'I can't budge another inch!'

Effie swears very loudly. She's craning her neck to catch another glimpse of him. 'We've lost him,' she curses, and turns to give me a very black look.

She's about to say something else, too, when the most horrific noise reaches us from across the dunes. It's Martin. He's screaming.

'What . . .?'

And there're other noises, too. Fleshy, rending noises. Tearing, sucking noises. Teeth and fangs and the chortling glee of something not quite human. Or, no longer human.

'By Christ . . .' Cleavis breathes.

Effie clutches at my arm. Martin shrieks again and again; his last, desperate cries emerging as shock waves we can just about feel as they batter us, and they puncture the perfect stillness of the bay. They die down to gurgles. And we can hear a gibbering shriek that all three of us recognise at once:

Womanzee!

We catch only the tiniest glimpse of Jessie. The three of us are frozen to the spot. Clutching each other. Too scared to give chase. I don't think it would be a good idea to pursue her anyway. When we catch sight of her she's capering like a sprite: feral and dripping with gore. Martin is obviously stone dead and limp in her arms. She's dragging him away at great speed towards the shore and, presumably, her cave. Soon, the shadows have swallowed them up.

'Home,' Henry says thickly. He urges Effie and me to come to our senses. 'We must go home at once.'

'Oh my word,' Effie moans. 'She . . . just did away with him!'

'I knew it,' Cleavis says grimly. 'I knew it when we saw her last night. I knew she would end up doing something like this.'

As we turn to plodge back up the sands Effie and I

exchange a strange look. I don't know if we're accepting blame for what's happened to Martin, or if we are both racked with guilt, or what. I just don't know. But we both keep quiet about Jessie. I wish I'd never told Henry she used to be my friend.

As we struggle back up the slimy steps to the pier, I can still hear Martin's screams in my head.

No one has come running. Surely all of Whitby must have heard his cries? But no. If they heard them, they've ignored them. They've snuggled into their bedclothes and tried to block out their night terrors.

'Jessie,' Henry mutters. 'You said her name was Jessie, didn't you?'

I nod unhappily. He buttons his lip as we hurry back down the pier. Effie is straggling behind thoughtfully. 'It feels awful, to have left Martin's body back there,' she whispers. 'Even if he *was* a murderer.'

There was nothing of him left. Jessie had taken the body. And then, the grisly thought strikes me that we have to tell Robert about this at once. We don't want him going out to his aunt's cave – happily taking her breakfast – and finding her sitting there, gnawing on the remains of his friend.

'Robert is going to be devastated,' I tell Effie. 'He won't have it that Jessie's regressed so far.'

'She's a danger to us all,' Henry says. Now, as we step off

the pier, on to the cliff edge, we see that a thick sea mist is coming in behind us. It's rolling in to cover the whole town. I greet it with a weird lifting of my spirits – as if the mist could wipe over and obscure the terrible thing that's happened tonight.

If only.

We hurry through the streets of town. They are quieter than usual. Only a few drunks and one or two mysterious figures flitting across the narrow alleys. The three of us hurry straight to my place, by unspoken agreement. We don't say anything more until we're in the side passage and I am unlocking my door. We stumble into the warmth and comfort of my home, groaning with relief.

Soon, we're installed in my attic. Effie and Henry slump in the comfy chairs by the stove and I'm bringing them tea laced with whisky. I pull up a wooden chair and sit by them.

Even in the midst of all this business, it still feels good to sit with my two best friends in my attic. Henry is sipping his tea and looking about with interest, his bright eyes gleaming. I think he likes my home, for all its cramped confines and its clutter. But I can tell his mind is on other things. He's still dwelling on the horror we witnessed on the sands.

'There's a sort of poetic justice to it,' Effie says harshly.

'Oh, Effie,' I say. 'He might have deserved it, but I wouldn't have wished that on anyone.'

Henry darts Effie an annoyed look. 'You know where that creature lives, don't you?'

For a second she is affronted by his tone. 'We do indeed. We took her kippers on Monday morning.'

'You *fed* her?'

Suddenly I can appreciate how this must look to Henry Cleavis. Crazy spinsters feeding dangerous monsters. 'She used to be our friend, Henry. She was human, once.'

'Most monsters were,' he ruminates darkly. 'That's what makes them monstrous. Not their ugliness or savagery. It's the loss of their humanity and their souls.'

I absorb this quietly. For a second I feel irked by him for his easy expertise. What does he really know about this business of being a monster?

What about those of us who were *born* monsters? Who never had a soul in the first place, and so never had one to lose? What about those of us who have had to try so hard, and work so consistently, at turning ourselves into human beings?

I bridle for a while and don't say anything.

Effie cackles bitterly. 'This town is full of monsters, Henry. You'll find that out.'

'You need to tell me where she is hiding,' he says.

'Why?' Effie narrows her eyes at him. 'What are *you* going to do?'

'You saw how dangerous she is. She ripped that poor boy apart with her bare hands. She came running out of nowhere. She crept up on us and attacked like that. No one is safe! She needs to be dealt with.'

'What are you going to do, Henry?' I am very struck by the quiet determination in his voice.

'I shall eliminate her,' he says calmly.

'Eliminate?' Effie echoes. She looks him up and down. 'Are you sure you can manage the job?'

'Of course I can,' he says, with just an edge of crossness in his tone. 'That's what I do. It's what I've always done. I eliminate monsters.'

'Oh,' says Effie. 'I thought you translated ancient poems?'

'I moonlight,' Henry says, with grim humour. 'And I've been dealing with creatures like Jessie for years.'

I moan, rubbing my tired face. 'You can't just kill her . . .'

He looks at me sharply. 'What do you suggest I do, then?'

'I mean, it won't be as easy as all that. She's . . . she's undead. She returned to life.'

'That's right.' Effie snorts with laughter. 'We watched her ourselves, didn't we? Crawling out of the grave. She burst her way right out of the coffin and hauled herself back on to the earth. Hell kicked her out, didn't it, Brenda?'

I nod, and slowly sip my tea.

Henry is looking at us both and I don't like his

expression. He wants to know how we can know so much about this. Why are we tangled up in it so thoroughly? I watch him suppress his feelings of revulsion. He smiles pleasantly. 'I have despatched zombies before,' he says. 'And I shall do so again. Now, my dears. It's very late. And it's been the most extraordinary evening. If you don't mind, I think I'll make my way home to the Miramar.'

Effie and I watch him get up and stretch. He puts down his mug and straightens his waistcoat.

Effie and I look at each other. The question hangs silently between us: are we just going to stand by and let him destroy Jessie?

I'm tossing and turning all night.

The noises come. This night they decide to redouble their efforts. They plague me through the pre-dawn hours. That thumping, skittering noise in the hallway is back. Right outside my door. The spider-octopus thing, dancing on the drugget at the top of the hall stairs.

Wrong. The spider-thing is coming into my room. There is a sharp squeak and a long-drawn-out squeal. The light shifts slightly. Pitter-patter, pitter-patter. Something comes across the floorboards on tiny feet. It's coming closer to me and I'm rigid there in bed. I'm icy. I can't budge an inch, even if my life depended on it.

Then: patter-patter-patter and the thing moves away from my bedside. I feel as if it's been looking up at me. Checking on me. Then toddling off. Away from me. Exploring on its own. What is this thing?

And why am I too stupidly scared to get up and see what it is? It fills me with dread, as nothing else does.

Those are my last thoughts before I drop mercifully into oblivion.

But I wake early and straight away I know what I have to do. I get up and drag on some clothes. I don't exactly dress with meticulous care this morning. I just need to be covered in my usual human disguise. My thoughts are fixed on getting to Robert. I phone ahead and warn him. Check that he's not already left for the harbour mouth; that he isn't visiting Jessie's cave this morning. My heart leaps up when he comes to the phone. At least I've spared him the horror of getting there and finding Jessie crouched on the beach, eating human flesh like a latter-day version of the Scots cannibal, Sawney Bean. On the other end of the phone Robert sounds confused and worried by my call. I tell him there are things he needs to know, and I have to tell him face to face.

I set off at once. He's suggested a small greasy-spoon café quite near to the Miramar. He often goes there for breakfast, so he knows it's open and that we won't be disturbed.

I scoot out of my establishment and scurry up the hill that will take me to him. There aren't many people about, to see my haste and harried face.

When I get there he's sitting hunched over two steaming beakers of tea. His hair's all mussed up and his collar's standing up out of his jumper awkwardly.

'Jessie is in terrible danger for her life,' I tell him, once I'm settled on the squeaky vinyl seat. I lower my voice under the genial chitchat of Radio 2, which blares out through speakers. Robert frowns at me and I quickly tell my tale. I tell him about me and Henry witnessing her rampage in the Silver Slipper amusement arcade. Then I tell him about our meeting with Martin and his confession – and then its unfortunate sequel. Martin fleeing across the stodgy sands. Jessie pelting out of nowhere. Striking him down. Slashing him to bits with her claw-like hands and vicious teeth. Dragging him off across the clinking shale of the beach towards her cave.

'Oh, my God,' Robert says slowly. 'She *killed* him? Are you sure?'

I nod. 'Of course we are. The three of us were standing there, Robert.'

'But are you sure, Brenda? You really saw all of this?'

'It was dark, of course, and we were all in the shadows from the cliffs. But we saw enough. We heard Martin's cries and his death throes. Then we could see Jessie. She was like a thing possessed, Robert. We saw her hefting up Martin's body like a side of beef . . .'

Robert stares down at his greasy tea. 'I've tried to protect her. I've tried to get through to her. To tell her what would happen if . . . if she went too far. But her mind is gone, Brenda. She is completely feral. She's hardly my aunty at all now.'

'Oh, Robert,' I say. 'Jessie will always be your aunty. You have to believe that. And she will always care for you. It's just that . . . well, she's gone a little bit wild. That's all.'

'That's all!' he barks, too loudly, and sobs. 'And what about Martin? Have you told the police? The authorities? Won't they just go straight out and shoot her?'

'Ah.' I feel myself looking shifty. 'We haven't reported his death. We haven't said a word. The three of us decided not to.'

Robert narrows his eyes. 'How come?'

'Henry says he wants to deal with this . . . in his own way.'

'What does that mean?'

'I don't know yet,' I say. 'But he went all strange and determined-looking. He says that fighting monsters is his job. Monsters and things without souls are his business.'

'But Jessie has a soul still!' Robert grasps my hand and

won't let go. 'Can't we make them see, Brenda? She isn't really evil! She hasn't lost her soul!'

I look at him and I don't know what to say.

Because now, as it all settles in, I don't believe that's true. I think Jessie has lost everything. There is nothing of Robert's aunty left now.

The poor boy is clinging on to nothing.

There are more rooms in the Hotel Miramar than I'd have thought possible. The corridors are narrow and dark and they smell of ginger biscuits. I have to keep squeezing past busy chambermaids, who block the way with their little trolleys of cleaning things and miniature toiletries. I shouldn't really be up here, uninvited, but Robert let me in. Urgent business.

At last I'm standing in front of room 163. I take a deep breath. Fancy me falling for the bloke who wants to clean up the town, I sigh. I go and give my heart away and it's to the feller who wants to destroy one of my friends who is going through a rough patch. Admittedly, a pretty bad rough patch, but still. I knock hesitantly on the plywood door. Have I really given my heart away? Is that what I've done?

Henry Cleavis looks sheepish and tired when he opens the door to me. He shoos me in and glances furtively up and down the passageway. Who does he expect is following me?

I scurry in and sit on the edge of the bed, which is too soft and squashy for comfort.

Three things strike me first off. First: the dashing figure Henry cuts in his paisley silk dressing gown and his loosely knotted cravat. Quite the gentleman adventurer. Second, I don't think much of the décor in Sheila's hotel. Rather dated, almost sleazy – patterned nylon sheets and wood-effect fitted cabinets, indeed. And third – and this is the shocker – I realise that there are weapons everywhere. Henry has unpacked all his luggage and he's got a veritable arsenal laid out on every surface. He's polishing them up – these gleaming daggers, machetes, nunchakus – and readying himself for war. I'm sitting there watching him buff up an elephant gun.

He has noticed the look on my face. 'Now, Brenda,' he says, 'I'm not wanting some long conflab about this. On the nature of good and evil. And whether we can, um, call Jessie an innocent savage or not.'

'How did you know what I was going to say?'

He gives a sharp bark of a laugh, shoving some kind of rod down the length of the gun. 'Because I know *you*, my dear. *Think about it from the monster's point of view, Henry. She doesn't mean it. Doesn't mean the things she does.*'

'But that's true!' I burst out.

He shrugs. 'Doesn't matter. She still needs to be dealt

with. Whether she intends to do harm or not. Can't have her running about Whitby taking bites out of people, can we?'

His face creases up into the gentlest, sweetest of smiles and he comes to sit next to me on the too-squashy bed. How can he be so lovely, and still be talking about murder? It's him with the savage streak, really, isn't it? It's him who's cold-blooded. Now his arm's gone round my shoulder. Bless him, he can't even reach the whole way. I dwarf the poor feller.

'I know she's your friend, Brenda. It's very loyal of you, this. Arguing on her behalf. But this is why I am here in Whitby, you know.' He gestures round at the room, and its deadly display of armaments. 'I'm here to deal with the monsters. There's an unusually high level of, um. Activity, I suppose we'd call it.'

I stare at my sensible shoes and my thick tights miserably. I know exactly what he's talking about. I even contribute to that statistic. It looks as though Henry and I are on different sides, this time.

'Look at me, Brenda,' he says. He gently tilts my face so that I'm looking straight at him, into his eyes. They are wise, full of compassion. Like warm caramel, they are. He's pushed his smooth, whiskery face right up to mine. I feel a bit uncomfortable, truth be told. It's startling, this intimacy lark. I'm out of practice. I feel myself flinch under his steady gaze. He's too close. He'll see all the lumps and blotches under my make-up. He'll see right through me. The puckers and gathers of the scars under my chin, and up the left-hand side of my face: all the great jagged zigzags that craze my complexion. In the seedy half-light of mid-morning in this hotel room, I feel as if he is studying me.

Henry leans forward slowly and kisses me on the end of my nose. I blink in surprise. He has drawn away before I even realise it.

'I think a lot of you, you know,' he tells me. 'And I would never let anything hurt you. You know that, don't you?'

I nod, dumbly. It's as if he's robbed me of speech, of volition. Inwardly, I curse myself. I've let this little feller put me off my stroke. I came here to warn him, to tell him to leave poor Jessie alone. To abandon his monster-killing schemes. Instead he has felled me with a single blow. It's humiliating! It wasn't even a kiss on the lips. Not an ounce of high passion anywhere in it. A tender peck on my mighty nose and he's stolen my gumption and my ire. I get up to go, and shuffle dazedly to the door.

'I'll be in touch,' is all he says, going back to his gun-polishing. Outside, heading for the lift, I'm thinking: there must be some magic in this. Some kind of spell he's put on me. I swooned! I bloody well swooned when he leaned in for the kill! I'm furious, but my heart's beating like mad as I ride down to the foyer. Silly old woman!

Downstairs I find a whole lot of bustle and busyness going on. There's a huge black van at the front and Robert has abandoned the desk in order to give instructions to the garden furniture men. The name of the furniture manufacturers, *Danby's*, is emblazoned in gold script down the side of the van, and on the front of the men's overalls.

Danby's? A shudder of dread passes through me. That was the name of the owner of the Deadly Boutique. Surely it can't be the same man? Could he have branched out into garden furnishings? I hope not. I hope it's a coincidence. The recurrence of the name seems like an ill omen and I try to shake the thought away.

The men are carrying between them the most exquisite tables and chairs, all woven out of blond bamboo. They are taking them round to the back of the hotel in a grand procession to the beer garden, where Robert is in charge. He is issuing instructions as to where everything should be placed for now. Afterwards he will finesse the layout, he tells me, and create the paradisal sanctuary that Sheila requires for her barbecues.

'It's going to be marvellous,' I tell him, watching men manhandling ornate chairs.

Robert stares into my face for a moment. 'He's got to you, hasn't he?'

'Who?' I say. 'What do you mean?'

'Cleavis. He's put you in a funny mood.'

'Mood?' But it's true, though. I know what he means. My head's swimming, even now that I'm out in the sunshine and away from the giddy dusk of his room. What's he done to me? What have I allowed him to do?

Robert looks piqued. 'Did you warn him? Did you tell him to keep away from Jessie?'

I am a bit shamefaced at this. I mumble, 'Of course I did. But he's like . . . a man on a mission . . .'

'It's others in this town he should be going after,' Robert says darkly. 'Mrs Claus, for instance. Why isn't he gunning for her, eh? Now we know she was the one really responsible for the murder of Rosie Twist. He should be dealing with her.'

'You're right,' I tell him. 'That's what we should tell Henry.'

'Have you heard what she's planning? It's the most wickedly hypocritical thing I've ever heard of.' Robert pauses here, to help extricate one of the large wickerwork chairs, which has become entangled in the box hedge as the men try to haul it through.

'What is she planning?' I ask him.

'Tomorrow evening,' he says, 'Mrs Claus and all her elves are going to hold a service of commemoration for Rosie Twist. Outside the Christmas Hotel, because that's where Rosie got shoved off the cliff.'

'But that's awful! Mrs Claus was the one who had her shoved!'

'Mrs Claus just wants to get into the papers. Wants people to think well of her.' Robert's face is hard with fury. 'It's her who's the monster. Not my Aunt Jessie.'

What surprises me over the next day or so is Effie's behaviour. I know she doesn't think much of Jessie. I know she thinks that, in accordance with our mission to guard the Bitch's Maw, Jessie should be dealt with. But, as far as she is concerned, Jessie is our problem. She belongs to us, and the town. It isn't up to some interloper to come in and do away with our womanzee.

She tails Henry Cleavis round the town. Wherever he goes the rest of that day, Effie is always right behind him. At first he isn't even aware of this shadow in her twinset and stout walking shoes. Henry is determined and tooled up. He has all kinds of weapons secreted about his person and he wanders around the town, and across the beaches, in search of Jessie. And Effie is there, dogging his footsteps at every turn, all of Thursday and then into Friday.

She tells me what she's been up to, Friday morning, in the Walrus and the Carpenter. We're having tea and buttery fingers of cinnamon toast.

'So he hasn't found her yet?' I ask.

'Not a chance.' Effie cackles. 'I kept on his back till after midnight. Followed him all the way back to the Miramar. He looked so dejected! And exhausted, humping all his knives and guns around in his little bag.'

All of yesterday I was busy at work, at home. I've got a rush on. Every room is booked all of a sudden, and the work has piled up at my place. In a way I am glad, though, that I was able to keep out of it. I wouldn't have wanted to be trailing after Henry.

'He never saw you at all?'

'Oh, he did in the end.' Effie grins, crunching into the crystallised sugar on her toast and wrinkling her nose. 'He turned round in the street and shouted at me! Really! It was so embarrassing. This was on his lonely, defeated walk back to his hotel in the early hours. There weren't many people to witness it, but I was still embarrassed. I was crouching on the ground, behind a car. He called me over like a tutting, disapproving headmaster.' But Effie doesn't look as if she cares that much, not really. 'He's got no right to hunt our Jessie down. I told him so, there and then. Silly old fool. Who does he think he is?'

'I'm just glad things have gone a bit quiet on the womanzee front,' I say. 'Perhaps it will all blow over . . .'

Effie looks perturbed. 'She's had a taste of human flesh now, remember. I don't think that's the last time she'll kill.'

Effie's right. And I remember the swiftness and savagery of her attack on Martin the elf, down on the beach. If I close my eyes I can still hear those ghastly noises. I can see the startled look on that boy's face as Jessie lunges out of nowhere. Or am I imagining that in retrospect?

'But what's our plan?' I ask her. 'We don't want to let Cleavis kill her, or send her back to hell. But what are we going to do about her?'

Here Effie bites her lip. 'We're her protectors, in a way, aren't we? We were told that hell will spill certain of its denizens into this town, and our job is to look out for them. I take that to mean that we are their protectors, rather than their destroyers. We are here to make sure they don't cause too much bother.'

I nod slowly. 'I think you're right.'

'I've thought about this a lot, these past few days. Since Jessie has gone to the bad. I'm sure that is our role here.'

In that case, I think, we're not doing that good a job of it, are we? That's what goes unspoken between us at this point. We look at each other a bit guiltily and finish up our toast.

Effie pays our bill because it's her turn. Then we wend our way up the cobbled lane to the foot of the one hundred and ninety-nine steps. Quite a lot of tourists about today. It's hard going, just fighting our way up our usual route.

Effie tells me that she wants to go down on to the sands, to check out Jessie's cave.

'Right now?' I ask uncertainly.

Grimly, she nods. She's a brave woman. Bearding the womanzee in her den. But she's right. We need to see if she's there. And what state she's in.

We veer off past the holiday cottages and the kipper shop. We amble along easily under the great shadow of the rocks. And then we slip down on to the beach, where there is no one about. It's deserted here and bleak. It's like walking across the surface of the moon. Robert was very wise in finding his aunt a hideout here.

To cover our nerves we start talking about the memorial event to be held this evening on the western cliff. 'What's Mrs Claus playing at?'

'Good press, no doubt,' says Effie, stumbling a little on the rocks. 'But the ironic thing is, with Rosie Twist dead, there's no one to write about her noble gesture.' It's true, *The Willing Spirit* has gone completely silent since Rosie came a cropper.

We draw in close to the cliffs, peering at the dark mouths of the cell-like caves and trying to remember which is Jessie's. I hope she's taken to sleeping in the daytime, like any self-respecting member of the undead.

'There's the remains of a fire.' Effie points. 'She must be

in the cave there, look.' As we approach we see various signs of her recent presence. There are hanks of matted hair clinging to the jagged rocks. The fire's ashes are dead and cold: it hasn't been lit for days. We find charred and chewed bones. Dribbles and spots of browning blood. 'This is it,' Effie whispers.

And so we creep closer to the cave mouth.

There's a stench here. An awful animal stink. This is what she has come to. A whole lifetime of struggle and toil, and she ends up here. Crouching in the dark and coming out at night to terrorise the town.

Effie pauses in the entrance. I can hear her swallow before she perks up: 'Jessie?' Her voice is rather shrill. 'Jessie, dear, are you there?'

She's going to come bounding out, I think. I look at Effie's frail and slightly stooped back, thinking: she won't stand a chance. When Jessie comes screeching and tearing out of there with her claws outstretched, Effie hasn't got a hope. For a moment I marvel at my friend's courage. Then I step up to stand beside her in the entrance.

'I don't think she's there,' I say, after some moments of staring into the darkness. 'I think she's abandoned this hideout.' Something about the desolate smell of the place makes me think this. Jessie has moved on. Perhaps she's hiding further inside the system of caves, within the cliffs.

Perhaps she's in the sewers under the old part of town. She's drawn even further away from society as if even she has realised that she has passed beyond the human pale.

'Let's go, Effie,' I say at last. I hate to admit it, but I am relieved when Effie decides we can stop looking into the cave. I'm glad she doesn't suggest crouching and squeezing ourselves into that low aperture in the rock. I have a horror of being confined. I don't think I could go any further into that hole, not knowing what was in there waiting for us.

I'm happy to turn, with Effie, and leave the beach behind.

Neither of us were great fans of Rosie Twist, but we end up going to the memorial event anyway.

'It's just the way things are, here in town,' Effie says when she calls for me, early Friday evening. 'If we didn't go, tongues would certainly wag and, given the mysterious circumstances of that idiot's death, we don't want that.'

Once more I bow to Effie's wisdom and throw on a light cardy.

When we get there we realise that it's a bigger event than we expected, with some kind of makeshift stage set up on the grass outside the Christmas Hotel, and folding chairs laid out in neat rows. Most of these are already occupied by the great and the good. There are also a great many pensioners from the Christmas Hotel, wearing party hats. I don't think they even know why they are there. We spot Sheila Manchu floating about in a kaftan-type affair, being treated like some kind of celebrity. She's there with Robert in his leather flying jacket. He looks like her minder and my heart gives a swift pang of jealousy as we all kiss each other hello.

'I'm here, much as I hate to attend one of Mrs Claus's dos,' Sheila whispers. In the open air and in public, she is a much quieter, more demure person than you would think. She looks insubstantial, somehow, like an old photographic negative that could fade under the strong sunlight. She grasps Effie's skinny arm. 'Do you think it could be Mrs Claus writing the letters? Do you? I do. I know everyone says she's had one herself, but I think she's bluffing. There's only her who could do such a thing. Who would know so much . . .'

Robert tries to shush her as a small band on the podium starts to play a soothing medley of golden oldies. This is our signal to take up our places. A troop of elves are marching out of the hotel and bringing with them the gargantuan Mrs Claus in her motorised chair. This is a new chair she's got, bedecked with holly and ivy. She is wreathed in smiles. She bestows upon us all a ghastly, benevolent grin as the elves accompany her over the road and on to the grass and, at last, up on to the podium. We poor saps are left to applaud her stately progress. Then someone is tugging at my cardigan from behind. I turn and there's Henry Cleavis. He has squashed himself into the row behind, between two old dears in paper party hats, who are singing along to the memorial medley.

'Oh, hello,' I say, sounding less than delighted to see him. He picks up on this immediately.

'Look, are we going to fall out?' he barks. 'Over this Jessie business? I'd rather um. I'd rather not, Brenda. Seems a damn silly thing to fight over.'

I glare at him, and so does Effie, craning round to look at him. 'Have some respect,' she hisses. 'This is a memorial service.'

Cleavis winces. The two old women either side are singing along to 'Una Paloma Blanca'. I wonder if these songs were all favourites of Rosie Twist's and, if so, how Mrs Claus knows that.

'Have you found Jessie?' I ask Henry. I give him the once-over and imagine that the pockets, sleeves and hidden compartments of his three-piece worsted suit are bulging with what must be his knives and guns and whatnots. It can't be all that easy to walk about the place all tooled up like that.

'No luck yet,' he says grimly. 'But I'm not giving up, Brenda. She needs to be put an end to. Mercifully.'

I roll my eyes.

'Don't look at me like that,' he snaps, pulling on his silvery moustache. 'I'm only doing my duty. You remember. That's what I always do.'

Now this really infuriates me. The music is coming to a gentle climax and the crowd is clapping and purring its approval and I am yelling at Henry: 'It might be old hat for you, Henry, but as it happens, my memory's not as good as yours. So I'm very sorry if I'm bothering you.' And I turn away abruptly, pulling my cardigan tight around me. Effie nudges me and gives me a nod.

Just then Mrs Claus takes the stand and holds up her hands for silence. Now, I can't stand the sight of the bloated old bag, but I'm glad of the interruption.

Her tribute to Rosie Twist goes on for some time. It's like watching *This Is Your Life*. At one point she has the elves singing Whitney Houston a cappella. And then she announces plans for *The Willing Spirit* in Rosie's absence. Without her, the newspaper is nothing. An empty organ. (Can she have that metaphor right, I wonder?) And so Mrs Claus, she magnanimously announces, is taking over the local paper herself. She and her private staff will see to it that we get our weekly, free dose of local news, opinion and gossip. There is a huge wave of giddy applause at this. Beside me, Effie, Sheila and Robert aren't looking quite so pleased. 'Corruption!' Effie mouths at me. 'Now she controls the press!'

I want to point out that it's only a free weekly rag, but I don't say anything.

'I hope that *The Willing Spirit* itself will prove to be the best, most fitting, and most durable memorial to Rosie Twist that she could possibly have,' Mrs Claus is saying in a quavering tone. Her several chins are quivering busily and I know it's all put on. There's not a shred of real human feeling in that terrible woman. She's got this town in the palm of her hand. Effie and the others are right to be concerned.

Then, as the crowd falls silent for a few minutes' prayer and reflection, I give out the most almighty squawk of horror. I try to stop myself, but it's out before I can even think about it. Heads up. Cries of alarm. I'm pointing and crying out.

'Brenda! Control yourself!' Effie cries, and in this weird, distended moment, I'm aware of Mrs Claus's head jolting out of her prayer. I'm aware of Henry Cleavis behind me, jumping into action, all prepared to protect me. Most people are watching me freak out, but none of them know yet what I've seen.

'Glooooooooooopppp!'

Jessie has come amongst us.

She is here! She must have clambered, paw by monkey's paw, up the cliff face and bided her time. She waited till most people were concentrating on their prayers. And then

— the womanzee is suddenly here! And she is loping, slavering and gibbering, towards the front of the stage with murderous intent.

'Aunt Jessie!' Robert yells out.

'By Christ!' barks Cleavis, right in my ear.

'Gloooooooopp!'

Jessie causes a great Mexican wave of horror to ripple out from the front row. Even Mrs Claus is shrieking over the tannoy at the sight of the womanzee who, if I'm not very much mistaken, is working herself up to go into a rampage. Pensioners begin to scatter. Chairs are overturned. Pandemonium is starting to break out. Someone is shouting for calm, and Mrs Claus doesn't help matters: 'Stop her! Shoot her! Arrest her!'

'Gloooop!' Jessie bellows back.

And suddenly Robert's aunt is transfixed by the sight of Mrs Claus: on full, extravagant display up there on the podium. As everyone else turns to flee and I struggle forward, with Effie and the others at my heels, I can see that Jessie's primitive mind is turning and churning over the sight of this woman before her. Mrs Claus. Her erstwhile employer. Whose hotel Jessie died in, apparently from exhaustion, while she was doing the downstairs dusting. Jessie lets rip a primordial screech.

'Glooopp! Glooooop! GlooooooOOOOOoooOOOooppp!'

'Get her away from me!' howls Mrs Claus, and her terrified elves hasten to help her.

But Jessie is fast. She vaults the rows of folding chairs. She is preternaturally nimble and can cover distances like this in a scant few seconds. We are all seemingly frozen as events spin rapidly out of control.

I dart forward; Effie darts forward; Robert darts forward.

Sheila falls back a bit and, as I find out later, Henry Cleavis has snapped into desperate action. It turns out that he has only one deadly weapon about his portly person. It is a small silver handgun loaded with very special bullets. They are tipped with local jet.

'Gloooop!' Jessie screams as she reaches the podium. Her nails slash and sizzle on the air, striking out at the elves as they gather hopelessly around Mrs Claus, who thrashes and bellows for protection.

'Stop!' Effie shouts. 'Jessie, you must stop this at once!'

For a second I think she might have got through to the beast woman. Some inkling of humanity might have sparked in those deep-set eyes. Jessie pauses, dripping with elf blood. She casts aside her latest victim and even seems to consider Effie's words.

'We can help you, Jessie,' Effie says. 'Your nephew is here. So is Brenda. We are your friends, Jessie. You don't need to kill . . .'

But at that moment Mrs Claus gives a faint mew of fear and an expression of sheer animal hatred asserts itself again over Jessie's ruined features. She prepares to go in for the kill.

And Henry Cleavis – standing on a chair behind us – fires his gun at her.

All I'm aware of is a sudden, dense cloud of something acrid.

Then the sharp, nasty crack.

And then, weirdly, *Effie* jerks upwards like a puppet. She crumples up instantly on to the grass. And, on the podium, the womanzee takes the special jet-tipped bullet full in the chest.

She leaps backwards and none of us actually sees this at the time, but Mrs Claus later records it for posterity, in her first ever editorial on the front page of *The Willing Spirit*. Jessie the womanzee struggles to her feet, bleeding copiously. She turns and she staggers towards the cliff edge from which Rosie Twist herself plummeted. Perhaps there is a kind of poetic justice or irony in this, writes Mrs Claus – who clearly wants to pin Rosie's death on the innocently monstrous Jessie – but, in exactly the same place, the creature flings herself to her death.

Only Mrs Claus is watching as Jessie topples into the nothingness and the booming surf below. None of the rest of us – not even Robert – can see this at the time.

We are gathered around Effie. She is all crooked and sprawled on the grass. The pool of blood around her head seems enormous and horribly thick and dark.

There is an impossible amount of blood, I'm thinking. She's certainly dead.

Cleavis has slain her!

'It's a flesh wound,' he's babbling, and I'm wondering what other kind there can be. 'She's all right,' he says. 'I think she'll be all right. The bullet just grazed her . . .'

But as we stand there, shocked to the core, waiting for the ambulance and the professionals to come, Effie looks drained of all life and colour. It's as if she's been carved out of pale wax. Her bony features are weirdly calm.

And I feel sure that my friend has been inadvertently killed.

Chapter Three
Enter the Smudgelings

I'm not going to the hospital today. I was there all of Friday night. I walked out that way again yesterday. It's a little way out of town. Quite awkward to get to without a car. And there's not much to see, even when you're there.

Effie's still out cold.

Late Friday night I was at her bedside with Henry. He was grey with remorse. He looked like a beached fish, dead on the slab. He looked worse than Effie did. 'I never meant, you know I never. I never meant to hurt her. It was a freak. A freak accident.' He kept muttering away like that. It got on my nerves after a while, if I'm honest. As if the only important thing was to get himself off the hook. I told him to button it, in the end. We stood there in silence, watching

Effie. She was looking so serene in that bed. All hooked up with tubes and whatnot. The machines blinking away as though they were keeping her going, and her head massive with pristine bandages.

She looked so tired and tiny, lying there. A proper old woman. You could see just how old and defenceless she really is, as if that wilfulness of hers had fled from her.

We stood guard over Effie, and waited for what would happen next.

Mrs Claus had seen to everything. She had talked to the police. And I saw at once one more manifestation of her power in Whitby. The police gathered about her after the event and she told them – dictated to them – precisely what had gone on. They accepted her version without hesitation. It was an accident that had happened, and that was an end to it. The police obeyed her and went away.

Well, I was pretty stricken myself, but I overheard some of this and I was staggered. Mrs Claus had everyone in her back pocket. She could tell everyone and anyone what to do. I caught her eye, in all the fuss of loading Effie on to the ambulance. Mrs Claus winked at me. A leering, conspiratorial wink that made me shudder. She had made the police go away. We can deal with this ourselves, thank you.

In our haste to get help for Effie, we had all forgotten

about Jessie. It was only as Henry and I stood vigil alongside Effie's bed that I remembered, with a sudden, sharp sob. Robert hadn't come with us to the hospital. I hadn't seen him since those terrible few moments. It had all been such a panic, such a blur.

Events have a way of dashing on ahead of me. Sometimes my mind seems slow to catch up.

On Saturday I was standing by Effie's bed and it came to me in a horrible flash just where I was. A hospital. Amongst all of that awful machinery, all geared towards prolonging and repairing human life. I dashed to the lavvy and thought I was going to throw up. But I hadn't eaten anything for days. Just a packet of fruit gums out of the waiting room machine. Delayed shock, Cleavis said wisely, rubbing my back, when I returned to him. But it was more than that. Hospitals terrify me. I've avoided them all through my long life. I can't bear to be near doctors and nurses and all the nasty, meticulous things that they do.

I had to go home.

We couldn't do anything more for Effie. It was just a case of waiting for her to wake up. No one knew how long she would lie like that, unconscious. Her body was repairing itself. She needed rest. We weren't doing her any good, and we weren't helping at all, by hanging around and watching her.

Henry walked me back into town early Saturday afternoon. I felt as if I was dressed in rags. I was desperate to get home. It was almost a distateful eagerness to be bathed and changed and in my own place again. Cleavis, too, looked worn out by events. He still looked terribly guilty. The few words I said were to assuage his monstrous guilt. As I watched him trog off up the front path of the Hotel Miramar, though, I was thinking: he shot Effie! Your man friend's bullet grazed your best friend's temple! He could have killed her stone dead!

Best not to go over these things too much in your mind.

I stumbled into town, down the long, gentle declivity towards the bay. I really didn't want to see anyone I knew. The streets were quiet for early spring, and no one on them knew my face. I dashed along at a fair clip, key at the ready. Luckily, there was no Leena and Raf outside their shop. They'd definitely try to hold me up with their questions about Effie.

I hurried up my side passage and unlocked my door.

And there it was.

I blinked down at the welcome mat. The post must have been delivered late this morning, I remember thinking. There wasn't anything here when I left for the hospital. But I'd been so distracted, dragging myself back and forth to Effie's bedside, taking her night clothes and whatever else I thought she might need, that I mightn't have noticed this plain white envelope on my doormat. It might have been there for a day or so. But I doubted it. Gingerly, I picked it up.

As I ripped it open my heart was thudding. Dread was coursing through my veins. I yanked out the single sheet of paper and read the few words that were typed there, on some ancient machine, by the looks of it.

Who the devil do you think you are, woman? You've got no one fooled. You ancient trollop. You're not even a proper woman! You're not even human! And you dare to think that you blend in so well. You have the gall to think that people accept you! But they don't. They snigger behind your back. They think you are a freak. And not just an ugly freak. Not just some unfortunate woman with a lumpy old body and one leg fatter than the other. They know your secret. I know your secret. People here know just how freakish and unnatural you are. Monster! Harlot! Spawn of Satan! We'll get you out of this place, eventually. We'll have you driven out of town.

And that was it. I read it through quickly, once. My eyes misted up towards the end and I clutched the banister for support. Then I got a grip on myself and read it again.

I had the impulse to destroy it, there and then. I wanted to shred the vile thing into a million pieces. But I reined myself in. It was evidence.

In the twenty-four hours since then, I've just about memorised the contents of that letter. I've tried to get on with things as best I can. I've cleaned my establishment top to bottom. I've made everything immaculate, including myself. I've whizzed up this delicious soup in the blender, thumped away at my rough puff pastry, and stuffed my chicken with unusual force. All to distract myself, and to rid my thoughts of this awful taint.

I sit in the garden with my glass of wine. I hurry in to fetch the rest of the bottle. The gazpacho is chilling in my biggest tureen and lunch is ready to go. I cool my heels, waiting for Henry. I'm going to show him the letter. I've nothing to hide from him.

I'm trying out something new, and I've stuffed the chicken with pearl barley and raisins. It's just as I'm basting the bird with honey and lemon that I start to wonder if it will taste too much like a cough remedy. Never mind. I bang it in the oven. He'll be grateful for it either way, I'm sure. Henry doesn't look as if he's had much home cooking in recent years.

I'm making him a Bakewell pudding for afters. A fat crust of rough puff pastry with a glistening interior of sweet eggy batter and crimson jam. He's going to love it. He'll be curling his toes up in pleasure. Those clever old eyes of his will be twinkling away.

It's even sunny enough for me to set up my picnic table in the secluded back garden. I hoisted out the best chairs and laid everything out just so. I want this to be perfect.

Of course, I'm merely imposing calm on disaster. However organised I'm being in preparing lunch, my mind's going back and forth like the shuggy boats at the fair. It's whirling like the prancing horses on the carousels. When most of my preparations are over, I'm half an hour early. We're starting with gazpacho, so there's nothing to warm up. I sit everything ready and slosh myself a glass of white burgundy.

He arrives and we sit and for a while I am kept busy, serving up our lunch and dashing back and forth. Henry is the perfect guest: pleased about everything, and sitting there, letting me get on with it. He exclaims over each course in turn and praises me lavishly.

It's as we spoon up our desserts with cream that I pass him my poison pen letter. He reads it as he eats and his eyebrows creep higher and higher in alarm.

When he is finished he holds it aloft quizzically. His eyes narrow, as if he can X-ray it and read its very fibres for clues. He doesn't embarrass me by alluding to its contents, for which I am grateful. But now he harrumphs and says, 'How many people here in Whitby know the truth about you, Brenda? Hm?'

I stammer. 'About me? I . . . um . . .'

'Come on,' he says. 'This letter of yours narrows down the field of poison pen suspects quite considerably. Does it not? Spawn of Satan, et cetera. Um . . . this allusion to your not being human or natural, and so on. Bang on the money, are they not? Now, there can't be many to whom you have disclosed . . . your unusual pedigree.'

I feel myself go tight-lipped indeed. 'Hardly any. And some seem to know without my having told them. Mrs Claus, for instance. And you, Henry. You seem to know all about me.'

He gives a gracious little nod. 'Who else?'

'Well . . . people I trust. Robert. And . . . Effie. Effie knows about me.'

'Ahhh,' sighs Cleavis, tapping the frail sheet against his chin. He stares into space for a while. 'Effie. I see. And you told her, did you . . .? All about . . . your situation?'

Situation! I like that! 'Everything,' I say. 'It all came out last year. I ended up telling her the whole lot.'

'You must really trust her then,' Cleavis says.

This makes me feel foolish and dull, as I take the tray of dirty pots and plates back indoors. I unload them and put the coffee on, setting out dinky cups and filling up the silver pot. Was I a fool to trust Effie? She's my friend. I couldn't help the truth's coming tumbling out. Especially not in the circumstances of the time. We were both prisoners of Mrs Claus, up at the top of the Christmas Hotel. It was Mrs Claus who gave the game away about my 'situation' as Henry so gallantly puts it. She blew my cover for me, and so I ended up having to tell Effie the whole, tawdry saga, while we were tied up together in a musty attic. I told her the long, incredible tale of my life. Where I came from. And who made me. And why.

But Effie wouldn't betray me. Surely not. She wouldn't use those disclosures of mine — painful as they were — to taunt me now. I'm sure of it. I feel rotten for even suspecting it, what with Effie lying senseless in the county hospital.

There is no way Effie wrote those letters.

Is there?

Outside in my garden, and Cleavis is back on the scent.

'Tell me, Brenda. Does Effie have an old typewriter?'

'For business correspondence.' I nod miserably. 'An old death trap machine in the office at the top of her house.' I clatter my spoon down and start stacking dishes up on the tray. 'Why does this have to happen now? When she's in hospital, and I can't even ask her?'

'Perhaps it isn't her at all,' Cleavis says gently. 'After all, by the time you received the letter, Effie was already in hospital. How could she have delivered it to you, hm? No, I am sure she is quite innocent in this. I apologise for even considering it.'

Gracious of him, again. But I am thinking about the letter, half wedged under the mat. It could have been there the day before. I've been in such a kerfuffle, with all the goings-on. And I'm thinking now: Effie might well have dropped it through my letter box earlier. And I never noticed it until today.

I screw up my eyes and take a deep breath. I listen to the breezes shushing the tall trees about, making a noise like the sea itself. I can hear the wood pigeons crying out their usual 'To-do! to-do! to-do!' And I think about Effie. Do I really believe that my best friend is capable of secretly and stealthily tapping out these nasty notes to inhabitants of this town? Setting out to hurt people? To make them feel paranoid and even scared?

'I'm really not sure what to think any more,' I tell Henry.

He nods very patiently. 'We can't rule her out yet. And . . . you know, Brenda. I haven't seen much of her, and I know she is your best friend. But from the tiny experience of her I have, I do wonder . . .'

'What?'

'Perhaps,' says Henry. 'If she was, perhaps, at some point, feeling very miserable and lonely and anguished . . . in a weak moment she might just have . . . let all her bile out in letter form . . . I can almost imagine it. She seems so very pent-up and . . . Oh, I don't know. Is that a bad thing to say?'

I glance at him. Yes, I think. It's a downright awful thing to say.

Then he becomes tender, solicitous. 'My dear. Why don't we drop the topic? Unfortunate, this. I'm sure your friend is quite innocent in the matter of these vile epistles. I'm sure.'

'Hmmm.' I pour the coffee out, bridling a bit. Why is there always some mystery? Why is there always something horrible going on? This afternoon it's balmy and warm. The garden is perfect and I'm here with my new man friend. Why must all these horrible thoughts and possibilities be running through my mind?

'Have you talked to Robert since I shot his aunt?' Cleavis asks, looking shifty.

I shake my head. That's something else I'm dreading. Poor Robert! My continuing friendship with Cleavis is bound to cause a rift between us.

'It's a bit awkward.' Cleavis harrumphs. 'Him working at the Miramar. My being a guest there. My having shot one of his relatives.'

'Have they found her body?' I ask.

Cleavis tersely shakes his head.

I imagine poor Jessie, careering all that way down the cliff, into the thrashing, freezing North Sea. Poor Jessie, felled at last. She's had no luck, that woman. And all for what? Trying to do herself up and make the best of herself. Rewarded like this! Transformed into a monster; a primitive beast. Shot like a mad dog and chucked into the sea!

That's what humans do to you. If they can't control you and box you in. They simply get rid of you. And my heart jumps a little at the thought that Jessie's body hasn't turned up.

There's just a chance, isn't there, that she's more resilient than anyone knows? Isn't there just a chance that the womanzee still breathes?

But Cleavis looks pleased with himself, at a monster-hunting job well done. It's one thing that stands between us and any chance of happiness, I suppose. I hated him for roaming about the town with those weapons. I hated the way he whipped out his pistol and bang! there goes Jessie, without a second thought.

My expression must be a savage one. I must be frowning at him across the picnic table, because he asks me what the matter is.

'*I* am a monster, Henry,' I say. I take a deep, ragged

breath, surprised at my own words. 'What happens when you decide it's time to hunt *me* down?'

He laughs at me. He guffaws. Then he realises that I'm not joining in. I'm serious. 'You're no monster. My dear! Oh, Brenda! You're not a monster at all.'

'By any rational definition, I most certainly am. I am unnatural. Not of woman born. Stitched together. Patched together. Flung together with loving care by the greatest scientist of his age. I am almost two hundred years old, Henry. Of course I'm a monster! I'm a classic!'

He slurps at his coffee, crunching up the grounds in embarrassment. 'Well. Um. Yes. Of course I'm aware of. You told me of. Um. Yes. But not a *nasty* monster. Not one that needs to be dealt with. Or put out of the way. You're no danger to anyone, are you now?'

I can feel my eyes sparkle dangerously as I catch and hold his gaze. His expression wavers. I can see how much I disconcert him. 'Are you sure about that?' I ask him. 'Mightn't you come running after me one day, with your harpoon gun, your mistletoe and garlic, your jet-tipped and silver-tipped bullets?' I sound almost mocking. Challenging.

'Never, my dear,' he tells me. 'Even if I was instructed to. Even if you were deemed to be the most dangerous woman in Britain. I wouldn't hunt you down. I wouldn't harm a hair on your head.'

I don't point out to him that this is a wig. I'm completely bald up top.

'You know that I wouldn't hurt you,' he says now. 'You've known that from the start.'

'The start?' I say. 'I'm not sure I remember the start.'

Cleavis smiles. 'Oh, I do.'

'All those years ago. Sixty or more, as you've helpfully pointed out . . .' Cleavis smiles ruefully at this. 'I was living in rooms in the old college. My younger brother John had moved in with me, acting as a sort of secretary, though he wasn't much use. I had him dealing with my correspondence and generally tidying the place up. Kept him out of mischief, I suppose. And he loved the life, too. The ancient town. Everything mildewy, fusty. Crammed with erudition. And all us musty old bachelors gadding about the place in our crow-like robes. Dashing about the place on our bikes. He loved all that, did John. And he loved my friends, too. He would even attend our regular meetings. Thursday nights. He loved to play host. He'd pop out to the buttery to fetch a jug of beer for us. He'd listen with the rest of us. Bated breath. As Professor Tyler read us another chapter, say, all about his elves and fairies and whatnot. Or William Freer gave us one of his interminable epic poems. John was always included. One of the founding members, I'd say. One of the very first Smudgelings. And it was his enthusiasm that kept us going. We took it for granted, the sitting together, talking and reading and making up stories. To John it was all a novelty. He thought we were so lucky. Living the life we did. And so we were.

'So. I am thinking about after the war, aren't I? Everyone is returned, it seems. Amongst our group, anyway. I've been nowhere. I've been in the home guard. Tyler has been a warden. John's leg has never been the same. He's discharged now. Under my care. The undergraduates are coming back. There are more demands on our time. The old town is changing. We can all feel it. But the Smudgelings are trying to keep their little bit of it just the same as ever. That's important to us. We believe we are preserving something. Keeping something going. I don't know what that was now, looking back. The old stories, I suppose. The wellspring of myth itself. Does that sound silly, Brenda?'

I shake my head.

'So we read our poems and our stories, our works in progress, to each other. Monday lunchtimes we would meet in the Book and Candle, the hard core of us. Tyler liked a pint or two. And on Thursday evenings, come rain or shine, we would meet for one of our long, long sessions of listening and arguing the toss. Often we would meet in my rooms. That's when John was happiest. When we were playing host to all the others. When he really felt he had a place. Other times, we would be out at the Tyler residence. It was a large, ramshackle house, further out in the town. Almost in the suburbs, John would complain, as we marched out there. I can hear him now, groaning on. That particular night. In all the snow. It was halfway up our calves and coming down thicker and faster by the minute. We bent our heads against the oncoming, whirling snow and set a fair pace for Professor Tyler's house.

'John was joking about Tyler's wife, the formidable Edith. She was a brusque, disconcerting sort. None of us could imagine why the two of them had ever fallen into step, let alone shackled themselves together. Except the story went that she had nursed old Tyler back to health at the end of the last war. Perhaps it was out of sheer gratitude that she'd pulled him back from the brink of destruction? We heard that his war wounds were savage. And that was why he had brought her here, to this old, dank, university town that the ex-nurse hated so much. You could see it in her face when she allowed us in over the threshold on nights like this. Rolling her eyes at us. Tutting at us. Reg's funny university friends. Rum types. John seemed to find Tyler's wife rather amusing. He kept up an endless stream of Edith jokes and anecdotes as we struggled through the wintry park.

' "One thing," I interrupted. "She has been a great support to the venerable professor." I pictured the mismatched pair: Tyler skinny, ascetic, sour-looking. Edith all blowsy and frilly. Rather commonplace, in fact – though none of us would ever dare to voice that opinion. "She has looked after him and seen to it that his great work has gone on uninterrupted. His college duties, but also the real work. Why, without the protection of the impressive Edith, I doubt he would have progressed this far."

'John made a noise of agreement. The oncoming snow was too savage for me to turn and see his expression. "Seventeen years, though!" he said, whistling. "All that time on one book. Who knows, if it wasn't for Edith, he might have finished it by now?"

' "Rubbish," I scoffed. "Edith has been urging Reg to get it finished for years now. She's convinced he's dragging his heels just to spite her. She wants him to publish it and make pots of money for her. She wants the high life, does Edith. She's convinced what's-he-called – Disney – will want it when it's done. Just imagine! Imagine Tyler's face when she suggested it! Disney!"

' "Do you think he'll ever bring it out for the public?" John asked me. And I had to admit that I just didn't know. We were privileged, we few Smudgelings. For years we had been listening, in instalments, to *The True History of Planets*.

And, as the months and years went by, it had become increasingly clear that we were listening to something unique as it was evolving. Something very special indeed. Tonight, at the Tylers' residence, over cheese and port, we would hear more.

' "Is that Freer?" John asked suddenly, squinting into the swarming darkness. He faced out across the park, where the iron lamp stands had only just been replaced. They cast pools of dirty yellow light and, as John pointed, I could indeed see a dapper figure, bent almost double by the knifing wind.

' "It certainly looks like him," I murmured. "Shall we wait for him to catch up?"

'John shook his head quickly. "I'd rather not walk along with him, Henry, if you don't mind." I knew already that John didn't think much of our newest member, the London novelist William Freer. I felt sad about that, because Freer had been offered membership at my request. I found him fascinating as a writer, and as a man, even though he wasn't our usual sort. No stuffy academic, he. He lectured occasionally in Spitalfields, for the Workers' Educational Association. He talked about the Romantics, which Tyler had taken to ribbing him for, since nothing of consequence had been written – in Tyler's view – for at least a thousand years. But it was Freer's formidable, free-spirited intellect and imagination that I – and I hoped the other Smudgelings – valued him for.

'As we watched now, it was apparent that he was being met by another man. A dark figure, hard to make out. As if it was a fine, spring evening, they were standing together and seemingly passing the time of day.

' "How very peculiar," John said. "He's chatting away with that fellow in the cape."

' "Best not to disturb them," I said, and we hastened our footsteps past the park, and into a crescent of tall, elegant houses, wherein lay the Tyler residence.

'A housemaid came to answer our crashing and banging at the door. We were frozen, standing there in the porch, as it slowly filled up with drifting snow. The door opened a crack, letting out this wonderfully warm golden glow from within. And this new housemaid – just started work for Edith that week – gazed out at my brother and me. Her face was creased with a suspicious frown as she asked who we were.'

Now Cleavis smiles at me. 'It was hardly the politest of introductions, Brenda. But I can still see that moment, crisp as anything. Crisp as the snow down my starched collar. Sharp as the throb of my chilblains as you asked us – quite – gruffly – to step inside the hall.'

I choke up. '*I* . . .?'

Cleavis nods. 'Yes, you, Brenda. Don't you remember? You were the Tylers' new housemaid. All those years ago. You took our hats and coats. I was charmed from the moment I first clapped eyes on you.'

I gasp. A hollow, involuntary sound. And I remember. I can remember being the housemaid.

Now I'm back in my kitchen. I need a few minutes away from Henry, just to get myself together. I'm giving the dishes a quick rinsing, and then I'll steep them. It'll make them easier to do.

I was a housemaid. Of course I was. And not just for the Tylers in Cambridge. For various people, in many different houses, over the years. I have been a servant. I don't remember actually deciding to go to Cambridge. I can't recall exactly why I chose that city, but I do remember Tyler and his wife, Edith. She was an unsure, tetchy woman. She was young, trying to act older. She was out of her depth, and struggling to keep up. She was self-conscious and cruel. I once came upon her beating one of the other girls they had in doing the chores. I had to shove my way in and stop her.

As Henry told me his tale I was seeing everything through his eyes. I could see him and his brother in that snowy park. I could see them plodding heavily towards the lit-up windows of the Tylers' place. I could see myself on the doorstep: a glowering lummox in a servant's cap.

My first sight of Henry Cleavis that winter night had me responding much as my first recent sightings of him have done: I was drawn to him. He felt safe to me. But in those days I was less likely to trust anyone. If I liked the look of someone I was curt with them, stand-offish. I just about barked at him and his brother that Tyler was in the drawing room with one or two of the others. Waiting with the port and the fire raging. To me they were like little boys, playing silly boys' games, and at first I didn't have much patience with them.

But I listened to their welcomes and their hellos in that drawing room, as I stoked and banked up the fire. I bustled about, making busywork, listening all the while. Then I was intrigued: it was rare to hear Professor Tyler so animated. He could be such a glum and starchy presence, but when Cleavis was there and the Smudgelings were in session, his mood became expansive, even ebullient.

I can remember them talking about all sorts of things. I would pass back and forth, bringing and unloading trays, and I would try to look as if I was paying them or their conversations no heed. Of course I was, though. I was drinking up everything, whenever I went into that drawing room on those nights. All their peculiar conversations – all their learning, all the things they had made up. The dribs and drabs I heard in that room thrilled and disturbed me. They were talking about other times and other countries and, in my ignorance, I never knew if these things were real or not. To me, it was as if these clever men could bring just about anything into existence by the mere act of talking about it. They began to fascinate me and I was drawn to the stuffy warmth of the colloquy more than a servant should have been.

Edith scolded me out in the hallway. In that narrow passage, with stuffed fox heads and murky paintings in gilt frames, I hung my head as the coarse mistress of the house took me to task. I was to leave the Smudgelings in peace. No, they didn't want any more cake or biscuits or cocoa. I wasn't to find any more spurious excuses. They didn't want interrupting by the likes of me.

'Besides,' Edith snarled. 'A girl like you. What can you possibly understand about the things they say?'

'I know they are writing books, all of them,' I said. 'They're all writing about marvellous things. Impossible things. Professor Tyler is writing about the most marvellous of all. I have heard a little of his story, just a little . . .'

I watched the mistress's face cloud over. It was past one in the morning and the men were still chuntering away in the drawing room. Edith could have done without my beaming enthusiasm. I watched her temper snap, and her tiny hand go up to slap me. Instinctively I protected myself. My own, rather larger mitt reached up and grasped her wrist. She quivered and shook with frustration.

'Don't you listen to them!' she spat. 'It's not for the likes of you.'

I stared at her and let her wrist go. She rubbed it and glared back at me. 'How dare you grab me like that?'

I didn't say anything.

'You mustn't listen to what the men in there say, Brenda. It is wickedness. It is dangerous.'

Now, this was the first I'd heard of such an idea. 'Wickedness?'

She bit her lower lip. I could see how young she was, the mistress of this place. Tyler had grabbed her up and brought her down here to this mildewy place and she was out of her element. She was going to the bad, and she knew it. The place was distorting her nature. And now she was filled with paranoid speculation, superstition. 'I know they talk about magic. About terrible things. All of this . . . messing about with their manuscripts, with their made-up tales and so on . . . it is simply a cover. They are talking about sorcery, Brenda. You must stay away when they talk like this. And so must I. This isn't for the likes of us.'

I remember my insides thrumming with excitement at

her words. They were talking about sorcery and it scared poor Edith silly. But it had the opposite effect on me. The words were tantalising to me. They drew me to the very edge of their world and the dark things that they got up to.

'Reginald won't talk to me about it.' The mistress was gushing now, looking to me as if for my help and my reassurance. 'I ask him. He won't tell me anything. He won't say a word. He's been like this for months. I think he hates me now . . .'

'No, no, I'm sure that's wrong.' I found myself trying to calm her. Too soft-hearted, me. She'd just had a go at clouting me – and here I was, stroking her golden hair, which had dulled somewhat in recent weeks. I was hugging the wretched girl in the hallway of her big house. Trying to make her feel that her husband thought something of her. But I didn't really think he did. Not any more. He was a cold old fish, Reg Tyler. All he cared about was that book of his.

RAT-TAT-TAT on the door. A late member arriving in a flurry of sleet and ice. Both Edith and I jumped at the sharp rapping of his silver-headed cane against the door's paintwork. I hastened to answer.

And there stood a tall, impeccably dressed man of indeterminate age. He gave me a vulpine, suggestive smile. William Freer: the most recent addition to the Smudgeling roster. He was late because the London trains were delayed in this hellish storm. There were ice crystals on the black fur collar of his overcoat. As he whirled into the corridor I realised that the pang that went through me was one of fear, rather than attraction, though William Freer was a devilishly attractive man. Off came his coat for my safekeeping, and he was in a charcoal suit underneath, sharp as a pin. Edith hurried to welcome him. She stammered and she shook and she pretended to know Freer only slightly. This charade was obviously for my benefit. But I saw the looks they were giving each other and I knew it for a charade.

When I re-join Henry in my garden, the air has turned mellow. The sun slants through softly and lights up all the insects on the air. I'll be bitten to pieces if I stay out here. Somehow they are always drawn to me. I must have very delicious blood.

Henry Cleavis is looking at me as if he can discern something interesting in my face. He knows straight away that he has triggered my memories.

'You've started to remember.' He smiles with some satisfaction.

I nod and smile and really, it feels as though he's started an avalanche going in my head. A slow, stately avalanche, all rumbles and ominous trickles. Without him, I'd never have consciously thought back to being a housemaid. What's the point? Those years have long gone. But now Cleavis has reminded me of Reg and Edith and William Freer and the words and pictures have resurfaced. Or started to, anyway. It's shocked me that I can remember things word for word. My memories are like delicate bolts of lace: rotting with holes here and there, where they have been folded and stashed away. But in other places the fragile patterns and fine traceries are still discernible, holding the fabric in one piece.

I want Henry to go home now. He's smiling at me, proud of himself as if he's presented me with a wonderful gift. I find I can't return his grin, or give him thanks for this sudden access to my past. He's shown me a doorway, a hatchway leading further down into myself. My own savage interior. That's what he's done. Into a time when I was less good at being me, when I was so much younger. Why should I thank him for that? I want to concentrate on *now*. On today.

'I wonder what it is about your memory,' he muses. 'I wonder why it works differently from . . . from most human beings' . . .'

I shrug, and glower at him warningly. Surely, if he knows me so well, he knows better than to go into this. He should know I don't like talking about such things.

'The analogy would be with computer hardware, I suppose.' Henry warms to his theme. 'You're the second owner of your mind, if you think about it. The first one must have been wiped, I suppose, so that you could fill it up with your own thoughts. Like a hard drive, as I suppose they would say today, hm?' Another thought seizes him and his eyes light up. 'I wonder if each of your constituent parts has its own memory? Hm? Of its original, um, owner? Wouldn't that be marvellous? There's no reason why not. The body and all its bits has its own intelligence, its own intuitions, does it not? There is a twitchy, deep-rooted wisdom to what our bodies know. My, Brenda! You must be a mass of conflicting emotions and ideas and feelings, why . . . all the time!'

'*Get out*,' I tell him. 'Go home, Henry.' I try to modify my sudden bellow, my evident crossness, by gentling my tone and yawning. 'I've really come over very tired.' It's only early, but I don't care. I've had enough of him and his whiffling by now. I hoist myself out of my deckchair and he follows, politely mystified by the vehemence in my tone.

'Will you accompany me to Sheila's first barbecue night?' he asks. 'It's tomorrow evening and she wants to show off her new facilities.'

I nod quickly, feigning a migraine. He's given me the

creeps, the way he talked about me, my body and everything. What does he know about anything?

As he toddles off, so pleased with himself, Cleavis doesn't even know that he is spoiling things between us. Shooting Jessie. Grazing Effie's temple with the same jet-tipped bullet and putting her into a coma. Reviving my unwanted memories. He goes up on his tiptoes to kiss my grease-painted cheek before he leaves.

I have an early night because I want to be up and about at the crack of dawn, in order to visit Effie. I've started to feel guilty for not going this afternoon. What if she woke and came to her senses? Remembered that the last thing she was aware of was Henry firing his gun into the crowd? Wildly, like a madman, like an assassin? And then she heard that I was giving him lunch? Going to such an effort for the silly old fool? What would she say?

She wouldn't be impressed.

So my dreams come early. The shallow side of midnight. And I'm back in that silvery winter in Cambridge, when the ponds in the park were frozen black, and the denuded trees stuck out like strange Chinese writing. Those funny hieroglyphic things they use. There was writing everywhere in the snowy dark.

I dream about the suave William Freer. With the thrilling voice. The large, cool hands. The furry collar round his cloak. That way he had of talking to you, as if you were the only important person in the room. In the world, even. It was a seducer's way of carrying on. A con-man, a charlatan, a proper Casanova. Well, I was never going to be taken in by him. I might have looked like a naive working woman to him. An uneducated servant. But by then I was a hundred and twenty years old, and I'd seen a thing or two.

Edith and the Smudgelings were taken in by him. He swooped into their lives, their homes and all the while he was mocking them. I can sense that so clearly in my dream of William Freer. He acted so solicitous and kind, but in my dream there's a touch of the pantomime villain about him. The old silent movie feller, with his cloak and his twirling 'tache. He thought the Smudgelings – Henry, Reg, and all of them – were bumbling, parochial fools. Stuffed to the gills, self-satisfied and smug out there on the eerie, eely Fens, tamped down with useless knowledge. Writing silly fairy tales for each other. But there was something he wanted and something he desperately needed from them. Otherwise, why waste his time?

It was *Edith*. I woke with a shock in my dark bedroom. It was *Edith* he wanted.

I could see them plain as day. Not that night, some other night, deeper and later into that winter. Freer and Edith were canoodling in the hallway. Playing with fire. Anyone might have caught them. But it was just me, popping through with ginger cake and tea on a silver tray, and I hardly counted. I was barely sentient in Edith's eyes, though Freer spared me a lascivious, tormenting smile as I edged past them. He had Edith clutched to him, under his cloak, and, until she noticed me passing through, she was squealing with pleasurable fear. Then they sprang apart.

She loved him. As I sit there in my bed, I remember that well. Edith hated Tyler by then. She once sat drunk at the kitchen table, demanding cooking sherry and unwisely telling me and Mrs Ford, the cook, how much she had grown to hate her professor.

'My life was meant to be different. I was a nurse. I was his nurse. He promised me the world, you know. For bringing him back alive. For bringing him paper and pens so that he could work on the ward, even though he wasn't allowed to. Not really. He needed to be resting. But I could see all this need in his face. He begged me. He was older than me. Not as much as you would think, looking at us now . . .' Edith had burped softly at this, wafting away the cooking sherry fumes, and the cook and I stared at her dough-like face. The eyes like little dried fruits stuck into the softness. Her spiteful little mouth red as preserved cherries. We looked at her and neither of us liked her, really, since she had been so cruel to us. But her admissions –

especially those about her love for the satanic Freer –
completely thrilled us and held us rapt.

'Will you run away with him, ma'am?' asked the
cook.

'I should run away.' Edith scowled. 'I don't belong here.
This damp place. I belong on the northern coast. Where I
grew up. Where I worked in the hospital and met my
nemesis, my husband . . . I should go back to Whitby.'

Whitby! Of course! Of course that's where Tyler met his
nurse. Where he recuperated from his head injuries during
the Great War. It was where he first started work on his
opus, *The True History of Planets.* It was too neat to be just
a coincidence, surely. I hadn't made the connection up till
now, sitting with the heavy bedclothes bunched about me,
sixty years later. Here I am, in this town I was drawn to by
supernatural means. Here is Cleavis, investigating, killing
monsters, in the town where his great friend first started out
on his momentous path into fantasy: into the world of the
Smudgelings. There are lines and glimmers of connections
here. I can't quite see them properly. They're like threads of
tinsel, twisting and turning in the light. My brain's all
messed up, with the extra work I'm making it do. It isn't
used to digging around like this and—

Tap, tappety, tap-tap-tap.

All I need.

Skittering and scratting. Tiny feet falling over themselves in the dark. Drunken feet coming to get me in the dark. Breaking once more into the sanctuary at the top of my house. Skitter scatter tap tap tap. I'm so used to it now. It still sends a shock right through me, though.

Tap tappety tap.

Like having malign goblins dancing on your grave. Taunting you.

But I must sleep. I must show them they can't scare me any more. I don't care. I must sleep blithely, deeply, dreamlessly. No more digging around, no more of the past surfacing and washing up on the shore. Enough of that. I have to get up early and go to the hospital and see how Effie is.

Effie the poison pen letter perpetrator. But surely I can't believe that?

No, I refuse to. Until she wakes and is in a position to defend herself. That's only fair.

Who else but Effie knows the nature of my secrets? Who else could have written me that horrible note?

Tap tap tap.

Only Mrs Claus. Robert. Henry Cleavis.

Horrible mystery, when almost all of the suspects are your friends.

I'm so worn out with it all even my haunting can't keep

me awake. I slump into dreams again and, despite myself, I'm in the company of William Freer and Edith Tyler. They are smooching and canoodling in the gaslit hallway, while the other Smudgelings carry on their meeting elsewhere. I am watching them through a crack in the door that leads to the servants' quarters. And I watch Edith giving herself away to this evil interloper. She also gives him a package tied up with string. A manuscript, thick with handwritten pages. I watch Freer stow it away in his carpet bag and he turns and leaves the Tyler residence hurriedly, into the night, without saying goodbye to his host or the others.

I remember Edith's face. Stricken by the temporary loss of him. And wondering whether she had done the right thing. Too late now, girl, I thought at the time, and I would have loved to have known what was in the parcel.

After that, this night, there's only swimming in darkness and voices I can't quite make out. Then the sun is washing through my attic windows in a great tide of golden light.

I'm sitting with Effie and there's no change. Her head's all bandaged up as if she's taken to wearing a turban, and she has retreated far into herself. That's what the nurse has told me, putting a consoling arm on my shoulder as she goes round. My friend has gone far into herself, out of shock. I nod rather dumbly, and I'm wondering about the jet that Henry used to tip his bullets and how Effie told me several of her ancestors were seen off with just that noxious substance. Inimical to evil. But Effie isn't evil, is she? She's my friend.

Seems useless bringing fruit, but I did. I knew better than to bring flowers, of which she doesn't approve. She once said something about the absurdity of placing genitalia in vases for display, only she mouthed rather than said the word 'genitalia'. Not a very Effie word. She could be so harsh. So judgemental.

But I still don't believe that she was typing out these nasty letters.

In the shop this morning, Leena and Raf watching me warily. Bursting to ask. 'You've had one as well, haven't you? We heard on the grapevine. Do you know who sent it? Have you uncovered the culprit?'

I could do the proper detective thing, I suppose. While she lies here helpless I could get Effie's keys out of her bag and I could get into her home. I could go there under the pretext of airing her rooms, guarding against intruders. But I should go up to the dusty office in her attic and have a good look at her clapped-out typewriter. I should compare the keys, the machine's idiosyncrasies. Easy work to check out a typewriter, as Sherlock Holmes once pointed out. They each have their very own fingerprint. So I would easily be able to see whether it was the one which tapped out my letter. There was a dodgy s in the letter. A slightly misaligned key.

But somehow I can't bring myself to go and do it. So I don't. And why? Because I wouldn't be able to bear it if the letter matched the machine. I couldn't bear to find Effie out. I would rather not know. And so I put off the obvious solution as if it hasn't occurred to me and, ironically, hear Effie's caustic voice in my head: 'You'll never make a real investigator, Brenda.'

Well, in this case, I don't want to. I don't want to have my suspicions confirmed.

A gulf is separating Effie and me. More than the distance between the half-dead and the semi-alive. The undead and the unconscious. The revived and the comatose. A much bigger distance than that. Now that I have seemingly thrown in my lot with Henry Cleavis (though the last time I saw him I was throwing him out of my garden), a gap of sympathy has opened up between my friend and me. When she wakes up (and I just know she will: she has to) she'll know that my man friend shot Jessie dead and she will not be able to forgive that. She will not be able to understand how *I* can.

What will I say? I was giving him Sunday lunch. I was treating him like an old and dear friend. We talked and talked for hours and I let him stir my memories round. Up they came like the murk at the bottom of a pond, turning the clear water cloudy. Effie will want to know why and how I can trust him. And give myself away to him.

I kiss her cheek gently, as if I don't really want her to wake up at all. And I plod heavy-limbed out of her stark private room. Gladly I leave the hospital behind and walk back to town.

Jessie – the real Jessie – had gone for ever, hadn't she? I am pretty sure of that. There was precious little left of the woman we had known. The erstwhile glamour puss and waitress, turned to bitterness and gall amongst the endless baubles and tinsel of the Christmas Hotel. That woman had gone, eaten away by the primitive womanzee possessing her. That's what Cleavis believes, and I must believe, too. He sees monstrousness as a canker, as a demonic form of possession, from which there is no going back. Not quite how I see it, of course. I'm nine-tenths monster myself. It's a very ordinary thing to be, in some ways. It's all about how you comport yourself in public.

Oh, dear. I'm starting to think I should have done something. I should have realised Henry was about to shoot. I should have been quicker. My reflexes are second to none. I could have elbowed him aside. Ruined his shot. I know I could have. But then what? Have him hit some innocent face in the crowd?

And . . . I cling to the faint hope. Perhaps Jessie isn't dead. Possessed as she is of inhuman strength and capabilities . . . maybe she even survived her bloody drop into the briny?

We will find out, I am sure. A shudder runs through me then, and somehow I know I'm right. The day is warming up and I'm too hot in my good wool coat, but for some reason I am shivering. And I have a very distinct impression that Jessie still lives. She is waiting somewhere, out there. She will return to us.

That's just as well. A presentiment. Good news, at any rate, to tell Effie when she comes out of her coma. I can tell Robert, too, when I see him this evening, at Sheila Manchu's barbecue. I trust my instincts. I have learned to believe in what they tell me, even if what they tell me seems impossible at times.

And that's why I believe these flashbacks I've been getting, at Henry's prompting. I know they're true. I can feel it in my waters. Whole conversations are coming back, word for word. I can even smell the musty silk carpets in the Tyler household, such a nuisance to keep clean. That heavy old furniture from his mother's house. Polishing it in his study while he was at his college. Me, in his study, the venerable professor's sanctum sanctorum. Of course it never occurred to either of them I would have any interest in his papers.

He used to write on the backs of old examination papers. Very frugal, was Reg, and he was right to be, after the war. He wrote in this very scratchy script, like runes, or something. So I had to squint and peer sideways at what he had written.

And such strange things he had written. His novel, *The True History of Planets*, was immense and disorderly. It had hundreds of characters and situations. There was very little consistency, very few jokes. Sometimes I was hardly sure what I was reading, scanning those sheets, one eye anxiously on the door for Edith. The few bits I did manage to make sense of filled me with a queer sort of dread. Stuff about old gods and gateways, far-flung dimensions, star-spanning creatures that interfered with humankind. All that funny business, coming out of his head, I thought! Just imagine what he dreams about! That dome of a brilliant skull of his. It seemed eggshell thin. All his precious secrets within. I feared brash Edith would smash it, turning over in bed, as easily as she smashed the shell of her breakfast egg, spraying bits everywhere, leaving it for me to clean up.

I suppose I even had a little protective crush on Reg Tyler, too, and his wonderful, strange book, as I did on Henry Cleavis. I had a crush on all the Smudgelings. I loved what they did. I imagined being among their number. Having their privileges — of class, gender, intelligence, wherewithal, everything – and being able to join them in their weekly get-togethers. It seemed to me they were making a voyage of discovery across the vast stretches of the human soul. The limits of the possible and the made up. Does that sound silly? Nevertheless, it was a voyage I felt myself barred from. I was – and am – lowly and inhuman. I could merely serve the tea in china cups and the cake and the port. And I could listen for scraps of the erudite and the fabulous, and that would have to content me.

When I arrive for Sheila's barbecue I don't get a chance to have a word with Robert. He is smart in his black outfit, but he is curt with me. He marches about between the hotel and the beer garden and I feel desolate inside when he nods me a hello and doesn't stop to talk. Things will never be the same again between us. He did everything he could to save his aunty, and I am one of those who betrayed her. That's how he will see it.

I'm in a light frock with a cardy over my shoulders, in case it turns cool. I wish I hadn't come out at all.

There's a jovial feeling – a spirit of revelry and light-heartedness – here at the Miramar this evening that hardly fits my own mood. Every one of Sheila's guests, and various well-wishers from town, have gathered to attend the opening of her beer garden. At first I think they're all drunk, the way they're carrying on. But I don't think they are. Not yet. They are just happy to be here, in this arcadian place with all the bamboo trellising and the wickerwork furniture. I must admit, Sheila's done a nice job. No expense spared. There's a blazing fire, for decoration more than anything, because the actual barbecuing seems to be going on at a rather futuristic-looking machine in one corner. There, hanks of bloody meat and festoons of fresh sausages are waiting to be scorched.

Henry bustles up and draws me away, to sit with him at a small wicker table by the dog roses. As he pats my hands I tell him I feel as if I've lost Robert's friendship for ever – because of him. He is sympathetic, but I can't help feeling that he's brushing the topic aside. As ever, Henry is dead set on what it is he wants to discuss. 'How is your memory doing?' he asks earnestly, leaning in.

I frown at him. He seems so ardent. 'It's all right,' I grumble. Somewhere in the garden, music starts up. Some kind of wartime jazz, presumably for the oldies. I feel like telling him that my memories are no business of his. I feel a stab of rebellion then. But I know it's no use. Of course it's his business.

'Do you remember how we went to London on the train together, hm?' he asks. He's still patting my hands, in a rather insinuating manner.

I shake my head. 'No, I don't remember that. Not at all. Together? London? Surely you aren't suggesting . . .'

Henry Cleavis gives an almost ribald chuckle – which surprises me. 'It was all in the line of duty, Brenda. Nothing suspect. Nothing untoward.'

'I'm glad to hear it,' I say stiffly, as delicious cooking smells start to waft across the noisy beer garden. But am I glad? Wouldn't I have adored it if Cleavis had whisked me away for a dirty weekend? I almost blush to imagine it. I'm finished with all the romance business these days, of course, but back then I think I would have gone off with Henry at the drop of a hat. If he had clicked his fingers I'd have run off with him, to London or anywhere.

Because, of course, I was very drawn to him, then. There was something about him that put me at my ease. The others – especially Tyler – treated me like a servant. They barely treated me like a person. I was an ungainly lummox bustling about. I couldn't understand a word they said, and so they needn't modify their speech or hold their tongues while I served them their nightcaps and their midnight snacks. And so I learned far more about the Smudgelings than I was meant to. They'd have been horrified to know how much I knew.

There is dancing starting in Sheila's beer garden. I sit there swaying and aching, wishing more than anything that

Henry would ask me up. There's a knot of revellers, all silhouetted and glamorous against the trellis and the rose bushes. They jostle and make merry. What would Effie say? You don't need a man to ask you up to dance. Don't be ridiculous, woman! If you want to dance, get up there and dance! But my heart's heavy tonight. I feel as though I'm wearing a corset of iron. Clodhopping boots of lead. I couldn't dance if I tried.

'I remember going to you . . . with my suspicions,' I tell Henry quietly, sipping the cocktails that are brought to us.

'Good.' He nods.

'The next time the Smudgelings convened at your college. A little after that night when Freer turned up so late. A few weeks later and it was even snowier, darker. A week before Christmas that year. And I called you out into the hallway. I had to tell you. What I thought was the truth.'

'Which was . . . ?' What a teacher Henry Cleavis sounds like just now. Drawing the answers out of me. So encouraging and sparkly.

'Parts of Professor Tyler's manuscript were missing. The old feller hadn't even noticed, so set was he on the pieces he was writing. He was so closely focused, so myopic and trusting, he never looked behind him. And his sour-faced wife was betraying him. I had watched her. Giving sheaves of his precious manuscript away – to that wicked man, Freer. Her lover!'

Henry nods, very pleased with me. He sucks up green foaming cocktail through his 'tache. 'You've done very well, Brenda. You've recalled quite a lot. Was it very disturbing, to have all of this past life come back to you?'

I shake my head quickly. 'When you have as many memories as I have, you have to stash them away a little deeper. It takes longer, but it doesn't always hurt to bring them out again.' Now I'm lying, and I can see that Henry knows it.

'Do you remember that I listened to you? I believed in you? I let you take me aside and tell me that one of our Smudgelings was an evil man? A villain?'

I smile. 'Yes, I do remember that. I was staggered. I could tell you were a decent sort, but . . . I hardly expected to be believed so easily . . .'

'I think I already knew that Freer was up to no good.' Henry sighs. 'And it was all my fault. It had been I – so naively trusting and silly – who had read William Freer's peculiar, satanic novels and lapped them up like a schoolboy. Though Tyler and some of the others were against it – hating his writing, his ideas – I campaigned to have him join us. I thought the knowledge he seemed to have, of evil, of magic and the devil, would stand us in good stead. Would help us in our fight. The good fight. Um.' Henry looks at me bleakly, and then he smiles. 'Because, of course, you realised almost straight away that we weren't just a writers' circle, didn't you? More than a gathering of friends and academics?'

'I did.'

'You knew what the Smudgelings were really up to, in their ongoing battle against the creatures of the night. We were godly and righteous crusaders against the darkness. And, of course, coming at it from a slightly different angle, you yourself were caught up in that struggle too, weren't you? You still are, Brenda. And so am I.'

Henry's voice has dropped to a seductive murmur, under all the hullaballoo of the barbecue. Which, I suddenly realise, is no mean feat. The barbecue around us is a rather boisterous affair. The guests have been whipped into a gluttonous and celebratory frenzy. They abandoned knives and forks a while ago, and the dancing is no longer confined to the dance floor. There's something curious going on in this beer garden, but it's as if Henry and I are no longer even part of this scene. We aren't infected by the atmosphere because we are caught up in the past. We are plunging backwards and now we can focus on little else but the sound of our own voices.

'And we worked together then?' I ask. 'We went to London?'

'We chased Freer. We went after him. For Tyler's manuscript. We wanted to know why it was so important to him that he had to purloin the only extant copy. We went to get it back. That very night.'

'I'm sorry, I'm not sure I can recall any of that,' I say. Now I'm ravenous, as the cooking smells thicken on the dusky air. The sharp excitements of the night are getting to me, and stirring my juices up. There are too many distractions here in the beer garden of Sheila Manchu. I shake my head to clear it. 'But it's like there's a great big wall in my mind at that point. I just don't remember . . .'

Henry nods understandingly. 'That is why I would like, um, permission. To try to get to the truth. By taking us both somewhere quieter and less frenetic, and hypnotising you.'

It turns out that I am an easy subject. Who would have thought it? I fondly imagined I would be all defences and strong fortifications. But, it turns out, as I sit there in my bobbly green armchair at home, later that night, it takes only a matter of minutes for me to go under. I am even aware of what I am saying as I say it, though it's as though the words are speaking themselves.

It's like watching myself on a screen, somehow. And it's shocking, the detail that the past comes up in. Suddenly, I'm right back in 1946.

'I am keeping a close eye on Edith Tyler. I know she is planning something special. I am on the alert, waiting for her to move. Once or twice her lover, Freer, comes by in the afternoon, while Professor Tyler is in college. Again she slips him individual chapters of Tyler's novel. They are handwritten in that scratchy lettering and my heart boils with anger when I see Freer slipping away, into the snow, his lips hot with Edith's kisses and the professor's masterpiece under his cloak.

'And then comes the night of the flight to London.

'When it comes I am ready for the pursuit. Mrs Ford the cook is suspicious. I'm pulling on my old boots in the cellar kitchen and she's squawking at me. She knows something is up. I shouldn't be leaving tonight. I am needed here. But I won't listen to her. I'm tailing Edith Tyler, who has packed a compact weekend case and is slipping about the house like a shadow; like someone preparing to leave for the very last time. Reg is out for the evening. It is Thursday. He is at yours, Henry. At your college rooms, drinking sherry and talking with the rest of the Smudgelings. He has no idea his wife is about to leave him.

'I watch through a crack in the door. She's in the professor's study. She's in the drawer where the rest of his manuscript is waiting. She hefts the last remaining chunk of one hundred pages. That's the lot. Now she has taken everything and she looks pleased with herself as she puts it in her case, squashing down the top and snapping the clasps. What has Freer told her he will do with Tyler's book? Have it published himself, and halve the cash with her? Or is it just a bargaining tool? Bring me your husband's precious book and you can be mine, Edith? Either way, she's nicked it.

'And now she is out in the snowy streets of the suburbs. She's struggling in the direction of town, slipping and sliding in unsuitable shoes. I know she's meeting Freer and there's only one place she can be heading to – the train station.

'I am out of the house after her. All I know is that I won't let her get away with this. My loyalty is with the professor and the Smudgelings. I make a swift detour into the very centre of town, knowing that I'm surer on my feet than Edith is, in all this snow. I lumber heavily but quickly to the college where I know you reside, Henry.

'I only passed this way once before, when I first came to this ancient city. The pale, spectral buildings disturbed me. Their windows were dark and I felt that eyes were looking out at me, studying me. They were like castles, these colleges, and their inhabitants frowned at me and made me feel I had no place here. Tonight I can't afford to feel disconcerted. I duck through the portcullising of the porter's lodge. I try to keep to the shadows; ducking and flitting through courtyards and up smooth stone staircases and corridors. I follow the signs and dread the approach of anyone asking me what on earth I think I'm doing. How will I explain? I am Tyler's servant. Concerned for the theft of his manuscript; the absconding of his faithless wife?

'At last I find your set of rooms, Henry. I take a deep breath and bang, with both heavy fists, at your door. Panic is surging through me now, and I know I have to work hard to convince you of the urgency of my mission, otherwise Edith will get away. She must be aiming for the five to seven. The last train to London this evening. Freer lives in London. She is going to him.

'All of this comes out in a rush. You're clutching me by the shoulders in your shabby passageway. It smells of kippers and light ale and the brown-spotted must of old books. You look at me as if I'm on my last legs. You try to calm me like you would a startled horse, whispering and petting. I sit on a rickety chair and you bring me a glass of treacly sherry. I hear you making excuses to the other Smudgelings. You don't tell them I am here. You quietly close the door on your study, where the fire crackles and your friends gather and their low, murmuring voices are so reassuring, so safe. While, out here in the hallway, I am telling you an outlandish story to do with your best friend's wayward wife.

'You look shocked at first, pulling on your moustaches. "Freer left early this evening," you say at last. "He read us one of his poems – rather shorter than usual – and left about thirty minutes ago. It was quite surprising."

' "He's gone to the station to meet her!" I burst out. "They're running off together with the professor's book. Tell him! Tell Tyler!"

'But you are firm on this point. "Not yet," you say. "Let's sort this out as best we can, without upsetting the poor, betrayed professor."

'And next thing I know you've dragged out this colossal, rickety bike from under a heap of coats and papers. I'm scurrying down the courtyard after you and you're ringing the bell. Commanding me to get on the seat while you pedal. Well. It's a sturdy enough contraption, I suppose. They really knew how to make bikes in those days. But I think we're lucky to survive that trip out of the college and through the frosty heart of town. I try to keep my legs up and just give in to the momentum, and I think you do yourself a mischief, pedalling like a demon. We're going like the clappers through these narrow streets. You know all the quick routes and all the sly passages. We just about kill a number of unwary students as we bowl along.

'And then we're at the station. You leap with surprising athleticism over your handlebars, leaving me to clumsily tie up our steed, and you bustle us through the turnstiles, flinging money at the ticket booth. "No time for messing about," you're yelling. "We have to be on the—"

'The five to seven. It's standing there, resplendent, on Platform Two. Gleaming and black and puffed up in streaming plumes of its own hot steam. The guard is ready to put his flags up in the air, doors are slamming, he's about to give a sharp toot on his whistle and the engines are idling and ready to roar.

'You're shoving me across the platform, and we're barging through well-wishers and wavers. But we're aboard. We make it. I'm surprised at first. I'm not used to the plush confines of first class. It's all gilt and gas lamps. Thick carpets and flock wallpaper. It's a different world, up this end of the train. We pause in the corridor to catch our breath as the train shunts and pulls out of the cavernous station. We grin at each other because we've made it! We've actually done it! They are here somewhere, on this train. Edith and Freer are here, thinking they are safe. Thinking they are scot free. But we are on their tails. You and I grin at each other and my blood is surging like billy-o in my veins. I've not felt like this in years.

'Then it's time to get to business. We have to check out all the carriages. We have to find them.

'We split up. You head up the train, and I head down

towards the back. It's a process of opening up each of the compartments and thrusting your head through the door. Glaring at each of the startled occupants in turn. I don't allow myself enough time to stop and think. What am I doing? Making these well-heeled passengers jump up in alarm in their plush velvet seats. Here's my ghastly, troglodyte face peering at them in the gloom and the flick-flacking shadows as our train rumbles across the Fens.

'The first few carriages are quiet enough. Three nuns sit quietly together in one. Then an old woman and her young niece. They are startled by me. But I'm ignored by the four gentlemen who travel together in the next compartment: one of them is a huge, bearded beast of a man, expounding in a loud, hectoring voice and getting the others all involved in a heated argument. I move on quickly down the carriages, till the passengers I'm disturbing start to become a faceless and unhelpful blur. In another compartment a very old woman in a dove grey suit is knitting away thoughtfully.

'We have to get to Freer and Edith before we hit London and Liverpool Street station. Otherwise the metropolis will surely swallow them up. They'll be like rats down a bolthole, taking Tyler's book for ever.

'I pause in a shadowy, curtain-swagged niche between compartments. Why am I so bothered about this? Why so worked up?

'Because this, after all, is the reason I came to Cambridge. I know that now, as I struggle to calm down my ragged breathing and get a grip on my exhilaration. I was drawn to the old town, just to be involved in this escapade. Fate and sorcery. Something was acting upon me, without my even knowing it. I was destined to become embroiled in this very fandango! Me and Henry Cleavis, thrusting open carriage doors! Crying out our apologies and giving curt "Good evenings".

'Look at me, still in my housemaid's uniform, with my hair all straggly and my stockings round my ankles – I'm an adventurous slut, hot-footing it to London, with the villain of the piece in my sights—

'Ah. Did you hear? My hearing is rather better than most people's, thanks to my unusual anatomy. A female voice. "William? Are you there?" Coming down the corridor, through the satin and velvet and quavering slightly, unsure of herself as the carriage sways on the tracks. "William?" Has he abandoned her already, then? I shrink back. I can't let her see me. I nip back to the last compartment I peered into. The knitting woman tuts and stares, unsurprised, as I peer through the curtains. Outside, Edith Tyler is staggering along the way I have already come, clutching her case and sounding more and more desperate.

' "There's always strange goings-on on this train." The

old woman behind me is shaking her head and sighing. "I hope that young girl comes to no harm. I saw the man she boarded with and he's up to no good."

'I can only agree, wordlessly, with the old woman. She returns to knitting her bootees as I slip out, oh-so-carefully, after Edith. Edith must surely be wishing by now that she had stayed at home. You can tell by her pained, frightened tones above the clickety-clack of the tracks beneath us that she isn't best pleased. "William? Won't you tell me where you are?"

'And then she evidently hears something. A noise she recognises. She straightens up and cocks her ear. She bolts forward. And I am behind her, in her shadow. But I'm too late to save her.

'Like Edith, I can hear William Freer call out to her: "I am here, my darling. Compartment seven. Directly in front of you." And I can hear Edith sigh with such relief. He hasn't left her after all. She hasn't been dumped. For a moment then Edith had thought that Freer had simply used her, abandoned her and taken the spoils. But they will travel to London together, after all. And he will love her for ever, as he promised. "William," I hear her begin, in an upbraiding sort of voice I have heard her use many times before, "why did you leave me behind in the— Oh!"

'And that sharp note of surprise in her voice. It's almost

alarm. What has she seen? I creep closer. She's a dark, bell-shaped silhouette in the doorway. She sets down her case, and quickly tries to tidy her hair. "William? Will you introduce me to your friend?"

'Company, I wonder? Someone else involved? And I take the risk of being seen. I stick my neck out of the darkness. I crane forward as Edith steps into the compartment. I glimpse her beloved, the traitorous Freer, gesturing to the man that Edith hasn't yet met. His accomplice. His master, to whom Tyler's manuscript has been safely delivered this night.

'The way Edith touches up her tumbled locks like that, I can tell she finds this newcomer attractive. More dashing, even, than her lover Freer. Her tone goes gooey and girlish. "You never told me we would be accompanied on our journey to London, William."

'And then comes Freer's voice. "This is Tyler's wife, my lord. I have brought her with me, as well as the book. Clever, no? Impressive, yes? To whisk away the professor's most prized possessions like this? All in one night?"

'Edith slaps at Freer's hand almost playfully. "Possessions," she scoffs, and she doesn't yet perceive the danger she is in. The danger that I now know she is in. For William Freer is presenting her, with real formality and aplomb, to the tall, chalk-faced figure who shares this compartment with them. "May I introduce to you, my darling, my master? This is Kristoff Alucard. Count Alucard."

'And a stunned Edith drops a curtsy at this point. She always was a snob. Felled by titles, honours, good breeding and manners. Stuff like that. Bit of a clumsy curtsy, if you ask me. And, at first, I foolishly think Count Alucard is darting forward in order to lift her back to her feet.

'But he isn't. He has jumped on her.

'In those close, stuffy confines, he's leapt at her throat. Like a lion on a gazelle, except there was no pursuit. Edith simply vanishes under him, as if she has fallen under the train itself. Freer squawks in horror and tries to shove the door closed.

'But he has seen me! Freer's eyes lock with mine, standing here in the corridor. Freer has seen me! He yells out in shock and I leap backwards.

'And Alucard raises his face, all streaked with Edith Tyler's gore. And I realise I'm a goner. They can't let me get away now. Not after I've seen them . . . like this!

'And I have to run! I have to run! I HAVE TO RUN!'

I burst out of my trance. That's the only word for it.

Poor Cleavis has to deal with me. Shrieking and gibbering like the womanzee herself. I'm thrashing about in my armchair and Henry flaps about me in a vain attempt at pacifying me. But I'm wailing and moaning and it takes me some minutes to realise that I'm no longer back there. I'm not in 1946.

I'm not racing towards the metropolis on an antiquated steam engine. I haven't just seen my mistress's pale, perfect throat ripped out. Or watched her lover Freer's anguished, terrified expression as he saw it happen. And I haven't just come face to face with the burning, feral eyes of—

'*Alucard!*' I shriek. 'Henry, it was him! He was there—'

Then I'm up on my feet, swaying and gasping. 'I had that wall inside my memory. I couldn't see him. I couldn't even remember that . . . he was there . . . at the heart of this thing . . . *Alucard!*'

Henry is rubbing my back and murmuring noises at my ear. 'Can I get you anything, Brenda?'

Soon we're sitting at my kitchen table with a pot of tea. I calm down with the scent of cardamom and cloves. My head is still reeling with the vividness of being hypnotised. I can tell that Henry is somewhat surprised at his success, too.

'It's rather as I suspected,' he tells me at last, crunching into a ginger snap. 'I um. I sort of knew about Alucard's involvement. I wanted to see if you remembered.'

'You knew?' I burst out. 'Why didn't you warn me?' And

now, when I squinch up my eyes, I can feel myself frozen on the spot again, staring into their compartment. All the plush streaked with Edith's blood. How those two evil men ignored my shrieking. Freer clasping his lover. He made feeble attempts to revive her, but he must have known she was dead. Freer, I think, had quite lost his mind in the moment that his master turned on his mistress. Freer was a gibbering wreck from thenceforth.

He and Alucard slid open the black window and between them they bundled Edith's body out into the rattling night. THUMP, THUMP, THUMP as she bounced along the tracks at speed. Away down the embankment into darkened fields like so much old rubbish. Alucard had got what he wanted from her.

I HAD TO RUN! I HAD TO RUN! I was face to face with Alucard and I had to run!

'You know Kristoff Alucard?' I ask Henry quietly.

'My dear.' He laughs softly. 'I have been a member of the Smudgelings since the late thirties. We have been doing battle with the forces of darkness for over seventy years. Of course I have known Alucard. I knew him even before he adopted that ludicrous anagram. Our paths have crossed again and again.'

'He was here,' I say. 'Last year. But I didn't remember him. Not at first. He . . . seduced my best friend.'

'Effie?' Henry is incredulous.

'She has a house filled with old books. Rare texts. Things that don't exist anywhere else in the world. Magic things. That's what he was after. And a lot of good it did him.'

'It makes sense,' Henry muses, 'that he would return to Whitby. It was his first home in England, back in the 1890s. He has strong connections here.'

'Well,' I say, slurping my tea. 'He's gone now, anyway. Gone for ever. Effie and I saw him dragged off into hell.'

'Really?'

My head's all fuddled. 'I can't talk about it now. Too tired and shaken up.'

'Yes, of course, my dear. Um. But if you have any knowledge of Alucard, you really must let me, um, know.'

I stand up and gaze down at Henry's bald head. I'm a bit cross with him now. He drags me through that hellish trance, and now he's still telling me what to do. Well. I've made my mind up. He's not getting anything else out of me. At least, not tonight. Is that why he's here, I wonder, as I wash out our cups, and the teapot. Is he in Whitby on the trail of Alucard?

He touches my elbow. 'You look scared,' he tells me. Of course I deny it. 'The things you were dredging up are bound to be disturbing,' he adds.

'I saw Edith Tyler murdered,' I tell him, my voice

breaking now. I feel as if I'm about to burst into tears. This is ridiculous. Making a fool of myself. I've seen much worse things. Why are these particular memories getting to me? 'I can't get the pictures out of my head . . .'

Then Cleavis is hugging me. He has to reach right up to my neck. His arms are skinny and too short to go round me. He's straining upward like a wallflower trying to catch the sunlight. I don't care though. I've not had a cuddle like this in a long time and he means well. When he leaves go at last I feel a little better, and Henry asks me: 'Do you want me to stay?'

I flutter and stammer like a young girl. 'Oh, I'm all right, really . . .'

'I can sleep in the chair, there, if you have a rug to go over me. Obviously I'm not suggesting anything improper.'

A small shaft of disappointment goes through me as I go to the cupboard for spare pillows and covers. Of course we wouldn't be improper. Of course not.

But I'm glad Cleavis is going to stay with me. And stand watch over me through the night.

We take affable turns in my bathroom and he exclaims over its luxuriousness, its spotlessness. We tiptoe about with toothbrushes and towels and we're gentle with each other. I put on a soothing James Last record as we prepare to bed down for the night. And, at last, I lie under all my heaped blankets and I can hear him stirring across the other side of my attic room. And guess what? I love hearing him breathing there, and moving about, and settling down. I love having him with me as we say our good nights.

I ran to Cleavis for comfort, reassurance and safety back in 1946, as well.

As soon as I close my eyes I am back in my trance. I dreaded this, and knew it would be so. I burst out of my dreams of the past, shrieking and scared. But almost immediately I am back there. Backing away. Turning to run. Watching with appalled fascination as William Freer disposes of Edith's body and Alucard turns to me . . .

I run for my life. I pelt heavily down that narrow corridor, rucking the carpets, almost slipping. The guttering gas flames throw nightmarish shapes about me and I can hear Freer and Alucard yelling.

Alucard! He came after me. Haring down the length of that train. I was shrieking and disturbing all the other passengers. I wanted them to come out of their little rooms and see. The best way to put him off the chase and impede him, I thought, was to publicise him. And let everyone know he was here in their midst . . .

Alucard! A legend amongst monsters. Here on this train. The evil force behind this scheme, this adventure in which Henry and I found ourselves involved.

I whipped round as I moved from one carriage to the next – and saw that he had pulled down another window and I just caught a glimpse of his ankles disappearing into the patent black night. He slipped out like a shadow, like an eel shimmying swiftly into subaqueous realms. This disturbed me more than if he had just been running after me, somehow. He was out there, clinging to the thin metal skin of the train as we hurtled towards London. He could slip back in at any of the windows. He could find me and get me. I was a goner, I knew. After what I had seen . . .

Other passengers were coming out of compartments now, roused by my shrieks of alarm. They clustered and they besieged me. And I remember talking like one who had lost her wits.

And Henry was with me once more. He took charge of the situation immediately, throwing his arm about me and bundling me down the train's length, in the direction of the buffet car. Here it was warm and consoling and I could pretend I hadn't seen anything terrible. But I had. I knew I had, really, even as Henry poured me tea and wielded the sugar tongs (four, five, six sugar lumps for shock). He gazed at me earnestly and asked what had happened.

And all I could focus on was the rhythmic thumpety-thump of the rails on the tracks beneath us. Like the thumping of Edith's body being flung out and bouncing off the sides of the train and on to the swift, dark hardness outside. Thumpety-thump. Like my own second-hand heart, so jarred and alarmed I felt it would never go back to its normal pace. Thumpety-thump. Thumpety-thump. The bone china rattled on the table in front of us. The cutlery tinkled to that same rhythm. Henry was looking at me and he seemed scared, as though the look on my face told him I was going to start screaming once more. Thumpety-thump.

Alucard was standing behind him.

Of course, my own screams wake me again. And Henry jumps out of my armchair and dashes to my side.

'Oh, Henry, you've shaken me up proper, hypnotising me like that. I can't help remembering now, all the things I suppressed . . .'

He murmurs and pats and I realise he's saying something banal like, 'Better out than in, old girl.'

'Alucard walked into the dining car, easy as you like,' I said. 'He came in and stood behind you, as if nothing was amiss. Do you remember?'

Henry nods grimly. 'I do remember. But I think we should stop thinking about it all tonight—'

Thumpety-thump.

'What was that?' I gasp.

Thumpety-thumpety-thumpety thump.

The noise from my dream. A dreadful pulse. The

clanking of pistons. Of blood pumping out of severed arteries. How has this noise got outside my head? How is it here – so loud – in my attic?

Henry grips my arm. He's heard it too. How could he not? And he's scared as well.

Thumpety. Thumpety.

Tappety tap. Tappety tappety trip-trip-trap.

Then suddenly I know. I even relax a little, when I realise what the noises are. My usual late night visitation. My ordinary hauntings.

Tap tap tap tap. Out on the landing.

'Can you hear them?' I ask Henry.

'Of course!' he hisses. 'What is it? Do you have guests staying . . .?' But he knows I don't.

'This happens almost every night,' I say, sounding far more nonchalant about it than I feel. 'These noises come. They come in the room—'

And, as if on cue, the door squeaks and moans and the tapping noises approach us through the gloom. Warily, though, as if they are aware of the extra presence of Cleavis. Trip-trap-trap.

'Oh, my God,' Henry says thickly. 'How can you stand this? How can you?' He grips my hands. 'Can't we do something? Surely we can sort this out?'

'No,' I tell him fiercely. 'There's nothing to be done.'

'But surely—'

'No, Henry!' I am vehement, startling even myself.

Tap tap tap, all around the bed. Henry draws his feet up until he is sitting on my bed with me. The invisible intruders circle the four-poster as they always do. They swarm about me. They are even underneath me, with the dust balls and the old shoes. Henry Cleavis and I hold hands on top of the rumpled bed, clinging to my warmth and my calm as if we're on a life raft in an ocean of ghosts.

We sit like this for what seems like hours. The night starts to recede. The blackness of the open skylight comes a bit bluer. I can hear the birds starting up. The tap-tap-tapping grows less frequent, less pronounced, as if our torturers have grown bored with us. They are going away.

When they have been quiet for a while, Henry turns to look at me and I can now see his face in the bluish dawn. 'You really are haunted, aren't you?' he says.

'More than you'll ever know,' I tell him.

We wake up late, in the same room, all achy, stiff and guilty like teenagers. The phone is ringing. I don't think either of us meant to fall asleep, but we did, and both of us are startled and confused by the noise.

It's Robert. He's gabbling excitedly down the line at me. 'She's awake, Brenda! She's woken up!'

At first I don't know what he means. I think he's talking about his Aunty Jessie – and that the womanzee has been found and restored to miraculous life.

'I'm talking about Effie, Brenda! She's come out of the coma!'

'What?' I must sound so dopey.

'I went in to visit her really early this morning. I was sitting there, telling her all about recent events, and then her eyelids were fluttering and she was coming awake! It was amazing, Brenda. Next thing, she's surrounded by all these doctors and nurses. I came straight away to phone you . . .'

'This was just a few minutes ago, then?'

'Yes! She's awake, Brenda! She's going to be okay!'

I'm laughing now, with happiness and relief. Cleavis is standing by the armchair where he slept, clutching a blanket. He is bleary-eyed and confused. When I come off the phone I explain quickly to him, and hurry about, making preparations to go straight up to the hospital. Cleavis is left muttering pleasantries in my wake. I have put everything out of my mind now: my memories and my trance; the noises and revelations in the night. In the clear light of day – it's past ten o'clock! – none of that seems relevant now. I bustle Henry along, and make it plain that I want him to leave.

'Can we meet this evening, perhaps?' he asks me. 'I think we need to talk further.'

For a moment he sounds like a romantic suitor. Someone trying hard not to be shrugged off the morning after. Someone about to be sent away with a flea in his ear. I almost laugh. 'Of course,' I tell him, and we make plans for Cod Almighty this evening.

Next thing, though, I'm washed and changed and letting us out of my side door. And, sure enough, Leena and Raf are outside their shop, arranging wares. They give a wave and a nod, both plainly delighted to watch me leaving my house with a strange man. Of course he's my lover. And of course the news is going to be all round town by the time I get back. I give them a helpless little wave, and don't stop to tell them about Effie.

Henry wants to know whether he should come to the hospital with me. 'I don't think that's a good idea. She doesn't want one of the first people she sees to be the man who shot her.'

We're standing outside the Miramar hotel and Henry looks piqued. 'That was an accident! And it was only a graze!'

I frown at him. 'Anyway, I'll see you later.'

'You just look after yourself,' he tells me. 'And try to forget about that poison pen letter. And all the rest of it. Memories . . . and hauntings and such.'

I leave him and stump back to the main road out of

town, towards the hospital. He would go and have to remind me about my letter. Henry can be stupidly tactless at times. I just know Effie is going to be furious that I let him hypnotise me. Perhaps I'll not mention that to her. She doesn't hold with people messing about with other people's minds. 'The human mind is a very delicate thing,' I can hear her saying. 'Best not to tamper with it. Leave it well alone!' And, as I scurry along towards her, I hope that there'll be no permanent damage from the coma. I hope that she has come back to us whole: herself, again.

Robert meets me outside the main building, where he's having a sly fag. We hug each other hard and it's such a relief to be with him again. I couldn't have stood him being frosty with me for ever.

'She's resting now,' he tells me. 'She's fast asleep. But they reckon she's okay, Brenda. It's natural sleeping. She's out of danger!'

We go in to look at her. A nurse tries to explain everything to me, and I have to pretend to be Effie's next of kin in order to hear all the details. Still they go over my head, as I stand there, and survey the tiny body of my friend. Looking as if she's shrunk. It's like a little girl lying there. Her head's still huge, swollen under bandages. 'I'll bring her a nice turban in,' I say aloud. 'I'll buy her something stylish to go with her leaving-hospital outfit.' Of course, they still want to keep her in under observation for twenty-four hours. 'Did she say anything?' I ask the nurse.

'Just a few, nonsensical things, like things from dreams.' The nurse smiles ruefully. 'Nothing of any relevance.'

Then Robert and I are left sitting with the naturally-sleeping Effie for a few moments. I just about jump out of my skin when her eyes fly open and she fixes that cool, grey gaze on me. 'Did you bring that awful man with you?'

'Who?' I ask.

'Cleavis!' she hisses.

'No,' I tell her. 'He—'

But her eyes close again and she snores at me.

Robert walks with me back into town. 'I'd love to come for a cup of coffee with you, Brenda,' he says, 'but I really have got to get back to work. We've another big night in the beer garden tonight.'

'Another barbecue?'

'They're going to be every night now,' he tells me, looking a bit tired, now that I get a real look at him. 'Sheila is demanding that we do them every night. Now that the good weather is here, nobody wants to be shut up inside, it seems. The Yellow Peril was completely empty last night. They were all up in the beer garden, singing and drinking and dancing all night long.'

I think back to the previous night's inaugural barbecue. It was a curious do. I mean, it was enjoyable enough, but I didn't feel as much in the swing of it as everyone else. There was a tinge of hysteria in the good-natured crowd, I thought. As if everyone else had been drinking a good deal more than us. Something about that evening in the wickerwork garden had unnerved me, but I couldn't quite say what it was and, anyway, my mind had been on other things.

I wave Robert off as he turns to the Hotel Miramar. I hope he doesn't come across Henry. It's best if their paths don't cross just yet.

I head back home and start making a mental list of all the things I need to pick up from Effie's house to take in tomorrow. She'll go mad at me if I bring the wrong things.

And, perhaps, while I'm in there, I will check out her old typewriter in the office at the top of the house. I might as well. Just to check. See if it has a wonky s, like the one that tapped out my poison pen letter. I'll have a little look.

Just to prove it wasn't her.

Chapter Four
Dirty Deeds Down South

This is how it was. Now I know.

When Henry put me into that trance he had a good rummage through my memories. I am like a long disused and abandoned attic. He unlocked me. I'm chockablock with stories. I'm too full, in a sense. All you can do is open the door and see what comes tumbling out.

And now – the whole adventure in 1946 has come back to me very thoroughly. The whole lurid and ghastly saga.

Let me fill you in.

This night – the night before Effie returns from hospital – I'm supposed to be going out for a fish supper with Henry. I've smartened up and put on my lipstick. But I'm sitting at my kitchen table. And all these memories unwind.

*

The train rattles and shunts and screeches through the night.

I am sitting wedged into our little table in the buffet car and Cleavis is staring up at our enemy. I can feel Henry's leg jogging away under the tablecloth, so I know how scared he is. He acts pretty cool, though, as he faces off with Count Alucard.

The count stares down at us pityingly. Not a slicked-back hair is awry. His cloak hangs down in gorgeous satin folds of scarlet and black. He curls a feral lip at us just to show his jagged canines. And then the two of these fellers engage in the kind of banter always engaged in by mortal foes in to-dos like this.

'So . . . you thought you would follow me!'

'I'll follow you to the ends of the earth, accursed one! Give back what you have stolen!'

And I'm sitting there thinking: hang on! It was me who became aware that Edith was nicking chunks of Tyler manuscript. It was me who discovered she was going to run off with Freer. And I was the one who saw her being savagely murdered by this creature and it was me who was chased the length of this train by the Prince of the Undead. So why are the fellers doing all the talking?

'Why are you so keen to have Tyler's book?' I burst out.

They both turn, startled, to look at me. 'I mean, surely he's going to publish it eventually, and then you can just buy one, or borrow it from a library . . .'

Henry gives a hollow laugh. 'Somehow I don't think Alucard has a borrower's ticket.'

'But I still don't understand,' I say. 'Why go to all this palaver?'

'Why ask the sun why it shines? The moon why it waxes and wanes?' says Henry. 'He does things because they are wicked. That is his nature.'

Alucard frowns at Henry as though he's being particularly stupid. Then he turns the full force of his charm on to me: 'My dear, I'm afraid we haven't been properly introduced . . .?'

'Brenda,' I say, wondering whether I am wise to do so. His eyes smoulder like dying clinker and I ponder what it would be like to fall under his spell . . .

'Brenda what?' he says. He is staring right into me. He knows there is something strange about me.

'Just that,' I tell him firmly, and he sighs.

He continues: 'I would have thought it obvious that I am stealing Tyler's manuscript in order to prevent its being disseminated in the world.'

'Oh,' I say, nodding. 'I see.' Obvious, really.

'I am taking it to a friend who has a particular interest in it. And that's all there really is to this affair. Quite harmless, really.'

'Harmless!' I cry. 'You murdered Edith Tyler! I saw you!'

Alucard pulls his face, as if I am talking nonsense. 'She disembarked somewhere along the line, I know that much. But . . . murdered? I think not. Your imagination is somewhat overheated, Brenda. Possibly by all the lurid romances your type of girl reads belowstairs.'

'So . . .' Henry says. 'You are working for someone else. Alucard acting as another's servant! I never thought I would see the day!'

The vampire's face darkens as he scowls. Henry has hit a nerve. 'No slave, sir! Merely doing a favour!' His voice is dangerously low. 'And I come to warn you. To cease this pursuit immediately. The doings of Freer and myself are no concern of yours. If you dabble further, I shall have no hesitation in destroying both you and your charming companion here.' He leans in further and purrs at us. 'In fact, I will have every pleasure in bestowing upon you both full membership of the legion of the undead. Giving you a borrower's card, so to speak. It would be a particular pleasure to recruit a God-botherer like you, Cleavis.'

Henry splutters and heaves with fury at these words. I'm still inwardly quaking at Alucard's reference to his and Freer's 'doings', which seems an unfortunate way of referring to their plans. What's wrong with me? Why doesn't he scare me? I feel like laughing in the vamp's face. So I do. It bursts out of me, like some violent eructation.

'You stupid man,' I tell him. 'Do you think we'll give up as easily as that?'

Alucard narrows his beautiful, burning eyes at me. 'What?'

'We are both members of the Smudgelings,' I tell him, folding my arms. 'And we won't be scared off by the likes of you.'

Alucard won't attack me here. Not in the dining car, where others are eating and drinking sedately, as the train rushes busily through the night. He can't risk giving himself away here. Instead he turns brusquely to Cleavis: 'You should control your woman better. And since when did you allow female members of the servant class to join the Smudgelings?'

I get up to punch him, but he's gone – quick and slender as a shadow. Back to his carriage, and back to his craven lackey, Freer. Probably to gloat over their precious spoils.

When Henry Cleavis turns to me his face and voice are incredulous: 'Do you know who that was? Why were you provoking him like that? Do you know what he is capable of?'

I shrug lightly. 'He doesn't scare me. That's most of his

power, you know. People dying of fright just at the sight of him. But he's not that scary. I'm a bit disappointed, to tell you the truth.' I slurp up the last of my tea, which is cold now. I'm putting on a proper show of bravado for Henry. Inside I'm shaking like mad. I must really want to impress the professor, mustn't I? But I must admit, it was fun baiting Alucard. And what else should he expect, from the estranged daughter of Herr Doktor Frankenstein?

He's lucky I didn't smack him one, the old fop.

We start talking then, about how we're going to follow Freer and Alucard to their den – wherever it is – in London. Alucard could turn himself into a bat. He probably will. It's unusual for him, I suppose, to be taking public transport this far. But I suppose you can't carry much luggage, as a bat. I hadn't really thought of that before. So he needs his cringing myrmidons – the likes of Freer – to lug his stuff about for him, and it is the more earthbound Freer that we will follow.

As Cleavis talks about pursuing these ruthless monsters into the heart of the capital, my insides are quivering with excitement. Life's been quiet for too long in that old university town. I can't tell you how glad I am to be on the move, and in the thick of trouble once again.

This is what I'm like, back in those days. So keen! So brave!

Henry tells me there's less than half an hour till we hit the metropolis.

And, as we hurtle through the night, I stare out of the window at the flitting fields and hedges, the fragile rows of suburban houses. I feel so alienated from all of that, from everyday life.

It's as I'm sitting there that the voice calls out to me for the first time.

A soft voice, impossibly old. It's crying and begging. Imprisoned and tortured. Hopeless, helpless, and calling out to me across some huge distance.

'Did you hear that?' I ask Henry sharply.

He shakes his head. 'What?'

He hasn't heard it. That voice is calling out to me alone. As the train nears London, the voice grows stronger, though no less plaintive and scared. We are approaching its source, I realise.

'You must come to me, Brenda . . . Only you can free me . . . For it is foretold . . .'

Well, I think, as we hit the city's grimy outskirts. It's just one thing after another, isn't it?

In the press and confusion of Liverpool Street Henry and I become separated for a few moments. He is holding on to my hand. Laughable, really, in that his little hand is so much

223

smaller than mine. But at first he is fiercely holding on to me, as if protecting me, as we face the metropolitan crowds. I think we both feel out of our depth here, in the great smoky hollow darkness of the station concourse. We are bobbing about with our hearts in our mouths, while everyone around us is so heads-down, marching-onwards, set on their destinations. My sweaty hand slips out of Henry's grasp and I think we both panic a little.

Of course there is no sign of Alucard. He's the sort who's only seen when he wants to be. My hope is that we can latch on to Freer. But in all the mêlée we have lost him. He's a sneaky devil, Freer. I stop right there, in the middle of the crowd, and I could scream with frustration. This is hopeless. We don't stand a chance.

And then Henry is at my shoulder, with a fierce whisper in my ear. 'Look there!' And the game is on.

Foolish, arrogant Freer is coming out of a tobacconist's and pocketing his change, his purchases. We can see him clear as day, as he peers into the swarming masses, looking so shiftily about him. Then he turns on one slender heel and hurries for the exit. But we have got him in our sights and I lumber after Henry, who darts through the crowds after Freer.

The traffic is fierce. The pavements here are narrow and the buildings tall. The roads are teeming with overloaded buses spraying filthy slush everywhere. It's been a long time since I was in the capital – longer than I care to remember – but the heady, heart-pounding pressure of keeping up, keeping afloat, keeping your head above water is still with me. It's necessary to be determined and decisive, otherwise it's easy to panic in all this booming, terrible noise.

Henry's hand is back in mine and I'm holding on grimly.

We press on, for block after block, tumbling heedlessly across roads and through arcades and the canyons between huge buildings. As we go on, though, the streets become shabbier. The street lights are on, and they are a pale, dirty yellow. I can smell the Thames somewhere close. Freer is leading us somewhere filthy and grim, I just know it. He's leading us back to his mucky bolthole.

He's swinging his carpet bag almost jauntily in his hand.

When we get to a quieter street his pace slows somewhat. We pass the glowing windows of a rough-looking pub and we turn into a darker alleyway. Freer surprises me then by turning and catching us in the act of pursuit. He stops. We stop.

There's ten yards between us, but his mellifluous voice reaches us easily. He's used to speaking in the public lecture halls near here in Spitalfields. How beautifully modulated his voice is. You could almost believe every word he says. He smiles at us ingratiatingly. Henry and I stare at him, frozen.

'Is this really necessary?' Freer says. 'All of this subterfuge? This ridiculous gadding about?' There is something whining about his voice. There is a febrile cast to his eye. I realise I was right. Alucard killing Edith right before his eyes: it's driven Freer completely off his rocker. He gabbles on: 'Why don't I just give you the address of where I'm going and you could come along later on, rather than following me about like spies, hm? I mean, what do you hope to achieve?'

To my surprise Henry thrusts himself forward and covers the distance quite efficiently. Suddenly he's marched all the way up to Freer and he's bopped him one right on the nose. 'I used to box at school,' he tells me, quite cheerfully. 'Rather satisfying, really. Cuts through all this fellow's verbiage.' Then he hits him again, smartly, round the chops and Freer goes down easily. Henry sighs in a businesslike fashion and bends to pick up the carpet bag. He checks inside and there, presumably, is what we are chasing after. 'This is only about fifty pages of Reg's book,' he says gruffly, leaning over the groaning Freer. 'Where is the rest, hm?'

Freer is rolling about on the dirty cobbles, clutching his face. No action man, he. I'm a bit disappointed by that. I expected more of a barney.

'You don't know what you're doing,' Freer says harshly. 'You . . . shouldn't . . . you'll pay for this . . .'

'Yes, yes,' says Henry, passing me the scroll of fifty pages.

I stow them away inside my good winter coat. Henry grabs our twisting enemy by the scruff of his neck. 'I want you to lead us to your master. Alucard, or whoever it is you are both working for. I want you to take us there at once. And we are not leaving until all of Reg's work has been returned to our safe-keeping.'

Still Freer is writhing and moaning abjectly. 'You don't know what you're dabbling with! There are dark forces at work here. Things you can't possibly understand . . .'

'Hm,' says Henry. 'Possibly you're not listening to me.' He boxes Freer's ears, hard, in order to wake him out of his delirium. 'I feel like a guilty fool because of you, Freer. I petitioned my friends to let you join the Smudgelings, much against Tyler's advice. He said you were a shabby little satanist, in with a bad lot. And he was right, wasn't he? Now, I want to make amends. You're going to do precisely what I tell you to do.'

Now, as far as I'm concerned, this is all going rather well. I think Henry's getting on with things somewhat impressively. He's certainly surprised me with his strong-arm tactics. I never expected the venerable linguist to start slapping our foe about like that.

It's all going so well, in fact, that I have stupidly let my own guard drop. So entertained have I been by Henry's technique, I've stopped keeping an eye out. And that's when the gang of Chinese get us. Oh, I could kick myself. We've been grabbed by the tongs.

They come hurtling – a whole bunch of them, pigtailed, in satin pyjamas – screaming into the alley and overtaking us with arms and legs whirling about. Doing all their martial arts stuff. Of course we don't stand a chance, Henry and I. I do my best, swinging my deadly, heavy limbs about. I catch one or two of them and give them a hefty walloping. But they are so nimble! So small and agile! In seconds they've got Henry down on the slimy ground, and he's bellowing in protest.

I go very cold. We could be dead. They are ruthless, the likes of this lot. If they wanted they could have cut our throats already by now. The cobbles could be running with our frantic blood. But we have been spared. The gang's objective is obviously to rescue William Freer. He gives himself into their care and they carry him off swiftly and expertly and as I lie there, in the murky gloom, stinging with the nasty blows I've received, I'm irresistibly reminded of the spectacle of a colony of ants carrying off the recumbent form of a caterpillar. Back to their anthill, wherever that might be. Now they are gone. We have lost them.

I drag myself groaning over to Henry, who is livid and purple in the face.

'I still have the manuscript!' I tell him, grinning crazily. 'Our Asiatic friends didn't realise we had snatched it back.'

Henry sits up, looking mightily perplexed. 'Chinese involved. Vicious tongs. Very bad news, that.'

I nod at this and can only agree. In that moment I become aware of the mournful hooting and honking of boats on the Thames, somewhere near, beyond these dirty buildings. And I am aware of that great dense body of water and the seamy mists rising off it to obscure the night.

*

In a moment of madness Henry signs us in as Dr and Mrs Von Thal. So! I think. He's not averse to subterfuge. The lie comes so easily to his lips.

All we've come here for is to stop for the night and lick our wounds. Gather our resources and be ready to strike out in the hours before dawn. But we need to marshal our strength and plan our next moves. That is essential, we both agree. So . . . the next thing is, we're standing in the small but classy lobby of a discreet hotel not too far from the docks. The kind of place you wouldn't even suspect existed, unless you had someone like Henry with you. Someone who must have used it before.

I'm standing behind him thinking, we don't have any luggage. Oh, how must that look? And he bends to fill in our details, the gas lamp making his bald head shine. The hotelier seems not to give a jot. He produces keys for our room at the top of the building with a small, smart flourish and tells us breakfast is at seven. Henry turns to smile at me and I feel as if we are complicit in carrying out some dreadful misdemeanour. Dr and Mrs Von Thal, indeed. I wonder if I should fake an accent, just to make my alias complete? But instead I keep schtum as we navigate the twisting staircases.

I examine the room busily, trying not to look Cleavis in the eye. My aches and bruises are forgotten now as I turn back the covers on the large bed, and pull the cabbage rose curtains on the night. I'm blushing, I know I am.

Henry sits heavily in the tatty armchair in the corner and removes his shoes laboriously. He seems quite at home here, I realise. He's brought women here before, I think. Tarts. That's what he does. He lives the respectable life in Cambridge. The chaste, devout don in his bachelor's faded rooms. And then he comes here, to the wicked capital, and lives an occasional secret life in the underworld.

I sit on the very edge of the bed. What have I gone and got myself into? I'm in a room with this man. He's harmless-looking and he's kind. But what am I doing here? And how do I get myself into these things?

'I'm so sorry about all of this,' Henry Cleavis says at last. 'I am sorry to involve you in all this danger.'

He looks so concerned, bless him! I shrug heavily and the mattress jingle-jangles beneath me. 'I'm quite used to danger, Henry. My life so far has been a rather complicated one.'

'You're no ordinary housemaid, are you?'

I shake my head sadly. I watch him stand and take off his tweed jacket and waistcoat. He hangs them in the empty wardrobe. The empty wardrobes in places like this make me sad for some reason. Henry seems quite used to all of this, though. The bleakness of the place.

'I think we had better try to rest,' I say. 'Fix up our grazes and wounds, and then rest for a while.'

He comes to sit by me. He reaches over and pats my hand. 'You could have protested at any moment,' he says.

'About coming to London?'

'About coming to this room. Most girls would have been shocked at my suggestion. What we have done, using aliases to stay here, is quite shocking, you know.'

Girls! I laugh. I'm hardly a girl. 'I don't subscribe to the same ideas as most people,' I yawn, 'about what is shocking. This is just expedience, isn't it? We need to hide away and rest, and plot our next move.'

'You are a remarkable person, Brenda.' Now he's got a funny look in his eye. I have seen this sort of thing before. Perhaps I should nip it in the bud. 'No common housemaid, you.'

'That's very true,' I say.

And then he kisses me, very lightly, on the lips. It's such a hesitant, careful thing that it takes my breath away. I am used to fellers being quite gung-ho and so scared of rejection that they sort of flatten you against the wall when they first kiss you. They squash and prod you to prevent you from escaping. But Henry's kiss is an exploratory, fluttering thing: it comes with a question mark attached. He sits back and I blink, feeling his kiss scorching my lips. His gentleness has shocked me in a way that a swift, rapacious attack wouldn't have done. And the next thing – to my instant shame – is that I burst into loud, jagged tears.

Henry looks appalled. He leaps up. He flaps his arms. He doesn't know whether to embrace me and coddle me, or to run away to safety under the torrential onslaught of my tears. I'm bawling like the baby I never was. He sits and he reaches out tentatively to hold me and I fall helplessly on to him. I just about crush the life out of him, the poor devil.

'My dear . . . whatever is the matter?'

'Y-you're being so kind to m-me . . .' Oh, I sound pathetic. The whole hotel and all its seedy inhabitants, including the wry maître d' at the desk, will hear my shenanigans and think me crazy. I'm a lunatic whore that Henry's been unlucky enough to pick up and this thought makes me howl even harder. He pats and rubs my back and he even says 'There, there' until the violence of my breakdown subsides.

'I'm so embarrassed,' I tell him. The handkerchief he's given me is sopping.

'Don't be. You're a sensitive woman. I am mortified to have upset you like this. To have, um, insulted you. Your reputation. To have compromised you by bringing you here.'

And just then I want him to kiss me again. I'd like him to take me and hold me in his arms properly this time. I feel this sudden, giddy rush of excitement that I've never known in years and I realise that I want him to get me into this bed and have his wicked way with me. A new light must have come into my eyes because Henry is looking at me strangely. And, at once, he backs off.

'I will sleep in the chair,' he stammers. 'If you'll let me have one of the, um. Yes, blankets.'

I don't suppose all those tears and all that mucus are great aphrodisiacs.

Henry props himself in the faded armchair and I flop out, fully clothed, in the bed, which jangles horribly. So it's just as well, perhaps, that nothing has gone on between us. The lamps are turned down. We wait there in the semi-darkness for sleep to come. But with the street noise and the river noises comes the awareness that the whole of London is out there, with its dangers and its scheming enemies and all that life. It's quite hard for us to relax. And there's a tension in here, too, between us now. I want him to kiss me again, I realise. This time there would be no shock. I would feel no shame. I would relax into that surprising gentleness of his. I would have a suitable reply to that unspoken question.

So I drift off, into troubled dreams. Troubled, because I know that if I take this thing any further with Henry Cleavis, then there will be certain things I will have to explain to him. He will need to understand that I am not like any other woman he might have experience of. He would need to be warned.

And my dreams bring me face to face with my father. His long, handsome, lunatic face. Telling me that I am to remain loyal only to my husband. That the only reason I exist is to complement my husband, who was my father's first creation. I was invented so as to be the perfect partner for him. I am the perfect embodiment of that man's desires. My father knew my husband so well – inside out – that he could make that man's dreams into flesh. No one else will ever love you so well, I was told. No one else will ever love you at all.

But it never worked out, did it? I can see my husband in my mind again now. Handsome, too, in his own way. But he was never allowed anywhere near me. He never even held my hand before everything went to the bad.

See how easily these memories come out to disturb me? Memories over a hundred years old? That was a different world we were in. I have learned to live by myself on the earth since then. And I have proved my father wrong. I have known love outside our tight family unit. I have learned to love people – and they have loved me. I am sure they have.

I toss and turn on the rowdy mattress. I'm not even sure if I have slept, or whether I am turning these things over consciously as I lie in the semi-dark.

And then that voice comes to me again: the ancient, quavering, disembodied voice that I heard on the train tonight. It is stronger, reverberating inside my muddled skull. We are closer to its source and it is crying out for me: *'Brenda! Come to me! It is destined that we should meet!'*

Which is all very peculiar. And troubling. I can see I'm never going to get any proper rest tonight. I lie there and try to keep the memories, the nightmares and the mysterious voices at bay.

After a while I glance at the illuminated face of the clock and it's past three o'clock. So I must have slept. I sit up slowly and glance across at Henry, who looks so bundled up and uncomfortable on that chair. I should have insisted he slept in the bed with me. It's ridiculous, all these qualms and silly morals. He'll be one huge mass of aches and pains tomorrow. I should have taken the matter in hand. I should have dragged him into bed and told him what was what. I tut and shake my head at myself. Easy to be so confident and sure after the event.

I need a sip of water. There's only the water jug on the stand by the window. Just a mouthful. Just to wet my whistle. My dreams have left me parched. I get up, swaying, heavy-limbed, throbbing-headed. I lumber to the stand and take up a handful of freezing water. Actually, the whole room is much too cold. I'd protest about that, if I were Henry. A sharp, nasty frost has come over the city and I can see it hanging there, crystallised on the air. Glittering down there in the darkened streets. There is a film of cobwebby ice on the window pane and I reach out to chip at it, to scrape it with my nail.

Alucard is standing out there.

His face is level with my own as he hovers in the empty air. He grins at me and exposes those ludicrous canines and I lurch backwards and send the nightstand crashing to the bare boards. The jug and basin smash and I'm covered in frozen water. And I can still see Alucard there, standing easy as you like in the darkness, taunting me and laughing fit to burst.

Henry has come awake with a great yell and hurtles over to join me.

'Brenda! What—'

And he stops because Alucard has turned away in a swirl of frozen mist and I know Henry has caught a faint, chilling glimpse of his cloak and his dainty little feet as he streaks off into the night.

It's dawn and we're checking out of the discreet hotel. The sardonic-looking man is still behind the desk, and he looks me up and down. Does the man never sleep?

I feel rumpled and awkward. I feel as if there's a wall of silence between Henry and me and I don't know what to do about it. All we can do is focus on the task in hand.

Soon, we're sitting in a poky café he seems to know well. We're spooning sugar into huge mugs of thick tea and he's saying we should both order fried breakfasts, in order to put a lining on our stomachs, which is a disgusting phrase, but I know what he means. This morning it is bitterly cold. We walked a little way along the riverside and it really looked as if it was frozen over completely. The clothes I've come away in feel completely inadequate for the weather and, if I'm honest, I'm starting to regret this whole escapade. Danger and adventure I don't mind. Bitter cold, embarrassment and yesterday's clothes are another matter.

As we slurp our sweet, dark orange tea, Henry is turning through the pages of the chunk of Tyler manuscript we rescued last night. He squints at his friend's scratchy hieroglyphs and, to my surprise, invites me to scrutinise the pages too. 'What are we looking for?' I'm pleased that he's asked me: a lowly housemaid looking for clues in the text. He's the expert, surely?

'I'm not sure.' Henry sighs. 'But there has to be something here. Something of value. Something that makes this book Henry's been writing more than just a novel . . .'

I frown at the runic figures and only gradually do they become legible as English script. 'If Freer was going to such lengths to fetch these pages, in smuggled sheaves like this . . . and if they were worth having Edith Tyler murdered for . . .'

'Oh, good God,' says Henry, looking up at me. 'I'd managed to put that out of my mind. What are we going to tell Reg? Should we go back now and tell him?'

'No,' I say decisively. 'That's for the police. The poor man doesn't want us gallumphing in and telling him about all sorts of lurid stuff. We need to get on with things at this end. We have to find his book.'

Henry nods, looking stricken. 'I didn't know Edith well, but she seemed a decent sort. She was his nurse, you know. Years ago. When he started writing this thing . . . in Whitby . . .'

'Yes,' I say. 'I know all of that.'

'Freer was risking everything to get the book to

Alucard . . .' Henry shivers here. 'And Alucard tells us he is working, in turn, for another.' Henry waves to the waitress – a churlish-looking slattern who tuts at him and heads our way. 'We were attacked last night by Chinese men. That suggests only one thing to me.'

The waitress is poised above us with her grease-stained order book. 'Yes?'

'Two full English,' Henry tells her, smiling broadly at me. He makes the act of ordering breakfast seem like some sort of patriotic thing. The waitress tuts once more and slops away in her dirty mules.

I lower my voice so no one else will hear: 'What does our being attacked by Chinese men suggest?'

'That before long, one of our next ports of call should be Limehouse,' Henry says, and his smile fades gently away. 'And a whole lot of even more dangerous bother, if I know anything.'

A little later, when we're both chockablock with eggs and fatty bacon and my sides are aching and squashed with too much delicious bubble and squeak, we amble back to the riverside. It's still very early. The sky is streaky and pink and the seabirds are dive-bombing bravely and raucously. We talk a little about the previous night: about Alucard's nerve in hovering outside our window like that, trying to spook the pair of us. What we don't talk about is that chaste, burning little kiss we shared. The searing, frozen light of morning doesn't seem the right time to expose that moment to discussion. We both bury the memory for now and bustle along.

Henry has gone into lecturing mode. 'From what he has read to the Smudgelings over the years ... during our weekly meetings and so on ... From what I have, um, gathered during that time, Reg's book is a scientific fantasy of sorts. It has, for its setting, a vast number of other worlds. Each with their own complicated systems of flora and fauna, history, politics, natural laws. Reg has spent a long time working out all these devilishly complicated things ... They stagger me every time I, um, contemplate the scale of such an undertaking. He calls it *The True History of Planets*.'

I nod, watching the oily water and the traffic sliding over the bridges as we pass under and around them, one by one. 'I knew it was about different worlds,' I say. 'And what did Alucard say? He has been stealing it in order to prevent it from ever being finished and published? And sent out into the world? Why should he do that? To a made up novel about other planets?'

'There is other stuff in Reg's book,' Henry says, frowning. 'Stuff I was never all that comfortable with listening to, as a Christian. Darker things. Sacrilegious things. About wicked gods. Other planes of existence where these unholy

240

creatures dwell, and from which they are continually trying to escape . . . into our world . . .'

A shudder passes through me as Henry says this. I ignore my own shivers and decide to bait him instead. ' "As a Christian" indeed. Is your faith so shaky it can be rattled by a few spooky stories?'

'Sometimes, it is,' he says gloomily. 'Yes.'

I know what he means, though, from the few lurid bits of text that I've managed to take in, just flicking through Reginald Tyler's book. There's some rum stuff there, all right. I'm sure it would give me the willies too, if he was reading it out to me by the firelight on a winter's evening in that rumbling, professorial voice of his. I'd believe every word of it.

'Someone else takes it very seriously too,' Henry says. 'Whatever it is that Tyler is conjuring up with his words. It's dangerous stuff. Edith has died because of his book. That will hit Reg Tyler very hard.'

We walk in silence for a while.

Cleavis has the address on a tatty old card in his wallet. He's never been there before. He's never been invited. He's simply corresponded with Freer. Those exuberant, ideas-filled letters flying back and forth between the two of them make Cleavis feel foolish now. 'We gabbled together about the possibility of life on other planets. And all manner of things. Freer was always banging on about the other dimensions.'

'Oh, yes?' I say, loping alongside him.

'Planes of existence that are very close to us. We could penetrate the gauze between the worlds. Quite easily, if we tried. Freer said it was like the beaded curtain that shields the back room of a shop.'

I'm trying to follow his metaphor. I can hear excitement in Cleavis's tone. Freer has stirred his imagination. Cleavis is still under the thief's charlatan spell.

We trudge the early morning streets, looking for Freer's humble digs, and hawkers are setting up their barrows, and yelling out their wares. Street vendors are frying vast pans of spitting, dancing shrimps and serving them in paper cones. My eye gets caught by tailors' racks of petticoats and chemises, all frothing lace. I want more than anything for this to be an ordinary morning jaunt, and not an adventure at all. I want to be on the arm of my gallant beau, toddling happily along. Instead we are on the trail of monsters and madmen.

At last we find the right door. Freer's landlady is a withered, pickled-looking creature, instantly on the alert. Cleavis buys her off with crisp notes out of that wallet of his. The ghastly hag takes his bribe and ushers us into the dark hall and up the stairs. We follow her hallowe'en turnip head and her stooped, cadaverous body through the filth and the grime and the shadows.

Freer's room makes me sad, when we see it. He doesn't have much to show for his life. I can't help comparing this shabby mess with Tyler's grand residence, or the ramshackle, cosy bachelordom of the Cleavis brothers' rooms. There seems to be nothing in this room of Freer's that is worthy of a second glance.

The old landlady leaves us to it.

'Blood on the bed, look,' Cleavis hisses, stepping closer to the rank, twisted sheets and hairy blankets. There are large dark drops of blood on the thin carpet, too. I shiver as Cleavis dips his fingertips into one of the larger pools to see how fresh it might be. But my attention is snagged then by the desk and the papers scattered and crumpled across its surface and hastily shoved into unlocked drawers. Some instinct makes me dig deep through all of these papers. I glance at a few and can make neither head nor tail of Freer's scribbles. It's all gibberish to me. But I keep hoiking the papers out and, sure enough, I find one, two, three, four pages that are written in Reginald Tyler's distinctive hand. They have been hidden away at the very back of this drawer. Whoever has ransacked the room and spilled blood here has missed these particular Tyler originals.

Cleavis claps my back and grabs them off me. 'Oh, well done, Brenda! What a team! What a team!' He squints at Tyler's script in the squalid light. 'What's this about? Something something. His apotheosis. Blah. Something. Ancient of days. Something and . . . Goomba? Goomba? What's Goomba?'

At this single, apparently meaningless word, spoken thrice by the perplexed Henry Cleavis, I have what I can only describe as a sort of seizure.

It's a moment or two before Henry realises that I am standing there, frothing and lockjawed as if I've contracted rabies. I'm swaying on my heels and I'm about to keel over. And in my head I can hear the voice – ghostly, implacable – ringing hollowly through the millennia: *'Goomba waits! Come to me, Brenda! Come and help me! You can hear me, can't you? Goomba! Goomba!'*

Henry slaps me sharply across the chops. This jerks me out of the trance and shocks me so much that I punch him back. Pow. Right in the mush. When I come to my senses, there's my companion on the tangled, blood-spattered bed, ruefully rubbing his jaw.

'Sorry about that, Henry,' I tell him. 'But something was speaking to me. Inside my head. Trying to contact me. You broke the contact.'

'Hmm,' says Cleavis, looking at me with wariness and respect. I've got quite a hefty punch on me, I admit. I still feel woozy, though, after having that Goomba thing echoing in my noggin. Henry gets a portable stove going. He's brewing up tea in a silver-plated pot.

'I'm afraid he doesn't have proper English tea,' the professor sighs. 'Just this, um, spicy muck.' He holds up a purple and orange packet that catches my eye immediately. The aroma, as he brews up, is delicious, too: I can smell ginger, cardamom, garam masala, black pepper and lemon . . .

'Mm,' I clutch the mug to my face as if it's some special kind of remedy. 'Spicy tea. Where does it come from?'

Cleavis examines the packet. 'There's an address. In Limehouse. A tea shop. Hm.' Now he's tearing open the cardboard packaging, because he's found something scribbled hastily, in pencil, on one of the inner flaps. 'It says, "Goomba waits",' he tells me.

I nod. 'I thought it might,' I say, and slurp the deliciously heady brew.

It's a fair walk to get there, and we have to pass through some of the dingiest and most horrendously mucky back streets I have ever seen. And me, from the nineteenth century! But the East End takes the biscuit, really. Filthy place. And they're all looking at you, out of the corners of their eyes. They'd stab you in the back and ransack you, soon as look at you. Luckily, I'm like a giantess in these tiny streets, shuffling through the muck and detritus. The villainous poor round here are dwarfed by me. They skulk away, all sly and suspicious, and they leave us in peace.

'Terrible place.' Cleavis shudders.

'I've never liked down south much,' I tell him.

Then, at last, we find the tea shop we're looking for. Deep in the heart of Limehouse. There are colourful banners, flags and ethnic decorations almost everywhere you care to look, but there is still something dingy and depraved in the very air. It's not a very cheery place at all.

The shop's window display is of various types of tea and their multicoloured packets. 'This is the sort of place that could easily be used as a cover for something else,' Henry says. 'Opium and whatnot.'

He doesn't half enjoy coming across as the man of the world, does Henry. I think he's showing off for my benefit, so I flash him an encouraging smile as he opens the shop door and sets the little bell tinkling. In we go.

And I can hear the voice again: *'Goomba waits! Come to me, Brenda! Set Goomba free!'*

I get an instant headache. Like a weight of some kind, pressing down on my mind.

The shop's interior is dusky and there's a musky incense

burning, possibly to cover up other, inscrutable smells, and this ambience doesn't help my headache one bit.

Tiny little wrinkled Chinese feller, weighing out tea at the teak counter. Behind him are shelves of jars and tins. It all looks very proper so far. He welcomes us cautiously. Henry gives a smart little bow and offers our greetings. 'My lady friend is rather taken with your spicy tea. We'd like to purchase a quarter.'

'Spicy?' asks the man. 'You want special spicy tea?'

I'm not sure what Henry's game is. So, Freer bought his tea from here. What does that prove? He had a hankering for exotic spices, same as I have. Doesn't mean anything untoward is going on. There's a bead curtain over the doorway to the back room, though. Henry obviously thinks something far more interesting is going on back there. He knows more about these things than I do.

And Goomba. Freer – or someone – had written Goomba on that packet. What is Goomba? Is it Goomba's voice inside my head? Goomba wants to be free, doesn't he? Is he some kind of captive here?

'That's slightly over,' says the man, examining his scales.

'That's all right,' says Henry. 'Actually, I wonder if you could help us. We're looking for a friend of ours who was a customer here. A William Freer? Long, stringy feller, rather refined way of talking, all put on. Have you heard of him at all?'

'No, sir,' says the shop owner quickly.

I've had enough of letting Henry do all the talking. 'What about Goomba, eh? Does that name ring any bells, sunshine?'

This does the trick. The little man's eyes widen and he starts to gibber. 'Goomba! Goomba!' he cries, scattering bits of loose black tea all across the counter.

'Oh, really, Brenda.' Cleavis tuts. 'Not very subtle that, was it?'

I shrug. 'It got results.' Now the man is juddering and frothing, just as I did when Goomba's haunting voice was resounding in my head. Except this feller looks absolutely terrified. 'I'm liking this less and less,' I tell Henry. 'I'm not even sure I want to know who or what Goomba is.'

'These Eastern peoples.' Henry sighs. 'They are so damned excitable.' He reaches calmly across the counter and takes the little man by both shoulders, shaking him roughly. 'Now, look here, little chap. I wonder if—'

And then: CRACK. That's it. Someone has come up behind us and coshed first Henry, and then myself, right across the back of our heads.

With something hard.

We're out sparko.

Obviously we've been asking too many questions. It's often the way in situations like this. Shove your nose in too far; make one too many query; haplessly mention the name of the malign semi-deity at the root of the deadly trap – and you'll get right up the villainous nose of Mr Big. He'll have one of his lackeys come after you with a big stick. And WHAM: out you go.

You'll wake up in a dripping, nasty, pestilential cellar deep underground. One of those vile, cavernous spaces far, far beneath the slimy streets of Limehouse. Way underneath that old tea shop. Hidden away where no one could ever find you. You are lost to the world, grimy, sore, bruised and rueful. Henry and I regain our consciousness in a prison cell with only a little, feeble light coming through the slatted door.

'Sorry about this, Henry,' I tell him, reaching across to pat his arm. 'It's my fault, letting my mouth run off like that. I should have let you handle it.' We are lying on damp and dirty straw. I can feel his warm breath on my face and it still smells of his full English breakfast. It's weirdly reassuring, lying here with my Henry: my fellow adventurer.

'Never mind, old thing,' he says. 'You came straight to the point, and asked about Goomba. I have to admire your directness.'

'Now what?' I ask.

'We have to marshal our, um, strength. And set about getting out of this cell.' Slowly, Cleavis's features become apparent to me in the gloom. He looks so serious, bless him. 'And we have to find out whose underground base of operations this is. Who it is that Freer, and Alucard, have been working for.'

'Good plan,' I say. 'Shall I try to force the door?' Ouch. I sit up and find that I am aching more than I thought I was.

'Sssh,' Henry says. 'We're not alone in here.'

He's sensed something. Someone. Lying on a pallet of straw on the other side of the dank room. Now I can see them too, stirring and sitting up. Their frightened eyes catch faint sparks of light. Before I know it, Cleavis is on his feet. He darts across the cell and then he's boxing the poor feller's ears.

'Cleavis! Stop it! That's not helping anyone!'

The man is yelping and trying to pull himself away. And then, as I join them, I see who it is. Freer. Holding his head in his hands and moaning now.

'Perhaps you've got a point,' I tell Henry. 'I think I'll give him a slap, too.'

'Nooo!' cries Freer, eyeing my pan shovel hands.

'We are going to have a little talk, you and us,' Cleavis says in a very calm voice, kneeling down beside our fellow captive. 'We want to know all about what's going on. We want to know what it is you've been doing with Tyler's manuscript.'

At this, Freer bursts into loud, viscous sobs. 'I should never have done it! I was an idiot! Taken in by their promises, their compliments . . .'

'I don't doubt it,' says Cleavis. 'I imagine you lapped up every single drop of their noxious flattery. Such is your wont. You are a very shallow, very dangerous little man. But why, Freer? Why did they want Tyler's book so badly? Why have you let it fall into the hands of scum like Alucard? And these Chinese?'

Freer is wrestling with himself, twisting and sweating on the straw. He gasps and shudders, as if the truth is trying to force its way out of his body. He is sweating and heaving and I wonder what it is that's wrong with him. He's never been like this before. Poison? Opium? And then I realise. He's so pale. He's fading away to nothing. Alucard has been at him, hasn't he? He has sucked him almost dry. His own devoted servant, and that bloodsucker has drained him nearly blue.

At last Freer gets his thoughts together enough to tell us: 'Tyler's book is dangerous. Alucard . . . and our master . . . believe that Tyler has come too close to the real truth of the universe. In his writings . . . his researches . . . he is giving away the secrets of the diabolical creatures who . . . exist . . . in the beyond . . .'

'Rubbish,' Cleavis sneers. 'It's all out of his head. Tyler has told me that much himself. He dreams half of it up. When he's out on his bike, or half asleep. It's not real, you fools! How can it be real?'

'It is truer than Tyler himself knows,' Freer whispers.

'Cock,' says Cleavis, and laughs in Freer's blanched face.

Freer chokes in frustration and he coughs explosively. Blood appears at the corners of his mouth. I feel something warm and wet spatter my cheek. 'Henry,' I break in. 'Let's just listen to him, eh? You might find it ridiculous, but . . .'

Henry nods reluctantly, and Freer continues, shakily: 'When Tyler was wounded, at the end of the Great War. It was a head injury. He had a hole in his skull. Under that thin skin of his. His brain, though, was open to the elements. He was nursed back to health in a hospital near Whitby, on the north Yorkshire coast. They thought the fresh air would be bracing, healing, and so it was. They thought his skull would knit back together. But it didn't. It never did. It was open. His brain was open to . . . whispers, echoes, hauntings . . . suggestions . . .'

I'm nodding, I realise, as I listen to Freer. I know he is speaking the truth.

'Whitby,' says Freer, 'is a very odd place. So close to the

many openings. To the gateways and gauzes. To hell, and other lands. It's so near to them all. And Tyler – lying there, sensitive, that delicate mind of his so receptive. Well. He just drank it all up. He was laid open, there in Whitby, to the vibrations and the secrets of the cosmos.'

'My God,' Henry Cleavis says, after a pause. 'I always knew there was something a bit . . . off key about Reg Tyler. Are you saying that everything he writes really *is* true? That he really *is* writing down the secrets of the universe?'

'I think that's exactly what he's saying,' I say. 'And I think he means that certain people aren't too happy with Tyler because of that. They want to stop him.'

'Alucard,' Freer bursts out, spitting more of that ominous, dark blood. 'He betrayed me. He has slain me, I think. Unless I rise again. I don't know. But I have been a fool, Cleavis. I repent of it all now. And I am sorry. I have betrayed us all to Alucard . . . and his devilish master. His demon lord. I am so sorry. You will have to clean up my messes. You must stop them.' Freer is in some great discomfort now and I don't think he is going to last. He starts to thrash and gabble.

'Who is this demon lord?' Cleavis demands, still shaking him. 'And if it was such a big deal, why didn't they just have Tyler murdered? I know what the tongs are like. Couldn't they have just sent trained scorpions? Or vicious baboon assassins?'

'Sssh, Henry,' I tell him. 'He's fading. Listen to what he tells us.'

'I saved . . . I saved some pages . . .' Freer gasps. 'As insurance. I hid them in my desk, in my room . . . I don't think they will have found them. Even when they came for me . . . and took me . . . they weren't that thorough. I don't think they found those crucial, missing pages . . . the pages about . . . about . . .'

He can't get the word out. Or, perhaps, he daren't get the word out. I decide to help him, old Freer. I lean close and I gently whisper: 'Goomba? Is that the word you want?'

Freer goes rigid. The blood froths and bubbles out of his mouth. He shrieks: 'Goomba! Goomba! Goomba must be free! Help him! Help him be free!'

And then Freer jerks one last time. He sags and falls silent. We let go and take a step back. Cleavis brushes his hands as clean as he can get them. 'I do hope he doesn't rise again. We've got enough on our plates as it is.'

'What do you think Goomba is?' I ask, as Cleavis starts to pace gloomily around the room.

'I think the answers are in those pages that Freer stashed away.'

I pull them out of my bosom. 'A lot of it's gibberish, I

think.' I squint up, trying hard to read in this terrible light.

And that's when someone on the outside starts to clatter the locks and bolts holding us in. The heavy door squeals open and there's suddenly more light. Henry and I turn, blinking, to face our captors.

'Who are you?' Henry barks. 'What do you want with us?' I know he's trying to sound menacing, but there's a squeak in his voice. A tinge of fright. The Chinese who are advancing on us through the open doorway can hardly fail to hear it. Meanwhile I'm tucking away the precious pages from Tyler's book. Crackle, crinkle, down they go, back down my bosom. And God help any man who comes after them.

One of the men starts barking at us: 'You will come with us. Our master wishes to see you.'

They're about to manhandle us. They come towards us, ready to drag us out of the cell. But I'm in no mood now to be told what to do. My dander is up good and proper. Looks like it's time for another punch-up. CLATTER and CRUNCH go the heads of the two closest Chinese. SMASH and POW go their fragile skulls against the damp brick walls. There seem to be dozens of them, suddenly! Crowding out this tiny space! Where the devil are they coming from? Whirling like dervishes. They're kicking and lashing out, with all that fancy-dancing fighting they do. But Henry and I aren't having any of that. CRUNCH! SPLATTER! POW! go more of their inscrutable little heads.

And I'm out in the corridor. I'm out of the cell. 'Henry? Where are you?' SOCK! POW! ZOWEE! He's nowhere to be seen. But I can hear him call. He yells out lustily and I know he's doing okay for now. And I'm fighting a path through the hordes of—

GOOMBA!

The voice is back. It tolls inside my head like a colossal bell.

'COME TO GOOMBA, BRENDA!'

I am back in that epileptic stupor I went into before. Of all the times! Right here and now, in the midst of a punch-up! I try to gather my senses. I must do, or I'll be overcome in this place. I'll go under in this brawl and I'll be killed in the stampede. I'm foolish for letting my guard slip for even a second—

But I can't help it. The voice is crying out inside me. Somehow it obliterates all other considerations. I have to follow it. I must obey!

'Brenda! Brenda – where are you going?'

Cleavis has glimpsed me turning away. I'm shoving all the little assailants away from me. Their blows rain down on me, but I brush them aside. It is as if nothing can touch me.

And that's how I feel inside. Impervious. My whole being is subsumed to some other purpose.

'Brenda! What are you doing, woman?'

Still Cleavis battles on. He's flagging now. He's not as young as he was. Within seconds he will be beaten, and these little men will have their way with him. His is a lost cause. And I am walking away, leaden as a sleepwalker, and as determined. I am deaf to his entreaties and his puzzled cries. 'Brenda! What are you doing? Don't leave me! Please! BRENDA!'

But I have gone. I have stalked off down one of these dripping stone corridors. The Chinese have left me in peace. They don't like the determined cast to my eye. They know I will murder any who stand in my way. Off I go, guided by my inner voice, and Cleavis is left behind.

Left behind – for how long? How long before I see him again?

But right now I let the thought of Henry drop from my mind. I walk and walk, deeper into this vile labyrinth. I pass the locked doors of other cells, behind which moulder the remains of much older and forgotten prisoners. They do not concern me today. I stumble on, zombie-like. On and on into the greasy, guttering lamplight. Until I stand before another wooden door, locked and shackled with rusted chains. There's nothing special about this door. Nothing to make it stand out against all the others I have passed. But the voice inside my head tells me that this is the one. I have been led to it. I have a job to do here.

'Here Goomba waits! Open the door! At last!'

I raise both bloodied fists above my head. I can feel my strength flowing through me. I feel supernaturally charged. Impossibly strong. I have the barest of seconds to wonder what is happening to me. What has possessed me? And then I inflict the heaviest of all possible blows on this sealed door. The wood splinters easily at my touch. The bricks and mortar crumble. The rusty iron turns to powder. I step into the cell . . . expecting what?

The recumbent form of some demi-god? The mysterious deity who has called me to his side?

Is that what I expect to face?

Yes, it is. I expect him to be sleeping here, like an exiled Satan. Like a Prometheus, bound to a rock. I expect him to be beautiful, terrible. And grateful.

I step forward and what do I see?

Leaves. Whispering leaves and millions of them. Glossy and sepulchral vegetation. There's a sort of garden here, trapped underground. The dark cell is crammed with plant life and at first it's hard to take in what I'm seeing. How does something of such lustrous, immaculate green survive down here in the gloom?

The leaves are growing on thick spikes of bamboo and they rustle and rattle as I approach, as if a high wind was coursing through the room.

'Brenda! Goomba! Brenda! Goomba!'

The voice in my head has gone crazy. It will repeat only my name and its name in this raucous, triumphant shout. And I know now that the voice comes from this room, and its source is this plant itself.

The bamboo is singing to me!

I stand there, rapt with shock.

'Goomba! Brenda! GOOMBA!'

And I'm not at all sure what to do. I am spared from thinking about it any further by the advent of another noise. The sharp squeaking of the door through which I've just entered. A stealthy tread right on my heels.

In a panic I whip round, and there is Alucard, all suave and smug. His collar stands high around his gleaming white face and he gives me a flash of those seductive fangs.

Doesn't do much for me, I'm afraid. He thinks that everyone is easy meat. Not this girl.

'Beautiful, is it not?' Alucard purrs.

'Where's it from?' I ask him. 'How did it get here?'

'Goomba is from a very long way away,' Alucard says. 'Another world entirely. And my partner in this affair is very keen to prevent him escaping back to that world. He has need of him here.'

'GOOMBA! ESCAPE! HELP GOOMBA, BRENDA!'

I frown. I'm trying to block that ringing voice out of my mind, while I concentrate on what this dapper cadaver Alucard is telling me. 'Why does your partner want him? It's only a houseplant, surely . . .?'

Alucard smiles. 'Don't play the fool, Brenda. Even you must sense that this being possesses great power. My partner believes he can tap into that cosmic might. And bring about his own empire on earth.'

'I see,' I tell him. 'How dreary of him. And, um, who is your partner, eh? I don't believe you've told me. I'm surprised to see you working for some other party . . .?'

Alucard scowls. 'You'll find out soon enough.' He makes as if to lead me from this cell where Goomba is kept. The leaves set up a fierce rustling, and the bamboo spears rattle like sabres. And to be honest, I'm a bit miffed at the way Alucard is speaking to me: as if he's recaptured me. As if he's in charge.

So then I do something I've been hankering to do, ever since I first met him. I spring forward and punch him one, right up the hooter. POW. He wasn't expecting that. Undead or not, I can still make him smart. His aristocratic neb gives a satisfying crunch under my knuckles. Alucard howls and jumps back. He's still off his guard. I pursue, give him a shove and kick him in the balls. He turns into smoke. POOF.

'Not fair!' I bellow, pursuing him into the rank corridor as he disperses away from me. He hangs about like a noxious yellow gas. 'Show yourself! Manifest! I haven't finished yet!' I don't know where all this bravery of mine is coming from, but it's pumping through my veins and I love it.

Alucard is suddenly standing right behind me. He jumps as if to seize me by the throat. Ha! Swift elbow to the ribs, I think. Crrr-rack. He yelps. He's useless! He's not used to dames who'll put up a fight. Now I've got hold of his cloak and I'm whipping it about and twisting it into a rope. Boot him up the arse as he goes spinning past. What a fop! What a softy! I never knew he'd be so—

And here come the Chinese, dashing down the stairs. It seems like scores of them, coming to help Alucard. They're on me! Jumping up and piling on. I'm weighted down by them. I brush them off and lash out, but there're just too many. They're laughing evilly, enjoying this. I think they're going to kill me.

'No!' Alucard cries, still panting with exertion. 'Don't destroy her. Not yet.'

I'm on the slimy floor, bleeding all over the place. I've had it now. I'm looking up into all these savage faces and they're all mad keen to finish me off. In my head, the

Goomba voice has receded and it echoes plaintively. '*Free Goomba, Brenda!*' But it is a hollow voice now. It knows that I am defeated.

Alucard bends to sneer in my face. 'You monstrous bitch,' he curses. And he gathers me in his arms and sweeps me up into the murky air.

We are flying through the tunnels. The fetid breeze streams past and I feel helpless now, held in the vampire's arms. I am weightless and lifeless and now I hardly care where he takes me, and how he disposes of me. As we fly he suckles at my neck and perhaps, as the blood pumps out into his gasping throat, he is filling me up with poison, bile and despair. It really feels like that, as we spiral into bigger and bigger subterranean chambers, deeper and deeper under the capital.

I feel I am utterly lost and all there is left for me is to be disposed of. A sack of body parts. Ill-fitting, ill-used. A creature that should never have been alive in the first place, dumped underground and left to rot at last.

'My partner in this venture,' Alucard whispers. 'Here he is. It is too late for you, my dear. You will never have the pleasure of his company now.'

He pops me on to a shelf of rock and – he's had so much blood out of me now – I simply lie there limply, like an old dishrag. I am aware that we are in a vast stone chamber, lit weirdly in yellow and green. There's a terrible reek of incense and drugs.

Below, there is an opulent throne room. Ancient antiques sit hugger-mugger with banks of futuristic equipment. This is the secret base of Alucard's partner. We are here in the heart of his wicked machinations.

I long to be down there. I want to be confronting our enemy, too, alongside Henry. I want to be in on that final act.

But Alucard is draining what feels like the last few drops of my stagnating blood. I can't move. I am turned to sand, or stone. I'm lying desiccated here, helpless. Then off pops my attacker, sated at last.

He forgets about me in a flash, and he soars down to be greeted by the savage-looking coot on the throne downstairs.

'Alucard,' comes a voice I have never heard before.

The vamp lands gracefully beside him, lips still slobbery with my gore. 'I am here.' He inclines his head respectfully at his partner.

A bald man in a satin nightie. Trailing moustache and eyes that blaze with a lethal understanding of how this savage universe really works. Alucard's current partner in crime.

Mu-Mu Manchu.

And Mu-Mu looks furious. 'Our secrets are escaping from us, Alucard. Goomba's messages are seeping out into the world. He is asking for help. For release. Claiming that we are keeping him captive here.'

'Well, we are,' says Alucard.

'But he is attracting the likes of this creature,' snaps Mu-Mu.

And, down there, kneeling before the might of these men-monsters, is Henry Cleavis. He's in tatters and chains and he looks hopeless with his head bowed. He raises it slowly to glare back at Mu-Mu and Alucard. 'Not just me,' Cleavis spits. 'Others. I don't know what it is exactly that you two are up to, but believe me, it will be stopped. If not by me and . . . my friend, then others will come.'

Alucard sneers. 'You don't even know what it is we are doing. And what friend? Brenda? That gallumphing beast woman?' He chuckles, pressing his ghastly face close to poor Henry's. 'She is dead. I've sucked her myself. Drained her to the last drop.'

Henry stiffens. 'I-I don't believe you!'

'She was quite delicious.' Alucard grins. 'Something of a vintage.'

Cleavis howls. 'Nooo! Brenda! I don't believe you! Where is her body? She can't be dead! She's escaped . . . She's eluded you . . . She's . . .' And his voice breaks into gruff sobs.

I want to call out to him. Henry! Henry, I'm here. Stranded on this ledge. Almost too weak to move. I can't budge. I can barely breathe just now.

'Enough of this!' Mu-Mu cries in his harsh, grating voice. 'Alucard, you bore me with your incessant appetite and vanity. We need focus on our main task. We need to gain access to Goomba's secrets. Now that we have nearly all of the book . . .'

'Shall I return to the university and take Tyler himself?' Alucard asks.

'Oh, yes,' Mu-Mu murmurs. 'And perhaps, to help us, we could enlist the services of our professor here . . .'

Mu-Mu and Alucard round on Henry Cleavis.

But Cleavis sits cowed no more! He leaps up, on to his feet. He shrugs off the ropes he has managed to untie. In a heartbeat he has a short, ornamental knife in his hand. It slashes and flashes on the murky air as he rounds on his captors . . .

Yes! Henry! Do them in!

Get them, Henry!

Now the chamber is whirling about me. I have to pull myself together to do something to help Henry. And yet I can't move. I can't budge an inch to get myself off this ledge of rock. I am scraped and torn and I hang in tatters. Alucard has sapped me of all energy and volition. I might as well be dead. I am no use to anyone.

The savage cries and clashes of the fight below are the last things I am aware of.

The darkness reaches up to gather me at last. Oblivion, hopelessness. They catch up with me and claim me as their own. It is as if I give in to this despair quite gladly, and the scene below vanishes from my sight. It fades away as though someone blew out the candles.

And what happens next?

Time must pass. I lie there and lie there and then . . .

I come back to life.

I come bursting out of that useless, hopeless despair like a bat out of hell. I'm not finished yet. I have changed my mind. I am not ready to die just yet.

I turn and I plunge towards the light. I come bursting back to the surface of myself and I struggle to open my eyes again. And—

And.

And I am too late.

I return to consciousness and it is all over.

This secret base is cold and dark now.

Everyone has gone.

I do not know what has become of Henry. Perhaps he is

dead. At the last he will have thought I abandoned him. I could howl with rage and frustration at this as I sit up and stare down at the empty chamber below.

And what about Goomba? His words no longer ring out inside my head. Is he destroyed, too? I can't hear his interior voice. It no longer calls to me.

All of these swarming, ebbing, fading thoughts are pushed aside as I get up on my feet. One thought alone starts to dominate my mind. My sense of self-preservation has taken over. That selfish instinct is so deeply ingrained in me that it is no surprise to me that, when my consciousness returns, I find that I am already running away. How much later is it? How strong am I? Can I survive long enough to get out of this place?

I turn and I pelt headlong down the tunnel at my back, and into the sewers. The stench is indescribable. My senses swirl and I could easily lie down and die right here. But something drives me on. Life drives me on. My greedy desire for life and more life. Greed for this hideously prolonged life of mine.

So my arms and legs move like pistons, even though the air rasps bloodily, searingly, in my lungs. Rats scatter at my pounding steps. I can see light, though.

I can see—

*

So . . . the story has it I lay like one dead at the open mouth of the sewer.

They found me on the banks of the Thames, coddled in filth. Like a golem made of clay I lay there, with the precious spark of life just about extinguished. I had thrust myself out into the light and the relatively fresh air and I collapsed. Fish-belly white and bled almost to death.

I was found by the poorest of the poor. They were digging in the black muck of the mudflats for treasure. Kids. Urchins who lived in the warehouses, safe from the prying eyes of the law. It was they who saved me. They dragged my hideous carcass home. Thinking, maybe, they would sell me to the circus, or a freak show. I was certainly a curio. But they nursed me and fed me and they grew attached to me, this wretched gang.

I was their very own monster-woman; a full-grown baby from the infernal depths, and they wouldn't have parted with me for the world.

I must have been with them for months. I don't quite remember. My wits had gone. My memory had gone, almost completely. I had no idea where I had been fleeing from. Or whom. If someone had told me I had fled from Alucard, Mu-Mu Manchu and an alien creature made from bamboo, I'd have laughed in their faces.

Instead, I and my rescuers believed that I was a woman

from the bowels of the earth. I was a monster forged in hell and spat out by the devil, into London. Those kids loved me for that. I was their talisman and their mascot. Their very own she-beast.

And if Henry Cleavis had died down there, I never knew. I didn't even know who he was any more, so I could hardly feel guilty or concerned, could I?

I never even thought about that dear, befuddled face of his again until . . . until . . .

Until now.

These past few weeks. When I saw him again, across the dance floor at the Yellow Peril. And he brought my memory back. My memory came back bit by bit. It's a slow process. I've been pulling myself together so carefully, so gradually.

And it's only now that I've remembered the whole story.

That is how it was.

Now I know.

The whole adventure in 1946 has come back very thoroughly to me. The whole lurid and ghastly saga.

This night – the night before Effie returns from hospital – I'm supposed to be going out for a fish supper with Henry. I've smartened up and put on my lipstick. But I'm sitting at my kitchen table. And all these memories unwind. Everything from being on the train and looking up at Alucard as he baits Henry. Pursuing Freer through the East End. And winding up underground and being attacked and sucked dry and running for my life and being saved by children. All of it comes back. And how I failed Henry. How I thought he would be dead.

Henry! He's alive! He saved himself!

And my heart leaps up. Even at this old news. News that's sixty years old.

My Henry lives!

When I come to my senses, I see by the kitchen clock that I am very late. There's all this banging at the door downstairs. I dash down and thrust open the door.

In an instant he can see by my face that I've had some sort of horrible epiphany. I grasp him to my bosom. 'You're alive! You're alive! You didn't die! They didn't kill you!'

Henry is very confused by this at first. But he listens. He tries to soothe me. And gradually he realises what it is I have remembered, and what has put me in this state. He tries to tell me what I need to know. His voice is muffled in my chest.

'I was quite used to violent muffle mumble scenes like muffle mumble that one. And, of course, I had a mumble muffle muffle about my muffle mumble person, so I whipped it out muffle mumble muffle Mu-Mu in the head. Good enough to muffle mumble facilitate muffle escape.

It was mumble mumble who I thought muffle dead, Brenda!'

I don't manage to take in all the details. Something about making his escape from that deadly underground pleasure palace of Mu-Mu's. Henry had some kind of ornamental or ceremonial dagger secreted about his person. And he attacked Mu-Mu and caused some unholy fracas to break out. Hurrah! It was the kind of frantic to-do that Cleavis loved to be involved in. He gabbles away some more of the details — boasting, I do believe, about his fighting prowess — but I'm too busy hugging him and swinging him about in my tiny hallway. He's like a rag doll in my arms. I'm gabbling like mad. I'm trying to explain to him about Alucard attacking me, the coward. Setting the Chinese on to me. Sucking my blood. Leaving me for dead. I want Henry to know that I never abandoned him. That I would never have done anything of the sort.

I stand Henry back on his own feet and he looks up at me. He doesn't say much. He hardly says anything.

Suddenly I know there is understanding between us. It's a very gentle, sweet feeling that rushes through me then. I feel very peaceful. It's astonishing. This is what it feels like, to understand one another. It's a very quiet thing.

He reaches up to hug me. He pats my broad back and I cry. I am only just absorbing the shock of our adventures, some sixty years on. All that horror is starting to hit me, full force. I sob and ruin my make-up and Henry pats me.

I think what a good man he is.

Chapter Five
Stitched Up

I'm like a burglar, messing about with someone's desk and their private affairs. Even worse: it's Effie's desk, and Effie's private affairs.

Here goes. I roll the sheet into the ancient typewriter. Clatter, squawk, squawk, the roller goes.

My breath catches in my throat. I hold it there, not daring to exhale, inhale, or anything at all. I'm trying not to knock into anything or to make any kind of noise, even though there's no one else in this whole tall building.

What am I even doing here? What am I hoping to prove?

What I would really like would be for my suspicions to be wrong. I'd like to prove the very opposite of what I think is going to be the truth.

Quickly, I tap out a long lines of s's.
SSSSSsssssSSSSSsssssSSSS.

And it looks like one long hiss of disappointment. Or suppressed shock. SSSSSSSSsssss. I step back from the clattery machine and I start to breathe again, raggedly, and my heart thumps like crazy.

Oh, surely not. Surely she hasn't. Surely she couldn't have. But there's the proof. The wonky s. Same paper, same typeface as my letter. Same as the others, too, I'm willing to bet. I'm staring at the evidence with my own eyes, and I'm still trying to convince myself otherwise.

Effie is the holder of all the secrets. The taunter of the shamed recipients. She's the one who's stirred up all the bother. She's caused mayhem and tears and even murder. And she had the nerve to shove herself forward as investigator.

Effie is the author of those vile poison pen letters.

And she is my friend!

I know what Effie's like. She can have a cruel tongue on her at times. She can be snitty and peevish and she's been known to start fights. She's hardly ever tactful at all, and people are used to her being rather cutting. But that's just Effie. That's how she's apparently always been.

If pushed, I would say she's a misanthrope. Borderline depressive, perhaps. Certainly a snob. But can I really picture her, hunched over her desk in the lamplight, at the top of her dilapidated house? Crowing with ribald merriment as she taps out these letters brimming with hatred and bile? Can I imagine her deliberately causing all this upset, all across Whitby?

The very idea makes me shiver.

So what do I do? Do I confront her? I know I have to. I have to know the truth now. But how can I turn on her, and start accusing her, when she's fresh out of her hospital bed?

Bide your time, Brenda, I tell myself. Gird your loins and grit your teeth.

So here we are.

Effie is coming home and she's wearing a turban of turquoise silk I bought her in town. I bought it before I tried out her typewriter and confirmed my darkest suspicions. I'm not sure I would bother now but, as it was, I went into the shop that I call the Posh Ladies' shop. We've sometimes had a snoop round there together, in the hushed, sepulchral, luxurious gloom. We've marvelled at the garments and their prices. What a snooty bunch they've got in there, serving on. When we go in, Effie puts on a voice so lah-di-dah it could leave a scratch on glass. I just blush. I don't feel I belong in there and I scurry out without buying anything. This time, though, I popped in and chose Effie a turban, as promised, to cover up the dressings and to protect her still-sore head.

And so I am there when she comes out of hospital. All the while I keep my thoughts to myself. These furious and mutinous thoughts beat at my brows like an oncoming migraine. Effie and her terrible missives!

Robert and I wheel her carefully out of the main entrance in a chair, towards the taxi. With her rhinestone-encrusted sunglasses and her glamorous headgear, she's like a film star at Cannes, squinting at the curious world outside.

I must be compassionate, I keep thinking. My poor friend has been through a ghastly ordeal. She has been in a coma. She has been hovering in the netherworld between life and death.

Robert is very good. He is expert at manhandling elderly ladies into the backs of cabs. He keeps up a stream of friendly chatter as we get my friend comfortably installed.

Once we're all sitting side by side on the plush upholstery, Effie turns to me and says: 'You're very quiet, Brenda.' Robert is getting into the front, and giving the driver Effie's address. 'Aren't you glad to see me?' Her thin, pale face is set at a quizzical angle. I can't see her eyes under those black glasses. Inside I am cringing. I stammer my reply and I give myself away immediately. Effie can see that there is something wrong.

'Of course I'm glad you're out and you're better again,' I say, sounding nervously insincere, even to my own ears.

Effie squinches up her mouth and starts bragging. 'It was touch and go, the doctors said. Apparently they are all amazed by me. I am some sort of medical miracle. Fancy that! Me!'

We fall quiet. An awkward quiet, I think. The taxi shunts through the town traffic, all the winding way down the hill to the harbour. Effie takes huge lungfuls of sea air, as if she has been away for months. Then she is tense and keeps glancing at me. I know she wants us to be alone. She wants to quiz me.

And I want to quiz her, too, don't I?

As we get into the thick of town and we can hear the gulls screeching over the harbour mouth, we pull close to our little row of houses. And now I lean across and tell Effie what it is I have decided to do. I tell her in a voice that will brook no dissent: 'You are *not* seeing to yourself. You will need some help about the place. For a few days, at least. I'm going to help. I'm moving into your place for a couple of nights.'

Effie glares at me for a moment, and then relents. She shrugs. 'Whatever you like, Brenda,' she says. Then she adds, more quietly, 'I'm very grateful.'

I'm taking over a bundle of bedding and all the things I'll need for a few nights away from my home. I'm starting to wish I'd never offered to stay now. And I really hope my allergies don't flare up while I'm there. Effie's place can be dusty and – I have to say – quite grimy. It's strange to me, how someone so proper and fussy can live the way she does.

What a dreary house it is! Crammed with all the leftover tat from her witchy forebears. It's quite a struggle, with all my pillows and continental quilt, to get through the rooms to the upper floor. En route I knock over a couple of what I'm sure Effie will claim were very dear knick-knacks.

She watches me as I make up a bed for myself in the small room next to hers. She's gone quiet, now that we are alone. Shy, almost.

As I'm stretching out sheets and acting so breezy, I'm wondering what it's going to be like, sharing each other's company like this. I'm feeling awkward around her, and not just because my man friend shot her in the head.

I finish up and resist the temptation to have a good go round with the Hoover and the furniture polish. I settle us both in her meagre kitchen and brew us up a pot of tea.

'At least,' Effie says thoughtfully, stirring her cup, 'while you're staying here, you won't be bothered by your . . . nocturnal visitors.'

I just boggle at this. I hadn't even thought of that. And, while the truth of what she's saying sinks in, I'm also stung by the suggestion. That I'm here out of self-interest. How dare she!

'The thought hadn't crossed my mind,' I say stiffly. 'Like I say, I'm here to help you manage.' Then I distract us both, telling her I thought I'd make my famous lamb stew for dinner, with lots of fresh rosemary and thyme and peppery dumplings. Effie nods her bright blue turban dazedly, as if she's not at all bothered.

'Sounds very nice,' she says. 'Are your hauntings still as bad?'

'I suppose so,' I say.

'You should get them looked into. Like I did last year. Get an exorcist, or a cable TV show or something. Professionals.'

'No thanks,' I tell her, with a tight smile, and gollop down the last of my spicy tea, which makes my eyes smart.

'And what about your other haunting? Your other visitor, eh? Are you seeing much of him?'

Of course she means Henry. But I don't want a row with her. I certainly don't want her to make me choose sides. And I could imagine Effie doing just that. 'It's either him or me, Brenda. You can't have us both in your life. You should choose either your dearest friend, or the horrible old man who shot her.' It would be impossible.

'Speaking of Henry,' I suddenly start. 'He met Mu-Mu! We both did, in a manner of speaking. Ages ago. 1946. My memory has started to come back.'

'Who?' says Effie tetchily.

'Mu-Mu! Sheila's husband. We were both in the clutches of Mu-Mu in Limehouse!'

'Oh yes?' Effie smiles sweetly and sceptically.

'But it's true. I remember most of it now. We were trapped down there and there was all sorts going on. It all came back when Henry stirred up my memories, and put me in a trance . . .'

Effie sits up in alarm. 'What? He did what?'

'He hypnotised me, to unearth my—'

'You fool, Brenda! How could you trust him? How could you let him tamper with your mind?'

'I'm sure there was nothing untoward—' But now I'm stammering and sounding foolish and I'm floundering helplessly beneath Effie's withering gaze.

'He is a man on some kind of mission, is Cleavis,' Effie says. 'He'll stop at nothing – hypnotism, brainwashing, murder – in order to get what he wants.'

'Surely not . . .'

Effie snorts and tosses her head. Suddenly she looks very dignified and beautiful. And I am beneath contempt. I sigh.

'All that hogwash about Mu-Mu,' she snaps. 'Can't you see, Brenda? It's probably all made up, by him. It's all my eye and Peggy Martin!'

I'm not sure who Peggy Martin is. Then I realise it's some weird, idiomatic phrase of Effie's. I hate her now. I get this pent-up force of irksomeness rearing up in me and I have to have a go back at her. 'It was all real, Effie. Real as you and me sitting here talking. We had the most glorious adventure in Limehouse in the forties. And I'll tell you something else for nothing, missus. Your fancy man was there. Kristoff Alucard. And it wasn't very pretty. You wouldn't be half so keen on him if you'd seen the things he was up to. He was depraved and wicked. He attacked me! He drained me dry!'

Effie stiffens in her chair. Now she looks furious. 'Brenda,' she warns.

'He abandoned me and, now I think on, it was down to him that Henry and I were separated for all those years! Your precious feller ruined my life, in effect! And here he was last year, flaunting and sashaying about, cracking on that he had mended his ways. Being all nice to me. All sweet-talking to you. And he must have known that my memory was gone. That I couldn't remember the blood-curdling things he had done to me . . .'

Well. I must have gone rather shrill and hysterical. Effie feels she has to lean across and slap my face. She's got very dainty hands but by jingo it stings. I shut up.

'You asked for that, Brenda. Bad-mouthing Kristoff. He repented of his past sins. You've no right to drag them up now. Not when he's not here to answer you.'

'Ha!' I bark. 'He's in hell! That's where he is! You make it sound like he's gone on a cruise to the Maldives or something! He's in hell, Effie, and I hope they're making him pay down there.'

Effie grinds her teeth. 'I think, some day, we'll all have to make a visit there, won't we? And we'll all have to pay, eh, Brenda?'

Stand-off. We're glaring at each other across her mucky kitchen table. There's a deadly pause. Then the invalided Effie sags back in her chair.

'Oh, dear. It's made me feel faint, all this gnashing of teeth. I'm going for a nap. The doctors told me not to upset myself. And you've got me all worked up, Brenda.'

Instantly I'm shamefaced. Fancy us, fighting over men. It's ridiculous. 'I'm sorry, Effie,' I mumble.

'Never mind, my dear,' she says weakly, and then I have to help her to her room. She weighs nothing in my hefty arms. I install her in her bed and promise to wake her for dinner. Then I dash out of the place to buy the makings of my stew.

My dinner is a huge success. Even if I say so myself. And I have to say so myself, because Effie won't. She doesn't pass comment on anything. Not even what a relief it is, eating proper food again. My gorgeous lamb and dumplings, all herby and melt-in-your-mouth. Here's this old dame, she's been on a saline drip for days on end. She's been wasting away, turning stringy and thin, and that can't have been much fun. Can't she summon up a bit more enthusiasm for all my delicious, steaming, molten veg, dolloped with piquant mint jelly?

But no. Face like a slapped bum all the way through. We finish up with jam roly-poly and custard – all hand-done. Not a smile cracks her mush. We sip Madeira out of little crystal glasses I found in one of her many armoires. Still she keeps quiet and she's studying me, I feel, across the lavish dinner service.

'All right, lady,' she says at last. 'Out with it.'

I'm flabbergasted. I'm siding up as she says it, and I have to set the dishes down in astonishment. 'What?'

'Something's on your mind. Under all your helpfulness, your concern and your care and attention, there's something preying on you, Brenda. Something to do with me. You're furious with me, aren't you?'

'Um,' I say, not very edifyingly, and suddenly I want to scurry into the kitchen.

'Spit it out. I'm not putting up with this . . . this . . . sulking for a moment longer.'

'Sulking!' I cry. 'It's you who's sulking, you miserable old stick!'

'I've a good right to sulk!' she shouts right back. 'I've been shot!'

'Don't go on about it!' I bellow at her, much louder than I mean to. 'Did *I* shoot you? Was I the one?'

'We're getting off the point,' Effie snaps. 'What's up? Why have you got the hump with me?' Her eyes are black, like little nuggets of Whitby jet. Smouldering at me.

I take a deep breath. I just have to tell her. That's all. Okay. I'll tell her. I'll ask her straight out. 'It was you, wasn't it, Effie? All along. It was you sending out those terrible letters to everyone.'

I watch her keenly for her reaction.

And now it is Effie's turn to look flabbergasted.

It takes a good portion of the evening to talk it through. Effie can't believe that I have accused her.

'I thought we were friends!' she keeps crying out, through her sobs. Each time she says it, I feel lashed with shame. 'I thought you were my friend!'

We move from room to room, round the upstairs of Effie's house, as she gets up and staggers about, throwing her hands up in the air, and I follow. I try to reason with her; I try to console her. 'I thought you were my friend!'

'But Effie . . .' I try to say. 'All the evidence . . .'

'Evidence, pah!' she cries, rounding on me. 'Evidence can be made to say anything!'

I'm not so sure about that. I'm bursting to tell her about

the typewriter and the dodgy 's', but she isn't having any of it. She is seething with anguish and can't listen properly at all.

'I am your friend, Effie. You have to believe me.'

'Some friend! Accusing me! Laying all this . . . horror at my door!'

'I didn't want to believe it,' I say. 'At first I couldn't believe it. But the evidence . . .'

'Stop going on about the evidence!' she yells. 'I don't care about that!' She comes right up close to me and thrusts her beaky nose in my face. 'I want to know whether you really believe, deep down in your bones, that I really could be responsible for sending out those horrible letters to people? That I could have done such a thing?'

'No! Yes! I don't know!' I throw up my hands.

'Hmm.' Effie bridles. 'I can see that we have got what they call "issues".' She looks me up and down. 'Who do you think you are, eh, lady? Moving here, next door to me. Getting me involved in the most lurid and hair-raising capers ever dreamed up. Getting me to risk life, limb and sanity on a practically daily basis . . . and then you have the gall! The gall to call me your friend! And the sheer brass neck to then accuse me and pillory me for something I just haven't done!'

I go quiet. Effie has stopped shouting now. She's sagged into her favourite chair and she's sobbing.

'I don't care what the evidence suggests, Brenda. I simply didn't write those notes. I would never, ever do such a thing. And I wish that you had had more faith in me.'

I hang my head. Poor Effie! Her lying there in a coma, and I've already been judge and jury and gone and hanged her. No wonder she's cross.

'What's the answer, then?' I ask her. 'What's been going on?'

'We shall have to think,' she says, rapping a knuckle against her perfect, porcelain teeth. 'There is something cunning here. Something strange.' The knottiness of the problem is distracting her from her temper, and I'm glad. 'Fetch the note you say you received,' she tells me suddenly. 'I want to examine it for myself.'

By now it is dark out. As I descend the many levels of Effie's narrow house I can see that the sea mist has crept up from the harbour and there's a terrible nip in the air as I step outside. How late is it? I've lost all track of time while I've been ensconsed with the volatile Effie. No matter. I hurry on my way, back to mine, to fetch the letter.

I've tucked it away in the safe in my bedroom. I'm not sure why I've hidden it so securely. Weird, really. I open up the small safe and take out the single sheet of paper. While I'm there I stare at my other treasure for a few moments. Just a few trinkets, a couple of mementos. I turn them over and savour them for a few moments. Not a lot to show for a life as long as mine, but there are some fine things tucked away here in my safe. Waiting for a rainy day.

I've just slammed and locked the safe door in my dark bedroom when I hear the noises. The night-time noises. Surely they've started early? Scritch and scratch and thud thud thud. It's been a few nights since I've heard them this clear. And, if I'm not mistaken, there is a new determination and clarity of purpose in their ghostly hullaballoo this evening. Thud, thud, thud. Creaking treads on the attic steps. Whump and thump. Pitter. Patter.

I am frozen, of course. Unlike my usual night-time hauntings, these have come while I am dressed and up and about. In a way, I have no excuse for not going to see what it is making all these extraneous noises. I can't just lie back and pull the bedclothes over my head, attempting to block it all out. I can't just lie rigid in terror and wait for it all to go away. This evening the onus is on me to be brave. To go and see what it actually is plaguing my night-time hours. To get to the bottom of this other mystery in my life.

I swallow all my bravado down. I crush my poison pen letter into my bosom. I try to quell my heaving heart and I dash, full pelt, through the darkened rooms of my flat. I don't even give myself time to think. Whump. Tinkle. Tap tap tap. And I fling open the door on to the landing.

Nothing. There's nothing there. And the house is silent once more.

I stand suspended at the top of my stairs, breathing raggedly. I could howl with frustration, I really could. This is torment and torture! Who can be doing this to me? I don't deserve this! I am trembling with frustration, fatigue and fright. I'm itching to put a stop to all this. But my enemy, my tormentor, is too swift and clever for me. I'm left like this, wrung out and panting.

The attic ladder is down. The attic hatchway is open. I never left them like that. Somebody has left them like this in their haste. Concrete proof. They've left proof behind, Brenda. They have come from – or gone up to – your attic.

My attic? But what's up there? Old rubbish! Necessary supplies. Loads of old gubbins that no one, surely, could want. No one in their right mind.

I don't want to go up there. I won't go up there. I'll leave it till daytime to go up to my attic and check it out. I'm not doing it now. Why should I? It'll all be the same in the morning. Why give myself the willies all over again? What am I, some weird kind of masochist? No, leave it for now, Brenda. Block it all out of your mind. Get back to Effie's with your poison pen letter. Get back to the job in hand. What was that again? Ah yes. False accusations and losing the friendship of the witch next door.

And so my own home is no longer my safest haven. This thought could make me cry, as I dash out of the B&B and lock it up behind me. That place has been my sanctuary. And now I can't wait to get out of it.

But: best hide all traces of my upset. I don't want it to be complicating matters with Effie. In the lamplit street I hastily rub away my tears and hope that they've not done too much damage to my make-up. They probably have, though. I bet I look a sight. But I straighten myself up and head back to Effie's. It's late, and there's so much to talk about. And I haven't cleared up after dinner yet. There's washing-up and recriminations still to come.

Effie has had time, now, to think about what she wants to say to me. When I get back she accepts the letter I have brought, and sits me down.

'You don't know what it's been like here, Brenda. You really don't know what my life has been like. You've come here and, to you, this town is your perfect home. On the surface of it, everything seems wonderful. Everything is fine. And why shouldn't it be? This place is idyllic, in a frosty, foggy, windswept, spooky kind of way. So you are content. Your life settles so nicely about you, into gentle busyness and consoling routine. You are needed and wanted here. You make friends. You have days out. You even attempt to solve a mystery or two. How pleased you are with yourself, for managing to feel at home at last, after all these years. Clever Brenda.

'But – think on. Some of us aren't as clever, or as lucky. Some of us aren't as happy here. Do you think I'm pleased with my life, Brenda? And with what I've managed to achieve here? I've never wandered the whole wide world, as you claim to have done. I've not lived through two bloody, eventful centuries, right in the thick of it, as you have been. I've never seen tumult and turmoil as you have done. What have I seen?

'Bugger all, that's what.

'I have seen the sun set and rise again over Whitby's ragged rocks and crumbling roofs. I've seen the sea mist creep in and creep out again. I've seen the insides of this decrepit place. This wretched home of mine and all its accumulated junk. I've seen the haughty expressions on the portraits of all my dead aunts. I've seen them watching me, every day of my life. And this has been the full extent of my life, Brenda. Scraping a living in this place. Not much excitement. Just struggling along.

'Now, you must realise that your coming here was quite a big deal for me. I made a friend. I never had many friends before. Not to speak of. I had been warned by my many aunts not to trust people on the outside. But I knew at once that we would get on, Brenda.

'You may think of me as a cold old fish, but I welcomed your friendship. I tried to meet you halfway. I tried to trust you. And you repaid that trust. When you told me all your secrets. About your past and everything. I was so touched by that. I mean, I was appalled and amazed, of course. But I was touched, too. That you felt you could open up to me like that. I blushed with the sheer pleasure of it. Somebody's secrets. Freely told to me. Entrusted to me.

'And you were there all through that funny business, when I foolishly thought I had fallen in love. When that damned gigolo Alucard swept in and turned my head. Throughout all that, you were there for me. I felt I could depend on you for anything.

'I thought you understood, Brenda. Understood what it meant to me, to be trusted. How I would never take the idea of that lightly.

'You see, I come from a long line of witches and wicked crones. Everyone here knows that's been my family's business. We have been tortured, celebrated, consulted, tolerated, spurned and burned. We have been cast out, brought back, demonised and exorcised. Forgotten about, chased out, coaxed back, dug up and installed as local treasures. What we *never* were – none of us – was *trusted*. But you trusted me, Brenda. You gallumphing, addle-brained, monstrous idiot. You loved me enough to trust me.

And tonight you have gone and chucked that back in my face.

'And that's all I have got to say on the matter.'

We sit looking at each other for a moment. All the way through Effie's speech I've sat there silent, not daring to move a muscle. I never reacted to anything. I never tried to break in or anything. All those words came spilling out of her. One continuous rush of words. Like they were dammed up inside her. Like this was the real letter that she might have written to me. I look away from her.

She glances down at the poison pen letter I have received and pushed into her hands. She spares it a quick glance. '*I didn't write this, Brenda. Of course I didn't.*'

This is an unfamiliar bed. So I toss and I turn. I try the pillows round this way and that. My back aches if I lie this particular way. My head feels wrong if I try it like that. All my bones are cricking and cracking like a walk through wintry woods. It's a narrow bed. A clapped-out bed in a room no bigger than a cupboard, and obviously unoccupied since the death of one of Effie's maiden aunts. There's a little light spilling under the paper blind, and that only serves to illuminate the horrid engravings framed on the walls. I can't make head or tail of the subject matter and, frankly, I don't want to. I wish I was home next door, in my own luxurious attic. I am here out of compassion and a sense of duty. And guilt, of course. Great big steaming dumplings of guilt, served up with gravy and mint jelly.

Poor Effie. I wish I had never doubted her.

This house of hers smells of vinegar and dust. As if everything has been pickled and inexpertly preserved. It's not much of a life she's had.

At this point I try lying on my front. This is a novel position and not one that's at all comfortable, or conducive to sleep. I give a great moan and turn over to face the cold, clammy wall. And that's when the noises start up.

Tappity-tap. Trip-trap.

No. It can't be.

Tap tap tap.

Never in a month of Sundays!

Trip-tappity. Trip trap trap.

Those are *my* ghosts. Those are the noises that *my* visitors make.

Thud thud crash thud.

They can't be here. They simply can't. I refuse to believe in them. I pull the duvet up to my chin, hoping to block them out. My pulse and heartbeat are racing, raging and banging in my ears, so I can't hear anything for a while anyway. But then:

Thumpety thump. Scritch. Scratch.

They have come to the wrong house. How can that be? Thud thud thud.

I hope they don't wake Effie. She needs natural, deep, replenishing sleep. What good will it do her recovery if she keeps being woken all the time? I hope she's not disturbed by this. All this palaver. This crashing about on the bare boards of the landing . . . this toe-curling screeching of doors. I hope she's not sitting up, bolt upright in bed, as I am now.

Trap trap trap.

I wonder . . . Could these be different ghosts? Could they be the spirits that already haunt this house? Effie's forebears, parading up and down the upper rooms. Could it be them? If it were, I could gladly sleep again, sound in my bed. I know that those ghosts are only here to protect the place and that Effie is quite used to them. I know they do not mean her any harm.

Tappity tap tap.

But, no. These aren't her dead relatives. These are the miniature footfalls and the tiny thuds, clatters and bangs of the presences I am used to by now. They have followed me here. They have pursued me to another house and they have come here to taunt me and torment me. I am meant to be helping Effie, I think. And here I am, bringing unholy shades into her home. I am responsible for this.

More upset for Effie! And I will simply have to do something.

Tappity tap.

I have no choice. I sit up again and throw back the bedclothes.

Trembling all over, I get out of the narrow bed.

I am absolutely terrified. Chilled to the marrow. I feel I am about to face something that I have deliberately hidden from and avoided for months on end. Each night I have tried to ignore these visitors. I have blocked my senses to their eerie hullaballoo.

Now I ease myself across the confines of the room and glide to the bedroom door. It is time for me to confront the source of that endless, infernal noise. So I thrust open the door.

The noises are worse. They're getting louder, more insistent. I totter up the hallway, slipping a little on the mouldering silk rugs. Why didn't I put something on my feet?

'Brenda?' It's Effie. She is outside her own bedroom door. Whispering hoarsely at me and clinging to the shadows. My heart goes out to her immediately. She has obviously sprung straight out of her bed. Scared as hell. She hasn't put her turban on. Her dressings have fallen loose. Her wispy old lady's hair stands up fluffily in the moonlight.

'It's me,' I say, going to her. 'It's okay.'

'Those sounds,' she says, and pokes her head out of the shadows, to look up the next staircase: the one that leads to the very top of her house. It is from up there that the noises are coming. As if in response, they redouble their clattering racket. TAP-TAP-TAPPITY-TAP.

'I don't know,' I tell her. 'I think . . . I think they have followed me. They are the same as the ones I hear . . . at home.'

She nods, taking this news in calmly. 'Usually I sleep so well,' she tells me. She shrugs her thin shoulders. She's only wearing her thin cotton nightie. I want to tell her to get back to bed. That I will look into this by myself. But somehow I know she wouldn't go. And, really, I am glad she is there. She looks at me. 'I was lying awake and thinking tonight. Even before the noises started up. I was fretting.'

'What about?'

'About whether we would still be friends.'

'What?'

'After our row and everything.'

'Oh, Effie.' Without even thinking about it, I grab her in a vast hug. You'd expect her to complain and wriggle free like a cat, but she doesn't. 'Of course we'll still be friends. And it wasn't a row. I was just being silly. And insensitive.'

CRASH! Thud-thud. Scritch-scratch.

Effie pats my arm. 'I appreciate that. Shall we go and investigate now?'

I nod. Investigating is . . . Well. It might not be what we do best, exactly. But it's what we're both happiest doing. And it's with a perverse and brave delight that we broach that top flight of stairs. With the noises of my ghosts ringing in our ears. We manage to advance up the staircase side by side, neither one of us having to take the lead.

On the top landing there are a number of doors. It is obvious which one the spirits are haunting. 'The office.' Effie nods at the furthest door.

Tap – tap – tap – tap.

The door is already slightly open. We tiptoe over and I give it a gentle push.

Screech. I know that her office is an L-shaped room. As we peer round the door frame we can't see the whole thing yet. We can't see the desk. Someone or something could be hiding right behind the door, ready to jump out and get us.

But what we can see, straight away, is that the window is open. On the sloping ceiling, right under the roof, the large window has been wedged open, and the raggy old curtains are billowing inwards. The temperature is lethally cold. It's the kind of sudden drop that makes you want to turn tail and run like hell. Something unearthly has got into the house.

Scritch scratch. Tap tap tap.

They are still here. Moving around in this room. Either they don't know that we have cornered them, or they don't care. Brave souls. Strong and hardy spirits. They don't give a toss that they have been rumbled.

Scritch. Tap. Tappity-tap.

Squawk squawk. Squawk. Ting! Ting!

Effie seizes my arm. Then I realise. Someone's typing. Someone's tapping away on Effie's old typewriter. The carriage squawks again. Tap tap tap. Ting!

We've got them red-handed. That's what the pressure of Effie's grip on my arm means. We've got them! We've caught them! Don't you realise? The culprit! At the typewriter! We've got them now!

And before I can think twice about it, I slam my hand on to the ancient light switch.

One single bulb comes on, over the desk. We round the corner and its brightness is startling. The cobwebs and grime and accumulated clutter leap out at us with hideous clarity. But we stagger into the light to face our enemy and . . .

There's the desk. There's the heap of white paper spread out on the blotter. There's the rusted old typewriter.

And there's the culprit.

Effie gags at the sight. I'm no less alarmed, but I am silent in shock. We stand there swaying, watching, mesmerised.

It's two hands. That's all it is. Two disembodied hands hovering in mid-air. They pause with fingertips at the keys of the typewriter, as if considering their next words carefully. They give the impression of knowing they have been seen. They flex their fingers and I am horrified to catch a glimpse of the ragged, bloody stumps of the wrists, with tendons hanging out like old knitting wool.

Effie starts to wail. I nudge her hard.

The hands fly up and yank the page out of the typewriter's carriage. They dive for freedom and land heavily on the dusty floorboards. Scatter! Tappity-tap tap THUD THUD THUD. And there are other things moving about. I jump heavily to one side as a foot comes blindly nosing across the floor, following the nimble hands like a faithful guard dog. Now I let out a shriek, and two moth-like ears come fluttering down from the light bulb, where they have been transfixed for a few moments. The dirty light shows up the blood vessels inside their waxy skin and looks almost pretty. I shriek again and fall backwards.

We are blocking the exit – the open window – for these disembodied parts.

Before we know it there's a great crash as another window gets kicked in. There is a whole naked leg there, doing the kicking. A dancer's leg, high-kicking its violent way to freedom. It's performing a macabre cancan: clearing the shards that hang in the frame. And then all the bits and pieces – hands and ears and feet and who knows what else – go jumping out into the night. How many storeys up are we? But these body parts are heedless. Off they go. Into the dark.

And, in seconds, Effie and I are left alone. It is as if we have disturbed a roost of starlings, and they have fled with noisy alacrity.

Effie and I pick ourselves up and we're mute with shock. At last she moves to her desk and turns over some of the typed sheets. 'More letters,' she whispers. 'Drafts of more hideous, threatening, poisonous letters. To you, and me, and Sheila, and . . .' She crumples them up and sobs. 'What were they, Brenda?' she cries. 'What on earth have we disturbed here?'

'Ah,' I say. 'Um.'

She turns and there is a shrewd look in her eye. 'You know, don't you, Brenda? You know what those hideous . . . remains were, don't you?'

'Um,' I say, in a not particularly helpful fashion. I move over to the smashed window. In my mind's eye I've still got the image of that long, pale, dancing leg kicking in the smutty pane. And all the smaller body parts jumping through the frame after it.

I peer through the broken window, feeling the full force of the night breezes on my face. My whole head feels slack and putty-like. And I can see them – those horrible body parts – dexterously finding their way down the walls. They clamber down drainpipes. They hop from sill to sill. They rustle through the long grasses of the gardens at the back. The ears flitter-flutter and superintend the escape. The long leg slinks along like a snake. And they are making their way home, up the walls of the dark house next door. They clamber and toil up its walls, from handhold to foothold, to the attic sanctuary of their own house. My house. That's where they belong.

My heart feels so heavy in my chest. I feel sick with dread and . . . a weird kind of loving pride.

'What were they, Brenda?' Effie asks, in a determined tone.

I can't lie to her. I turn to her in the silence, as the bare bulb swings above our heads. I tell her: 'They are my spare parts.' I give a small cough of embarrassment.

She sits heavily on her swivel chair. Under the stark light her features are hawk-like and her fluffy hair seems almost transparent. 'Your what?'

I take a deep breath. 'They come from my attic. They are under lock and key usually. I don't know how they have . . . come to life like this. I don't know how they've got out.'

Effie's eyes are wide. You can see all the white around her irises. 'You have spare body parts in your attic?' she asks, very slowly.

'Of course,' I say. 'When my father abandoned me in his castle . . . I was left alone, half dead, half finished. I had to look after myself, didn't I? I took whatever I could from his laboratory. I filled two big cases with what I could find. Things that I knew would come in handy.'

'Hands? Legs?' she gasps.

'Of course. Things wear out, when you live as long as I do. Some thick twine, that's all I need. I've become quite adept at, erm, putting myself back together again.'

'Oh, my goodness,' Effie says. 'I think I'm going to throw up.'

I hasten over to rub her back, but she pulls away from me. All I can think is that it's just as well she didn't see any of the other spares. The internals. They would have made an even less palatable sight, hopping about on the rooftops in the night – the hearts and lungs and kidneys and so on.

'But they've got a life of their own . . .' Effie says.

I frown. 'Yes, that's quite disturbing. Before, they used to twitch and jump about a bit. Give the odd spasm. But this is new. All this . . . escaping and breaking and entering. And writing letters to people!' In a sudden, hysterical moment I feel like laughing. I was being haunted by my own spare

302

parts! That was all! These weeks of night terrors and sweats and wanting to scream. Now I know what it was! Just my own hands and feet and bits and pieces. Nothing that could really do me any harm.

'So then . . . it was you, really, wasn't it, writing the letters . . .?' Effie looks at me uncertainly.

'No!' I cry. 'Of course not! I never knew anything about it!'

'But . . .'

'They just got out. They escaped and they . . . ran amok. They caused mischief. They tapped into my unconscious dreams and desires and they . . .' A terrible shudder goes through me. I feel nauseous at the thought of those hands and other parts going about in the night, blindly and unconsciously acting out my hidden desires. Tap-tap-tapping into my baser instincts. It is a truly horrible thought, and one that dries the words up in my throat.

'Lock them up,' Effie says. 'Get stronger locks on your attic. You have to make sure they don't get out again.'

'I will,' I say.

'Another mystery solved,' Effie says, almost sarcastically. 'Now we know, at least, who it was, plaguing the town with those letters.'

We are both shivering in the harbour winds that are rushing through the attic. I close one window, and find some old cardboard to cover the smashed one.

All the while, as I work, and Effie sits there trembling, I am still thinking about my spare parts. So is Effie. She laughs bitterly. 'Your body parts,' she says, 'are revolting. Do you get it? Do you get it, Brenda?' She laughs louder, ripping up the last of the incriminating letters.

I don't think it's all that funny. She wouldn't be laughing so much if it was her whose spares were coming to life and acting up.

But Effie doesn't have spares. No one else in the world has spares the way I have. Of course they don't.

Effie says, 'I think we can say this investigation is closed now, Brenda. What do you think?' I get a wry look from Effie then. 'But I reckon we ought to keep quiet about the outcome, eh? We don't want all of this . . . getting out, do we?'

I can only agree with her.

Chapter Six
The Wickerwork Man

Saturday morning, I run into Robert at the butcher's, where he seems to be buying unholy quantities of meat. He is also full of questions about Effie, and Henry, and everything that's been going on. He's ahead of me in the queue, and I raise an eyebrow as he reels off his order for five dozen pork chops and a gross of sausages.

'It's barbecues every night,' Robert explains.

'Ah,' I say. Which reminds me. 'We'll see you this evening, I reckon. If you're not run off your feet. We're coming to the barbecue tonight. Effie is very keen.'

'That's good.' He smiles. 'I'm glad she's wanting to get out and about a bit more.' Then a shadow seems to flit across his face. 'I will warn you, though. These evenings in

Sheila's beer garden . . . they can get a bit rowdy.' Now he seems almost furtive, as if realising he is speaking out of turn.

'I think Effie is about ready for a little excitement,' I tell him. 'After hospital, and being cooped up and all. Only yesterday she was saying to me, she can't wait to be back in the swing of things. To see a bit of life again.'

'Hmm,' says Robert vaguely. 'She might see more than she bargains for, up at the Hotel Miramar.'

Now we are holding up the queue, as the butcher bags up the chops and sausages and whatnot. He's looking for a box big enough for Robert to carry it all in. The people behind us mutter impatiently and I touch Robert's arm, and lean in closer. I see that I'm touching the black armband he's wearing in memory of his Aunty Jessie, so I move my hand a little. 'What is it? What's up? Sheila's not started holding parties for swingers again, has she?'

'No, no, nothing like that.' He frowns. 'But there's something I can't quite put my finger on. There's an atmosphere. A presence, almost. I don't know. Perhaps I'm being ridiculous.'

'Perhaps,' I say. 'But we're best off trusting our instincts, I think.'

'Even Mrs Claus felt it.'

'I'm sorry?'

'She came to Sheila's barbecue one night. Brought some of the elves. She sat in the bamboo garden on her motorised scooter and what do you think she told me on her way out?'

He's looking at me earnestly. I shake my head, urging him on.

'She said she had felt something decadent . . . something wicked in the very air of the place. Mrs Claus had wanted to be away from there, and back home at her Christmas Hotel . . . because the Miramar's beer garden, she said, was steeped in . . . *evil.*' He boggles his eyes at me. 'Even Mrs Claus – wicked as she is – felt something untoward.'

She's got no right to talk, I think. 'Oh, she probably just doesn't like the competition.' I laugh.

'It's more than that,' Robert says.

I nod seriously. 'Well. We'll see. We'll be there tonight, Effie and me.'

'Good,' he says, and sounds genuinely reassured. Then he goes staggering out of the shop, bearing his vast freight of meat.

The two of us are all dolled up in our finery. Effie, in particular, has gone to a lot of effort. She's in an antique velvet frock she has brought out of deep storage. It's a striking outfit, but now she's fretting about the barbecue being smoky and stinking up our glad rags. She's still in her glamorous turban from the Posh Ladies' shop and its colour tones in nicely with the rest of her ensemble.

As we toil up the hill to the Miramar, she's full of beans. 'I want to make the most of being out of a coma. I've wasted too much time in my life. I've been a recluse. Hiding away in that house of mine, under all that dusty tat. Doing the bidding of ghosts from the past. I've been like some dotty old spinster.'

She's setting a brisk pace up the hill, and I have to hasten to catch up.

She goes on: 'No wonder I was so easily buttered up by that elegant charlatan, Alucard, last year. I'd seen nothing of life! I was easy prey! Well, not any more. I'm going to be more cynical and worldly-wise. And I'm going to get more in the thick of things!'

A shiver has gone through me at the very mention of Alucard's name. I haven't tried to tell Effie any more about my recovered memories of 1946. I don't think she would be all that receptive to them. I don't want to keep banging on about the way Alucard attacked me. It seems too much like rubbing it in.

When we get to the Miramar we see that it's all been decked out in bunting and fairy lights, as if there's some big festival on. Already there is music pumping out from some elaborate speaker system. The Rolling Stones, I believe. That stirs a particular memory for me, as we scoot around the hedges of the side garden. Something about Princess Margaret in the sixties and the Stones, but it's not very clear, and not at all pertinent to the matter in hand. We pass by a few of the Miramar revellers and they are grinning at us in welcome, holding their paper plates and plastic tumblers of beer.

We find our way into the beer garden, just as dusk descends across the town. Most of the wickerwork tables are already taken, but we find that a small one in the corner has been reserved especially for us. Robert's work, I imagine. Tall wax tapers are blazing away, creating a homely glow. I leave our handbags safely with Effie and fetch some drinks for us at the al fresco bar, and examine the griddle, where the chef is starting to cook huge quantities of meat. To be honest, my stomach rolls over at the sight of all those sausage links and dripping, fatty hanks of flesh. I might just stick to the salads, which look rather nice.

'What's this? Lager?' Effie frowns when I bring our drinks.

'It's all they're offering,' I tell her, and then I freeze. 'Ah. Hello.'

Henry Cleavis is standing right in front of our table. Dapper in a velvet jacket and a silk cravat. His polished head gleams in the gentle torchlight as he bids us good evening.

He stammers when he greets Effie, and he eyes her blue silk turban guiltily.

'Oh, it's you,' she says stiffly.

'Effie, what can I say?' Henry begins gallantly. 'I can only hope you find it in your heart to forgive me.'

Effie tosses her head. 'It's not as easy as that, is it, Professor Cleavis?'

'Isn't it?' I feel quite sorry for Henry. He's transfixed beneath that basilisk stare of Effie's.

'I know very well that your bullet grazed my temple out of sheer mischance and bad luck,' she tells him. 'Of course I realise that. I'm not a fool. And, if that were all, I could forgive you.'

'Well, then,' he says hopefully.

'But you were aiming at Jessie. You were intent on destroying her. Which, indeed, you did. You assassinated the womanzee in cold blood, and I was injured as you carried out that wicked act.'

'It needed to be done,' Cleavis says levelly. 'She was a danger to everyone. My job is to rid the world of monsters. That has always been my job, Ms Jacobs. Ever since the days of the Smudgelings.'

Effie's tone becomes rather lofty and grand. 'And what you do not understand, dear Professor Cleavis, is that this town has always been plagued by monsters. It wouldn't be the same town were that not true. We pride ourselves on our misfits and monsters and we deal with them in our own way. We do not shoot them in the head. Nor do we rely on passing vigilantes or strangers for help.'

'I see,' says Cleavis, swallowing hard. 'And so you would have let the womanzee roam about freely?'

Stupidly, I pipe up then: 'Yes, Effie. You were the one, warning Robert. Saying that Jessie shouldn't be hiding out in those caves . . . that she was a danger to everyone . . .'

Effie shoots me a glance. 'We deal with these things ourselves. We know what to do. We don't need help from . . . outsiders.' She glares at Cleavis.

'I'm an outsider, too, then,' I say. 'I've not been here long.'

'Oh, *you* belong all right,' Effie says.

'Look, let me fetch some food for you,' Henry says. 'And more drinks. I'd like to discuss this further with you. I want to know more about this place. I want to understand Whitby and what goes on here . . .'

Effie tosses her head snootily once more, but she has relented, I can tell. She passes Henry our emptied plastic beakers and we tell him what we want to eat. I have fully decided now to stick to the salads and the vegetables. Henry dashes off happily to gather our orders.

'He's not so bad,' Effie tells me, out of the corner of her mouth. 'He's okay.'

I sit back in my wicker chair and beam at this. Maybe she won't mind so much if Henry and I start seeing each other . . . properly. Perhaps there won't be any friction between them. My head swims slightly at the thought of being happy like that. Henry as a full-time boyfriend kind of thing. Boyfriend! And him over a hundred years old! I watch him shuffle along at the vast griddle, balancing three plates and chatting away with the other hotel guests. I glance around at the arcadian splendour of Sheila's beer garden, as the shadows start to lengthen and the whole place takes on a golden, glamorous atmosphere. There are glowing paper lanterns in the trees, rustling and bobbing in the night breezes. Chinese things, presumably in memory of the dastardly Mu-Mu.

Robert comes to greet us and he hugs us both warmly. He tells us to enjoy ourselves tonight and, if I'm honest, I don't know what he means about the atmosphere of the place. There's nothing diabolic about it. It's just us oldsters having fun. True, when you look around, the others might seem a bit greedy: the way they tuck into their chops and kebabs. Otherwise respectable-looking people are sitting there with sticky meat juices all down their chins, and even down the front of their party clothes. They tear at the barbecued meat hungrily, even rapaciously. I turn to remark on this to Effie, and find her wolfing her own hank of steak with unseemly relish. Henry grins at me through a mouthful of sausage.

'The meat is marvellous, Brenda. Are you sure you don't want me to fetch you any?'

'I'll stick to my chickpeas and couscous, thank you very much.'

As the night advances, they are all up on their feet. Dancing the night away under the diamante stars. I demur, and Effie and Henry seem to bury the hatchet, getting up to have a bop in the cleared central space of the garden.

There is a dizzying, manic energy to the scene. A fizzing, spitting, highly charged ambience. I can't quite put my finger on it. I sit here, trying to analyse it, in the shadow of the box hedges, on my creaking wickerwork chair.

And, as I sit there, a warm breeze comes shushing through the bushes. A gently exotic whisper, that seems spiced with the idea of distant lands. The party noise fades away and I hear instead other, less familiar noises. I stiffen and the chair creaks beneath me. The table crackles. It is as if the wickerwork is twisting of its own volition. A great shudder of foreboding goes through me. I don't understand.

But then the party noise around me surges loudly once more. The breeze drops and those eerie sounds are blocked out by Boney M, I believe it is. Effie is standing beside me, grasping my hand, asking me to come and dance with them, which I do. I get up, laughing, and hook my bag over one arm, passing Effie hers. We join Henry on the dance floor, in the midst of the seething crowd. He is scarlet with effort as he tries to keep up with the dancing. There's nothing I can do but fling myself into it. There's nothing like a nice bop for casting out the cobwebs.

The three of us are there until three in the morning.

In the early hours Henry Cleavis and I are stalking through the plush corridors of Sheila Manchu's hotel. The thick carpet muffles our footsteps and we're being ever so furtive. It's like a dream. It's tinged with that woolly feeling of things being not quite right. These moments are suffused with taboo, somehow.

Henry's in a red velvet smoking jacket and he's holding a candle in a little brass holder. I'm in my best frock and I'm clinging on to his arm.

No sign of any other guests in the Hotel Miramar. It must be very, very late. We descend into the basement. Down the black staircase that leads to the Yellow Peril. The late night music has been silenced. The good vibrations have been stilled.

There's nothing more macabre than a deserted night club, I decide, as we pick our way across the beer-sticky floor.

We find the door to Sheila's office. Her inner sanctum. This is where Effie and I were brought that night – it seems so long ago now – when Sheila told us all about her poison pen letter. And we as good as promised to get to the bottom of that mystery. Well. We did. There'll be no more nasty letters, at any rate.

But what are Henry and I doing, poking around in this place, and going through Sheila's private things? He's holding the dripping candle over her papers. He's rifling through drawers and tugging at the filing cabinet. 'It's Mu-Mu's papers we want,' he says. 'The papers he stole, all that time ago.'

This has me nodding in agreement. And there's something I want to tell Henry now . . . something about stolen papers . . . but the thought is gone before I can vocalise it. This is like one of those horrible, treacly nightmares, in which you can't quite master your own body or even your words.

Now Henry has found the shrine, at the very back of Sheila's office. He thrusts open the doors to reveal the display of creepy souvenirs within.

It looks even worse in the dark, lit only by candle flame. 'Good grief.' Henry coughs, and almost drops his light.

Hidden right at the back, beneath the silken robe, is an extra surprise. The skull of Mu-Mu Manchu itself, glowing an unearthly green. Its sockets flash with malevolent power as the shadows scurry back and forth and a spider, disturbed by the light, plops out of his calm home within the boneless cavity of Mu-Mu's nose.

'How revolting,' Henry comments briefly. And then, steeling his nerve, he thrusts his hand into the shrine. He starts poking about amongst the trinkets and the jewels, and all the leftover bits and pieces of Mu-Mu. What's he looking for? What is he doing? I grasp his arm involuntarily, as if to stop him. It seems almost blasphemous, this rootling about in Sheila's holy of holies.

Henry is staring into the blank black sockets of his ancient foe. 'I beat him at last, Brenda,' he whispers. 'Now I can stare him in the eye, and there are no eyes there.'

I sniff sadly. 'That's the great thing about longevity, Henry. Like mine – or yours. You get to outlive your enemies. Though Mu-Mu, of course, lasted quite a long time himself.'

'But he's gone.' Henry sighs. 'He went without ever succeeding in conquering the whole of the western world. Oh, you may chuckle. But he came rather close, on more than one occasion. He had terrible powers. Otherworldly powers we just didn't understand at the time. Something . . . from beyond . . . a force . . . that he was learning to harness . . .'

Someone has come up behind us. When they speak, suddenly, it makes the two of us jump. Henry's arms lash out spasmodically, knocking several of the holy relics off the shelves.

'What are you doing here? Why have you come here?'

It's Sheila Manchu. Looking stricken and wild in her satin nightdress. She's all fluffed up with feathers and indignation. Her mascara is smudged by sleep and her hands are hooked like talons, reaching out to rip us to shreds.

'Run!' yells Henry Cleavis, and we both try to dodge the widow's savage onslaught.

As we pelt out of there, and dash back through the sepulchral gloom of the Yellow Peril, the reality of it all is melting away as a deep, throbbing voice comes into my head. It resounds there, as if my own skull was as hollow as that of Mu-Mu Manchu.

'Freee me, Brenndaa. Now you have a chance of freeing meee again. Last time you failed. I have come again, Brenndaa. You must . . . you will . . . freee meee.'

And some time later, I sit up in bed. Suddenly, shocked.

The voice ebbs away. But I definitely heard it. It was definitely there, communicating with me, as I slept. My heart hammers like mad.

Where am I? I'm sitting up in bed. My bed. It's my own

bed. I'm home. I'm swathed and sweltering in my own sumptuous bedclothes. I'm safe at home. It's morning. None of these nightmares or messages or whatever they are can touch me now. I'm at home. Safe in this sanctuary of my own. Good.

Then I turn, realising that the mattress is sagging a little more than usual. I turn and see – with a small gasp of horror – that Henry is lying there, curled up beside me, fast asleep and in his vest.

All I can do is get on with my day.

This is a slack time, and there's no one staying at my B&B, thank goodness. I don't know what my paying guests would make of my having fancy men staying over through the night. But I've new people arriving in the middle of next week, and I have a fair amount of preparation to get under way. Today I'm cleaning down my kitchen and nothing – not even last night's various adventures – is going to deter me.

So there I am, down in the kitchen, on my hands and knees, scouring the tiled floor. I'm scrubbing away in order to keep my mind from ticking over, too. I don't want to think too much just yet. I certainly don't want to start going over last night.

Henry was in my bed! I woke up with him in my bed! In his vest! What did we do? Anything?

There's nothing I can do to stop the horror of that thought crowding into my mind. I scour and bleach and clean and polish, and still those rumbling, purple clouds come rolling across my horizon. Tempting thoughts. Intriguing thoughts. Horrible thoughts. What did we do? What happened? Why can't I remember?

Quite some time after I'm up and about, I hear signs of life from upstairs. Henry stomping around my attic bedroom. I try to block out those noises as he clatters and bangs about in the unfamiliar space. He'll be all headachy and swimmy, just as I am.

And I wonder if he'll be wondering what happened as well. Or possibly he will remember. And I just know I won't be able to face him or look him in the eye, when . . .

He puts his head round the kitchen door.

'Er. Hello. I. Um.'

I've got my bum in the air. Hardly dignified. I jump up and spill the frothy water across the tiles.

'Oh. Good morning. Tea, or, er, coffee?'

He looks at me bleakly. 'No. I'll go. I. Um.'

'Yes, all right. I.'

We look at each other. There's about twenty miles and six decades between us. We stand there, frozen by the sight of each other.

'Did we?' I ask.

'No,' he says. 'Um. That is. Um.'

'I thought we hadn't.' I nod, and smile awkwardly. Of course nothing mucky went on. I'd have known. Of course I would have. It's over twenty-five years since any man's had his paws on my body. It would come as a right shock if it happened again. And I would know if he'd been anywhere near.

Still we stand there, mortified at the sight of each other. I'm thinking of him lying there in his slightly yellow vest.

'I'll go. Um,' he says, and he is gone.

When I hear the door slam downstairs I dash straight to my phone. Effie answers first ring and she is agog.

'He's just left,' I tell her.

'What? Oh, Brenda!' she cries, but I can tell she's amused.

'Nothing happened!' I protest. 'And the weird thing is . . . I don't remember anything at all. Last night . . . sort of . . . *frizzled* away in my memory. One moment we were dancing around together and . . . then . . .'

'Quite,' says Effie. 'I suppose it was those noxious cocktails your chum Robert started bringing us from the Tikki Bar.'

'Perhaps,' I say, though it doesn't feel as if I was particularly drunk. No, this is something else.

'I'm calling a meeting,' Effie says briskly. 'Because I can't hang about listening to your terrible gossip all morning. I've work to do. What about seven tonight at Cod Almighty? My shout.'

It's not often she offers to pay. I agree hurriedly and she's off the phone in a flash. Well. Effie's back to full strength, it seems. There is something all fired-up and zestful in her tone. Her night out seems to have done her a lot of good.

I wish I could say the same about me. I feel strung out and wrung out. My whole battered body feels as though it wants to yawn. No, it's not quite that. I feel thinned out . . . and hungry, somehow. Hollowed out. I am . . . yearning for something or other. I'm not sure what it is. Oh, dear. Best to blot it all out. And immerse myself in kitchen cleaning. That's the best way.

I'm just about to start again when the phone gives its shrill ring. I can't afford to ignore it, in case it's a booking. But it's Robert, whispering mysteriously at the front desk at the Miramar.

'Did you feel it?' he asks.

'I'm not sure what you mean.'

'Last night it was more potent than ever. The air itself seemed thick with it.'

'I'm not sure,' I say. 'I certainly felt something. But all in all, it was a very pleasant evening.'

'It's getting stronger, whatever it is,' says Robert, and he sounds as disturbed as I've ever heard him. 'A kind of . . . voodoo thing . . . in the air.'

'A voodoo thing?' I laugh.

'Voodoo,' he says firmly. 'And I don't like it one bit.'

Effie has never done this to me before.

I sit there in my hat and coat, full of hell. I'm in our specially reserved booth at Cod Almighty, and I'm there with ten minutes to spare. I'm still there forty-five minutes later, in case the poor old thing is running late. But, no. She's stood me up.

This has never happened before.

What if something's happened to her?

I make my excuses and shoot home. Raf and Leena from the shop under me are locking up early and leaving. 'We're off to Sheila Manchu's barbecue,' Leena tells me. She's all done up in a new sari, all wafty sea green and gauzy.

'You're vegetarians!' I say, but they shrug and bustle off happily.

When I get in, my phone is going. 'It's Robert, Brenda. I'm sorry to ring you, but it's Effie. She's here at the Miramar again and she's got a weird fervid glint in her eye.'

'Fervid?' I don't like the sound of that at all. 'Is Henry there?'

I can feel the frost in Robert's tone at the mention of my beau. 'I haven't noticed him. I think you'd better get up here, Brenda. People are starting to act rather oddly.'

I don't get a chance to ask him, in what way *odd*, exactly? Lucky I'm in my glad rags already. I smarm on a bit more lipstick and I lock up again. My blood is thrumming with excitement as I hurry back out, and up the hill towards the Miramar.

When I arrive I find that things are proceeding a little differently from the way they were last night. There is still the same warm, welcoming atmosphere. The same blazing candles and fairy lights. The music is still pounding away, from speakers hidden in the hedges. The griddle is going and the bar is busy but the main difference is that the wickerwork tables and chairs are empty. People aren't sitting nicely at the new garden furniture and waiting politely for the evening to begin. They are already up, out of their places and in the middle together.

Now, I've been English for a long time, and I know that it takes several hours and a good few drinks for the English to abandon their reserve and to actually enjoy themselves. Something, I know, is definitely up.

They aren't dancing, however. That isn't why the barbecue guests are thronging in the central area of the beer garden. They seem to be working together, busily, on the dark lawn. I recognise a few faces: the butcher and his wife, the Reverend Mr Small, Raf and Leena. There must be about thirty-odd of them, pitching in and . . . building something.

Is that why they are here? To do some kind of DIY? It seems rather improbable. But here they are. Spread out on the lawn with a whole host of tools and heaps of old wood. Banging and tapping and hammering bits together. The noise is quite fearsome. Clattering and banging in time with the Stones' 'Sympathy for the Devil' – which, in itself, isn't massively consoling.

No, it isn't just any old heaps of old wood they are using. These aren't old planks and bits of furniture from inside, as I first suspected. They are using the wickerwork furniture. They are hammering together the spanking new chairs and tables that Sheila Manchu has only just purchased. Sheila will go crackers! What do they think they're doing? Mindlessly smashing and splicing together chunks of woven bamboo.

They are building something.

I turn and suddenly I see the rest of the barbecue crowd, amassed by the bar. They are holding up their frothing cocktails, apparently saluting this impromptu DIY. I crane my neck to see my friends.

And there is Effie. She is right in the thick of it, wearing her turban and another exotic dress from her bottomless wardrobe. She looks feverish and golden in the guttering torchlight. I can hear her now, exhorting the DIY people to work faster, faster.

'Build him! Build him!' she is hissing at the party guests.

I don't like the look of this at all.

I veer away from the lot of them, hoping not to be seen, and hurry towards the Hotel Miramar itself. I need to find someone with sense. Robert, or Henry. Surely they can't have succumbed to all this fervid voodoo mind control nonsense?

At my back, as I scurry away, the rapping and tapping of DIY and the low, chanting murmur of the crowd is starting to drown out the speaker system.

Sheila Manchu is at the indoors bar, looking shaky and mixing herself a very tall glass of gin and tonic. She looks as smudgy and wild as she did the last time I saw her. Her white hair hangs in unruly tatters and, at first, she seems relieved to see me. Which I'm glad about. I'm a bit embarrassed about her finding Henry and me poking about in her holy of holies. She hurriedly pours me a drink of my own.

'What's going on?'

Sheila gives a very fake laugh. 'Oh, I think it's just a bit of fun, really. They're making something. I don't know what it is they're up to . . .'

I glare at her suspiciously. She is trying too hard to seem unconcerned. But they are destroying all her expensive garden furniture out there. She has thrown open her beer garden and her guests are going bonkers. What is the matter with her? I watch her narrowly as she glugs down the gin.

'Sheila . . .' I say. 'They seem possessed. And Effie is out there, behaving very strangely indeed.'

'Have you asked her why?'

'I didn't want to,' I admit. 'She has a funny glint in her eye.'

'Fervid?' Sheila asks worriedly. 'Hm. I've seen this before.'

From the bar area we can see the picture window in the conservatory. I stare for a bit at the weird scene out there. The party guests are redoubling their efforts, knocking bits of wickerwork together and passing them over for further work, as if there is some grander design they have in mind. As if there is some final shape for their unwieldy jigsaw pieces to take on.

'What are they making, Sheila? What are they doing?'

Sheila looks stricken. 'I really don't know. I think they've flipped.'

Now the bigger wickerwork pieces are coming together,

bang in the middle of the lawn. Sheila and I drift closer to the window, in order to see. The people out there in the gathering gloom look like ancient Egyptians toiling to put up the pyramids. Or children building up a bonfire . . . piling and piling the wood into a heap . . . or nailing together the pieces for a home-made crucifixion . . .

'I think we should stop them,' I say.

'How?' Sheila says nervously. 'It's got out of hand. They won't listen to us. I should have known. I should never have bought that . . . that garden furniture.'

I look at her. 'You know what's causing this, don't you?'

Sheila shakes her head mournfully. I grasp her by the feathery sleeves of her satiny frock, and I drag her to the emergency exit. I kick open the door and tug her out into the dark garden, where the noise is rising even more hectically. The records have stopped playing, and it's the guests making all this manic kerfuffle. I can hear Effie's voice still screeching: 'Build him! Build him!'

'Tell me what's behind this, Sheila,' I say warningly. 'What is it about this garden furniture of yours?'

Sheila whimpers. She's got the gin bottle tucked under her arm. It slips and crashes on the paving flags. 'I can't explain! I can't tell you!'

'You better had, lady.'

She stares into my face. Her eyes are swimming with tears. 'We should destroy the garden furniture. Before it's too late. *He* is coming.'

'What are you talking about?' I am having to shout now, over the noise of the crowd. They have joined in with the rhythmic, primitive chanting started by Effie: 'Build him higher! Build him! Build him! Build him up!'

'He's coming after me! He wants revenge!' Sheila is shrieking and attempting to free herself from my grasp. She stumbles on the bottle she's broken and I can see she has cut herself. She's desperate to be away. Her dress rips in my grasp.

'Sheila, what are you on about?' I bellow, right in her face. I chance my arm. 'Is it Mu-Mu? Is it Alucard?'

She twists about and shakes her head. 'Noo! Nooo!' she cries.

And then, suddenly, all of the banging and hullaballoo of construction abruptly stops.

Something is happening. I let go of Sheila and hurry round the box hedges. I still keep out of sight of that demented crowd. I peer round and they are all gathering about and murmuring at their seemingly completed handiwork.

It is an effigy of something that is not quite a man. They have built it incredibly quickly and accurately. There is something superhuman about what they have accomplished here, and they are suitably pleased with themselves.

I stare at the thing. It has a recognisable, if rudimentary, semi-human shape. Its head is huge and hollow and its thick arms are upraised, stretching out. There are two black holes for its eyes. And it is all made out of twisted, splintered, spliced-together wickerwork.

Effie and the others are clustered about the effigy. They raise their arms in supplication.

How have they managed it? How have a ragbag assortment of Whitby residents managed, in less than an hour or so, to rig up this bamboo monstrosity? The statue has a weird look to it. Its dark, hollow eyes draw me in. Its clumsy hands seem to be reaching out to me.

Sheila totters up behind me on her bleeding heels. A chill silence reigns through her beer garden. She brushes past me. 'Sheila . . .' I hiss.

But, like the others, Sheila is beyond sense now. She mutters: 'Goomba . . .' in a low voice. She shuffles ahead of me, to be with the others.

'Sheila!' I cry out. 'What did you say?'

'Woorrrshiiip hiiimmm . . .' Sheila groans. Then she is lost in the mêlée of her party guests.

The rest of them are taking up her eerie, ecstatic chant. 'Woorrrshiiip hiiimmm!'

'Sheila!' I yell, as she is swallowed up in the crazy, candlelit gloom.

Did she really say the name I thought she said?

Of course she did. I should have known by now. I should have realised. And now there is no doubt, as the beer garden resounds with the mindless cries of the party-goers:

'Gooommmbaaa! Gooommmbaaa! Woorrrsshiiip Gooommmbaaa!'

Now they are all swaying. The wax tapers spit tall flames. Shadows dance and flicker across the hulking wooden brute of an effigy.

And I turn and flee.

I'm bustling through the dark spaces of the lobby of the Miramar. Someone catches me up in their arms and I shriek. Of course, my nerves are completely jangled by now. I pummel at the chest of whoever is holding me, but their grip is firm. 'I think she's doolally like the rest of them,' says Henry.

'Surely not,' says Robert, steadfast, standing behind me.

I'm so relieved it's them I could cry. 'I'm not doolally! I'm okay! It's me, Brenda!'

'We know that.' Henry chuckles. 'Quickly. We have to get out.'

'I know!' I gasp. 'Have you seen what's going on out there?'

'I told you it was all headed somewhere spooky,' Robert says.

'They've got a big wickerwork effigy . . . and Effie is behaving in the oddest manner . . .'

The noise at our backs from the beer garden is even fiercer still. 'There's nothing we can do about them tonight,' Henry says. 'I suggest we make our escape before they realise that we haven't been . . . put under the influence, as it were.'

'But *Effie* . . .'

'She'll be all right,' Henry says, though how he can be sure I really don't know.

And so we make our escape from the Hotel Miramar and the lurid spectacle of pagan rites in its back garden. It's not even all that late, I realise, as we scurry through town, down the hill towards my place. The three of us catch a few funny looks from people out and about on the streets. We must look wild and white-faced with shock.

Weirdly, one thing I'm pleased about is that Henry and Robert seem to be getting on. They must have settled their differences. This, I realise, as we huff and puff our way to my B&B, is extremely important to me. These are the two men of whom I am fondest in all the world. They are like my little surrogate family of men, and they make me feel very secure – all of these being rather novel feelings for me. I've not had much chance to rely on anyone much in the past. But here they are – co-operating – and sort-of rescuing me from the infernal rites at the Miramar. And Robert is talking to Henry, even though Henry shot his Aunty Jessie.

Henry's got hold of one of my arms and it's as if he's frogmarching me home. I feel the pressure of his grip on me and I can't help but have a flashback to waking up with him in his old vest. Inappropriate just at the moment, I know – but I think all that primal heat and ceremony has got into me just a little.

'Goomba, Henry!' I suddenly cry out, in the middle of the street. 'Did you hear them? They were all chanting "Goomba"!'

Henry is grim-lipped. 'I did indeed.'

'Goomba's the name of the . . . thing that Mu-Mu had hidden away under Limehouse.'

'Quite,' says my companion tersely. 'But I don't think we should be discussing this out on the street.'

'Oh,' I say, 'of course.'

We've reached my house. I fumble in my bag for keys, reflecting that Henry is so much more professional in his investigations than Effie and I are. Professionalism takes some of the fun out of it, I think.

Robert follows us into my dimly lit hallway. 'Brenda, would you mind putting me up overnight? I don't want to go back to the Miramar while they're all acting up like that. God knows what they'll get up to.'

I'm flicking on lights and thundering up the staircase, leading the way into my palatial home. It's so good to be in, with the door locked behind us. Safe in my B&B while Whitby goes mad around us. 'Of course!' I cry. 'You must both stay here as my guests. There is no way on earth I'd let you return to that madhouse.'

I bustle them into my kitchen and get the kettle going. I also fetch down the brandy and slosh it into three green glasses. I reckon we've all had a shock. I pass the drinks round and heave a deep sigh. We are safe, but I wish Effie was here with us. She would love all this. Escaping and sitting up late to make plans.

'Who wants an egg sandwich?' I ask, and they both do, having missed out on the barbecue part of this evening.

And so we sit up in the kitchen, eating, talking, drinking and trying to make plans. We go on, making less and less sense, until we are too tired to focus any more. And then I show my boys to their rooms, which are all perfectly made up, of course, and ready for new guests. Robert thanks me profusely, and Henry raises a quizzical eyebrow at the doorway of his room.

I slap him firmly on the back. 'In you go, lovey.' And I send him on his way. 'We'll talk more at breakfast. Eight o'clock sharp. We'll get to the bottom of this Goomba business once and for all.'

As I head up to my attic, the air is heady with fried egg sandwiches, brandy, spicy tea, and talk of bamboo deities from beyond time and space.

I sleep pretty well, considering. I'm a bit woozy when I hop out of bed and swing into my usual star jumps and sit-ups. But I remind myself that I have my two impromptu guests to look after. Breakfast to make! Plans to get under way! And I'm excited, even though something terrible is going on just up the hill, and Effie seems to be in danger.

I try her number on the phone, and there's no answer. A jolt of guilt goes through me. How could we have run away last night, and just left her there?

As I sit in my claw-footed tub in gallons of steam I stew it all over.

And there's that voice again: '*Free me, Brenda. You are the one who knows. You must find a way . . . to freeeee meeeeee.*'

I shake my head to clear it. Goomba's voice is calling out to me – to me specifically – just as he did all those years ago in Limehouse, as Henry and I approached the lair of Mu-Mu Manchu. But just as I didn't understand then, I'm mystified now. How can I free Goomba? And would that be such a good thing anyway, given that he's got everyone in his thrall and behaving extremely oddly?

I simply have to face the day and see what it brings, that's all. I'm sure we can get it all sorted. No reason why not.

Porridge and bacon and scrambled eggs. The boys staying with me are bound to have healthy appetites. As I busy about and cook for them, though, they slurp hot sweet tea and bicker about the shooting of Jessie the womanzee. It's good that they clear the air at last, I suppose.

And there comes all this knocking at my side door.

'Effie!' I gasp, dropping the hot frying pan and rushing for the door. She has made it back! My heart leaps in relief and I stumble down the stairs.

'Where have you been, lady? We thought we were going to have to send for—' I fumble with locks and bolts and throw open the door. But it isn't Effie. It's Sheila Manchu in her tattered night attire, and she looks devastated. 'You look terrible, woman. You'd better come in.'

So now she is sitting at my kitchen table with a mug of tea. Her nails are all broken, I notice as she curls her fingers round the mug. Her hands are dirty with mud from her garden and they seem to be stuck with splinters of wickerwork.

'What's going on at the Miramar?' Henry asks her gently. He's got just the right tone for this subtle sort of probing.

She looks at the three of us and her eyes fill with panic.

'He wants to kill me! He won't stop until I'm dead! It's all about me! That's why he's here!' She sploshes her tea on the tablecloth.

'Start again,' Robert urges. 'Who do you mean? Who wants to kill you?'

'That *thing*,' she spits. 'Says it comes from the dawn of time. From beyond time and space. That's the one. It's come after me, it has. It's bided its time and it's found me at last. And now it's here and it's taking over all our minds . . .'

'Not ours,' Henry says proudly. 'I don't believe it's taking over any of *our* minds. What is it, exactly, this force from beyond time, hm?'

'*Goomba*,' she gasps, as if the word is being dragged out of her. 'It's some kind of god, Mu-Mu used to say. And it is *in* the garden furniture! It's *in* the tables and chairs!'

Robert's eyes widen at this, I can see. All three of us are prepared to accept what she says, though, however outlandish the tale. We have seen too much to start doubting now.

'And they have smashed up the furniture and made it into an image of their god. Goomba! Goomba has risen again, in my accursed beer garden!' Sheila's voice rises to a shriek at this point. Robert leans round to pat her back.

'How did this . . . spirit, this entity . . . get into the garden furniture?' Henry frowns.

Sheila struggles to regain her composure. 'My fault. It's all my fault. You see, I didn't make sure . . . I didn't do a good enough job . . . of having him destroyed in the first place.'

I make us a second pot of strong tea as we all settle to hear Sheila's dreadful story.

'Remember, Brenda, when I told you how I was the very young bride of Mu-Mu Manchu. I was seventeen and, by then, in the early seventies, he was well over a century old. But I didn't care! I loved him for who he was. His tremendous intellect and his magnetic personality. He was cankered and disappointed by then, of course. His career hadn't worked out quite how he had hoped in that, truth be told, he *wasn't* God-Emperor of the entire western world. And, unfortunately, everyone in Christendom wasn't *actually* kneeling at his feet and doing all his bidding.

'Looked at in one light, Mu-Mu was just a sad, skinny old man living in his secret hideaway under the streets of Limehouse. He wasn't even getting a pension from the British government. Everyone had forgotten about him. When I first met him, he was wasting away.'

I think – with a shudder – of that glowing skull in Sheila's cupboard-like shrine in her office.

'I fell in love with Mu-Mu, and he did with me, instantly.

I gave him a new lease of life, he said. I was young and spirited – I was waitressing in Soho. Nasty, tacky little clip joint. I was keen to get out of that world. Mu-Mu's faded glamour and his apparent riches fired my imagination. In him I saw escape from my tawdry lifestyle. But he was stuck in a rut, down there, under the ground, down in his cavern. He was letting his bitterness overtake him.'

Henry butts in gently, pushing her on in her tale: 'And Goomba?'

'I tried to talk my beloved into coming away from London. Leaving the dirty old Smoke behind. It was 1974. There was nothing left there for us. I talked up Yorkshire to him. The clean, healthy living. The lovely countryside. The views. I brought him some brochures down, and Mu-Mu seemed quite interested. He started to think seriously about what it might be like to retire to Whitby. Whitby was my suggestion, by the way. Little did I know what Mu-Mu knew about the place: what small sparks of recognition it fired in the mind of my godlike genius lover. But, of course, Mu-Mu remembered Tyler's connection with Whitby. How the professor had been inspired by this place to write his opus, unlocking the secrets of the galaxy.

'This strange town on the north-east coast, Mu-Mu knew, was rife with cosmic murmurs. It was a storehouse of secrets he would dearly love to crack. And so Mu-Mu listened seriously as I described how we would run away together to the seaside, and open a hotel.

' "But my dear," Mu-Mu confided in me one day, "we cannot leave these catacombs. Goomba is here. Goomba has been with me here, hidden from the world, since I first arrived in this country, at the very end of the last century." I frowned at this. "So?" I asked. I was a brash girl. Nothing scared me. "That bamboo plant?" I laughed. "Are you saying you'd throw over all our plans because of a plant?"

'I knew the plant in question and I hated it. Mu-Mu treated it with such reverent care, I thought it was ridiculous. It was the only thing about my beloved mastermind that irritated me. He had let this bamboo plant grow out of all control. It filled one entire room inside his underground palace, and he had his minions and lackeys tend it with such elaborate care that it made me almost envious. Imagine! Me! I was jealous of an out-of-control house plant! Even more ridiculous, I thought, was the way Mu-Mu named it "Goomba", and talked about it as if it was a member of the family.

' "It's out of control, Mu-Mu. You'll never be able to transplant it. It simply can't come on the van with the rest of our stuff. It can't come to Yorkshire with us, to our new life. It will just have to stay here." Well, I thought I was talking common sense. But Mu-Mu burst into frantic tears!

I had never seen him like that. So inconsolable. He sobbed like a maniac. "Goomba! I will never leave you!" he cried and I tried to shush him to no avail.

'I thought that my poor dear megalomaniac had, with his great age and disappointment, become rather feeble-minded. My incredulity grew as he explained to me that his overgrown bamboo plant came from another dimension, beyond time and space, and was possessed of tremendous power. And, if Mu-Mu could only unlock the secret of that power, then he was still in the running for the exalted position of God-Emperor of the entire planet Earth.

'I looked at him. His livid green eyes were as serious as I had ever seen them. I took a deep breath and I was, if I'm honest, sad for myself, mostly, in that moment. My hubby-to-be was bananas, and that was a hard truth to swallow.

'I patted him gently on his egg-like skull, and I tried to console him. I tried to convince him that I really didn't think his bamboo plant was going to help him rule the world. "But Professor Tyler knew!" Mu-Mu seethed, twisting about in my embrace. "He knew the secrets of Goomba! I'm sure he knew how to control him! How to use his powers!" Well, back then, I didn't even know who this Tyler was that he kept referring to. I know now, of course, that he was the man who had written all this guff about Goomba and various other gods from far-flung dimensions.

Well, I wished he'd never bothered. My lovely man friend was obsessed with this bamboo demon. And my plans for a nice retreat to Yorkshire and a hotel of my own were completely scuppered, so long as Mu-Mu stayed fixated on this Goomba malarkey.

'The hotel of my dreams – the Miramar – wouldn't be on the market for ever. I kept travelling up to inspect it. I examined it and I dreamed and I was in a lather of frustration at Mu-Mu and his silly plant. And all that – as I saw it then – mystical twaddle.

'So I took matters into my own hands. I bought an axe.

'I descended into my lover's secret hideaway in Limehouse. I sneaked past his guards and his myrmidons. And I managed to get into the sacrosanct room where Goomba had lain in wait all those decades, growing steadily and apparently murmuring sweet nothings into Mu-Mu's ears. So I did what I had to, in order to set my future husband and myself free. I set to work with my shiny axe. And I chopped the bamboo monster into a million pieces. Before the guards found me and dragged me away – oh! they were so horrified – I had succeeded in reducing Goomba to splinters! We were free! We could leave that place for ever!

'Poor Mu-Mu. When he heard what I had done . . . He should have been furious. He should have had me executed.

I saw the dangerous light in his eyes. And I knew that a younger, more determined Mu-Mu would have done just that. My silly life was forfeit, and I grew fearful. But I underestimated myself, and the extent to which I had this criminal genius wrapped around my little finger. Mu-Mu sagged back on to his throne. He stopped shouting at me. He ordered his guards to gather together all the little bits of Goomba and bury them safely, deep under Limehouse. And Mu-Mu looked at me and told me that I had got my own way. He would leave behind London and the last of his plans for world domination. And we would come to Whitby together. And he never spoke of Goomba again. And I almost forgot about the horrible thing.

'Until now. Until I foolishly ordered that wickerwork garden furniture. Goomba has found his way back into my life! And he is here in order to make me pay! He exists once more! And he wants my blood as revenge, I am sure of it!'

'But . . .' I break in. 'How on earth was Goomba turned into a set of wickerwork garden furniture?'

Sheila shakes her head tearfully. 'That I don't know. But he has found his way out into the world again. He must have taken control of Danby's Garden Furniture Manufacturers. His very essence must have called out to be revived and to be brought to my garden, from where he could take his revenge. There is no coincidence here.

Goomba has seen to it that he will destroy my world at last!'

Robert has moved over to the kitchen window. He is looking down into the street, frowning. 'People are drifting back home. They're like zombies, all dazed. It's your partygoers, Sheila! The influence has left them and they're coming home. There's Raf and Leena from downstairs, letting themselves into their shop. And there's Effie! Effie's back! She's exhausted-looking, but I think she's all right!'

So they return home from their night of revels.

All over Whitby, these droopy partygoers return to their homes and their families. There is about them a smell of barbecue smoke and cocktails . . . as well as a whiff of something alien, odd, dangerous. In no particular hurry, they drift their way through town, returning to their doors. No one hurries to their work. All their usual humdrum concerns are forgotten.

All they can really think about is the hulking effigy in the beer garden of Sheila Manchu. The prime concern in their minds is the image of that wonderful creation. Goomba stands still in that garden: poised on the brink of becoming. They know he is there waiting for them, and for the moment when the party and the midnight shenanigans can begin again.

We get to Effie before she makes it back to her house. Robert and I are out on the street, dragging her back to my alleyway. She mutters a few complaints and stares at us wildly, at first, as if she hardly recognises us. But then she relents, and her skinny little body falls limp. We bundle her up my stairs to the attic and get her installed in my comfiest armchair. Henry is brewing up the strongest coffee in the world, bringing over the silver-plated service on a tray with a huge grin. 'Here we go,' he says. 'This will knock her socks off and, I hope, bring her back to her senses.' We watch Effie grip the mug and slowly sip.

Henry's coffee doesn't do a great deal for Sheila, who is sitting on the sofa, rocking back and forth. She's still babbling about Mu-Mu and haunted garden furniture. I listen for a second and realise that she's wondering aloud once more how Goomba has managed to have himself made into sets of bamboo tables and chairs. How has he been so devilishly specific in taking his revenge against Sheila? This thought alone has her rocking and quivering with paranoiac fright.

I could tell her the answer, though. I think I know how dreadful things like that happen. And it's all because the world is a terrifying place and it teems with monstrous coincidence. Sheila is quite right to descend into paranoia and terror. The evil forces in the world are indeed ranged against us, and every day they seek new ways in which to do us harm.

'I think I've got some walnut cake in that tin,' I tell Robert. 'Fetch it out, would you? Effie might respond to something sweet. If cake doesn't work, we'll have to mix her a snowball. Eggnog in the top cupboard, there.'

Now Effie is hissing under her breath and we all lean in close. To my dismay she's saying: 'Woorrshiip hiimmm . . .' So it seems that she's still subsumed by all that nonsense. 'Gooommbbaaa . . .' moans High Priestess Effie. 'Gooommbbaaa!' And this sets off the other one. Sheila spills her coffee in the act of thrusting her arms into the air, joining in with Effie's chant: 'Woorrshiip Goooommba!'

'Oh, God,' says Henry weakly, and I know it's more of a feeble little prayer than it is a muttered curse. 'Can't we get them to stop?'

Robert is mixing up snowballs on the kitchen table, but I think that's probably a poor idea, now I see how demented these two are.

'He will take us with him,' says Effie. 'When he returns to the stars and the Interstitial Fold, Goomba will bear us with him . . .'

Sheila chimes in with this, as if it's an aspiration she shares with Effie. But I know this isn't something Effie's been particularly keen on doing before. This is mind control, I know it. Goomba has reached right into their souls and taken them over. Not even daylight, coffee and my best walnut cake can do any good. Robert hands them both a snowball and they drain them in one go. Effie sits there with her turban awry and an eggnog moustache, and the look in her eye is one that I find frankly blood-chilling.

I am glad I don't have a soul. It's at times like these – and only times like these – that I find myself actually glad of that unfortunate fact. Nothing can get to me. I can't be taken over like this. But now the onus is on me, of course, to sort the whole mess out. 'Robert, you stay here with the ladies,' I tell him, standing up decisively. 'Whatever you do, don't let them out. Keep a keen eye on them. Give them anything they need.'

'Goomba! Goomba!' chant Sheila and Effie in what can only be described as a samba rhythm.

'Okay.' Robert nods grimly. I notice he's fetched himself a snowball.

'Henry, come with me,' I say tersely, and lead him straight upstairs to my bedroom.

Because I have a plan. Sheila's tale of Goomba in Limehouse has set my thoughts running wildly and spectacularly and I have made a connection. A fantastic connection. I have had the most marvellous idea, and as I thunder up the stairs I'm hoping fiercely – with every fibre of my frazzled being – that it's going to bear fruit.

Henry lumbers up the stairs behind me. 'Oh, heavens. Um. Back in your bedroom, Brenda? I. Um.'

This brings me up short. I stop and turn to glare down at him. 'What about my bedroom?'

He looks down shamefacedly. His bristly eyebrows conceal the expression in those eyes of his as I stare down at his blushing bald head. 'We didn't really um. Did we? Anything? Did anything happen?'

'No,' I growl. 'And I'm not at all sure how you wound up in my bed anyway. I nearly had a coronary. You, lying heaped there in your old yellow vest.'

'Me too!' he gasps, starting to chuckle. 'When I woke. I um! What a shock!'

Now this has me miffed. 'Oh! Would it be so bad, eh? If something untoward happened?'

He is appalled that he's offended me. 'Goodness, no! Um. It would be a turn-up, though, wouldn't it? Um. After everything. All these years.'

'Anyway,' I break in. 'Past all that nonsense.'

'Quite. But still. Good pals and all, eh? Funny that — exhausted as we were — we just fell asleep like that together. Rather um. Sweet, no?'

I glower at him, still feeling obscurely offended. But there is work to do. 'Come on! In the attic! In my safe!'

Henry scurries after me. 'What is it? Something useful?'

'I hope so. Sheila reminded me. When she was talking about Tyler's book.' I am at the safe, clicking away at the familiar combination.

Henry tuts and shakes his head. 'Reg's bloody old book. Sometimes I wish he'd never bothered, you know. What a fuss it's caused! And he never even um, published it, after all that fuss.'

'I know. He died in . . . what? 1972? And the few privately printed copies were spread far and wide across the globe. What Sheila was saying had me thinking. That's what we need! We need Tyler's book in order to know how to deal with Goomba. All the secrets will be there. Mu-Mu was scared that they would get into the wrong hands . . . so there must have been something there . . . something about how to put a stop to Goomba . . .'

'I don't have a copy.' Henry sighs. 'I wish I had. But I never had a copy of Tyler's *The True History of Planets*. Not even the British Library has one. It's as if they all went up in a puff of smoke.'

'Hm . . .' I swing open the door of my safe. 'I was in here fetching something the other day. And hunting through all these precious bits of bric-a-brac.'

Henry shuffles nearer, and I instinctively hold him at bay. 'What have you got in there?'

'All the oddments and remnants of a long life spent

having wild and supernatural adventures,' I tell him. 'There are things here I daren't even tell you about. Anyway, I glimpsed something out of the corner of my eye the other day. And I never consciously realised what it was. Only just today I made the connection.'

'And?' says Henry eagerly.

Then I find what I've been looking for. It's a bundle of greasy and water-damaged papers held together by string. They are almost solid, like papier mâché, but I know this is what I am looking for. 'When I was fished out of the Thames by those children in 1946, following our misadventures in Limehouse . . . a bundle of papers was found upon my person. I was babbling and crazy and my memory had gone. I couldn't read anything for years afterwards, you know. But these were all the personal effects I had left to me. So I hung on to them, like something talismanic. It was very strange. Superstitious. And so I've still got these papers. And I've never opened them up, in order to see what is inside.'

Henry's eyes are out on stalks. You can see his fingers itching, keen to grab the bundle out of my grasp. 'Do you think . . .? Could it possibly be . . .?'

I shrug carefully. My hands tremble as I take the papers to my bedside table. 'I think they are the pages we found in Freer's bedsit. The ones Mu-Mu was missing. Do you remember? I shoved them down my cleavage – and I left them there. Little knowing how precious and useful they might one day be!'

I can sense Henry holding his breath.

What we expect to see is page after page of Tyler's tight, unreadable script. Luckily Henry is an expert. He mastered Tyler's personal hieroglyphics a long time ago.

I start peeling away the pages. They resist, and then open up with an almost audible crack. I half expect them to crumble to dust in my shaking hands.

Here they are. I hope this is it. I hope the solution to our whole quandary lies here for the taking, right in the palm of my hand.

'Well?' Like the fussy old academic bloodhound he is, Henry shoves his cold nose forward, quivering, in order to see. 'Is it? Is it Tyler?'

I am staring into my hands. I can't believe what I'm looking at. Fruit scones. Steak and kidney pie. Spotted Dick. 'I'm afraid not.' I'm holding a handful of ancient recipes.

'Oh,' says Henry, deflated. 'Never mind.' He pats my shoulder heavily. 'It was um. Worth a try, old girl.'

Now I'm furious with myself for getting both our hopes up. What on earth made me think this useless bunch of scribbled recipes could have been the answer to our prayers? It would have been too neat. I'm a fool. I caught a glimpse of ruined old papers and assumed they were the crucial pages. But no. Things never work out as tidily as that.

A weight of despondency rolls over me. Henry watches it happen, compassion crinkling his eyes. 'We'll sort it out anyway,' he tells me softly. 'Together. And remember: you don't have to do this on your own. It isn't you who has to come up with the answer to everything, Brenda.'

Downstairs we have something of a situation, since the two ladies are up on their feet and they want to go out. They are still in their dazed, trance-like state and, although they aren't very forceful about it, we know they would rather be out of here. They get up, we push them back down. They slump down, and then get back up on their feet again.

'Need to go . . . Goomba calls usss . . .'

'We need to . . . Yesss, Goombaaa . . .'

It's quite distressing, watching them flounder like this. Robert is worn out with keeping them in the room. He's been alone with these two pale ladies and it's taking it out of him. They seem to me like two giant moths, daft and determined, batting at obstacles.

'Let's . . . let them out,' Robert says, looking pained. 'We can't really keep them here, can we? Not against their wills.'

Now Effie and Sheila are getting worse. They are moaning continuously and waving their arms about in the air.

I fold my own arms steadfastly. 'I don't think it's a good idea to let them out and about while they're in this state.'

'They aren't in their right minds,' Henry puts in. 'They might do themselves a mischief.'

Robert has got hold of Effie by her arms, and he's trying to draw her back to the settee. Suddenly she uses all her strength to shrug him away. He backs off. 'We can't stop them going, if that's what they want to do. They won't come to any real harm, will they? All this talk of Goomba . . . We don't know what it is, really. We don't know what it actually means. And maybe . . . maybe it isn't even anything really bad? It almost sounds quite nice . . . what they're saying about going to other planets and stuff . . .'

I narrow my eyes at him. 'Now, don't *you* start, Robert.'

'I *do* feel a bit strange,' he says.

'Be strong!'

'And *I* don't feel exactly, um. Tip-top,' Henry adds.

Oh dear. At this rate I'm going to be the only one in all of Whitby who hasn't succumbed to the psychic blandishments of Goomba.

'Right,' I tell them. 'Let's tie the two old ladies up.'

*

352

That afternoon the booming voice of Goomba calls out to me, louder than I've ever heard it. It's almost pitiful, the way he sounds.

'Freeee meeeee!'

It makes my heart turn over with pity. It brings tears up, all spiky in my eyes. But I refuse to listen to him going on. I try my damnedest to block him out.

'Breeennndaaa! Listen to Gooommmbaaa!'

I mean, he can't intend anything good, can he? He must be up to something really nasty. He just has to be, what with the way he's trying to control everybody, and the extraordinary way he is making them carry on . . .

So I resist him with every atom of my mortal being. And because I am soulless, he can't reach into me and take me over. He simply can't do it. That sorcery of his – elemental, cosmic, arboreal, vegetable, whatever it is – it passes straight through my hollow body, and there isn't anything he can do about it. I can sense his bristling outrage at that. I can hear the thrashing, twisting wickerwork fibres, just about snapping with frustration.

Not as benign as all that, then, Goomba . . . reaching out to me . . . hoping to take possession . . .

'Gooommmbaaa . . . Come to Gooommmbaaa, Brennndaaa!'

Fat chance, chum, I throw back at him.

*

Dusk comes early. Sea mist drifts in from the harbour. A savage chill seeps right through my house. I am upstairs in the lavatory when all the noise starts from the attic.

Oh, no. That's all I need. My spare parts playing up again.

Pitter patter. Scritch scratch. Tap tap tappety tap.

'Go away!' I hiss at the ceiling. I get up and flush the loo, drowning out the insistent noise of them over my head. 'Pipe down! I've got guests in! We don't want to be hearing all your nonsense! We've got enough on our plates . . .' And isn't that the truth. But the noises continue unabated, and I imagine those dismembered hands and legs, organs and extremities, jumping up and down for attention in the dark. Frenzied and ghastly.

Trip-trap. Tappity-tap.

Henry is waiting for me on the landing, looking grim. 'Is that your ghosts playing up again?'

I remember that I never actually told him that Effie and I solved that particular mystery. Now I'm blushing. 'I reckon so,' I say. 'Never rains but it pours, eh?'

'It's awful.' Henry shudders. 'Those two old ladies like zombies down there, chuntering on. And I think Robert's getting taken over, too, now. I keep fighting Goomba off . . . but I don't know how long I can keep it um, up. Frankly. Um. And now your ghosts!'

CRAAASH. That's the new, hefty locks I fixed to the attic hatchway.

They've smashed them open. Easy as anything.

Really, I don't know my own strength.

The lock falls away and the hatch is thrust rudely open. Poor Henry. He's so shocked at this he jumps about a foot into the air. Lets out a squeal of fright. What comes next startles him even more, of course.

But not me. I know what's coming next. Not that that makes it any easier to deal with.

My spare parts are letting themselves down from the attic. They are furious and determined.

The pale, slightly blue hands lead the way, spanning the rungs of the ladder and trailing gory tendons. The slithering dancer's leg follows, as do various smaller bits and pieces – a bulbous nose, a greenish pancreas, several loose fingers.

Henry presses himself against the far wall of the hallway and gibbers gently. He knocks an arrangement of dried flowers off a console table and leaves them where they lie. His wild eyes look to me for reassurance and I can only nod: yes, you really *are* seeing this. A mass exodus of body parts from my attic. We both watch a long string of glistening purple intestines undulate their elegant way on to the landing.

They breeze right by us, that's the funny thing. They

aren't doing their usual gleeful haunting and taunting. The spare parts are going straight downstairs, as if they are on some kind of mission.

Henry gags. 'What are they?' he cries. 'What in God's name are you keeping up there, Brenda?'

I frown at him for this. Hardly tactful of him. But I let it pass for now. 'We have to follow them,' I tell him.

I have a hunch my parts know what they are doing. They are quite conscious of everything that's been going on, and there is something that they feel they have to tell us. As I think I've already said, my parts are extra sensitive.

The hands hover, waiting at my door. I step over the leg, the pancreas and the foot and I heft my front door open. Out they all tumble, into the misty teatime dusk.

'Good heavens,' Henry says, looking sickly. 'Are we really going outside with these ... things? With this ghastly menagerie?'

I ignore him. He really isn't trying to spare my feelings, is he?

The street outside is deserted. There is a curious atmosphere, as if all of Whitby is holding its breath. Soon, I know, the revellers will leave their homes once more, and head towards the Hotel Miramar in order to worship Goomba again.

And my body parts have something they want to tell me.

I can feel their insistence, like an itch all over me. I tremble and twitch as I follow them, into the main street and . . . lo and behold! To the front door of Effie's home and junk emporium.

What's in here, then? What is it we are being led to?

The nimble leg dances forward and, quick as a flash, it kicks in a pane of glass in Effie's front door. The hands spring through the smashed shards and deal with the lock. We're in.

'You're like some, um, terrible version of Snow White,' Henry whispers at me. 'But whereas she had little singing birds and fauns and rabbits scurrying about her, um. You've got bits of cadavers fluttering around you.'

I stiffen at his words. But I don't reply. What a horrible thing to say. Does he even know he's been so horrible? He is stunned and fascinated and repelled by my body parts and he hardly knows what he's saying. That's what I think, to excuse him for now.

We snake through Effie's downstairs junk shop. A hundred dragging, tap-tap-tapping noises. Tiny footsteps. The liquid slouch of the internal organs on the dusty boards. Upstairs we go, up the wooden hill to Bedfordshire. Three storeys up, to Effie's top rooms.

'Old Effie lives in a pretty Gothic style, too,' Henry comments – again, rather rudely.

The spare parts have led us to one of her rooms of books. These rooms are lined almost completely with shelves, as high as the tall ceilings. The collections housed here have belonged to generations of Jacobs women, and they are testament to the many and varied arcane enthusiasms of Effie's female forebears. Most of these texts are about the supernatural, and about seemingly impossible things. They are all bound in supple leather and reek of old mould and mystery.

'I wonder what they've brought us here for . . .' I muse. I must have seen something once, when browsing these shelves. Something my conscious mind has forgotten. These spare hands of mine rove along an upper shelf, hovering and prying, and reading the gold embossed titles as if they are printed in Braille.

'Quite a collection,' says Cleavis. His voice has dropped to a reverent hush. He's right. I'm sure the books that Effie has here would fetch a fortune from the right collector. I bet Effie herself doesn't know half of what is concealed here. Henry is rapt with a bibliophile's suspense.

And it is one very obscure, fat black book that we are here in order to disinter this evening. The hands find it and they seem to dance a horrid little jig in mid-air when they come across it. It's a plain, rather small thing but, as soon as I see what it is, I realise what my spare parts have been playing at, and I thank them with all my hearts.

It's *The True History of Planets* by Professor Reginald Tyler. Privately printed in an edition of twenty-five, in 1954.

Henry Cleavis gives out an astonished gasp as the hands slide the book gently out of its hiding place, and present it to us.

Together we take the book to the desk by the window. A green lamp casts a calming light upon the beautifully preserved pages. Both Henry and I draw up wooden chairs and we prepare to study.

Their work done, my spare parts withdraw from the room. Subtle, expert servants, they don't even wait to be dismissed. They slip into the shadows. I am vaguely aware of the tip-tap-tap of them. The slap-slap-slap of them. The squelch-drag-squelch of them, as they hop off back down the stairs. They make their careful way back to my house, and their place, roosting and waiting in my attic.

But I put all thought of my disembodied bits out of my mind for now, as Henry flicks through the pages of Professor Tyler's strange old book.

Back then, when I worked for the professor in 1946, and when I was privy to some of those meetings of the Smudgelings, I thought the stories that Tyler told were marvellous. He had a knack and a zest for storytelling that would make the breath catch in my throat as I bustled about the place, quiet as a mouse, collecting up the crockery and the leftovers. He held his fellows enthralled with his supernatural tales.

But this book . . . I shake my head sadly. No wonder the book never came out. No wonder it was privately printed in a strangely tiny edition. The pages that Cleavis is flicking through seem to bear very little relation to the full-blooded and fantastical tales that Tyler wove in those dimly lit studies of the past. What is this we are looking at? It's not really a novel. It's a parade of grotesques. It's an episodic ragbag of images, thoughts and ideas. And such strange ideas! And sketches. Horrid little sketches in pen and ink, of slimy, tentacled, horned and shaggy, thorny and leafy gods from other dimensions.

'Tyler must have gone crazy,' I whisper.

'This is what was transmitting itself right into his brain.' Cleavis sighs. 'I had no idea it was so awful. They are like the ravings of a madman. There's no coherence here. No thesis or plot. Just wild speculations and ludicrous claims about how the cosmos is populated and controlled.' I can feel Henry shivering, as he presses closer to me and to the nasty little book itself. 'But Mu-Mu believed all this was true. He thought that something . . . something about Whitby itself . . . made Tyler and his head wound, his fractured skull . . . vulnerable and receptive to these secrets.'

'Is the cosmos really ruled by . . . giant squid things and bamboo monsters?' I ask him, not really expecting an answer.

'I'm not sure,' Henry purrs. 'It certainly looks like it, doesn't it?'

There's a noise then, down in the street. I jump. I get up to see, to peer down through the musty panes and into the milky street light below. It's my side door. Someone slamming it shut behind them. And then I see them. Moving like sleepwalkers, sure of purpose, chillingly docile as they glide along. Effie, Sheila and, bringing up the rear, Robert. All of them on their way to greet Goomba. Both Henry and I sigh at the sight, as our friends join other, similar figures in the main street.

'I have an awful feeling that disaster is about to strike,' Henry says. 'They are building up *towards* something, at the Miramar. I just know it.'

'We have to go up there. We have to follow them and prevent it.' Inwardly, I marvel at the steely determination in my voice. I'm rather proud of myself.

'Indeed,' Henry says. 'But let's finish our researches here. The precious pages about um. Goomba. We must learn what Reg knew about this entity. And see what Mu-Mu wanted to conceal . . .'

And so we carry on searching the pages.

We find one of Tyler's demented, scratchy drawings, towards the end of his book. It appears to depict a prehistoric swamp in China, several million years before Christ. Rising out of the murky bog are huge, knotty spears of bamboo, spiking up in every direction. One particular plant seems to have a face. It is the most malignant face I have ever seen, and that's saying something. Its eyes seem to glow right out of the page.

Henry starts simultaneously translating and paraphrasing Tyler's erratic text: 'He says Goomba is a tree god of tremendous power and wiles. He slipped through to this dimension millennia ago. He floated through space, looking for somewhere to plant himself . . . and came to Earth in a terrible lightning storm at what we would probably call the dawn of time. Anyway. Um. A nasty piece of work. All he wants, though, according to this . . . is to go home. Back to his dimension.'

'I've gathered that much,' I say. 'What does it say about sending him there?'

'It says Goomba needs help. He can't do much by himself. He is possessed of tremendous power – for good and evil – but can't do a great deal of his own accord. And so he needs to enslave the minds of mankind. And his aim is to get them to send him back to the stars.'

'How?' I gasp. 'Ritual? Sacrifice? Dancing and barbecues?'

As Henry reads ahead, his eyes widen. 'You're almost right, Brenda. Um. He requires sacrifice. His old bamboo body needs to be burned up to cinders, and this will send him on his way to the stars.'

'That sounds all right,' I say. 'If it just means sacrificing himself . . .'

Henry shakes his head. He turns the page. Another picture by Tyler. This time showing the wickerwork man that the revellers have erected on the lawn of Sheila Manchu. It is remarkable for being faithful to the recent construction in every single detail, from its towering, imposing size to the hideous expression on that box-like head.

'Look inside the hollow head,' Henry says quietly. 'There's someone in there. Being burned to death, along with Goomba. Tyler calls this person the "pilot". And they have to die, too, in order to help Goomba return home.'

'No,' I say. 'We're not having that.' I grasp Henry's wrist, hard. 'We're not letting him do it.'

'Indeed,' says Henry, quickly surveying the rest of the chapter. There's nothing further to add from the text. We have learned everything Professor Tyler seemed to know about our foe.

'This has gone far enough,' I say, getting up. 'If that's where it's headed – to ritual murder – it's time I went and put a stop to it.'

Henry looks at me curiously. Admiration in his eyes, perhaps. I can't be sure. He might be wary of me. Afraid, even.

Meanwhile, I'm saying all this, but I haven't got a clue, yet, how I'm going to go about it.

As we approach the Miramar we realise that this particular night has its own distinctive smell. A woody, acrid scent that comes wafting down the hill and through the mist. 'Bonfires . . .' Henry whispers. This sends a jolt of panic into my heart. They have already started the burnings! We must hurry. The two of us double our pace, breathing raggedly.

Henry leads the way straight round to the back of the hotel. He seems to know a quick way through the gardens to where Goomba has been built. Once we are over the low wall and edging round the box hedges we come face to face with the thick, curling smoke.

'We're too late . . .' I say, but then I realise that it is all eerily quiet.

Henry presses on.

And then we can see them, through a gap in the foliage, where we crouch and observe for a few moments.

A crowd of people, all ages and types, are waiting patiently. They are queueing to pay tribute to Goomba. Each of them has a piece of old furniture. They are carrying hat stands, foot stools, broken chairs. One poor old man has a whole door on his back, and looks as though he's being squashed under its weight. They drag their tributes to the feet of the statue and pile them round his base.

We have to crane our necks to see Goomba properly. When we do, I realise with a gasp that he is indeed already on fire. All the wooden detritus and old furniture stacked around him is crackling and glowing with golden flames. Suffocating grey fumes are rolling over all around the beer garden, but no one seems at all alarmed. Goomba himself towers above all of this. He is bigger than ever, it seems. He has swollen to monstrous size and malevolent godhood. Now those two hollow eyes are glowing a fearsome red. The weird thing is, though, that the savage, uprushing flames from his bonfire nest don't appear to be affecting Goomba yet. He simply sits there, licked by them. It's as if Goomba is basking in flame and relishing its fiery tang.

'Look,' Henry says. 'The head. It's like a cage. Big enough to shove someone in.'

There's a ladder running up to a little door in the side of Goomba's head. None of this is aflame yet. There is still time for some victim to be dragged up there and shoved inside. But not if I can help it.

As I prepare to dash into the deadly mêlée, I trip over something on the lawn. I pick it up. A kind of plastic gun thing. A nozzle! Attached to a hose. Yards and yards of cold, dripping hose. What luck! Some gardener has just dropped it here. 'It's got five settings,' I tell Henry, with some satisfaction. 'It's really powerful. I can go in there and put out the flames and douse the wood and . . .'

'They won't let you,' Henry says. 'Look at them. They are out of their minds. They are enslaved to that hideous, wretched creature. If you try to spoil their fun, they'll rip you to pieces, Brenda.'

'Huh! What do you suggest, then?'

'Perhaps . . . there *ought* to be a sacrifice. If we are to believe what Reg wrote in his book. Um. I see no reason to doubt him. If we want Goomba to leave Earth for ever . . . then perhaps one of us *should* make the um. *Ultimate sacrifice.*'

I can hardly believe my ears. Cleavis looks like he means what he's saying, though. His chubby features are grim in the dancing firelight. How can he be so glum and defeatist? I feel like giving him a blast with the cold water, to bring him to his senses. But maybe that's it. Maybe Goomba is at last getting to him. Even Henry's brilliant, iconoclastic mind. Even its barriers are being slowly eroded by the force of Goomba's will.

'Sacrifice indeed!' I yell at him. 'Not on your nelly, Henry!'

No one is going to stop me trying. I heft the nozzle of the hose like a machine gun. I leave Henry in the box hedge shadows and I run full pelt into the deadly beer garden. I am amazed that none of the revellers try to stop me as I go dashing past them. 'Right!' I yell, and twist the hose nozzle to full.

The flames hiss and roar with fury. The smoke turns black immediately as the wood gets damp. A mist of rain is flung everywhere around the beer garden and I find myself shrieking with laughter as the acolytes howl in displeasure. I am raining on their – well, not their parade exactly. I am raining on their pagan rites to an alien bamboo god. That's what it is.

And then Goomba himself shrieks out loud as the water lashes against his swollen wooden form and the flames are driven back. His branchlike arms flex and thrash; his clumsy, sinister fingers ward me off.

'Brennnddaaaa! Noooo! You muusssst heeelllp Gooommmbaaaa!'

Henry has run up right behind me. Hot on my heels he yells: 'Brenda! You'll make it worse!'

'How can it be worse?' I shout back. 'Look, I'm doing something practical. I'm sick of all this fannying about waiting!'

I try to make out the figures of the revellers as they

surround us. They are pressing in on us, through the hissing smoke and steam. Rip us to pieces, Henry said, and I am sure he's right. They are stamping and thrashing about in the mud. I drive them back with fierce blasts of freezing water.

Then the water pressure gives out. All of a sudden, it just stops.

I whip my head round, and there is Sheila Manchu. She is standing by the outside garden tap. She glares at me. Her eyes are a venomous, unearthly red.

'You dare to jeopardise the apotheosis of Goomba?'

'What?' I'm on the point of really losing my temper now. 'Sheila! Stop being possessed! Stop being so weird! You've got a mind of your own! This Goomba thing wants to destroy you! It wants revenge on you, remember?'

'Goomba just wants to go home to the stars,' Sheila says, in an ethereal voice. 'I badly misunderstood Goomba. I wickedly tried to destroy him. But he was reincarnated as chairs and tables, and now I have a chance to make it up to him. By sending him home. By offering him unholy sacrifice . . .'

I watch the zombie-like followers picking themselves up. Some are piling up fresh wood and attempting to light it once more. The rest of them are turning their attentions to Henry and me.

Bumbling Henry pipes up then. 'And this um, sacrifice. Goomba's going to burn him up into a frazzle, is he? Use him as some kind of fuel. To help him slip through the dimensions and return home . . .'

'It's my fault.' I curse myself. 'I should have listened to Robert. He knew something funny was happening here. I should have known! And I had that voice in my head . . . Goomba going on at me . . . I should have known!'

Suddenly I am aware of a deathly cackle, cutting through the fumes and the noise. Effie is standing there, baleful and beautiful as a high priestess. Robert stands by her and they both are glaring at me as if they hate my guts.

'You are powerless to stop Goomba,' Effie spits at me. 'You always were. You foolish little woman. You were always *nothing*. A clay effigy of a woman, fashioned by a madman. Merely a rough approximation to human, *female* life. How could you ever hope to stop Goomba in his plans? How could you ever stand by your feeble promise to protect all life here in Whitby?' The possessed Effie flings back her head and laughs like a madwoman. Robert and Sheila and all the others join in.

I scald over with shame and I feel like simply turning tail and fleeing from this dreadful place. Henry puts a heavy, consoling hand on my shoulder and I shrug him off. I don't want him calling me 'old thing' and being all solicitous just now.

Right now I want action.

Then, breaking into our scene, the huge and shattering voice of Goomba comes booming out of the wooden effigy. *'Gooommmbaaa will speeaaak to youooo!'*

We are swept along on a tide of zombie neighbours. They are all filthy now, from building the pyre and the mud I was whipping up everywhere. Only Henry and I aren't wearing madly ecstatic expressions at the sound of Goomba's voice.

'I am almost at the critical moment,' says the creature, *'of making my departure from this world, at long last.'*

A ragged cheer at this, from his exhausted acolytes.

'You have served me well, you human beings from the place known as Whitby. Goomba has waited many thousands of years to be served so well. You will be rewarded too, in time.'

I pipe up then. 'Hello? Goomba? Could I have a word?'

The wooden god's eyes blaze. He is an awesome sight, it has to be said, with those hungry flames ravishing him, and growing ever higher.

'Who addresses Goomba?' the creature demands. *'Who still has a will of their own?'* His twiggy claws flex irritably.

'Ah, that'll be me,' I shout.

'Brendaaa,' he groans. *'You promised meee. I called out to you for help . . . I thought you were going to save meee . . .'*

'I promised you nothing,' I yell. 'I pitied you, being trapped underground by Mu-Mu. I listened to your cries in my head. I had no choice but to listen. And maybe I would indeed have helped you. But not now, Goomba. Not now that I know you are planning to sacrifice someone in order to get your own way.'

Goomba lets out an ear-splitting cry of rage. *Bring him forth! Bring forth the sacrificial pilot!'*

Now Effie, Sheila, and the other wild-haired women take up a ragged chant. Beside me, Henry has gone oddly stiff.

'Oh, no, Henry,' I whisper. 'Not you.'

'I'm . . . afraid so, old thing. Um.' He is struggling to maintain control of himself. His movements are jerky and heavy, as if he is battling some incredible, invisible force. 'I knew it. I knew it would be me. Um. In the end.'

The worshippers pounce and Henry is dragged away from me. He hangs his head in shame and helplessness. I shriek and howl my complaints, but the crowd lays hands on me and holds me back. I am pinned to the ground. And they are forcing Henry to walk right up to that bonfire. He climbs up the rickety ladder. He is shoved inside the very head of Goomba. A huge cry of satisfaction comes from the bamboo god then, and his acolytes echo it.

I sit up and struggle to see Henry, silhouetted, slumped

inside the creature's head. He has just given up. He knows that if he does this thing, then Goomba will go. We will all be saved.

'Burn him! Burn him!' shrieks Effie. She sways and exhorts the crowd to sing with her. 'Send Goomba home! Send him home!'

I am buried under their stampeding feet as they surge dangerously close to Goomba. I am trampled underfoot and for a moment I, too, feel like giving up. It seems absolutely hopeless.

'Burn him! Come home! Burn him!' Goomba's cracked voice shudders through the very ground beneath us.

The bonfire makes such a vast noise. More cries go up as the flames start to rise. Goomba shrieks in orgasmic pain and triumph.

And I decide, *no*. I'm *not* putting up with this.

Henry is my friend, and precious few of those have stuck with me over the years.

I simply have to save him.

But I am dragged down in the slimy, ashy mud. A creature of clay, as High Priestess Effie told me. I can barely lift myself on to my knees to see what is happening. I'm a mass of pain where the heedless acolytes have kicked and pummelled and trampled over me in their haste to rush to the burning.

But I struggle and I heave and, at last, I get myself up on my feet.

Now it's my turn to bellow in triumph.

Before I know it I'm on the rampage.

I see red. I lash out with both flailing fists. I crack jaws. Snap arms. Despatch a few swift, deadly kicks up the arse. I cut a swathe through the crowd and they shrink back in fear, and so they should.

'Get baaaaack! Do not approach Goooommmbaaa!' howls Effie, keeping herself a safe distance from me. She knows I'm a devil in a hand-to-hand fight. 'Keeep away from Gooommbaaa!'

Goomba himself is oblivious of what's happening. He moans and twists in the flames. I gasp then, because the flames look terribly high by now. Henry can't have many minutes left.

I plunge forward. I hunch my shoulders and plough through the crowd, buffeted by the force of the heat. I make my way to one side of the burning pyre where, as I suspected, the flames haven't been quite so successful in catching the wood. Suddenly – before I can even question the wisdom of it – I am standing on the heap of branches at Goomba's feet. And I can see there's a way – still relatively untouched by flame – up which I can climb. There are footholds and handholds, all up the back of the creature.

I am yanking myself up the hot, twisting branches of the wooden god's calves, then the thicker, woven bamboo of his thighs.

'Stooooop heeerrrr!' shrieks Effie, above all the thunderous noise. But none of them would dare to follow me now. They shrink back; I can see them through the gaps in the wicker. They watch, appalled, as I clamber upwards.

I am almost flung off, a couple of times. I ache and sweat like mad. I scale up his neck, hand over hand, praying that Goomba isn't able to somehow throw me off. But I am strong and determined. I reach the head, which is latticed and woven from bamboo. Quite ingenious, really, the way his acolytes built him.

But there is no time. I rattle on the wooden bars of the cage. I half squeeze my bulky self through a gap and I yell to get Henry's attention. 'Henry Cleavis!' I shout. 'Don't just sit there! Don't give up!'

But can he hear me over Goomba's savage, primordial cries?

We're both going to be burned to cinders together. This is it for both of us.

Henry is slumped by one of the glowing eye cavities. He looks just about dead with heat exhaustion and mind control.

'Henry, it's me! I've come to get you out of here!'

He jerks awake at the sound of my voice. 'What . . .?'

Below, the noise is horrendous. The crowd is baying for my blood. I am blaspheming against Goomba by being here, by attempting this.

'Get away, Brenda,' Henry splutters. He waves at me feebly. 'We need to be rid of Goomba. This is the only way. But you . . . you need to save yourself, Brenda. You're too precious . . .' Henry's face contorts as he forces out the words. He is struggling to retain control of his own mind.

I wrench apart the bamboo, finding that it splits and shreds quite satisfyingly in my fists. 'I won't leave you, Henry,' I shout. 'You're coming down from here with me.' It's hard to catch my breath, though, in the choking black fumes. My eyes are stinging like crazy, but I reach my hands out to him. I have to be strong.

'The flames are too high!' Henry cries. 'We'll never make it down!'

Then he catches my eye. Through the streaming tears and liquid fury of the air, he sees my expression. He knows how serious I am. He knows I won't climb back down without him. My clothes are smouldering. It's starting to hurt. But I am not budging until he staggers to his feet.

He comes close enough for me to grab hold of his arms and drag him across the cell. The whole construction is starting to rock. Goomba must have realised that something is going on. Something that jeopardises his plan. The fearsome red orbs of those eyes are flashing horribly. 'Thank you, Brenda.' Henry coughs. I help him haul himself through the gap in the wood. I hang on by one arm as he yanks himself free.

And then we are out in the air. Suspended above the garden. Still in mortal danger. But at least Goomba is deprived of his pilot.

Together Henry and I climb backwards down the body of Goomba. Henry shakes and almost drops off the side as the great creature twists and shudders, but I grab him each time.

We jump the last few yards on to the churned-up lawn. We're coughing our guts up. But Henry is safe. I help him to his feet and hold him in a bear hug.

He says something, right in my ear, but I don't hear it. There is an almighty racket from Goomba's worshippers. They don't sound very happy at all.

'Gooommbaaa!' cries High Priestess Effie. 'Talk to us! Speak to us! Why have you gone so quiet?'

It's true. The creature has stopped his howling protest. All we can hear is the fire and the noise of the human crowd.

Henry steps forward and says, 'The effigy is dead. Goomba is no more.'

'Nooo,' Effie gasps. Her lackeys wail and gnash their teeth. Then Effie's eyes are flashing that terrible red. 'Goomba!' she shrieks. 'Goomba is gone! And he took *none* of us with him . . . to the stars!'

And then Effie collapses on to the ruined lawn.

Henry and I go running, and all the others crowd round her. Effie is lying too close to the spitting flames. Her velvet frock is starting to scorch and, together, we only just manage to get her away before she goes up in a flash.

The servants of Goomba suddenly stop in their tracks.

It is as if everyone remembers something very important, all at the same time. They jerk awake and stare about themselves.

'Oh, crikey,' says Robert, looking alarmed at the scene around him.

Then he and Henry and I cluster about Effie. 'Give her air,' Henry says. 'Step back.' He claps me quickly on the shoulder. 'Well done, you. You've saved us all, you know.'

I don't get a chance to bask in that moment. We all watch as a weird, will-o'-the-wisp thing comes whooshing out of Effie's unconscious body. It is like smoke, pouring out of her. It joins the smoke from the pyre as the wickerwork effigy finally catches light and is suffused in flame. All that smoke plunges upward into the dense night sky.

What remains of Goomba crackles and shivers and blazes

away. I can hear the ex-acolytes calling out in pain and frantic confusion. Sheila Manchu sounds the most alarmed and confused of them all, as she regains her wits, and stares in horror at the devastation of her beer garden.

As the next hour ticks by, hardly anything remains of what was on the pyre.

Ambulances come and go. We all gabble excitedly about what has happened. We watch Effie come to, and she's got no memory of what she's been up to. She just looks amazed to be her own self again and I know I'll face some stiff questions in the morning.

Robert comes over to me at one point and says, 'This was all you, wasn't it?'

'Hm?' I smile. My wig is hanging on by threads, and I must look a terrible sight.

'You've rescued us all again, haven't you, Brenda?' he asks.

'I wouldn't go that far,' I say. 'Not quite.'

Sheila totters over and Henry has to support her. 'Has Goomba gone?' she asks me.

'Oh yes,' Henry says. 'Brenda sent him away for ever. But not where he wanted to go. Without a pilot, he just burned up. There'll be nothing left of him.'

It makes me feel a bit sad, really, as Henry says this.

But then there is a crowd gathering about me, congratulating me, and asking me how I knew what to do. And

I'm aware of Effie glaring at me across the beer garden, furious at being left out at the end.

It's several days later that things start to feel as if they are getting back to normal.

I have some new guests to look after in my B&B, and that helps. I clean the place from top to bottom prior to their arrival, and fuss over them a bit – perhaps too much – once they are under my roof.

I don't see anything of Henry. I can't quite face going up to the Miramar for a few days. I've seen quite enough of it. And he doesn't come to see me, either. I think we are giving each other a little bit of – as they say – space.

There is an embarrassing editorial in *The Willing Spirit* written by Mrs Claus. It gushes on about my bravery in rescuing Henry and all the others from the out-of-control bonfire. Of course the paper plays down the supernatural element. But I am a heroine of the town, nevertheless. I get greeted in the street once my picture's been on the front of the local rag and, I have to say it, I quite enjoy the whole thing.

I'm having cinnamon toast and a pot of tea with Effie in the Walrus and the Carpenter on the morning the paper comes out, and I can tell she's miffed about it. I turn the subject to her instead. I ask her: 'Are you back to normal now? No bad after-effects from your . . . possession?' I lower my voice towards the end of the question.

Effie rolls her eyes. 'Of course there're not. Of course I'm back to normal. Though I don't know why you insist on making such a big deal about it all.'

She doesn't remember details. She didn't see the worst of it. Perhaps that's just as well. Another terrifying affair sorted out, and no ill effects.

Effie crunches down irritably on her golden toast. I think what's mollified her more than anything is my telling her that we found a rare copy of Tyler's book hidden away on her shelves. And she was glad to hear that it was the information in that book which ultimately saved the day. She positively beamed at this bit of news. 'Ah well,' she said. 'Those books have always been rather special and precious to me.'

That's Effie for you. You have to keep her sweet.

She rolls her eyes again as the café door shoots open, and we are joined by Robert.

'I knew I'd find you here at this time,' he says, sitting with us. He looks all windswept and handsome as we bunk along the banquette for him.

'These teatimes of ours are sacrosanct, young man,' Effie tells him haughtily. 'We don't expect all and sundry to come joining us.'

He suppresses a smile at this. 'There's something I need

to tell Brenda.' Now he looks at me seriously. Of course it has to be bad news. My heart plummets and I put down my china cup. No one looks at you like that without its being bad news.

'What is it?'

He swallows. 'Henry has gone. He checked out late this morning. Took all his stuff with him, all his bags.'

'What?' gasps Effie. I hang my head. I knew it would be this.

'He took a taxi to the station. He was catching the train south. He didn't leave any messages or anything. I asked him . . . but he said no. No messages.' Robert looks at me. 'I'm so sorry, Brenda.'

'He's gone?' caws Effie. 'Just like that? Without a by-your-leave, or an excuse, or . . .?'

Robert shakes his head. I try to shush Effie.

'But what about Brenda?' Effie cries, scandalised. 'He can't just leave her! Not without saying goodbye, even!'

I pat her arm. She's getting too loud. Heads are turning. 'He can if he wants, Effie. He didn't make any . . . I don't know, promises, or anything, did he? It wasn't like we had . . . any kind of understanding . . .'

'Yes, but,' Effie says. She looks completely shocked. I'm obscurely pleased that she is so angry on my behalf.

'There's no use me whingeing about it.' I sigh. 'Henry is

his own person. He always was. And anyway, Effie, it was you who said – didn't you – that he was only here for work.'

'Well,' she says. 'That's true, but . . .'

'So maybe he thinks his work here is over. Monster-hunting. The deed is done. The adventure is over. It's time to go.'

Effie opens her mouth to speak, and closes it. There's nothing more to say.

Robert gets up again. 'I'm sorry for bringing bad news. But I knew I had to tell you. When he said he wasn't leaving you a message . . . I just knew I had to come and find you . . .'

I pat his hand. 'Thank you, lovely.'

And Robert goes, back into the streets of the ramshackle old town.

I look at Effie and see that she's dying to take umbrage again. She's dying to say that she never liked Henry all along. She knew he was going to let me down. Break my heart.

'So here we are,' I tell her, mock cheerfully. 'Two batty old spinsters in a quiet northern town. Looking for excitement again.'

She tuts. 'I wouldn't be too keen on finding excitement. Not just yet.'

We finish our tea, pay our bill, and link arms as we walk

back through town, over the bridge and across the harbour.

'It was my spare parts that did his head in,' I say.

'I beg your pardon?'

'When Henry came face to face with all my spares. When he saw them busying about like that. Like the Sorcerer's Apprentice. He couldn't handle it. He couldn't face the truth of what I am. I mean, he knows all right. He's always known. But seeing the truth of it. That I'm not your average old lady. I think that put him right off me, to be honest.'

We stroll along slowly, past lobster pots and fishing boats, and the gulls are shrieking and diving about us. Effie mulls over what I've said. She knows it's right. Even Cleavis – a man so used to monsters – couldn't cope with the idea of what I really am. And so he has run out on me, and I'm alone again.

Effie surprises me then. 'Well, it's his loss,' she says briskly.

Which sounds, to me, uncannily close to a compliment.

But it's not over yet.

When I get back to mine and find the post on the doormat, my first thought is: oh, not silly buggers again. No more poison pen letters, please!

Because I don't recognise the stationery or the handwriting on the letter that's lying there for me.

Horrible, jagged handwriting. Crude letters on cheap paper.

I open it up and hold my breath as I read. Even before I start, I know it's going to be something awful.

And it is.

You are mine. And I want to see you. All these years. Years and years. We've never really met. But you are mine.

And I have rites. Conjugal rites.

You are mine and I am coming to see you. I know where you are now. I have been looking. Now I know where you are.

And I am on my way.

Your husband is coming to get you.

*

Can't wait for the next instalment
of the adventures of Brenda and Effie?
Read the first two chapters of
Conjugal Rites right now:

Chapter One
A Familiar Voice

The ladies were poised over their walnut cake and morning coffee in their favourite café, *The Walrus and the Carpenter*. The café was in the oldest part of town, at the foot of the 199 steps that led up to the ancient abbey.

Inside it was small, cramped and chintzy. Effie was petite and hardly noticed this, but Brenda was on the large side and today she felt a bit squeezed in. As they talked their voices blended with the tinkling of spoons and crockery, and they weren't aware of the young waitress eavesdropping on their every word as she dithered about the room.

Brenda was saying, 'I don't see how you ever make any money out of that junk shop of yours.'

Effie's eyes bulged slightly. 'Junk! That's nice, I must say.'

'You know what I mean. Nick-nacks.'

'Antique collectables, I'll have you know, Brenda.' Effie looked her friend up and down. What would Brenda know about taste?

'Hmm. What I mean is, you're hardly ever open. Only about two hours a day. And you absolutely hate browsers, don't you? You don't exactly encourage them.'

Effie shuddered. 'It's true. I can't stand the way they just . . . loiter about.'

'How do you survive?' All Brenda knew was that in order to make a living out of her own establishment, the cosy Guest House right next door to Effie, she had to work her socks off all the time.

'I have my means,' Effie pursed her lips and sipped her coffee. 'Anyway, money is overrated. I don't have many wants.'

'Oh, I do,' Brenda smiled. 'Besides, I like to be up and doing. I like work.'

'Well. It takes all sorts, doesn't it?' Effie looked up sharply then as the young waitress pounced on their table and, with a great clatter, started to clear their used dishes on to her tray. There was something odd about her manner. Effie had noticed the way the girl had been hovering around their table.

'And how was that, ladies? Anything else I can get for you, is there?'

'No, indeed,' said Effie. 'That walnut cake was rather less moist than we're used to.'

The waitress said cheerily, 'Changed our supplier, didn't we? And we're not very satisfied, either.'

'See, Brenda? Everything's slipping. Hell in a handbasket, is the phrase that comes to mind.'

Brenda was pulling her old woollen coat back on. 'Well, we'd know about that, wouldn't we?'

As the ladies were standing up to go, it was as if the waitress could hold herself back no longer. She burst out: 'Excuse me, it's Effie Jacobs, isn't it?'

Effie frowned. this young woman was new to *The Walrus and the Carpenter*. The regular staff all knew Effie and they would never behave so oddly forward. 'It is. What of it?'

The waitress grinned and gave a slight squeal. 'I thought I recognised your voice! Oh my God! You're famous! You're a celebrity!'

Effie experienced a moment of alarm. She picked up her handbag. 'Don't be ridiculous.'

'But you are!'

'My dear, I—'

'Wait till I tell the others . . .'

Brenda was completely confused by now, looking from Effie to the waitress and back again. 'I don't understand! It's just Effie! We're in here every week and no one ever notices her! Why's she suddenly famous . . .?'

The young waitress stared into Brenda's perplexed face. 'What? Don't you know?'

Now Effie was trying to bustle them both out into the street. 'She's being ridiculous, Brenda. Let's go . . .' She ushered Brenda to the door, horribly aware that they were being stared at by ladies at the other tables.

The waitress wouldn't stop. She called after them: 'The Night Owls, that's why! That's why she's a celebrity now. Isn't that right, Effie?'

Effie thrust open the café door. 'Come along, Brenda,' she said firmly.

Brenda was wedged in the doorway. 'But I . . . Effie, what's she on about?'

'She's quite clearly off her rocker. She's probably on some form of recreational drug. What's Whitby coming to?'

The young waitress could see by now that, for whatever reason, she had embarrassed Effie. Strange. You'd have thought the old woman would be proud of her new-found fame. The girl shrugged and picked up her heavy tray. 'Oh well. Bye then, Effie. I'll listen out for you! You'll be on again, won't you? On The Night Owls . . .?'

Effie tossed her head and slammed the door behind her. *Crash tinkle* went the bell.

Chapter Two
You Don't Need to Know

They were out on the chilly, cobbled street, clip-clopping down the hill towards the harbour. As they mingled with the mid-morning crowd Effie was the more purposeful. Brenda felt that she was being rather furtive and cross.

'What was that all about?' she asked, willing her friend to slow down a little.

'She was quite clearly mixing me up with somebody else.'

'She seemed very sure of herself. And she knew your name.'

Effie gave a short sigh of impatience. 'Never mind, Brenda. It's nothing.'

Here they had to pause at the bridge as the crowds surged back and forth. The gulls were wheeling and screeching and the Esk was a startling sheet of blue. It was a brilliant morning. Brenda thought Effie looked pinched, worried and somewhat exhausted. She appeared to be even older than she usually did.

'You've gone and got yourself involved in something, haven't you?'

'Now stop it, Brenda.'

A gap opened in the shoppers and sightseers, and Effie darted into it. Brenda wouldn't be put off and dogged her heels across the bridge. 'What is it, some new investigation? You really love it, don't you? You're never happy unless there's something spooky you can go shoving your beaky old nose into . . .'

'I like that!'

Brenda was glad to have irked her. Now they were plunging into the warren of shopping streets on the west side of the town. Effie was really hurrying along, forcing Brenda to call out at her back, louder than she would have liked: 'What are The Night Owls?'

'Hm?'

'The waitress mentioned The Night Owls. Twice. What are they?'

Effie was the picture of exasperation. She clutched her bag to her and the two ladies stood glaring at each other on the pavement. 'Oh, nothing, Brenda. Just leave it, will you?

Now look, I've an appointment at Rini's for a shampoo and set. I'm saying goodbye to you here.'

Brenda felt as if she was being dismissed. She raised her eyebrows and said in a very level voice, 'See you later, then.'

Effie softened somewhat. She looked up into her friend's trusting face and quietly murmured, 'Look, I'm not being secretive. It's just . . . it's not a mystery. It's not something spooky. You just don't need to know what it is, Brenda.'

'I see.' She wasn't in the slightest bit mollified.

'Bye then,' Effie said, with a tight smile, and darted into a back alley that led through a quick way to Rini's Salon.

Now you can buy any of these other bestselling
Headline books from your bookshop
or *direct from the publisher*.

FREE P&P AND UK DELIVERY
(Overseas and Ireland £3.50 per book)

The Voice of the Night	Dean Koontz	£7.99
Die for Me	Karen Rose	£6.99
Power Play	Joseph Finder	£6.99
Virus	Sarah Langan	£6.99
Dead Sexy	Tate Hallaway	£6.99
Contract	Simon Spurrier	£7.99
Death's Door	Quintin Jardine	£7.99
Friday Night in Beast House	Richard Laymon	£7.99
A Passion for Killing	Barbara Nadel	£6.99

TO ORDER SIMPLY CALL THIS NUMBER

01235 400 414

or visit our website: <u>www.headline.co.uk</u>

Prices and availability subject to change without notice.